Midland

Also by the Author

Habitus
52 Ways to Magic America
Soft Apocalypse: Twelve Tales from the Turn of the Millennium
The Book of Ash

Midland

James Flint

Unbound

This edition first published in 2019

Unbound
6th Floor Mutual House,
70 Conduit Street,
London W1S 2GF

www.unbound.com

Text design by Ellipsis, Glasgow

A CIP record for this book is available from the British Library

ISBN 978-1-78352-595-9 (trade pbk)
ISBN 978-1-78352-597-3 (ebook)
ISBN 978-1-78352-596-6 (limited edition)

Printed in Great Britain by CPI Group (UK)

For my father, for my family, for all families:
this brief history of Warwickshire

With thanks to the friends of *Midland*:

Lise Bird
Jon Bradshaw
Kate Brooke
Jack Browning
Tara Cemlyn-Jones
Gervase Clifton-Bligh
Neville Dastur
Garth Edward
Marie Flint
Sean Geer
Amit Gupta
Steve Jelley
Hari Kunzru
Andy May
Tom McCarthy
Rupert Mellor
Ali Miremadi
Oliver Morton
Simon Prosser & Anya Serota
Elaine Pyke
Ben Rapp
Ben Richards
Dianne Trahan Browning
Sarah Waters

With special thanks to Simon Bishop

And in the wood, where often you and I
Upon faint primrose beds were wont to lie,
Emptying our bosoms of their counsel sweet,
There my Lysander and myself shall meet,
And thence from Athens turn away our eyes,
To seek new friends and stranger companies.

William Shakespeare
A Midsummer Night's Dream

Midland

WHALE

ALEX WOLD FOUND OUT about Tony Nolan's death at the end of an already tumultuous week. First had come the confirmation of his wife Mia's second pregnancy. Great news, wonderful news, another person in the world, another child. Mia seemed happy, he was happy. The usual hurdles had yet to be overcome, of course. But Mia was healthy, sensible and strong, and Alex didn't doubt that Rufus would soon have a baby brother or sister to keep him company, and that he himself would be heading up a family unit that was solid and foursquare.

A couple of days after the test had shown positive he'd been travelling back along the Embankment in a taxi when something strange occurred. The traffic had come to a standstill. Alongside the hold-up the entire pavement was jammed with people all of whom, for no reason that Alex could readily perceive, were looking out towards the river.

Incapable of sitting by while something interesting was happening, Alex abandoned the cab and insinuated his way into the crowd until he reached the concrete parapet that ran along the water's edge. The tide was out and people were also gathered on the slick mudbanks that had emerged; one man, dressed in a dark blue fleece, was actually standing up to his waist in the water.

All eyes were on three small boats that bobbed in an awkward configuration a few dozen yards from the shore. Why, Alex didn't know.

He bent his head to the schoolboy standing next to him.

'What's going on?'

'There's a whale.'

'What?'

'In the river. There's a whale. It's come in from the sea.'

Another boy, dressed like his companion in creased black trousers, battered black trainers and a sky-blue hoodie with his school's logo on the back, was eager to prove he knew all about it too.

'It's lost. Must've swum in from the ocean by mistake. They're trying to get it back before it swims onto the mud and gets stuck. It was up by the Houses of Parliament before, so it's going back I think.'

Alex glanced from water to boy and back again. As his gaze travelled to the river for the second time a hot cloud of water-saturated air jetted upwards about fifty metres from where he stood. At its base he could just make out a blowhole, set in its square of rubber sheen. Once, twice, three times it gasped, and on the third respiration a rhombus of flesh, dark as the mudflats, broke the surface a car's length away. There it was. The whale.

For possibly the first time since he'd joined Sovereign Brothers eight years previously, Alex's mind stopped chewing on the matter of his next trade. Pushing back through the bodies, he worked his way around to a stone staircase that led down onto the beach. He had a fight to descend – the steps were crammed – but with a combination of elbows and *excuse-me*s and a little aid from gravity, the slime left by the retreating waters was soon sucking at his hand-stitched leather loafers and oozing its way through the turn-ups of his bespoke wool flannel suit.

It was a perfect January day. The spokes of the London Eye shone with the glycerine light of the low winter sun. Big Ben stood cold and proud above the traffic, rendered timeless by the refrigerated air. News helicopters hovered at the old clock's shoulders like winged familiars, their spinning rotors patiently processing the sky, almost but not quite achieving thought. And the river shone beneath the Victorian arches of the bridges, slapping and sucking at the weedy brickwork as the tide went out, grinning and gurgling as it slowly slackened its grip.

In the midst of all this beauty the whale seemed like hope, like a conciliatory messenger sent upstream by the senate of the seas. Here they were, the people of England, gathering to greet it, to embrace it, to send it back from whence it came with tidings of peace and love. Festival was in the air. People were happy and amazed. People were good, the universe was good. Today had become one of those rare days on which the laws of combat were suspended and, for a brief period, death was not the truth of things.

Alex was swept up by it all in a manner he hadn't experienced for years. Perhaps it was the news of a second child finally sinking in, perhaps just the energy of the moment, but standing here on the chilly silver mud he felt alive with enthusiasm, abuzz in root and branch. He felt – wow – he felt young. Not that he'd noticed feeling old, particularly, but until this moment he hadn't realised quite how tuneless his existence had become. The brushed-steel lifts and glass-sided corridors of the investment bank's offices in Aldgate, the enervating, dehydrating hours he spent in business class, the long list of deals and trades that had seemed so exciting at the start but felt automatic, with even the double-plays and kickbacks hardwired into their routines . . . he was tiring of it, and had been working so hard that he hadn't noticed the tiredness creeping in.

It was a pitfall of finance. You spent so much time living in the future, so much time planning for the day when you cashed in your chips and walked away to pursue a more pleasurable lifestyle, that you forgot to enjoy the money you were so assiduously making. And then by the time you did walk away the stress and the fifteen-hour days had sapped your health so much that you were already half-dead. This was how you became a grey man, Alex reflected, on and on, round and round until your life was summed up by a spreadsheet and you were felled by cancer or a coronary aged fifty-five. That was Alex Wold, class of '91, a good guy and $NPV(A) = (1-(1+r)^{-n})P/r$. That was how you lost your soul.

He should have noticed when sex with Mia, beautiful Mia, had started to become perfunctory, when his libido had begun to leaf back through a few pages from the secret diaries of the bad old days. The black Filofax, as his main man Freddie Winston – currently making serious money over at HSBC – liked to refer to it. Only idle, that leafing, only a perusal, but it was a warning sign, a *vulnerability indicator*, and he'd have done well to pay it more attention that he did.

So he emailed Patricia from his BlackBerry, instructed her to reschedule his meetings for that afternoon, and turned his attention to the four tonnes of eternity now thrashing and bobbing in a panicked spiral thirty metres from the water's edge.

The whale didn't disappoint. Alex had never been this close to one before. He'd waited in the restaurant on the quay that one time in Montauk when he'd had the opportunity. He'd wanted to go on the boat trip, but he knew from bitter experience he had no sea legs and so stayed and ordered beer and chowder while Lucía and Carlos from Sovereign's New York office made the trip without him. Both of them gone now in the Twin Towers, while he'd been cavorting with Mia on a beach in Brazil. Christ, what a waste. The memory of the two of them was suddenly physical, a ferrous taste around the tongue, an actual lump in the throat.

Then the bottlenose broke the water and triggered Samuel Barber's *Agnus Dei*, one of the pieces Alex favoured when he needed to float his mind free of the hopeless matrix of sclerotic rush-hour roads, to start playing unbidden in his head as clearly as if he was listening to it while sitting in his Porsche.

His reverie continued while the whale breathed and disappeared. When it surfaced a second time, perhaps half as distant as before, the people on the parapet started shouting: 'Go back! Go back!' and the man waist-deep in the water began to splash and wave his arms. Before he knew what he was doing, Alex was plunging forward into the river. Cheers went up behind him as, one shoe already sucked from his foot, he pushed into the oily swirl, lungs constricting as the ancient river licked round his legs. Panting with the unexpected effort, he made fists of his hands, set his jaw, and strode on – seven strides, eight – until he drew level with the other man.

'Come to help?' the stranger said cheerily, as if they were standing in the park trying to launch a kite.

'Yes, I suppose so,' answered Alex, his voice weaker than usual in the face of the Thames. 'What's the plan?'

'Trying to keep the fella from beaching himself on the mud. This here's the edge of the bank. After that it drops off pretty fast.' He grinned. 'I don't recommend you go any further out, in other words. I did, and I nearly went under.' He pointed to a high-water mark that ran across his fleece at the level of his armpits. 'There's quite an undertow.'

Alex could feel it even now, tugging at his feet. The famously treacherous current, responsible for dragging so many thousands to their deaths: swimmers, suicides, drunken boatmen, unwary children, foolish dogs, luckless rats . . . and maybe even the odd whale.

This one though, this one they were going to save. He could feel it. He'd saved many things in his career. Once he'd saved an entire pension fund through a spectacularly audacious piece of hedging, securing his first six-figure bonus in the process – nice work if you can get it. He'd lost things too, of course, though he'd learned to brush these to one side. There had been some moral compunction in the beginning – the time he'd helped asset-strip a business, a family-owned retooling operation, he still remembered that one, the awful calls and letters from the eldest son. Or the time he'd sat by as the company suppressed a damning health and safety report on a chemical plant outside of Merthyr Tydfil in order to maintain the share price. But the culture at Sovereign Brothers was focused on the bigger picture. They knew, and soon he knew too, that the world was at war. The fleets and armies were companies and banks and brands and corporations, and Britain's survival as a nation depended on her ability to keep marshalling her forces as effectively as her numerous competitors marshalled theirs. There was no time for sentiment. No quarter could be given.

This thought reminded Alex of a conversation with his first boss at the investment bank, a veteran fund manager called Peter Bedway who had built his reputation (and considerable fortune) on the basis of his successful reading of the post-Big-Bang boom. Alex had been working under his supervision for about a year when the press began to fluster about a possible Chinese invasion of Taiwan. This was significant, because the fund that Alex was helping to coordinate was, at that time, very exposed to Taiwanese steel.

'Why aren't we getting out?' he had finally demanded of his superior, as the sabre rattling had been ratcheted up to what was in his eyes an unbearable level of intensity.

'There won't be a war,' Bedway had replied.

'How can you be so sure? There are troop movements on the mainland, the Americans have evidence of missiles being re-targeted . . .'

'There won't be a war.'

'I don't see how you can claim to know that.'

Bedway turned from his screen and stared at Alex with his disarmingly languid, almost bovine gaze. 'Tell me something,' he said. 'What's the price of rice been doing the last twelve months?'

Alex hesitated, then bashed a few words into his keyboard and hit return. A matrix of figures flashed up. He ran his eye down the relevant column.

'Nothing much.'

'Exactly. So no war.'

Alex looked blank.

'Look. China, despite being the world's largest rice producer, has so many mouths to feed that it's a net importer of rice. If it were to invade Taiwan there'd be an international outcry and in all likelihood the UN would impose sanctions, making it very hard for China to buy rice. Even if there were no sanctions, sellers would start to charge a premium, knowing that the Chinese would have no choice but to pay. The Chinese government understands this, and would therefore be buying extra rice to stockpile against that eventuality. That would be pushing up the global price – not a lot, maybe, if they were doing it carefully, but a bit. But the price has been relatively stable. So the Chinese are not buying rice, even surreptitiously. Ergo: no war.'

There was something priestly about Bedway. He was quite a short man with a delicate frame and a large head, and what was left of his hair was cropped so short as to make him effectively bald. He wore expensive suits but because of his size they seemed not to quite fit him, which lent him a monkish air and contributed to his slightly pious aura. He lived and breathed Sovereign Brothers, was often in the office till two or three in the morning then back in at seven, and as he actively enjoyed the denial of self this entailed it was an example he assumed, as a general rule mistakenly, that others were happy to follow.

Alex had been impressed by him and scared by him in turns. Bedway apparently derived all his personal satisfaction from his job. He was a vegetarian and even at big social events had never been known to drink more than a single glass of wine. And then, boom, one day he had died from a massive stroke aged – guess what? Fifty-five. To cap it off it had happened in the office. The cleaners had found him late one night, slumped back in his Aeron chair, his expressionless face illuminated by the Nikkei prices still ticking across his Bloomberg screen. All that calm . . . in the end it turned out to be little more than bottled stress. It was a cautionary tale.

There was a roar as the surface of the river burst open and the whale surfaced a mere three metres in front of Alex, like a U-boat from one of the many war films he'd watched as child. The animal's hide was so taut, so perfect and plastic, that it didn't seem possible that it belonged to anything alive.

'Go on,' said the fleece man in a sensible voice, loud and calm and firm. 'Back you go.' He rattled the water with his palms, an action which Alex, coming forward now, began to imitate. It felt ludicrous, standing there flapping at this miraculous beast as if it were a farmyard cow, but it was having an effect and instead of coming further towards the bank the whale slowed, raised its beak at the two men, and cawed like a bird. Alex had only ever heard one thing like it before in his life: the first sound that Rufus had made when he was born. Suddenly this creature from nightmares, from other dimensions and dark, undiscovered lagoons, was something that he understood. Tears stung his eyes.

'It's okay,' he said. 'It's all right.'

But the whale didn't think so. It cried again and raised its tail and with a slap that would have felled a bigger man than Alex it cuffed the water and propelled itself away in a violent curve. And so back it went towards the centre of the river.

As the molten body passed him, Alex reached out his hand and touched the creature's flank. Just a second's contact, but it was enough. The eely body felt elemental, felt like fire, and it warmed him sufficiently to keep him standing sentry in the water for another hour. By the time he got home late that afternoon, however, he was shivering. His BlackBerry had been ruined by the water, so he hadn't called ahead, and Mia couldn't believe it when he slopped into the hallway, carrying his ruined loafers in his hand. He then spent an hour following the whale's progress on Sky News while regaling a slightly bewildered Rufus with the tale of his adventure.

Mia was hardly less bewildered than the three-year-old. She thought it greatly out of character, this sudden sentimental concern her husband was displaying for the welfare of an animal. And now here he was, absconding from work and risking drowning and exposure to goodness knew what admixture of waterborne diseases. It was out of the ordinary, to say the very least.

The next day the little family altered its Saturday routine and went back to the Embankment to see how the rescue attempt was progressing. Alex wanted Rufus to see the creature, and he was also keen to show his son where he had stood, up to his waist in water, the previous afternoon.

The tide was in now and the muddy beach submerged, but the whale hadn't got much further back towards the sea. From what Alex could gather from members of the crowd – and there were a lot of people here now, many more than yesterday, enough certainly to make Mia feel claustrophobic and exasperated – all attempts to guide it there had failed. It had been swimming in increasingly chaotic circles in more or less the same part of the river for the last twenty-four long hours, and the specialists on the boats brought in to rescue it felt that it was going to stress itself to death if it carried on much longer. So a barge was being brought, equipped with crane and an inflatable pontoon so that they could lift the whale and support its body while they returned it to the sea.

Ignoring Mia's sighs, Alex hustled the three of them to the relevant side of the recently completed Hungerford footbridge, from which vantage point they watched the barge arrive.

'Why do they need the big yellow boxes?' asked Rufus, as the pontoon was being prepared.

'So the whale doesn't suffocate. It's so big and heavy that if you take it out of the water it can't support its body enough to get air into its lungs.'

'But how's it breathe?'

'It breathes air, like us. It's not a fish, it's a mammal. See that hole there on its head? That's like its nose. It breathes through that.'

'What's a mammal?'

'Well . . .' Alex thought about this for a second, seeing if he could dredge something up from long-forgotten school Biology lessons. 'It's an animal like you and me. Fish breathe underwater and lay eggs for babies. Mammals breathe air and have babies in their tummies. Like Mummy.'

He winked at his wife, who forced a smile. She wasn't overjoyed at being compared to the helpless lump of blubber now being hoisted out of the water, though it was fair to say it pretty much described the way she'd felt through the latter months of her last pregnancy. But then the stricken animal was lowered onto the deck, the crowd hurrahed and Mia – who had been on the stage herself before she'd become a mother – experienced a surge of fellow feeling for this unfortunate northern bottlenose. Poor thing, to get separated from its pod and wander deep into the heart of a city, ending up surrounded by this bizarre circus of kindness. It must feel so alone, so lost.

'Will it find its friends, when they take it back?' Rufus asked.

'I'm sure it will, *chéri*,' Mia sniffed. 'I'm sure it will.' But she wasn't sure at all, and she had to bow her three middle fingers and use the soft pads they presented to brush a tear from her cheek before the boy had a chance to see.

Alex saw, though. He stepped back, put his arm around her, and pulled her to him. She coughed out a little laugh.

'I'm so silly,' she whispered, as she extracted a ball of tissue from her sleeve and put it to her nose.

'No you're not. It's very moving. That's what I was trying to tell you yesterday.'

'The boat is moving, Dad, the boat is moving,' Rufus said. He was standing in front of them, peering down at the unfolding drama through the gaps between the railings.

'Yes, yes it is,' Alex agreed. And the three of them watched as the barge carried the whale and its rescuers, now busily occupied in hosing down their charge with torrents of water, directly underneath their feet.

'There he goes,' said Alex.

'There he goes, look Rufus, there he goes,' said Mia.

'There he goes,' Rufus echoed airily. 'Bye bye, Mr Whale. He'll be all right now, won't he, Dad?'

'He'll be fine,' Alex assured him. 'Don't worry.'

They didn't. Satisfied that the whale would soon be returned safely to his element, the Wolds left the bridge and got on with their day: coffee, cakes and newspapers in a favourite café off Sloane Square, a foray into Peter Jones to buy two tennis rackets and new trainers for Rufus, who had outgrown his favourite pair (which had battery-powered lights in the soles), and a trip to Waitrose to stock up on supplies. It wasn't till they were home preparing dinner that Alex switched on the dayroom television and heard the whale had died.

He was stunned. He couldn't take it in. That had not been supposed to happen. Not after he'd spent an afternoon up to his waist in water, trying to save its life. Not after the sacrifice of a fifteen-hundred-pound suit and a two-hundred-and-fifty-pound pair of shoes. Not after an afternoon AWOL from work and the problems *that* was going to cause. And especially not after he had spent an evening and an afternoon of quality time investing his son with the important life lessons concerning mankind's responsibility for the natural world. For a minute or two he couldn't even speak.

'Look Daddy, the whale,' said Rufus, pointing at the TV, which was showing footage shot earlier in the day. Mia, less affected than her husband by the news, put down the plastic bag of chlorine-washed salad that had only the day before been harvested from a polytunnel somewhere on the coast of southern Spain, grabbed the remote control, muted the sound and tugged her son away.

'The whale, I want to watch the whale,' Rufus wailed.

'The whale's gone home, baby, he's gone to join his friends.'

'I want to see him!'

'I know, sweetness, but he's gone. And you saw him earlier.'

Alex, it seemed, had regained the power of speech. 'I can't believe it, I can't believe it,' he was saying over and over, under his breath.

In the corner of the room, nestled inside a hand-tooled leather briefcase that, like the salad, had come from Spain, was his laptop. He unclipped the catch on the bag, retrieved the machine and bashed the words 'whale' and 'industry' into the search field of a browser. Immediately an orange diode on the router upstairs in his office began blinking furiously as the thousands of writhing giblets of data that had been squirted into the networks by a gigantic bank of flash RAMs in Docklands started to arrive.

'How come we can slaughter thousands of whales every year but not save just one?' he muttered. 'What's wrong with us?'

Mia said something about there being quotas, but she was more concerned with getting Rufus to turn away from the truth of the world and focus on his colouring set.

Alex wasn't listening anyway. He was thinking about his brother. He'd probably be watching this. Knowing Matthew, he'd been on the pontoon with the whale, hosing the damn thing down. Was that why he'd got in the water in the first place? Some weird subconscious urge to connect with his brother? Because for sure they did not connect, and had not done so for too many years.

It preyed on Alex's mind, this, all the more since Rufus had been born. Before then, Matthew's antipathy towards him had been dismissible: sibling rivalry, an annoying phase. But now that he wanted Matthew to be a proper uncle and them all to be a proper family, his brother's attitude was getting in the way. They'd been close as boys, fortunate to have a big house and garden to play in and the Warwickshire countryside to explore. Camping out in the woods, sledging down Round Hill, making dens in the cow parsley, sneaking cigarettes in the shed – it had been good. Happy. Idyllic even. And then that had all changed.

Matthew disapproved of what Alex did for a living, of course. Environmental considerations simply did not impinge on share prices, on whether you bought or sold. Sure, if a business traded on that sort of image, fashionable now in certain sectors, it might have an impact. Or if you were involved in one of those 'ethically' weighted funds (which Alex was not). But otherwise? Not really. Other things did. But not that.

To people who had never experienced them, Alex liked to describe the markets as a vast, multi-courted and massively networked game of pelota. Most people, of course, had no more experience of pelota than they did of the markets. But pelota was easier and more fun to describe. Alex had only been to one pelota game, during his friend Carlos's stag trip to San Sebastián, that mini-Monaco on the northwest coast of Spain in whose harbour Napoleon and Wellington once faced off. A gastronome's paradise served by three times as many Michelin-starred restaurants as London, the six of them had gone there for the dining, the surfing and the casino. On the third day they'd taken a trip over the mountains, across the dusty Riojan plain, and into a valley town split by a shallow, rocky river where they'd pulled into the car park of a *frontón*.

Inside, two teams of two men used curved baskets fitted onto their hands like preposterous fingernails to hurl a hard little latex and leather ball down a long thin court along one side of which hundreds of men sat in steeply raked seating drinking cognac, smoking cigars and cheering.

Pelota, Carlos had explained, was not like other sports. In other sports there were clear favourites, competitors setting out to be as superior to the opposition as possible, with the bookies setting their odds accordingly. But with pelota it was the opposite. The odds always started at evens, the teams deliberately engineered by a supposedly impartial committee – advanced players paired with novices, strong players with weak – until all concerned were happy that the contest was evenly matched.

Once the game got under way, however, and the red or the blue team (always these colours) started to pull ahead, the odds changed – and that was the point. Now the betting began, live betting and hedging, on the unfolding game. The bookies stood at the front, their backs to the court, offering new odds on *rojo* or *azul* and scribbling bets onto little pink slips which they stuffed into split tennis balls and lobbed into the ranks of yelling spectators.

Unlike their counterparts at dog or horse tracks, the bookmakers didn't underwrite the bets themselves. Instead they acted as middlemen, matching bets between competing spectators. They'd only offer blue if someone else had placed at least as much with them for red. For someone to win, someone else must lose – the zero-sum aspect of the affair that most reminded Alex of the markets. That, and the raging crescendo of the betting as the game progressed, the intensity whipped up by the sound of the pelota cracking off the front wall like a pistol shot and the party-game frivolity of all the tennis balls flying to and fro. It was hysterical, laughable, and deadly serious all at once.

On the markets, of course, that frothiness was all largely hidden behind the endless banks of computer screens that had replaced the old-style trading floors, which these days looked much like any other offices. The Nymex in New York, where Alex had done a stint early in his career – and where he'd met Carlos – was one of the last to have that race-day atmosphere. After that he'd spent eighteen months as an energy trader for BP, where his job had been to 'trade the curve', which meant, essentially, placing bets on when a commodity – in this case oil, gas, coal, uranium – would be delivered, and at what price.

The curve stretched from tomorrow to about four years ahead. The closer the trade the steeper it was. Close trades – short trades – had higher liquidity, tended to be smaller in value, and came with less risk attached. Long trades were as a rule much larger. They took place in a much slower market, but the risk was proportionately larger since, over a four-year time span, the chances of the curve shifting shape were that much higher.

Even in the short term, volatility was a problem. Every morning Alex had to monitor the European weather reports: a cold snap in Germany meant more people would burn oil and the price would rise; rainfall over the Pyrenees translated into a boost in hydroelectric power and a fall-off in demand for fossil fuels. The hotter weather brought by global warming had people falling over themselves to install air-conditioning, changing the nature of summer energy demands, which could be expected to equal winter peaks for the first time. And it brought other, more unexpected changes too: rising river and coastal temperatures were taking local waters beyond the level that could be used to cool nuclear cores. This was a big issue in France, where the scorching summers meant less nuclear power available and more need for coal.

But weather was rock-solid reliable compared with the wild cards played by politics. A strike in one country might mean a sudden race to buy energy from a neighbour, causing prices to bounce around like a rubber ball. A shock election result might send the markets reeling one way while an asymmetrical event – an explosion in a refinery, a reactor leak, a terrorist attack – might send them reeling the other. Any trader worth his or her salt was alert to all these things and many more besides. Steering a fund through these kinds of rapids and maximising your bonus by coming out on top year on year was no easy task. Matthew was absolutely right that if you were trying to do this, environmental considerations were absolutely not part of your remit.

But Alex had stopped trading like that some time before. After he'd been hired by Sovereign Brothers in the late Nineties he'd moved across to structured credit: creating and tailoring huge bundles of loans, mainly mortgages, and selling them on as collateralised debt obligations – CDOs – to big pension funds and other institutional investors. It was a new game and he was in early, so by 2004 he had been made a managing director and put in charge of his own team. Perhaps because his father was in property and he was comfortable with the sector, his desk began to specialise in European commercial property bonds. An investor would call up and want to invest say £500 million in a triple-A-rated note yielding 2 per cent above LIBOR, and Alex's guys would go off and put the deal together, buying up a bunch of debts collateralised by specific mortgages – an office block in Cologne, a port development in Marseille, a business park outside Birmingham – often paying well over the going rate for the underlying square footage in the process. But that didn't bother them, even though the overblown prices they were paying might artificially inflate the local market: the yield was all that mattered. They'd group the bonds accordingly, sell the senior tranche to the enquiring client, and push the mezzanine and equity tranches out to other punters.

It was straightforward enough in principle, but things got more complicated when trying to project the risk profile of the various tranches over the lifespan of the CDO. Calculating the probabilities of the various tranches defaulting, and in what order, depended upon a complex set of mathematical concepts known as 'correlation'. And here Alex had an edge. Almost nobody on either the buy or sell sides really knew how correlation worked, but included in Alex's undergraduate degree in Philosophy and Mathematics had been modules in statistics and probability theory, for which he'd had a particular affinity. As a result, the cascading values of credit-default sequences were a relatively open book to him, and this gave him the confidence required to structure his products and sell the CDOs to clients, few of whom understood quite what they were buying, and fewer still of whom wanted to admit it.

He was doing well, but he still thought of himself as small fry. In Alex's London more than thirty thousand people were earning over half-a-million pounds a year, and much to his chagrin he wasn't quite yet one of them, was not yet a member of the exclusive club formed by the top 0.1 per cent of British earners, average income £1.1 million, combined income £33 billion – more than the individual GDPs of two-thirds of the world's countries. At the investment banks the likes of Michael Spencer, Guy Hands and Richard Gnodde were pulling in annual packages worth upwards of £10 million. Star traders like Chris Rokos, who to Alex's supreme annoyance was actually a year younger than he was, were making even more than that, as were Ian Wace and Paul Marshall, whose hedge fund, based just off the Strand, had earned them £50 million in pay and dividends over the previous two years.

Incredible though this was, by global standards it was not particularly remarkable. George Soros, Steve Cohen, Edward Lampert and Kenneth Griffin were earning around a billion dollars a year apiece. Ahead of them all was James Simons, a former mathematician and cryptologist whose Renaissance Technologies fund was rumoured to be earning him another half a billion on top of that.

Even to someone as financially literate as Alex, this was staggering. He was living in the London of the £65 million townhouse, the £15 million restaurant refit, the £2 million studio flat. It was a city that bore almost no relation to the one his father had briefly worked in as a young man. The post-war dream of a relatively equable, stable middle-class society was dreamt now by a dwindling rump of *Guardian* readers and almost no one else. The period that ran roughly between 1918 and 1978 was beginning to look, not like the brave new future it thought it was, but like an anomaly in history, a brief outbreak of social equality in a riven and polarised world that was now reverting to type.

And good riddance, was Alex's considered response. The dream had been a lie in any case, a bubble floating on the last of the blood that had been sucked out of the colonies before their husks had been cut adrift and Britain had retreated into itself like a gorged and aged spider. The great idealistic systems of the twentieth century had brought miseries and oppressions orders of magnitude more appalling than the worst horrors dreamt up by the market. To his eyes these were now being replaced by a kind of new Elizabethanism, a golden age of global trade whose overture rang out every second of every day from the vast electronic symphony of the market networks. And for this music Alex felt that we should all be profoundly grateful. Yes, there were losers, there was poverty, there was damage, there was exploitation. But look at what we'd gained! Look at London, how it had been transformed from a rubbish-strewn nightmare of stained, convoluted little streets wrapping themselves around islands of rotting, toxic concrete into its current glorious spectacle. Just to jog along the Thames, as Alex often did when he eventually escaped his desk at night, was to witness a panoply of joys: the Eye, the new bridge at Embankment with its rigging of blue light, the revamped South Bank, the Tate Modern, the Swiss Re Tower, the jukebox of Charing Cross, the helmet-like City Hall and the majestic office blocks that zagged beside it, the glade of towers that mapped the nexus of financial ley lines and confirmed Docklands as a global power centre, and even, further down, the Dome, Blair's mammary reply to Thatcher's pyramid-tipped phallus at One Canada Square, which everyone was supposed to hate but with which Alex had never had a problem.

But Matthew saw none of this. Alex had tried on many occasions to communicate his excitement about it all to him, but his brother just didn't want to hear it. Matthew's world had a moral shape, with his goddess Gaia at the top and everything else arranged around her in cowed subordination, and anyone that didn't like this schema he found impossible to tolerate.

The phone rang and Alex checked himself. His knees were locked, his elbows tense, his breathing shallow. His gaze, though directed at the television, hadn't registered anything that had been appearing on the screen for several minutes, and the news had long since left the whale behind. Even with the sound off he recognised the stories: a female PC shot in Manchester, an investigation into a toxic food dye. Big things, important things. Yet here he was, obsessing over one dead animal. Bedway, the whale . . . maybe he too was dangerously stressed?

Mia handed him the handset. 'It's your mother,' she said. Then, in a lower voice: 'She sounds upset.'

Still looking at the TV, Alex put the plastic speaker to his ear.

'Hi Mum.'

'Hello dear.'

'Everything okay?'

'Yes, yes, everything's fine. Well, that's not quite true. I'm afraid I've got some rather sad news.'

'Oh really? What's that?'

'Tony Nolan has passed away.'

Alex stood, reached for the remote, and switched off the television.

'Oh, Mum. That's awful.'

Mia looked up from helping Rufus with his picture.

'What is it?' she asked.

Matthew Wold had just boarded the Reading train at Gatwick when his mobile rang. He wasn't in the mood for talking but he dug it out of the pocket of his jeans and peered at the name on the little display. It was his sister. This was unusual, to say the least.

'Em?'

'Can you hear me?'

'Yeah.'

'It's not a great connection.'

'I'm on the train. Just flew in from Spain.'

'Oh, that's better. I can hear you now.'

'We're pulling out of the station. What's up?'

'Tony Nolan's had a heart attack,' said Emily.

Matthew's immediate response was irritation.

'Well there's a surprise,' he said.

'Well,' said Emily, 'it's pretty serious. He's dead.'

'Really?'

'Don't sound too upset! The funeral's on Friday. Mum and Dad are going. I thought it might be a good idea if you came up for the weekend – gave them some moral support.'

At that moment Matthew's phone emitted three sharp beeps. He looked at it: a low-battery icon was flashing on the screen, which then blipped out. Matthew swore, jammed the device back into his pocket and slumped down into a seat. Tony Nolan. That was the last person he wanted to think about right now. Why the big deal? Years had passed since his mother had been married to the guy. Decades even. Long before any of them had been born. And Dad would be there, and Emily. How much moral support did she need? What about his moral support? Had she thought about how he would feel about it? Because no doubt Caitlin would be coming back for the funeral as well.

To calm the distinct sense of panic he felt at the prospect of being in Warwickshire at the same time as his former girlfriend, Matthew reached for the copy of the *Observer* that another passenger had left rolled up on the table across the aisle. He scanned through the political and crime stories on the first few pages, flicking quickly past them until a small item on page five, about a whale that had become stranded after swimming up the Thames, caught his eye. As it was likely to, given that he worked for an environmental organisation called EcoPath and was returning from a visit to a research project investigating a severe cetacean die-off in the Mediterranean waters around Almerimar, a holiday resort on the coast of southern Spain.

As his easyJet flight had come into land at Almería a few days previously he'd been afforded a perfect view of the cause of the die-off. Slotted like motherboard components into the grey rock of the otherwise barren Andalucían landscape were fields. At least, they looked like fields, but they were somehow too neat, and they shone with a dull un-field-like gleam. It was only after he'd cleared immigration and was humming along the coastal highway in an air-conditioned coach that the source of the gleam became apparent: the acres of polythene sheeting that cocooned numberless rows of tomato, lettuce, strawberry and mange-tout plants, protecting them until their bounty could be dispatched to the refrigerated shelves of Europe's galaxy of supermarkets.

To the north of the highway then, these gigantic cloches; to the south, hotels and apartment blocks shaped like ziggurats, interspersed with lush green golf fairways laid like giant rugs from the lee of dunes right into the vast quarries that had been carved out of the hillsides to source gravel and stone for more buildings and roads. And along the top of the ridges thus formed, the highway itself: cars, trucks and coaches rolling along it like glinting beads of mercury.

A thick halo of haze strongly reminiscent of Los Angeles smog hung around Almerimar itself. It combined with the abstracted concrete architecture – white, colonnaded Moorish geometrics spliced with lozenges of rich terracotta tile and embellished with the viridian spurts of palms and yuccas – to give the place a sense of timelessness, the effect that of a visionary city perched on the cusp of an interstellar void from the cover of some science fiction paperback. But Matthew knew that this apparent isolation was an illusion. Like an infestation of mosquitoes, the greenhouses, golf courses and hotels all thrived upon the aquifer that extended beneath the apparently waterless desert, sucking the water up and lacing it with pesticides, fertiliser, domestic pollutants and human waste before flushing it out into the Mediterranean. Where the dolphins lived. The striped and bottlenose varieties that frequented the shores around Almerimar found themselves trapped between the twin rollers of this chemical pollution and decades of overfishing; unable to replenish their genetic stock as readily as their cousins in the open expanses of the Atlantic, they were being slowly crushed to death.

This at least was the hypothesis that the EcoPath mission had set out to substantiate. For ten years a single ship had plied this stretch of coast, collecting meticulous oceanographic data and photographing and videoing any cetaceans it could find. The skipper, Rodrigo, was half-Spanish, half-Dutch; his command was a two-masted nineteenth-century Norwegian herring boat named the *Litenese*. He and his wife Mariana had bought it from the Norwegian government for a krona back in the early Nineties and restored it themselves before putting it in the service of the institute. They had then sold their flat, moved onto the boat, and gone wherever EcoPath had sent them. The cetacean die-off mission had been their first and so far only assignment. Since they'd started it they'd had two children, who had been brought up on board. It was just as well that they liked dolphins.

Matthew's job was to manage projects such as this, which for the most part meant allocating the volunteers: generally middle-aged European or American professionals, many of them teachers, whose idea of a good time was paying for – or applying for funding to pay for – the privilege of spending a week or two working as research assistants. It was an eco-holiday with a purpose: once aboard the *Litenese* the guests would spend their stay collecting oceanographic data, taking and analysing videos and photographs of any cetaceans they came across, and adding the information to the study's logs. The volunteers got an exotic and interesting holiday; the environmental project got years of committed manpower of a quality that it couldn't otherwise afford.

Most of Matthew's work was conducted from his desk at the EcoPath head office in Oxford, but he had to visit each project annually to conduct an audit. He had been the *Litenese*'s liaison officer for the past five years now, and of all the operations he oversaw it was his favourite. But much as he loved his sojourns aboard the herring boat, they always left him with a lingering sense of unease.

It wasn't just his horror at the ecological transformations wrought by the Spanish property and agriculture booms that made him feel that way. It was worse than that. At bottom, he was envious – envious of Rodrigo and Mariana and their boat, their life, and their kids.

It was absurd. He'd known them long enough to count them as friends as well as colleagues. But still he couldn't help feeling that theirs was the life he should have lived.

Rodrigo's natural charisma didn't help. A beautiful man with softly sculpted good looks, golden curls knurling his head and sun-cured arms and legs, at thirty-three he was also one year Matthew's junior. He spoke five languages, three of them perfectly, and captained the *Litenese* with an easy grace. Mariana was equally gorgeous, a compelling composite of vulpine Iberian features, lustrous flamenco hair and a PhD in marine biology.

Their children, unsurprisingly, looked like they'd stumbled off the cover of a catalogue, and having spent most of their young lives at sea they tumbled about the boat with a level of assurance that verged on the uncanny. The first time Matthew had gone sailing with them a heavy swell had meant no dolphin sightings for anyone on board and a bad case of nausea for him. As he lay near the stern, clutching the poop rail pathetically and vomiting periodically over the side, Maaike – the girl, then about four – tottered happily to and fro across the decks, bringing him a succession of plastic dinosaurs which she seemed convinced would help alleviate the wretchedness of his condition. Which of course they didn't; they just lent it an extra dimension of existential angst.

Since then Matthew had spent enough time on boats of one kind or another for seasickness to no longer be a problem. But the jealousy and the sense of personal failure and inadequacy that accompanied it remained. So despite what was on the surface of it an amiable few days spent updating his files on the dolphin study blessed by remarkably settled weather for the time of year, he'd left the *Litenese* in a bitter mood.

At Reading Matthew changed trains for Oxford. By the time he reached his flat in Summertown, Max, his mongrel feline, was in need of food, water and attention – and someone to clean up the turd he'd laid on the worn laminate flooring of the tiny kitchen in silent protest at the length of the period that had elapsed since the upstairs neighbour had last come by to check on him.

Matthew swore at the sight and smell of Max's message and then – first things first – plugged in his phone. While electrons skipped into the battery he rattled some Science Diet into Max's dish, emptied his litter tray, dealt with the rogue stool and opened the back door to let in some fresh air. He was in the process of chiding the animal for destroying yet more of his already battered hall carpet, Max's favourite solitary pastime, when the mobile beeped. It lived.

He checked the screen: a voicemail from Emily. Standing with his head bent in order not to dislodge the power cable from its socket, he watched Max chase the gritty pellets around his bowl while his sister explained that he really actually did need to come home.

Christ what a pain. He couldn't leave Max again, not so soon. There'd be nothing left of the carpet. But he knew his family. They'd tell him they didn't mind whether he came home or not, and then when he didn't go they'd beat him up about it for months to come. And besides that, again, there was Caitlin.

Matthew poured himself a glass of water and took it into the bathroom, where he washed his face and cleaned his teeth. Three steps back across the hallway and he was in the bedroom, the larger of his flat's two rooms. The bed had not been made since he'd last slept there a week before. He didn't bother to switch on the light, just sat on the edge of the mattress while he kicked off his shoes, pulled off his hoodie, and removed his socks and jeans. Then he collapsed backwards, pulled the carapace of duvet up over his head, and assumed a semi-foetal position in which he remained for several hours, quite unable to sleep.

The church of Our Lady and St Benedict stands alone on its hill to the west of Wootton Wawen, set back from the road towards the edge of the deep cutting that accommodates the North Warwickshire commuter line. Miles Wold must have passed it by car or train hundreds if not thousands of times. But until today he had never actually set foot inside the place.

Built of clay brick trimmed with stone quoins, sills and lintels and capped by a simple, steeply pitched roof with no steeple, the church was small – small enough, in fact, to be somewhat dwarfed by its more handsome and older presbytery. Miles knew that Sheila and Tony had been regulars here – Sheila was on the Parish Pastoral Council – but he thought they might have chosen somewhere grander for the funeral: central Birmingham perhaps, or even Walsall, if Tony had wanted to go back to his roots.

Still, he shouldn't complain. Far easier to come here than to negotiate the M5 on a Friday morning. And as he and Margaret parked up and walked past the long line of luxury saloons that lined the roadway, Miles began to see the attraction. The position was commanding, with wonderful views over Wootton Park and the flood plain of the Alne, a landscape he had been told informed the geography of Tolkien's Middle Earth. For many centuries it had been Catholic country too, of course, dominated by the Throckmortons over at Coughton Court and the Fitzherberts here in Wootton itself, as evidenced by the ancient Catholic cemetery in the grounds of the local Hall, where Tony was presumably to be buried.

Once inside, the favourable impression continued. Miles found the spare and elegant interior more impressive in its quiet way than those of many more elaborate churches five times its size: plain white walls supporting a hammer-beam roof with its rafters, purlins, ribs and braces all revealed to view; a little narthex and a choir loft fenced with a balustrade of matching oak; a set of coloured bas-reliefs depicting the Stations of the Cross set in a broken frieze round the walls; and lovely stained-glass windows. Apart from a few icons set into niches, and the altarpiece – a gorgeous golden triptych that, like the stained glass, pre-dated the church itself – there wasn't really much at all. The overall impression was almost Protestant in its restraint. Which, Miles reflected, was probably the reason that he liked it.

He and Margaret had arrived in good time, but the place was already nearly full and plenty more mourners were still coming up the path, so they tucked themselves into seats on the central aisle, consulted the embossed order-of-service cards that had been placed on every seat, and tuned in to the atmosphere of rustling calm peculiar to funerals. Miles considered making a quip to Margaret about the suitability of an ex-wife's presence at such an event, but suppressed the urge, guessing (correctly) that it was unlikely to go down well. Anyway, times had changed. No one was too bothered by that sort of thing any more. All anyone of his generation seemed to care much about these days was their health. Everything else rather paled into insignificance.

The organist struck up Schubert's *Ave Maria* and the hushed chatter died away. Once an appropriate level of hush had been achieved the priest walked in, followed by a beetle-like assemblage of pallbearers with the coffin on their shoulders, Tony's son Sean among them. Miles couldn't help but notice that the six men struggled slightly as they set the casket on the bier beneath the chancel arch. Tony had been a substantial man in more ways than one.

While the priest sprinkled the holy water the rest of family filed in and took their seats. First Sheila, then the brothers, Patrick and Conor, then, goodness, was that Jamie Nolan? Unless he'd kept his mother's name, which was Blake, if memory served. Interesting that he'd put in an appearance. Come to see if there were any crumbs of inheritance lying around, no doubt. Miles wondered how Tony would have felt about that. And then Caitlin, bringing up the rear. Gosh, she looked thin. Positively bird-like. As she turned to sit Miles got a better view of her: cheeks hollow, big bruised pits around her eyes, some kind of bandage on her hand. She was clearly taking this much harder than the others. He hadn't remembered her and Tony being especially close. But maybe that was just it. If there were unresolved tensions, then that could make it much tougher when it came to the end.

It wouldn't surprise him. Soon after he'd helped the Nolans buy the house in Shelfield he'd played Tony a few times at squash.

They met on Saturday mornings in one of the courts at the recently erected sports complex just southwest of Stratford's town centre, next door to the impressive new Hilton International Hotel. Both these buildings, with their long low profiles, banks of windows, large car parks and unadorned, modern facades, were, Miles had remarked to his opponent the first time they'd played, good evidence of how the town was changing.

Tony had nodded, mopped the sweat from his forehead with the sweatband he wore on his wrist, and cracked the ball noisily against the rear wall.

'If you ask me it looks like one of my factories,' he'd said, meaning the hotel.

'That's the style, now, isn't it?' Miles had puffed, misreading the bounce and sending his return clattering onto the tin. 'Oh hell and damnation. What's that, seven-all?'

They were pretty evenly matched. Tony had more power and presence on the court, about which he thumped and sweated and glowered in an intimidating manner. Miles was taller and skinnier, almost effete in his mismatched kit and schoolboy plimsolls, but was possessed of a competitive focus and a cack-handed coordination that made him a tricky opponent.

He learned that day, though, that a victory over Tony Nolan came with consequences. As Miles had begun to edge an advantage in the game the businessman's temper had become increasingly frayed, and he'd begun stamping and swearing about the court like an angry child. Eventually, after lunging for and missing a particularly fine boast of Miles's that had landed right in the nick, Tony smashed his racket against the wall with such force that he broke it. He stomped out of the door and returned a few seconds later with another one, identical, a level of preparation that suggested to Miles that such behaviour was not altogether uncommon.

More amused than flustered, Miles took the advantage and, soon after, the match. Tony sped off to his next appointment with barely a word, clearly furious at his loss, and Miles had thought no more about it until a few days later, when a peculiar letter from Nolan's solicitor arrived at his office, quibbling the calculation of the fees he'd charged on the sale of the house.

Miles had been somewhat taken aback. Tony hadn't mentioned anything about it when they'd met, though he'd had plenty of opportunity. He showed it to the firm's lawyer, who confirmed it as an attempt to stir up trouble – perhaps Nolan's solicitor chancing his arm in order to try to justify his own no doubt hefty fee? His advice was to ignore it and wait to see what happened next, advice that Miles took, although when he and Tony met for their game the following Saturday he took care to fluff several key points and lose the match by a small margin.

'I think that makes us honours even,' Tony had smiled while they'd packed their kit away. 'I got a handle on those drop shots of yours this week. You rely on them a bit too much, you know. Leaves you vulnerable. You want to mix it up a bit more. Use more of the court.'

'Thanks,' Miles said. 'Good tip.'

He was now the angry one. It was one thing to be bullied into throwing a match, quite another to be patronised about it. Positive now that the solicitor's letter had been a subtle piece of gamesmanship, he resolved to win their next encounter come what may. But when they met again his irritation affected his focus and Tony confidently dispatched him.

'Still relying too much on those drop shots,' was the comment, which left Miles seething. But an opportunity for further redress never came, as Tony found an excuse to cancel the next Saturday, and the next, and after that life moved on. They didn't play again, and nor did Miles ever hear another peep from Tony's solicitor.

At the time he had refrained from mentioned this little psychodrama to Margaret, as she would almost certainly have told him that he was being paranoid. She was ready to forgive Nolan anything, he wasn't sure why – as far as Miles could see he'd been as much of a bastard to her as he was to everyone else. Anyway, the habits of former partners were not something one really discussed, not when one valued one's marital harmony.

The only time he'd ever seen her be really angry with him was the night that Sheila had shown up at their house in a terrible state with that big bruise under her eye. It had stuck in his mind because it had been Emily's birthday, and he'd had to do most of the clearing up from her little party himself while Margaret comforted wife number two in the guest room upstairs. What had Emily been? Ten, maybe? Yes, that must be right, because she hadn't yet started at Wardle's. Miles remembered the balloons. Helium ones, filled from a canister they'd bought, floating all over the living-room ceiling. The prettiest things, even if they did remind him of the barrage balloons sent up over Birmingham like Flash Gordon rocket ships to deflect the waves of Heinkel bombers. Though maybe those were filled with hydrogen, not helium. That must have been one of his earliest memories – amazing he could still remember them, more than sixty years on. But he could. He would have been Rufus's age. Just goes to show. Life sticks to you. He hoped Emily would remember her birthday balloons when she was his age. He'd read somewhere, in the *Telegraph* probably, that we were running out of helium. It was an element, so not something you could make, and once the Earth's stock had been used up, they weren't going to be able to get any more of it. Who'd have thought it? No more party balloons – you wouldn't want to put hydrogen in those. No more barrage balloons, either, hopefully. Dark days, those had been. Very dark.

Emily had offered to make dinner that night, so as evening approached she found herself in her parents' kitchen laying out a set of worn placemats decorated with watercolours of Calcutta street scenes from 1785, not long after the city had become the capital of British India. To these she added three wash-worn linen napkins; various items of stainless steel cutlery; three scratched silver coasters backed with battered cork; and a selection of tumblers from the assortment in the cupboard over the dishwasher.

While she was laying the table she switched on the radio. It was tuned to Radio 4. It was always tuned to Radio 4: the volume dial was polished with use, the tuning dial tarnished by time. The six o'clock pips blipped out of the little speakers and carried the world into the room, and immediately Emily's stomach started to rumble: so many of her childhood meals had been cued in by this sound that she'd developed a Pavlovian response to it. She took an apple from the fruit bowl and bit out a chunk, and at the same time reached into the vegetable rack and retrieved a brown bag of potatoes, which she carried over to the sink.

Though not yet green, the potatoes were soft with age. There would be more in the pantry, dug from the rows behind the house by the gardener in the autumn, then left to slowly rot for want of mouths to eat them. Why her mother still bothered Emily really didn't know. It was another family idiosyncrasy, like the ability to persist as if there was only one media outlet in the country rather than a cacophonous ecology of satellite, broadband and digital.

While she scrubbed and peeled she listened to the news. There was an item on the whale that had swum up the Thames, followed by a brief discussion about the plan to put its skeleton on show. She filled a pan with water from the filter tap, dosed it with salt, and slid the woody knuckles of potato in from off the chopping board. As she set the pan on the hot ring of the Aga, two hands to carry it carefully across the room, one foot to shift the dog that lay, spine extended, along the warm base of the oven, the doorbell – which was just that, a bell, welded to an ancient spring and operated by a wire threaded through the house's beams – jangled on its hinge.

The noise was bright and pleasing.

Emily dried her hands on the wrong towel and walked out of the kitchen, across the flags of the back hallway, and onto the parquet of the front hall. She half-expected her mother back from the shop, hands full of something, lips mouthing the latest episode in some developing village catastrophe. But it would have been odd for Margaret to use the front door: except for formal occasions the family came and went by way of the door at the side of the house, the one off the breakfast room.

Her hunch was right. Another woman stood in the porch, a slender, drawn young woman not quite Emily's age, a woman that Emily was not quite prepared to see. Light from the leaded glass standard lamp that illuminated the hallway caught her highlights and picked up the green of her eyes. She was tall, slender, had her father's lips, her mother's nose.

It was Caitlin.

'Hello!' Emily said, trying to hit a note somewhere between pleasant surprise and sympathetic concern. 'How are you?'

'Oh, I'm okay.'

'I looked for you at the vigil.'

'Yes – Sean said. I'm sorry. I was getting some rest.'

'You were up last night, weren't you?'

Caitlin gave a faint wince. 'That's right. I – is your mum here?'

'Mum? Not right now. She just popped down to the shop to get a couple of things before they close. She'll be back in a minute. Please, come in.'

'Okay.'

Caitlin stepped into the panelled hall and Emily led her past the doors to the living room, drawing room, study and conservatory, then underneath the staircase and through into the kitchen, the house's control centre and the necessary setting for any serious conversation.

'Fancy a glass of wine? I've just opened a bottle.'

'That'd be nice.'

At the sight of a visitor the dogs waggled happily. Harry jumped up, dark paws against Caitlin's pale trousers, so Emily shooed him and Pandora out of the second back door, the one that led from the kitchen proper to the vegetable garden, before pouring out two drinks.

On the Aga the potato water was beginning to steam.

'I'm really sorry about your dad.'

'Thanks.'

'Did everything go okay today? Mum said the church was packed.'

'There were a lot of people there. Dad knew everyone.'

'Alex and Matthew are both coming back, you know. For the weekend.'

'Are they?'

'They thought Mum might need the moral support.'

'Is she okay about it?'

'I think so. I mean her and Tony . . . it was a long time ago.'

'Right. It was. What about you, did you come back too?'

'Me? No. I was here anyway. I'm kind of between jobs. And flats. So I've moved back in for a bit while I sort myself out.'

Just then the dogs began to bark: they had heard Margaret's car pull up at the side of the house and they knew that her return meant food. Emily probed the potatoes, decided that they were done, carried them to the sink and dumped them into a colander. Behind her, Caitlin sat down at the unlaid end of the table, next to that week's as yet unopened edition of the *Birmingham Post*.

Margaret saw her as soon as she came into the breakfast room.

'Oh,' she said, stopping momentarily. 'Caitlin. So it's your car then, out the front?'

'Hello Mrs Wold,' Caitlin managed, her words obscured by the noise of the dogs.

'For goodness' sake call me Margaret,' said Margaret, who was still dressed in the navy jacket and pleated cream skirt she'd worn for the funeral. 'Are you staying for supper? There's plenty to eat. Lay an extra place for Caitlin, Emily. Oh – what did you do to your hand?'

Caitlin rubbed the large, untidy dressing taped into the V between her left thumb and forefinger. 'That? Nothing. It's just a burn. You know – cooking oil.'

'That doesn't sound very good. Burns can be so painful! Are you sure it's all right? We've got some very good cream if you need it.'

'No, really, it's fine.'

'Well if you need anything do say.'

Margaret began to bustle around the kitchen as if this was seventeen years earlier and Caitlin's mother had been late collecting her daughter after the school run. She retested the potatoes, seemed satisfied that they were cooked, transferred them into a bowl and then began to unload things from the fridge onto the kitchen table with brisk efficiency.

'There's salad and quiche and cold beef and some pork pie if you like. Or are you a vegetarian as well, these days? I can't think why Emily is. I really cannot understand it. It seems like such a silly way to live your life. You always struck me as far too sensible a girl to go in for those kinds of fads. Miles! Supper!'

She stopped, and smiled, and then suddenly sat in one of the chairs as tears rolled down her face.

'Mum . . .' said Emily, not quite sure how to react.

Margaret shook her head and pressed the thumb and little finger of her right hand against the lower rims of her eyes.

'I know he was an old sod, but I still had a soft spot for him.'

Caitlin took a box of tissues from the windowsill and offered them to Margaret, who took one, folded it, and used it rather daintily to wipe her nose. She was not a dainty woman, but she had grown up with a particular ideal of feminine beauty, and it was one that she still aspired to.

She sniffed and let out a kind of soft chuckle. 'I'm so silly. It should be you crying, not me. Oh, let those wretched dogs in will you, Emily, before they completely wreck the door?'

While Emily complied, Margaret turned to address Caitlin. 'How are you anyway, dear? How's your poor mother? Is she bearing up? I'm sure she's overwhelmed, poor thing, with the funeral and everything else to organise.'

There was a pause while Caitlin stared into her wine.

'Actually, that's sort of why I'm here. Things are a bit . . . weird, what with Jamie back from South America and everything.'

'Oh,' said Margaret. 'Yes. I thought I saw him at the church.'

'He flew in this morning. We had a bit of a row when everyone got home. It started off about the will, and then Jamie started saying awful things about Dad. And then Mum and Sean got angry.' Caitlin paused and Emily thought she might now need the tissues, but her eyes stayed dry. 'Anyway, I just wanted to ask if I could stay here for a day or two, while Mum and Jamie sort it out. I just really think I need a bit of space from everyone.'

A tartan rug lay folded over the lower half of the second divan in the guest bedroom, the one nearer the window. Caitlin had never liked tartan unless it was the Burberry kind, in which case it was okay if a bit trashy. But the other bed was encased in a pale green satin counterpane, sheeny as plastic and about as antiseptic, and of the two the one with the rug looked the more inviting.

She sat quietly for a while, listening. Downstairs there was noise: footsteps on the flags and parquet, the dogs skittering about, doors opening and closing. But there were no voices, or none that she could hear. It would be just like the Wolds to be too polite to discuss her while she was a guest in their house.

She allowed herself a smile at this, her first smile for quite some time. Then – an unpleasant feeling.

Someone – or something – was watching her.

It was a teddy bear. It was sitting in a cane chair positioned against the wall beside the door, which explained why she hadn't seen it when she'd first come in. One eye was missing but the other buttoned her neatly onto her rectangle of rug.

A buzz of recognition. Ochre fur in the half-light.

'Hello,' she said. 'You've lost an eye since we last met.' She went over, picked it up, inhaled its scent of bark and cloves.

Somewhere in its belly an antiquated voice box performed a somersault and groaned.

Maaaaaawww.

'Poor old thing. Still alive, if only just.'

Buried beneath that cornflake-coloured fur, caught among the hessian and wood shavings and colonies of dust mites, were memories of her and Matthew, lying side by side in afternoon sunshine on a bed in the room next door one afternoon when his parents had been out.

She'd teased him about the bear.

'Seventeen and still need a teddy?'

'It's a family heirloom,' he'd grumped in reply. 'It's worth a great deal of money.'

She'd said something about his liking to be watched, and he'd laughed and pushed her back and started to kiss her.

The bear's one-eyed stare was a wink. *I know what you did*, it said. *I wasn't there, but I know.*

She couldn't stand it. A large lace doily lay across the dresser, protecting its veneer from dust; she picked it up and draped it over the toy's stuffed head. But that just made it worse. The teddy now looked like a Pac-Man ghost with the additional feature of two stubby teddy-bear legs. Snatching back the cloth, she grabbed the bear by an arm and carried it over to the wardrobe, the odour of naphthalene blooming out as she pulled open the door. *There, bear: go in there* – with the phantom ball of long-forgotten shoes, out-of-fashion dresses and suits for a younger, more slender edition of Miles: former selves parcelled up in a row of polythene shrouds. *In there. That's where you belong. Not out here staring at me.*

Caitlin then went and sat, this second time, not back on the bed but in the chair by the dresser. By removing the doily she had revealed a polished surface in which she could see her face. She reached for her bag, took out a pack of cigarettes, and from inside the pack retrieved a tiny envelope of plain white paper. She opened this carefully and knocked a little pile of chalky powder onto the veneer.

A dune by the sea. Sand falling into the base of an hourglass.

Again into her bag for a short length of cocktail straw. A glance in the oval mirror on the back of the dresser, canted slightly upwards on its horizontal hinge. There she was, drawn but defiant, and behind her the wardrobe. More mirrors here, the two doors panelled with bevelled rectangles of silvered glass, the metal backing starting to pucker and speck in the corners. In the reflected reflection she could see her shoulder blades and the dome of the back of her head. Angular. Anonymous. Vulnerable.

That fucking bear was still watching her.

She got up, strode across to the cupboard, and pulled open the door. Polythene and naphthalene. The bear winked then groaned in protest as she turned it round to face the other way.

She shut the door, returned to the dresser and contemplated the small heap of powder. There had been many such heaps, but she could keep on turning the hourglass for ever.

Could she? Couldn't she?

The bear. Polythene and naphthalene.

I can still see you. I know what you did. Wink, wink.

On a sudden impulse Caitlin swept the powder off the dresser and onto the carpet then strode over to the basin in the corner. She spun the mottled faucets, rinsed off the white crust that frosted the blade of her hand and washed away what was left in the wrap. That was all that she had. There wouldn't be any more. She had made up her mind.

Stooping, trying to avoid wetting the dressing that covered

her burn, she splashed the cold water onto her face. It felt right. She looked in the mirror, a third mirror – this room was a hall of them – fixed to the wall over the splash back. Hollows and points, plastic points. Purple mussel shells beneath her eyes. No sleep last night. Or the previous. She pulled the skin taut.

It would all be all right.

Then . . . a flash of gold behind her, something scything past the legs of the chair she'd just vacated.

It was the larger of the two dogs. He'd sneaked into the room and was licking at the patch where she'd spilled the cocaine.

'Get off!' she hissed. The dog shot her his best bad-puppy grin. Were his eyes already starting to dilate?

She lunged for him but he pogo-ed past her and back out through the door he'd nosed open, launching himself at terrific speed down the main staircase and past Margaret, who was on her way up with a stack of clean sheets in her arms.

'Harry, what on earth are you doing? You *know* you shouldn't be up here.' She could see, as she negotiated the landing, that Caitlin's door was wide open. 'Has he been bothering you Caitlin? If he has I'll shut him out.'

'It's all right, Margaret, really. He's just playing.' Caitlin's voice quavered slightly. She'd been there less than two hours and was already doping the family pet. Good effort.

Below her Harry clattered through the hallway and galloped into the kitchen, where he instantly infected a dozing Pandora with his chemical excitement. They made a circuit out of the central unit, nearly knocked Emily over, and then shot back into the hall where a skidded turn across the parquet catapulted them into the conservatory. Across the tiles and through the metal-framed French doors they went, then on into the drawing room where a large Chinese-washed rug the colour of green tea absorbed the sound of their claws for a couple of seconds before they crossed back into the hall.

Up the main staircase they rumbled, slaloming around Margaret (now on her way down), then through the divider door onto the old servants' landing and down the backstairs in a potentially expensive tumble of tail, haunch, fang and paw.

'The dogs have gone mad!' Emily yelled.

'For goodness' sake let them out into the garden before they break something,' Margaret called.

Emily headed for the breakfast-room door. 'Are the front gates shut?' she shouted.

Caitlin, keen to make amends for the chaos she'd caused, went over to the window to check. It was dark outside, but there was light enough from the house and the moon to make out their shapes.

'Yes! They are.'

On the affirmative Emily flung open the door. The dogs rushed into the driveway and chased each other around to the front of the house, where they tore to and fro beneath the boughs of the cedar, kicking up rusty gouts of earth from its dead needle bed as they went.

Caitlin watched them from the window while her shout faded slowly back into the silence. It had hung in the air longer than she would have expected, caught somehow by the geometry of the wall, the angles of the room, the glass of the windows and mirrors.

I can see you.

I know what you did.

Wink, wink.

When Emily went to take the rubbish out to the bins round the side of the house a little while later, she found Caitlin out there, smoking.

'Hello.'

'Hey.'

'You okay?'

'Yes. Just thinking. Want one?' Caitlin offered her the pack.

'No thanks.'

Caitlin leant forwards to stub what was left of her cigarette against the brickwork, her eyes curtained by a falling loop of hair.

'When will your brothers get here?'

'Matthew's coming on the train in the morning, but Alex should arrive tonight. He said he'd drive up as soon as Rufus had been put to bed.'

'Rufus?'

'Their son. His and Mia's.'

'Oh yeah. I forgot.'

'I thought you were kind of friendly with Mia?'

'I guess we lost touch.' Caitlin shrugged. 'It happens when people have kids.'

'Hmm,' said Emily, knowing just what she meant. 'It does.'

Caitlin nodded. 'What about Matthew?'

'Not much change there,' Emily laughed. 'Not on his income.'

'Where does he live, these days?'

'In Oxford, though he travels a lot. He helps organise these long-term environmental projects. If it paid better it would be an awesome job.'

'Oh Matty. He always was a bleeding heart.' Caitlin lit a

second cigarette and blew a concentrated jet of smoke into the frigid air. 'And what about you?'

It was a question Emily dreaded because the only truly appropriate response would be to curl up on the floor and wail. She wasn't doing anything, but the reasons she wasn't doing anything – well, where did they begin? In her childhood, in her relationship with her mother, in her genetic code? In her fear of maths, in the crush she had on her fifth-form English teacher? In her subsequent decision to study English at Southampton? How many layers should she peel back? How far down should she go? Which, if any, counted as primary cause? Which, if any, could really be isolated from the continuum of lived experience? What about her decision to even go to university in the first place, instead of dropping out and going travelling and writing a novel about her experiences, like she'd really wanted to? Maybe her idea to do the journalism conversion course at London City after she had graduated and then, during that, the choice she'd made – for no better reason than her feeling haunted, possessed even, by the ghosts of the authors of all the books she'd read – to take the print journalism module rather than the television one, even though the latter, given the age she lived in, would surely have been the more rational option.

At first print hadn't seemed such a bad call. She'd emerged from City into the maelstrom of mid-1990s London, all Britpop and Blairism, when the fashion, music and art scenes were exploding, the Internet was arriving, and magazines and websites mushroomed out of any crevice large enough for three or more arts graduates to cram in some desks built out of crates and plug in their Macs.

Emily had dug out her trashiest jeans, combed charity shops for old band T-shirts, worn her hair in a side pony and started knocking out freelance pieces for anyone who would take them. And there were plenty of takers. It was a fairly straightforward matter to meet or phone or email the various commissioning editors, even the ones on the broadsheets, and place a review of a fashion show, a gig, a gadget or a new exhibition and get paid a couple of hundred pounds in return. Soon she was doing interviews with minor pop stars, up-and-coming artists and designers, self-styled dotcom entrepreneurs and newly minted celebrity chefs – interviews that were not only easier to write than reviews but also commanded higher rates.

Her contact book grew and she was out every night, which was just as well, as the room she rented in a shared house in Holloway was not a place she ever felt overjoyed to come back to. She had a series of flings, first with a fellow journalist, then with a DJ, then with a photographer, none of them serious but each upping the ante in terms of her levels of access to scenes and events not just in London but in glamorous cultural destinations: Paris, Venice, Barcelona, São Paulo, New York. By the time the Millennium turned she felt as much at the centre of everything as she'd ever expected to be.

And yet at the same time she felt more and more dissatisfied. She couldn't say her life was empty – it wasn't at all. Plenty of people would have killed to be in her position. But at the same it did feel a bit pointless. She'd gone into journalism to make a difference like the writers she idolised, not to cover celebrities and trends with a half-life of less than a season. It had been okay as a way to learn the ropes and to get to know London, but she was beginning to feel mired in ephemera, as if she was slowly sinking into a kind of media quicksand from which, if she didn't extricate herself soon, she would never escape.

But the more she struggled against it the more the tide of

banality sucked its way up her legs. She tried repeatedly to get commissions for weightier pieces about the exploitation of immigrant garment workers, or the impact of climate change on cotton harvests, or the use of child labour by major brands, but despite positive initial comments from the editors to whom she pitched her ideas, when she tried to follow up they'd all suggest she did something else instead, or would somehow always be in a meeting whenever she called, or would just stop answering her emails and voicemails altogether.

She spent the final night of 1999 hopscotching her way across London via a series of parties held by her art and fashion world connections, starting out in the east on the top floor of a semi-derelict 1960s factory block wedged between Regent's Canal and the Hackney bus depot, whose machine rooms and lathes had long since been displaced by artists' studios. Long external walkways ran the length of the building, connecting the different apartments and affording a view of the city that was neatly framed by the decorative iron filigree of the two Victorian gasometers situated on the other side of the waterway.

Standing in the cold, Emily sipped a vodka cranberry cocktail from a plastic cup and gazed out at the blaze of lights, trying to work out how she actually felt about living in the midst of this vast agglomeration, so different from the landscape she'd grown up in. She couldn't decide, but then she'd have plenty more opportunity that evening to ponder the answer.

As soon as she'd finished her drink it was time to move on, and as if on a walking tour of the compacted layers of London's industrial history, she and her friends left the studios and made their way past the City Farm and the abandoned Children's Hospital and through the Boundary Estate, Britain's first-ever council-housing development, built exactly a century earlier. At length they arrived in Shoreditch, their destination a seven-storey building that between the two world wars had been a distribution centre for Lipton's tea, then had been pressed into service as a vast bacon smokery, and now was in the throes of an architectural makeover that would transform it into a suitable home for advertising agencies, games companies and an exclusive private members' club.

On this particular evening the gutted first and second floors had been tricked out with pop-up bars and art installations and crammed with revellers. There were more cocktails here – this time in a higher class of plastic cup – and then they were on the move again: off to Old Street station to get the Underground to Charing Cross and walk from there down to the Embankment.

They arrived way too late, the crowds so dense already that however much they ducked and threaded there was no hope of getting down by the river. The best they could manage was to squeeze far enough down a rammed side street to get a partial view of the Millennium Wheel. Even so, when the fireworks began – the much-vaunted 'river of fire' – they were so bright that they entirely filled what Emily could see of the sky, maxing out the CCDs of the handheld video cameras that people all around them were using to capture the moment, flooding the little LED screens with washes of undifferentiated light.

The year 2000. It had finally arrived. It was both extraordinary to be alive at such a moment, to be officially living in what for so long had been thought of as 'the future', and at the same utterly banal. However far out Emily and her friends pushed the celebrations – and they pushed them a fairly long way, on from the Embankment to a party in the premises of an indie record label in Borough, then south to New Cross for a warehouse rave, then back to Somerset House for a posh New Year's breakfast laid on by some fashionistas, then to a house party in Highgate that rolled on for the rest of the day – at some point the New Year had to begin much like any New Year always did in the capital: with a hangover and the prospect of grinding a path through the slow months of bleak and enervating weather that, new epoch or not, lay ahead.

Within a few weeks Emily found herself really quite depressed. The millennial mood had carried her most of the way through January before it completely wore off, but in mid-February she went down with a stinking cold, and even when her system began to shift it she found it really hard to see the point in getting out of bed, let alone in trying to chase down any freelance work. It felt like the end of an era, not the beginning of one. Change was required but the Lemsips weren't cutting it and she had no better ideas about how to make something happen.

But then, at 10.43 on a morning when the sky seemed even lower and the drizzle more relentless and penetrating than usual, an email popped into her inbox. It was from someone called Heather Monk whose name was appended, by means of an @, to the domain address of a large, well-known, American-owned magazine publisher.

The email itself was quite formal and began with an apology for any unsolicited intrusion. It went on to say, in fairly short order, that Heather Monk was the publishing director of a new magazine for women, still in the planning stage but due to launch in September, and she'd been given Emily's name in connection with a vacancy she was looking to fill on the features desk. Might she be interested in coming in for a chat about the possibility of taking up a full-time editorial position on *Hudson*, as the new magazine was to be called?

Emily would have fallen out of her chair had she been sitting in one. As it was she was propped up on cushions on the futon in her bedsit, still in her pyjamas and dressing gown, her laptop gently warming her knees. Her hands were shaking so much she accidentally deleted the email while trying to hit 'reply'. Once she'd calmed down and retrieved it from the trash she spent two hours drafting and redrafting what eventually, by the time she'd stripped it down to something she was satisfied had been completely cleansed of even the faintest scent of desperation, amounted to a three-line reply. Then she got up, showered, got dressed and ate a sandwich before forcing herself to read it through once again. She added a missing conjunction, corrected a typo, told herself it was now in the hands of the gods, and pressed 'send'.

Hudson's offices were in an unpretentious but well-appointed building a short walk north of Victoria Station, on a quiet square in the triangle formed by Victoria Street, Buckingham Gate and the grounds of the Palace itself. It shared the address with several of its stable mates from the mini-empire, with one of which Emily had placed several pieces over the previous couple of years – the source of the recommendation to Heather Monk.

Ms Monk was a half-Jamaican Mancunian who had spent the last decade working for *Harper's Bazaar* in New York and had returned to London in order to take up the position at *Hudson*. A willowy 52-year-old with rosewood skin and a headful of ringlets so evenly curled they looked as if they'd been planed off her scalp, she clearly spent enough time in the gym to imagine (correctly) that she could get away with wearing pink hot pants to work. That surprised Emily, as did her broad and readily summoned smile. She found Monk compelling, impressive and terrifying in more or less equal measure – a good combination in a boss. Just as well, because after a second interview with the magazine's editor, Bronwyn Durrant, Emily was offered the job.

She signed the contract on March 10th, the day the NASDAQ closed above 5100 for the first time. Suddenly her depressive New Year hiatus was over and the new millennium was kicking back in on a positive note. As Emily walked back to the Tube through Victoria Station, she couldn't think of anything she'd ever been more grateful for than the stapled sheaf of paper in her bag. Flushed with relief more than any sense of self-congratulation, she went out that night with a couple of girlfriends and got impressively drunk.

She started at *Hudson* the following week. The magazine's demographic was 25–35-year-old educated urban women, adventurous and self-determined in their approach to career, sex and relationships, and Monk had made no secret of the fact that Emily had been approached because she fitted slap bang in the centre of that category. She was, in other words, the reader, and in that capacity she was encouraged in the many planning meetings she attended over the next few months to shoot from the hip about what she thought was cool, what she thought was next, what other magazines were missing.

She took the opportunity to repackage many of her previously rejected feature ideas and found them a useful currency, received for the most part positively by her new colleagues, of whom there were rather fewer than she'd imagined there would be. Apart from Bronwyn and her deputy, Miranda Walton, who confusingly shared a first name with the Picture Editor, Miranda Reid, there was the Managing Editor, Joss Williams, the Production Editor, Cathy Schwab, the Sales Executive Katharine Cosgrave, and the only man in senior editorial, Art Editor Elliot Sawyer. Next in the pecking order came the fashion desk, which comprised the Fashion and Beauty Editor, Becca Smedley, the Senior Fashion Editor, Andrea Glass, the Fashion Editor-at-Large, Ellen Moore – a formidable figure in the industry whose path Emily had crossed before – and the Executive Fashion and Beauty Director, Tina Childs (whatever she did). Then, as far as she could tell, came Features Editor Emily Wold, and after her the two men whose job it was to wrangle and corral the collective output of all of these women: Sub-Editor Christian Timmer and the Designer, Ed Williams (no relation to Joss).

Around this core hung a mist of creative consultants, contributing editors, assistants and interns. Up at the top of the building, positioned literally and metaphorically above them all, was Group Editor Brendan Mallory and the executive team that oversaw the operations of the various magazines on the various floors. Numbered among these minor deities was Heather Monk.

Of all these people the only one directly affiliated with Emily seemed to be a woman in her early forties called Marie-Louise Johnson, whose job description was Features Associate. Emily wasn't sure whether or not this was a salaried position, but either way Marie-Louise didn't seem to be in the office very much. Rather like Ellen Moore – though lacking the fashion maven's panache – Marie-Louise flitted in and out more or less at random, dropping idea bombs on Emily's desk. When she actually produced a piece it was little more than a set of semi-evolved ideas, notes and musings, often without structure or even punctuation. Nevertheless she seemed to consider these offerings outputs of such genius that Emily should be actively grateful for the chance to pull them together and finish them off on her behalf.

Emily had imagined when she'd taken the job that the Features Editor would be running a Features department, and that her time would be more or less equally divided between attending cherry-picked events and sitting at her desk making decisions on the work her minions should do. But it turned out that this was Bronwyn Durrant's role. Emily's lot, as Features Editor, wasn't to run a department; it was to be a department – and to do all of the work of that department more or less single-handed, including most of the subbing. Christian helped out when he could, but he was always being pulled in seven directions himself, and he worked so hard and seemed so permanently exhausted and put-upon that Emily felt guilty chasing him to do work she could spend yet another of her evenings in the office doing just as well herself.

As a result, despite her initial high hopes of finally getting to write the social-impact features she'd long been dreaming of, once September rolled around and *Hudson* hit the shelves Emily just never had the time to do them. The longer articles tended to come in courtesy of Marie-Louise or one or other of the contributing editors, and when Emily did float an idea of her own at an editorial meeting she usually found that it raised the hackles of the stone-hearted Katharine Cosgrave, whose mission in life seemed to be to nix anything that might in any way jeopardise the closing of an adjacent ad sale.

In the beginning Emily tried to battle this on principle. Shouldn't editorial take precedence over advertising? Wasn't the fierce independence of the editorial voice absolutely fundamental to the very ethos of their magazine? But as the months wore on and the circulation figures rolled in she began to realise that this was not the case; editorial independence was in simple fact a luxury that could only be afforded by a profitable balance sheet, because without that there would be no magazine.

Plus, of course, since she'd started, the NASDAQ – along with all around it – had done nothing but plummet from the heady heights it had briefly attained in March. The bang that kicked off the year 2000 had turned out to have come from the bursting of the dotcom balloon, and with billions daily melting off the value of media companies that had paid too much for Internet properties that now appeared worthless, it didn't seem a great time to go biting the hand that was feeding you if you were one of the lucky few getting fed.

But Emily was too busy to worry much about any of that. Her remit included pretty much any text that didn't fall into the big bins of beauty, health or fashion, and each month she had to find the copy for a large opening section with a page apiece on something cool and current in pop culture, theatre, books, TV, film, art, music, sport, design, cars, restaurants, consumer trends and celebrity style; the 'Hot or Not' snapshot of what the *Hudson* hive mind considered to be either coming in or going out; a short section on something science-y (but not too science-y); a short section on money and investment meant to be aspirational rather than actually helpful for anyone doing any real financial planning; a short section about the website *à la mode* along with a round-up of the latest gadgets; a short section on the environment ('Help save the polar bear by re-using your plastic bags!'); and, most important of all, a couple of big anchor profiles per issue of arty stars of some description – designers, actors, writers, chefs, singers, comedians, whatever. It was quite a list.

Most of this material was supposed to come more or less unbidden from the constellation of contributing writers and associate editors, but the reality was that after the flurry of enthusiasm that accompanied *Hudson*'s first few issues it rarely did, and Emily found herself having to chase and chase hard for ideas and contacts, let alone copy, which almost never came in on time, however firmly promised. When it did arrive it invariably required a great deal of editing and fact-checking to pull it into shape, and then as often as not would be spiked more or less on a whim by Bronwyn during an editorial meeting or scorned by Katharine at a sales review. That's if it even got that far, as it was generally sent back long before then by the humourless Miranda Walton, who saw herself as an indispensable filter and gatekeeper and was in the habit of validating this belief by returning Emily's copy on reflex, annotated with schoolmarmish comments and requests for new angles, side panels, and changes in emphasis that were as often as not reversed by Bronwyn to something approaching Emily's originals once a draft had been deemed worthy to be placed on the editor's desk. 'Placed' being the correct term, as Bronwyn had a horror of computers and wouldn't consider anything for sign-off in the magazine by looking at it on a screen, a tic that could only be serviced by having *Hudson*'s office printers chunking out pages round the clock and running a bill for toner cartridges that stretched into four figures every month.

Before she really knew it, therefore, and certainly without ever having an opportunity to stop and think about it, the demands of servicing the magazine's monthly cycle had completely annexed Emily's life. Any notion of working the forty-hour week specified in her contract went out of the window on day one and then might as well have emigrated for all the hope there was of ever seeing it again. When Emily wasn't in the office she was on her way to it, or coming back from it, or doing something related to it. She didn't even have the time to dislike her bedsit any longer, as she was barely ever in it – it had become a place to sleep and change her clothes. She even washed more at work than she did at 'home' – there were showers in *Hudson*'s building and they were hotter and far more powerful than the pathetic electric-panel affair in her house, which never maintained a consistent temperature long enough for her to rinse the conditioner from her hair without getting alternately scalded and frozen in the process.

She was supposed to have five weeks' holiday a year, but the pressures of her deadlines were such that she only managed to take three of them if she was lucky. She was supposed to have weekends off as well, but an extraordinary number of these also went west, either because she was in the office, was catching up on work at home, was frantically attending to the various pieces of bureaucratic admin generated by the turning cogs of modern life, or was just sleeping to try and restore some of her much-depleted energy.

After nearly three years of this, two of them punctuated by repeated management assurances that the situation was temporary and would improve, Emily woke up one Monday morning with a feverish cold, muscular aches that made her wonder if she'd got early-onset rheumatoid arthritis, and the absolute conviction that she was being exploited. For the first time since she'd started at *Hudson* she called in sick, staggered to the doctor's to get a note to prove it, then took the train to Warwickshire to her parents' house to recuperate, emailing Miranda only to tell her that she wouldn't be in for the rest of the week and that they should call Marie-Louise in for cover.

When she did return, bolstered by her mother's cooking and assurances that she was far too thin and clearly working far too hard, she sent a memo to Bronwyn and Miranda – cc-ing Heather Monk – making what to her seemed like a very clear-cut case, given that she was personally responsible for more than a third of the magazine's written editorial, for her to be authorised to hire a full-time assistant in order – she was careful to argue – to offset any future risk of her absence through accident or illness.

Her gamble was that the experience of relying on Marie-Louise to get through press week would have proved so horrific that the editorial team would acquiesce to her demands just to ensure that they never had to ask the hare-brained Features Associate to act in such a capacity again. And so it proved. Marie-Louise had been almost no help at all, and the extra workload had fallen squarely on the shoulders of Miranda Walton – who, whatever else Emily thought of her, was at least capable of handling it. She was also capable of reminding Emily of this fact for months afterwards, which she did, and of hinting heavily that she suspected Emily of cynically engineering the entire situation in order to create a crisis that she could subsequently manipulate to her advantage – an interpretation of events that Emily sometimes thought, in retrospect, might actually contain an element of truth. But Miranda was also capable of seeing that the risk to the production process of having Emily solely responsible for so much content was real and had to be addressed.

Emily didn't get her way immediately, of course. There was a meeting to discuss possible solutions to the problem, all of which involved, in the first instance, trying to give her extra rights to call on the time and resources of existing staff. But having got this far she wasn't going to be derailed as easily as that, and so she firmly pointed out all the reasons that this would not work – not the least of which was that it would get the backs up of people across the magazine, most of whom were quite as stressed as she was. The next tactic was to try and fob her off with an intern, but Emily had seen that one coming too and had a response lined up: that it was actually illegal not to pay someone if they had set tasks and responsibilities and did real work, even if this law was regularly flouted across the creative industries.

Finally a compromise was reached. Although hiring anyone

new was apparently completely out of the question with the HR budget maxed out for the rest of the financial year (Emily did consider suggesting that if Bronwyn learned to edit onscreen they pay an extra salary with the money saved on toner), there was a person who was becoming available following the termination of a project on one of *Hudson*'s sister magazines. She was a trained journalist, very capable, and already had a contract. It would help Heather out if Emily would take her on, and obviously it would help Emily as well.

So all of a sudden Emily had an assistant. Her name was Laetitia Scott and she was twenty-eight, so a couple of years younger than her new boss, though she looked older and styled herself older as well. While Emily tended to favour a smart pair of jeans, a blouse and a jacket, Laetitia sported power outfits from good labels that hinted at family money or an eye for bargains in factory outlets or on eBay. She was also painfully thin even by the magazine's standards, her frame so frail that it vibrated slightly when she spoke with conviction or tested it with a laugh. And unlike Emily she smoked, was one of the crew that regularly needed to step across to the little park in the square in front of *Hudson*'s building and flutter nervously around the little cigarette bin that the council had clamped to the railings. She was also a vegetarian, so she and Emily had that in common, even if she hardly seemed to touch her food. And she was clearly smart, with a capacious memory and a quick mind, and that counted for a lot.

Unfortunately, as Emily was soon to discover, she was also precious, ambitious, completely self-centred and utterly ruthless, perhaps pathologically so. As a package she reminded Emily just a little bit of Caitlin, which was not a flattering comparison given the way things would turn out.

Naturally Emily didn't tell Caitlin any of that. Instead she put the bag of rubbish in the dustbin, replaced its lid, said: 'Not much, really. I'm sort of between things right now,' and went back inside the house.

Hands easy on the wheel, Alex zigzagged through the chicane of the driveway and pulled up in front of the garage. As the cooling engine ticked quietly to itself he retrieved a black leather holdall from the Porsche's minuscule boot, hooked it over his shoulder like a cricketer hefting a kitbag, and strode towards the back door, feet crunching on the gravel.

He was in the kitchen fussing over the dogs when Emily appeared.

'Hey Al.'

'Hey Em.'

'Journey all right?'

'Yeah, not so bad. You good?'

'Yeah, I'm fine.'

'Mum?'

'Bearing up I think. She got a bit teary today, but I think it was a one-off.'

'Oh right. What brought that on?'

'Bit of a strange one. After the funeral, Caitlin showed up.'

Alex stopped petting the dogs and looked up. 'She came here?'

'She certainly did. She's here now.'

'Really?'

'Yeah. And she could be around for a day or two. Jamie's come back, and apparently there's been some sort of family row over the will. She wanted to keep out of it.'

'Crikey. Well, can't say I blame her. I'm going to get a beer. Want one?'

'No, thanks. I'm off to bed. I'll see you in the morning.'

''Night.'

''Night.'

Pondering the mystery of Caitlin's arrival, Alex disappeared through the door that let onto what the family called the back kitchen corridor. It connected to a large room called the freezer room, a half-forgotten game pantry that was too dark and too cold and too damp to ever get used for much of anything, and a third room lined with old teak cupboards. This was the 'brown cupboard room', and an investigation of its eponymous storage spaces would reveal a dozen tennis rackets of varying antiquity; some bats of varying purpose; a few mildew-stiff canvas bags rattling with calcified cricket pads and shrunken leather balls; several balled-up rugby shirts rich with moths and spiders; three dilapidated and nearly-valuable boxes of *Monopoly*, *Cluedo* and *Trivial Pursuit*, and an occasional shuttlecock, lurking amongst the clutter like the cocoon of a giant bug.

Alex bypassed this treasury of memories and headed for the freezer room, where a supermarket crate of lager lay on the cool quarry tiles. He snagged a can and returned with it to the kitchen, where he cracked it open and upended it into a smoky yellow tankard. Then he sat down at the breakfast table and kicked off his shoes, a schoolboy habit that he'd never grown out of: inside the house – any house – he preferred to be in his socks, even though it meant he wore them out in a matter of weeks. Flexing his arches and enjoying the sensation of evaporating sweat, he glanced through the copy of the *Birmingham Post* that was lying nearby. Then his father wandered in.

'Oh, hello Alex. You're here are you? How was the drive?'

'Fine thanks. I thought you'd be asleep! How're things here?'

'Oh you know. Can't complain.'

'How's Mum?'

'Bearing up I think. She's upstairs in bed, but I believe she's still awake if you want to stick your head in and say hello.'

'Yes, I'll do that. How about Caitlin? Em said she's staying.'

Miles brightened a little. 'Yes, she is. I didn't expect that, I have to say. She was here for dinner. So long since I've seen her. Nice girl, but a little self-absorbed. Though you'd expect that, at such a time. She didn't touch her meal.'

'Emily said there was some issue with the will?'

'It wouldn't surprise me.'

'But you've heard tell.'

Miles produced a thin smile and began tidying away odd items left over from dinner: the cheeseboard, a stack of dirty plates, his son's empty beer can.

'It seems Tony has been playing silly buggers with all concerned,' he said. 'But why let death change the habit of a lifetime?' Was this a reference to the deceased's brief marriage to Margaret? Alex wasn't sure.

'Yes, quite.'

'Talking of which, young Mr Blake has returned.'

'Emily told me. She said he and Sheila weren't seeing eye-to-eye.'

'Apparently not. Though I'm not sure Jamie ever saw eye-to-eye with anyone about anything.'

'I always got on him with him okay.'

'Ah, yes – the Mia connection.' His wife, Alex felt, was another person of whom his father had never quite approved.

'That's right. Though I was thinking back to when we were

teenagers. I didn't actually see him the time we went to his place in Brazil.'

Miles frowned with the effort of remembering. 'He wasn't at your wedding, was he?'

'No.'

'No – well, it would probably have upset your mother.'

This was true enough.

'I'd better go up and see her before it gets any later.'

'Yes. I'll follow you. Nice to have you home, anyway, Alex. In spite of the circumstances.'

'Thanks Dad. Nice to see you too.'

Tankard in hand, Alex wandered through the silent house, pausing in the hallway for a minute to absorb its presence before slowly climbing the main staircase and padding along the landing towards the short wide flight of carpeted steps that led up to Emily's bedroom and the box room – home, when he'd last lived here, not to boxes, but to the family computer. At the foot of these steps Alex turned right, stepping down through an archway into a small anteroom, off which led two doors. One belonged to his parents' dressing room, the other to their bedroom.

He knocked lightly on the latter.

'Mum?'

'Alex? Is that you dear?'

Alex pushed the door open and walked lightly into the room. A bedside lamp threw a damp glow against the walls, and before he saw his mother his eyes fell on a silver-framed portrait that had stood on the cherry veneer of the table in front of the window opposite for as long as he could remember.

It was a photograph of Margaret at twenty-six, dressed in sandals and a pale blue dress with a square smock neck, leaning against the kind of low weed-choked wall that generally bordered some picturesque stretch of estuary. One foot forward, the other bent and back, her neck slightly craned, she was smiling – toothily, benignly – at his father, the photographer. Miles had taken the picture the weekend he'd proposed, and it held an important place in the Wold family mythology because Margaret had already been pregnant with Alex at the time. This fact sat contrary to the couple's otherwise rather staid reputation and lent them a hint of Sixties rebellion they'd always rather revelled in. But it told another story too: that of Margaret's fear, in the wake of Tony's fruitful affair with Janice Blake, that she might be infertile, and as always when confronted with the photograph Alex faced the troubling thought that his prim mother would almost certainly never have allowed herself such sexual liberties if she'd hadn't been stalked by that particular spectre – and that he therefore owed his own existence, in a very real way, to the libidinal urges of one Mr Anthony Nolan, Esquire.

'Hi Mum.'

Margaret lowered her copy of *House and Garden* and peered at her son over the tops of her reading glasses.

'Hello dear. I thought I heard your car. Did you have a good journey?'

'Yes. Clear all the way.'

'How's everything in London? How's Mia? And Rufus?'

'They're fine, just fine. We went to see the whale.'

'Oh!' Margaret perked up at once. 'I was going to ask if you did. I heard all about it on the news, poor thing. Wasn't it sad?'

But Alex had got over his brief obsession with the whale, and despite having brought it up he didn't think that right now the topic was worth pursuing. He sat down on the edge of the bed and looked at his mother.

'How are *you* doing?'

'I'm fine.'

'Not too upset?'

'Over Tony? No, dear. I mean, yes, obviously, it's an awful shame. But anything else . . . it was all such a long time ago. I really didn't come into contact with him very much. The last few years your father saw more of him than I ever did.'

'Well as long as you're okay.'

'Yes, yes. It's Caitlin we should be worried about, I think.'

'It was nice of you to let her stay.'

'Well it seemed the least we could do,' Margaret said, folding her glasses into their case. 'Though I have to say it was a little unexpected. I would have thought she'd want to be with her own family at a time like this. But it seems that Jamie's come back and there's some huge upset over changes to the will.'

'So everyone says. Bit premature, isn't it? Same day as the funeral?'

'I think that's what Caitlin thought. I think she thought she'd leave them to it.'

Back in Chelsea, Mia's belly had started hurting again, just as it had in the early stages of her previous pregnancy. In becoming a mother she'd sacrificed any sense that her body fitted together. What had once been a lissom machine, the fleshed-out flux of a girl, was now a collection of disparate parts – and faulty, leaky parts at that. Add pain to the mix, mysterious pain that could signify an almost limitless range of possible horrors – or else nothing at all – and it seemed to take all of her energy just to hold on to any even vaguely coherent sense of who she was.

The discomfort woke her later that night. She slid out of bed, felt her way to the bathroom, lifted the seat, and slumped over the void. Another thing familiar from her previous pregnancy, this: the small-hours slash. Purge complete she wiped herself, rose to her feet, and let her nightdress fall back down round her knees.

Behind her the toilet floated like the stern of a small yacht. It wasn't set into the floor like the toilets of the houses she'd grown up in, but was cantilevered out of the wall behind it, a wall which – like the bath housing, the shower base, the two sinks and the medicine cabinet – had been cast *in situ* from concrete of the very finest quality, concrete that flowed around the room in a single, extruded mass from which the various fixtures and fittings emerged.

The construction had always reminded Mia of a French cartoon she used to watch as a child in Senegal. The cartoon was called *Barbapapa*, named for the father of a family of amorphous shape-changing beings who lived in a house of a similar nature. Inside it the various bits of furniture swelled from the walls and floors just as they did, in their way, in this room. When Mia had been small she'd wanted to live in a house just like that, just like the Barbapapa residence. And now, she supposed, she did. Except hers was even nicer.

Two sinks. Yes. They had two sinks. Barbapapa didn't have two sinks, though of course he didn't need them, as he or Barbamama could make a sink by extending their stomachs into bowl-like shapes whenever they chose. The question of what the Barba family did regarding drainage and sewage hadn't of course occurred to the childhood Mia. She looked at Alex's sink, on whose generous surround his razor, shaving dish, bottles of deodorant and aftershave had been tidily arranged by the cleaner. It was a little like living in a hotel, she thought. The notion made her happy: she'd always been very fond of hotels. And she loved this house. The young black architect they'd commissioned to do the renovations on the recommendation of a friend of a friend of Mia's who'd studied at the Architectural Association in Bedford Square had turned out to be an inspired choice. He'd gone on to become a media darling – a 'young Turk' – famous mainly for his open-plan layout of the tent that housed London's new art fair, held each October in Regent's Park.

'A miracle of topology,' *The Times*'s architecture critic had called it. 'It seems to actually fold the space in on itself.' Mia wasn't sure that she entirely agreed with this analysis even before Alex had quoted it to the point of irritation at their dinner parties. The art fair seemed to her little more than a very large marquee divided into cubicles, no more special than the layout of Ikea. But then Mia had not thought long or deeply about the endless time and motion studies that had gone into the design of Europe's favourite furniture outlet, which had parlayed the science of consumer behaviour into a cost/distribution ratio of which the most ruthless communist state would have been proud. Nor, for that matter, had she ever been to any other kind of trade fair. Her looks and natural poise had ensured she'd been steered well clear of such humdrum environments, where cheery businessmen swapped business cards and soft-shoed hacks hauled bulging, branded shoulder bags between the pit-stop smiles of the PRs and marketeers, all to squeeze a few more precious drops of green elixir from the cogs of capital as collectively they hauled them round.

Turning on her own hot tap, Mia rinsed her hands, looked into the mirror, and squeezed some rehydration gel onto the tips of her fingers – just under a hundred pounds a tube, from a specialist clinic in Belgravia. Carefully she massaged it into the skin around her eyes. What did she see? Did she see what Alex saw? Just what did Alex see, these days? She couldn't remember the last time he'd looked into her eyes. These days Rufus took all of their attention. They both looked at Rufus, Rufus looked back at them, and this was the way they'd come to communicate.

Yes. She supposed that's exactly what it was. Having a child. That's why you did it. That's how it worked. It was a kind of improvised theatre, everyone cast in roles they only half understood, trying to do what was expected of them, trying to reinvent themselves on the fly, trying to cope. It wasn't exactly what she'd planned for herself, that was for sure. If it hadn't been for Rufus, who knows? She might have had a lead role at the RSC by now and have brokered that into something sizeable in telly or even film. Her agent had been devastated – in the nicest possible way – when she'd told him she was pregnant. He'd always had such ambitions for her, but in the space of a few seconds she had seen that interest drain completely from his face. There had been talk of picking things up in a couple of years' time when the early stages of motherhood were out of the way – there followed a (short) list of famous actresses who'd managed this – but they both knew that her best chance of a breakthrough role was now, not later. Still, she hadn't given up hope just yet, if she could keep the wrinkles at bay. And if the gel didn't work, well, there were other things she could do. They could afford them.

The door swung open and a small figure came tottering in, rubbing his eyes with one hand and tugging at the soft fabric of his pyjama top with the other. It was Rufus, awake and out of bed. Mia bent to him and as she did her knees cracked.

'I can't sleep.'

'Nor can Mummy, darling. Come here now. Come on.'

She scooped him up and, rising, set him on her hip. He was

getting bigger. It wouldn't be long before she couldn't do this any more.

The child sank his face into the shelter of her neck and began to whine. She brushed the dark curls – her curls – back from his ear.

'*Viens, mon petit chou*. Shush now. Mummy's here.'

Leaving the bathroom light on so that she could see her way, she carried the child through the bedroom, across the landing and down the stairs to his room, where she coaxed him back into his bed. But she couldn't escape, not yet. He wanted her to read to him.

'Okay,' she agreed, 'but just five minutes.' And she reached over to the oiled oak bookshelves for the second volume of the Harry Potter saga and settled herself down beside him, arranging his Buzz Lightyear duvet so that it covered her legs as well as his.

'The next day, however, Harry barely grinned once,' she read, picking up where she'd left off earlier.

'No. Not that bit. The bit where Harry and Ron take the flying car to Hogwarts.'

'But we read that already.'

'But it's the good bit!'

Mia sighed and flicked forward to the page in question. A generation of kids growing up desperate to go to boarding school. Well, they had that covered. Rufus was already on the list for Winchester. That also wasn't quite what she'd envisaged when she'd been younger. The general idea then had been to bring children into a more open and equitable world. But somehow that ideal had got lost along the way, somewhere back with the modelling contracts, and the acting ambitions, and the need to find a husband who was capable of providing at least the basics of civilised living and security in a world that was far more off-balance and terrifying than she'd ever realised at sixteen.

Harry finally worked his magic and Rufus nodded off, although by this point Mia was wide awake. She ran her finger around the hairline of her sleeping son and wondered if that particular and ineffably perfect combination of mahogany curls and caramel skin would actually have existed if it hadn't been for the events of September 11, 2001. It was impossible not to have been transformed in some way by an event of such extraordinary intensity, and when Alex had called her a few days after their return from Brazil she'd had no hesitation in giving him permission to come and visit her precisely because of what they'd just been through. And when they'd ended up spending the night together, wrapped tightly like students in the single bed in her digs, their lovemaking had seemed a kind of affirmation in the face of all the lives that had been lost.

This fervour, of course, soon faded, but Alex came back again, and again, and as their situation began to renormalise Mia found that she really rather liked him. Then six weeks into her run at Stratford she had discovered that she was pregnant. She wanted children – she'd always wanted children – but now? With Alex? In the middle of the best job of her career? Even though the baby would arrive after the season was over, if she kept it then she would by then be starting to show. Hopefully it wouldn't be more than the seamstresses could cope with, but it was still going to be bloody embarrassing.

If she kept it? Was this even a question? She'd turned thirty that March. There was still time on the clock, but it seemed a little late in the day to have a termination. Two years before: maybe. Five years before: for sure. But not when she'd almost certainly be wanting to try and start a family before long anyway. Her mother and grandmother had both had an early menopause; she didn't want to be one of those older mums who had one child late on and then couldn't have another. And she certainly didn't want to be mucking about with IVF.

In the end, she decided that she wouldn't know until she told him. His reaction would be her gauge; by that she'd be able to calibrate her own decision. She waited until the next time he drove up to see her and told him in bed, right after they'd made love, making sure she watched his expression while she gave him the news. And the thing his face did, the very first thing, before there were words or thoughts or any of that ambivalent stuff, was to smile. Sure, later on there were hesitations, and qualifications, and manoeuvrings and misunderstandings, on her side as well as on his. But the first thing was that smile: that was the thing she would always remember, and that was the thing that sealed it. She would let him ask her to marry him, which before long he did. He couldn't not; not after the spectacular series of blowjobs she'd given him.

They tied the knot during a long weekend in New York right after her show came down, just the two of them, a gesture intended to both make up for lost time and to somehow symbolically close the circle opened for them on that terrible September day. They had a miniature ceremony in Central Park then the next day drove out to Long Island to visit the graves and the families of Alex's friends Carlos and Lucía. It was very poignant, but nonetheless getting hitched like that did manage to annoy both sets of parents, particularly Mia's mother, who still moaned to her at intervals about the need for them to have a proper party to celebrate. And now here she was, a yummy mummy in an extravagantly large Barbapapa town-house in Chelsea with two sinks in the master bathroom en suite and a second child on the way, living a part rather than acting one.

The pain in her belly was subsiding and now, unbelievably, she was feeling horny. Typical. The long hours Alex worked combined with Rufus's constant need for attention meant that sex, once a near-nightly delight, now seemed to happen about once a month. When they did make love she had to gear herself up to it and didn't really enjoy it very much. And now, all of a sudden, at two in the morning with her husband a hundred miles away, what she wanted more than anything was a really comprehensive fuck.

Sod it. She wasn't going to sit around at home all weekend. She'd drive up tomorrow and join him, maybe get Margaret and Miles to look after Rufus while she dragged him out for a sexy walk in the woods. It would be cold but they could take blankets. They used to do that kind of thing all the time. It was important to hold on to that stuff. It helped keep you young.

Caitlin did not appear for breakfast the next morning, so the four Wolds found themselves eating as a family. While he was making toast Alex's phone rang. It was Mia – she was missing him, and thought she'd bring Rufus for a visit.

'It's pointless us being in London, we've got nothing planned. We might as well all be together.'

'We could have all driven up together yesterday.'

'I didn't think about it then.'

Alex turned to his mother. 'Is it okay if Mia and Rufus come and stay?'

'Yes, of course it is,' said Margaret, as he'd known that she would. Alex sighed inwardly. He'd been looking forward to a child-free weekend. And with Caitlin in the house as well . . . it just might have been simpler if Mia wasn't around. He lifted the phone back to his ear.

'Sure. That'd be great.'

'Do you want us to come?'

'Yes, of course.'

'Because it sounds like you don't.'

'Not at all – it'll be nice. I was just worried you'd be bored. Caitlin's here too, by the way.'

'Caitlin? Really? At your parents' house?'

'Yeah. Some kind of family tension over at her place. Jamie's back and apparently it's all kicked off between him and Sheila. She's hiding in her room though – I haven't even seen her yet. Maybe you can find out a bit more from her when you get here.'

He ended the call, took his toast to the table, and reached for the Companies and Markets section of the Saturday *Financial Times*, which was muddled in with the various components of that day's *Telegraph*. No sooner had he sat down than the house landline rang. Miles tutted, got up from the table, and walked over to the sideboard to answer it.

'Wold,' he barked into the handset, and then proceeded to conduct an almost monosyllabic exchange with whoever it was that had called. 'Ah . . . hmm . . . yes . . . right . . . yes . . . see you . . . bye.'

'That was your brother,' he said to Alex when he was done. 'He'll be at Warwick Parkway at half past eleven. You couldn't spin over and pick him up, could you? I've got to pop out to a meeting this morning and it would save your mother a job.'

Alex nodded. Cast once more in the role of his father's errand boy; proof, if any were needed, that he was home.

After breakfast Alex retrieved his laptop from his bag and set it up on the kitchen table, figuring he might as well crack through some work emails before he set out for the station. But the house Wi-Fi didn't seem to be working, so he spent half an hour in his father's study hunting for the documentation belonging to the unfamiliar router and getting it to reconnect.

The study was on the ground floor at the front of the house, in between the dining room and hallway: it had doors that let onto both. The desk was in the large bay window, its chair positioned with its back to the view of the trunk and lower boughs of the cedar that sprang like a gigantic green toadstool from the needle-strewn expanse of the front lawn. At the other end of the room, which was decorated in something beige from Farrow & Ball and hung with a collection of framed prints and maps, a narrow archway let into a book-lined cubbyhole. This had previously been a tiny tool room, accessed from the stairwell via a peculiar little door inset with a leaded stained-glass window, but Miles and Margaret had knocked it through. The door had stayed, however, and had proved a source of irritation to all the Wold children, as its window allowed their father to see them from his desk whenever they slid down the rickety banister of the main staircase – one of their favourite activities, and one that was strictly forbidden.

Having got the router going again, Alex parked himself in Miles's chair and wondered – not for the first time – how on earth his father managed to work in it. It wasn't an office chair at all but a venerable oak armchair he'd picked up at some house auction or other, nice to look at but horribly uncomfortable to sit on. Miles had softened the hard, polished seat with a thin slab of cushion – almost as old as the chair by the look of it – but that actually made matters worse, because it slid around and made it impossible to hold one's position. Or maybe that was the point. Alex couldn't fathom which.

So it was uncomfortable, unstable, and on top of that the arms prevented it from being drawn up close to the desk, and on top of *that* it was the wrong height. It was, in short, not fit for purpose. It wasn't a surprise that what work Miles did in it was mostly done in his lap and that fact alone, Alex reflected, told you most of what you needed to know about the kind of working life he'd had. No one in Alex's world could operate that way. Computers wouldn't allow it, not even laptops, despite their name. The machines demanded sensible furniture and a sensible posture. Working like this, largely by hand, with piles of papers on every available surface, looked at best unprofessional, at worst chaotic.

Alex picked up the nearest of the piles and leafed through its contents. It was mostly particulars, mostly for houses in Redditch. This sort of thing was Miles's meat and drink, had been all Alex's life. His father's firm must have helped its clients buy and sell thousands of these kinds of places over the years. He put it back and picked up another. Land this time, deals covering several quite big chunks of land northwest of Snitterfield, including, to his surprise, the woods at the back of their house in which he, Matthew and Emily used to play as kids. By the look of it the buyer was the same in all cases – Tony Nolan's forestry project. That was more interesting. He hadn't known that Miles had been acting as Nolan's agent. But it made perfect sense.

Bored of the piles, Alex started on the desk drawers. The moment he opened the first one its rich musk of wood sap and linseed transported him right back to his childhood. Inside he found a collection of objects with which he'd long been familiar: a crappy 1980s solar-powered calculator that no longer worked, a magnifying glass he'd used a few times for torturing ants, a letter opener whose silver handle didn't properly fit its ivory blade, a few boxes of staples and paperclips, a decrepit hole-punch that had belonged to his grandfather, and a razor-sharp penknife that in contrast to the other items had actual utility. In the other drawers there was nothing much of note: envelopes and headed letter paper, chequebook stubs and old passports, a couple of empty photo albums, a stack of letters from HSBC . . .

Alex paused. A stack of letters from HSBC? Freddie Winston's bank? He took the letters out and placed them in his lap (he'd given up trying to sit at the desk). They were from the bank's retail arm, rather than the investment division to which Freddie belonged.

Twenty minutes later Alex was still reading through them, and what he read unnerved him. Two years earlier, no doubt with an expectation of having a project to both fund and occupy his retirement, Miles had set up a small company, named himself and Margaret as directors, and taken out a loan in order to buy several residential properties to rent. Nothing wrong with that, although the logic was questionable given that property prices were at all-time highs and it was hard to see how rents alone would stretch to cover the loan repayments. But capital accrual could in theory take care of that, and it was not the major problem. No. The problem, as Alex now identified it, was something different. It was the fact that the loan had been bundled, at the bank's behest, with an interest-rate swap.

An interest-rate swap was a complex instrument. Alex knew such crossbred beasts were being herded in volume through the derivative desks where they were served up to hedge funds and other banks looking to manage their own exposure on a loan or forward trade. But he hadn't quite realised that on the other side of the deal they were being packaged up on the high street for unsuspecting folk like his father.

Miles wouldn't have realised it either. As far as he had been made aware – if the correspondence Alex now held in his hand was anything to go by – he was being sold a 5 per cent loan with integrated insurance on which the maximum interest payable was capped at 7 per cent even if standard interbank rates should rise beyond that. What was not made clear, and was only referenced at all deep in the impenetrable booklet of terms that accompanied the paperwork, was what happened if interest rates should fall.

At that point the deal revealed its other face, the one beloved of the broker and the counterparty. For the trade that underpinned it was something called an asymmetric leveraged 'collar'. The collar in question was 2 per cent either side of the original 5 per cent rate. As long as the interbank rate, commonly known as LIBOR, stayed in this zone between 3 and 7 per cent, everything was fine. But if it dropped out of the collar, if LIBOR should fall below 3 per cent, then the rate Miles was obliged to pay would actually go up.

By what amount it would rise depended to some degree on the fee that the broker – the bank – had charged. If the deal was symmetrical, if the bank had insured against the same amount that Miles had borrowed with the counterparty, then the rates would go up proportionally. Under such an arrangement a fall to a LIBOR of 2 per cent would mean that Miles's rate would go up to 4 per cent; a LIBOR of 1 per cent and Miles's rate would rise to 5 per cent. But the kinds of bonus fees that could be charged for such arrangements were not, Alex knew, enough to satisfy the appetites of traders. They wanted to skim silly money off these kinds of deals, and because everyone knew that interest rates weren't going to fall they insured the total amount of the principal loan against interest-rate rises and insured double or even triple the amount of the principal against rate falls, and then pocketed the difference, earning the collar the adjective 'asymmetric' in the process. And they did this without bothering to make it clear to the end client that if LIBOR fell to 2 per cent he could end up paying 8 or 10 per cent interest on his loan, or even more. Because, the traders told themselves, it wasn't going to happen. The interbank rate had been around 4 or 5 per cent for years, and that was low, historically. No one could really remember it being any lower than that. And if it did, by some freak, fall below that point, chances were that by then all the traders involved would have long since moved to other desks, other jobs, other banks. Making the outcome for gulls like Miles, as far as they were concerned, pretty academic.

For Miles, of course, such an outcome would be very real indeed, as he would be the one person who would not be able to escape from its logic. In the event of a drop in rates his only way out of the collar he'd clipped round his neck would be to buy his way out by compensating the counterparty for their corresponding loss of income. Depending on the interest rate at the time of curtailment this could easily be 10 per cent of the principal. So: three hundred thousand pounds. Or more.

The sound of someone coming down the stairs broke Alex's focus. He slipped the letters back into their drawer, vacated the oak chair and nipped through the dining room back into the kitchen, where he busied himself making coffee. As he was priming the Gaggia, Caitlin walked in.

'Hello stranger,' he said.

'Hey.'

'Been a while, hasn't it?'

'Certainly has.'

'Fancy a latte?'

'Okay.'

Alex fetched a clean mug from the draining board, put the

machine through its cycle, foamed some milk, poured it in, and handed Caitlin the finished drink. 'Sugar's there, if you want it.' Her face was puffy; she didn't look great. Nor did the manky bandage she had on her hand. 'Rough night?'

'Couldn't really sleep.'

'I'm not surprised. I'm really sorry about your dad.'

She sipped the coffee. 'Thanks.'

'You want some toast? Or cereal?'

'Maybe later.' She pointed to the fruit bowl on the side. 'Mind if I take an apple?'

'Of course. Help yourself. Whatever you want.' She took one but didn't bite into it. 'I hear Jamie's back.'

'That's right.'

'How's he doing?'

'Oh he's just great.'

'Really?'

'He's over the moon. Why wouldn't he be?'

'I heard there was some issue with the will.'

'Something like that.'

'Well if you need to talk . . .'

'Reckon your parents would mind if I took a bath?'

'I'm sure that would be fine. You know where it is, right?'

'Yep.'

And then she was gone and Alex had to leave too, puzzling over her detachment and whatever it was she'd done to her hand as he located his car keys and headed out to pick up his brother.

The platform at Warwick Parkway sits atop a steep embankment, so when Matthew's train arrived and the passengers had spilled out of the carriages they all had to descend the metal staircase built around the shingled tower that houses the little station's solitary lift. Down they went, round and round, passing in and out of view before entering the glass and steel ticket office only to reappear a moment later in the car park via a set of automatic sliding doors.

Matthew was the last to emerge: beanie pulled down over his ears, rucksack on his back, jeans splaying over dirty trainers, mauve plastic cat carrier tucked beneath one arm.

'What's that?' Alex said, as he got out of the car to greet his brother.

'Cat,' said Matthew.

'Christ – what did you bring that for? It'll drive the dogs insane.'

'They're already insane. I couldn't get anyone to look after him.'

'Mum's going to be delighted.'

'She'll get over it.'

Matthew stowed his stuff; fortunately the cat box slotted fairly neatly onto the shelf behind the Porsche's two front seats. Then they climbed into the car.

Alex started the ignition and pulled away, enjoying the way the puckered leather seam on the inner circumference of the steering wheel ran through his fingers as he guided the machine out of the car park.

'How's the whale-watching?'

'It's not fucking whale-watching.'

'What's wrong with whale-watching?'

'Well, nothing, apart from the fact that there are so many tourist boats taking people out in places like Montauk that they're upsetting whale migration routes and damaging the animals' hearing with the vibrations from their engines.'

'Oh okay. I didn't know.'

'Don't tell me you've been on one of those dumb trips?'

Alex thought about his Montauk misadventure. 'Well, my friends went. I was sick.'

'I knew it.'

Distracted by the sudden appearance of the ghosts of Carlos and Lucía, Alex changed the subject. 'Hey, I have news,' he announced, as he crossed a main road and headed back into the lanes. 'Mia's pregnant.'

'Great,' said Matthew.

'Don't mention it to Mum and Dad – we haven't had the twelve-week scan yet. It's still early days. You're the first person I've told.'

'I'm flattered,' Matthew said, sounding anything but.

Alex reacted accordingly.

'You could at least say it like you mean it.'

'You know I think there's already too many people in the world.'

'What, so we can't have another child because it's bad for the environment?'

'You can do what you like. Just don't expect it to meet with my approval.'

Alex snorted, dropped the car into third, and whipped it round a tight, sharp corner. This was the back way to his parents' house and he loved to drive it. You had to be a bit careful, this time of day, what with all the locals trolling to and from the shops, but you could still hit it reasonably hard.

'You know that Caitlin's staying at our place?' He shouldn't have taken pleasure in saying it, but after his brother's reaction to his previous piece of news it was difficult to resist.

'*What?*'

Matthew, Alex noted, was suddenly exhibiting genuine concern.

'Apparently there's been some huge family row over the will, and she walked out.'

'What sort of row?'

'I don't know. I only saw her briefly this morning, before I came to get you. She doesn't seem to want to talk about it.'

Matthew turned his head and glowered out of the passenger window, tracing the outline of a cloud with his finger in the condensation on the glass. Houses flashed past: barn conversions, extended cottages, five- and six-bedroom properties occupied by lawyers, accountants, estate agents, marketing executives, car salesmen, stockbrokers, financial advisers. There were also, intermittently, farms: forlorn and slightly squalid places when compared with their gentrified neighbours, tongues of mud lolling out from their shambolic yards, rotting sheet-metal barns like giant air-raid shelters dwarfing the ill-maintained brick dwellings they overlooked.

'How's the documentary going?' Alex asked, referring to a project he knew Matthew had been working on in his spare time.

'Slowly. People don't seem that interested in doing anything.'

'They want to do things. Just not necessarily your things.'

'They want to do fuck all. We all do. It's too late, anyway. We're going to carry on consuming our way into disaster. We're on the downward slope now. The planet's going to burn, and we're all going to fry.'

'That's cheery.'

'It's what's going to happen.' Where he'd traced the clouds Matthew rubbed the glass clean with the heel of his hand. 'Will you slow down?' he snapped as his brother cut a bend finely enough for the tyres to nip the levee of grit on the edge of the verge.

'Why?'

'I don't like people driving too fast.'

'Would that be because you haven't got a car?'

'Just fucking slow down, will you?'

Alex grinned, depressed the accelerator even further and slalomed through his favourite S-bend. Then he lifted up his foot, dropped down a gear, and brought his speed under control.

'Sorry,' he said, turning to better stress his lack of sincerity. 'That last bit doesn't work if you take it too gently. By the way, I wanted to ask you . . .'

'Look out!'

Two horses with riders had swung into view: a girl on a placid piebald pony tagging along behind a young woman on a fine bay stallion. Alex rammed down on the brakes and the car vibrated as its anti-lock mechanisms kicked in. It wasn't enough: the surface of the lane was scarred by frost and heat and screed with rubble, the tyres couldn't grip, and inertia forced the vehicle into a skid. It didn't hit the horses but it did slide past them in a sharp diagonal, only coming to a halt when its wheels banged up against a kerb.

It wasn't over. The stallion, spooked, pranced and mashed the air with its hoofs. As its rider gripped furiously with her knees it wheeled about and gibbered down at Matthew, trapped white-eyed below it in the passenger seat. Then the pony took fright. Short of sight and dim of hearing, it hadn't been much affected by the skidding vehicle. But the stallion's rage was a different matter, and somewhere in its brain there pulsed the thought that it had better follow suit. It was old, though, and fat, and a little arthritic, and prancing hadn't been within its operational ambit even as a foal. Instead it bucked a bit and backed into the ditch, where it spiked its haunches on a collection of hawthorn splinters left by the last hedge cutter to have passed that way and cantered back in the direction it had come, the twelve-year-old on its back juddering like a solenoid. It was almost funny until she lost her stirrups, dropped the reins and tumbled to the ground, where she lay emitting a long, shrill wail of pain.

By this time the older rider had brought the stallion back under her control. Slipping from the saddle she hurried over to the girl, while behind her Alex and Matthew climbed gingerly from their cockpit.

'Is she all right?' Matthew asked.

'I think so,' said the instructor, who was comforting the screaming child while feeling up and down her arms for broken bones. 'No thanks to idiots like you. What in hell do you think you were doing? She could have been killed.'

'You shouldn't have a horse like that out walking on the road,' Alex smirked.

'What did you say?'

'What is it, a racehorse? It's obviously too highly-strung. God knows what damage it's done to my car.'

'Well if you hadn't been driving like a maniac . . .'

'I actually wasn't driving particularly fast.' He turned to Matthew. 'Was I?'

Matthew hesitated. The woman was staring at him, demanding a truthful answer, but he could feel his brother's presence by his side. Suddenly everything seemed to depend on him, on his word.

'Er, no,' he said finally. 'Not really.' The instructor shook her head, disgusted. 'Can I help you fetch the horses?' Matthew asked, ashamed.

'No. You can piss off. Both of you. Go on. Just piss off.'

They got back in the Porsche, and for the next two miles or

so Matthew's unspoken 'I told you so' hung in the air like a rancid fart.

'I know, I'm an arsehole,' said Alex, when he could stand the stink no longer.

'Yes, that's right, you are.'

'Thanks for backing me up there though.'

Matthew barely managed a shrug. He wished he understood why he hadn't sided with the riding instructor, even though he'd wanted to. To take his mind of it he produced a joint from the pocket of his jacket, which he waggled to and fro by the fold of paper at the fatter end as if willing his brother to notice. When Alex said nothing he engaged the cigarette lighter, to emphasise the point.

That did it. 'I hope you're not thinking of smoking that in here,' Alex said.

'Since when did you get so puritanical?'

'You know how I feel about that shit.'

'What, and you and your banker friends aren't all snurfing coke at all those posh dinner parties you all love so much?'

'Not my friends. And in any case, there's no smoking in the car. Of any kind.'

'Not even the fat cigar that comes with your massive Christmas bonus?'

'That more than anything.' The lighter popped up obligingly but Matthew ignored it, sighed, and returned the joint to his pocket. 'In any case, I should've thought you'd have wanted to see Caitlin with a clear head.'

'That's precisely the reason I want to get stoned.'

'I don't understand you.'

'You think how you think, I'll think how I think. Let's just leave it at that.'

The dogs were waiting in ambush in the hallway: they'd smelt cat before Matthew had even got out of the car. With the first crack of light round the doorframe they sparked into action, Max's whines coiling out of the slots in his box as Matthew held him just out of their reach.

'They're like cartoon crocodiles,' Alex laughed as the dogs jumped and snapped.

'You could always give me a hand.'

But Alex preferred to stand there and soak up the spectacle, watching Harry and Pandora continue to rage until Margaret came through from the kitchen and sent them packing with a couple of well-aimed slaps across their backsides.

'What did you bring the cat for, Matthew?'

'I've only just got back from a trip. I couldn't leave him on his own again. Not straight away.'

'You're going to have to keep it locked in your room.'

'That's fine.'

'It'll use a dirt box, will it?'

'It's a he, Mum. And yes, he will.'

'Well I hope so. I don't want to spend the weekend cleaning cat pee off the carpets.'

Matthew scowled and stomped on up the stairs. Ten seconds through the door and already his mother was on his case. Couldn't she have even said hello? Was it his fault the dogs weren't properly trained? God knows he'd expended enough energy trying to convince his parents to get someone in to teach them some modicum of obedience, given that his father had no interest in putting in the time himself and his mother did nothing but indulge them.

It was typical of their lackadaisical approach to everything, their lack of regard for the consequences of their actions or the feelings of those who might be affected by them. They didn't communicate, they never had, it was a source of constant amazement to him that they'd actually managed to . . .

'Hi.'

She was standing on the landing dressed in boots, jeans and a pointed Peruvian hat with long flaps that hung down over her ears, her hands in the pockets of a sheepskin body warmer.

Matthew watched her as she floated towards the cat carrier and bent down to get a better look inside. As her features loomed before the little mesh doorway Max stopped his yowling, licked around his teeth and blinked. Could she charm animals, as well?

'Hey kitty. Oh – he's only got one eye.'

'Yeah – I think he lost the other one to cat flu. But that was before I met him.'

'Poor thing.'

'It's tough about your dad,' Matthew said.

'Yep. It is a bit.'

'Where are you going?'

'I was going to go for a walk. I told Margaret I'd give the dogs a run.'

Matthew remembered the joint in his pocket.

'I was thinking of doing that too. Could use some fresh air.'

'Do you want to come?'

'Do you want me to?'

She shrugged.

'I'd better sort Max out first.'

'Max?'

Matthew lifted the cat box. 'He needs a litter tray. It'll just take me a minute. See you out the front in a sec.'

They went up the garden, through the back gate, and took the path that led round the edge of the wood, a route they'd last taken together some sixteen years earlier.

'I always thought they were a bit scary, these woods,' Caitlin said, as they came up over a rise that afforded a good view of the hillside, with its dense carapace of trees. 'Not like the ones near Round Hill.'

'They always seemed pretty friendly to me,' Matthew grumped. 'They used to frighten Emily though. Me and Alex left her alone in them one night, when we were camping together.'

'You never told me that.'

'I was embarrassed afterwards. About how mean it was. I don't think she's ever forgiven us.'

'I'm not surprised.'

They walked on a little farther, following a sheep track that wound between tussocks of grass shaped like giant emerald anemones, past a hawthorn hedge and a badger sett. The air was still and cold, undisturbed by birds or insects, the track beneath their feet baked hard by frost, the dogs running ahead of them, darting from scent to scent.

'It's very old, you know, this wood. That's why it's got such an atmosphere. People reckon that it's one of the few remaining pockets of the old Forest of Arden. You know, in Shakespeare's time a squirrel could cross from one side of the county to the other without ever touching the ground.'

Caitlin smirked. 'Dad used to shoot squirrels.'

'Really?'

'Yeah, he hated them. When I was little he used to call them "tree-rats". He had this air-rifle, and if he saw them in the garden he'd take pot shots at them out of his bedroom window.'

'So much for Tony the Tree-Hugger.'

'You mean his planting project?' Caitlin laughed. 'Yeah, the squirrel-shooting doesn't exactly fit well with that. Though I don't think he ever actually hit one. He had a rubbish aim. It's got quite big, you know, his forest. Loads of farmland all round where we live is fenced off for saplings now. I think he was even buying fields up over this way.'

'Well he's got a long way to go if he's trying to recreate the Forest of Arden. It used to go all the way up to Tamworth.' Matthew caught himself. 'Oh – I meant "had". "Had" a long way to go. Sorry. That was thoughtless.'

'It's okay. I still haven't quite got my head round the fact he's gone.'

'Why do they need to fence the trees in?' Matthew asked, keen to move the conversation forward.

'It's the deer. They strip the bark off the saplings and kill them otherwise. Trouble is that the areas are so big and the fences take so long to erect that the deer end up getting fenced in. So then they have to get all these blokes to come and chase them out again. It's quite a hassle.'

'Sounds it. I'm surprised they don't just shoot them.'

He meant it cynically, but Caitlin didn't take it that way. 'They do, sometimes, but there are quite strict rules about culling. It all has to be done by the book.'

Matthew reached into the zippered breast pocket of his jacket and produced the joint, which he lit and passed it to Caitlin. The two of them walked on around the edge of the field, passing it backwards and forwards in silence.

'You're in telly, these days, aren't you?' Matthew asked, at length, hauling himself back from thoughts of the past.

'Sort of.'

'We've been trying to get someone to make a documentary about one of our EcoPath projects.'

'How have you got on?'

'I've been to see people at a few production companies.'

'And?'

'It's extraordinary. The environment is front-page news these days. But unless it's got a celebrity attached or you can get sex in the title, no one wants to know.'

'Sex, fame and property. That's what it's all about.'

'The whole thing's been a colossal waste of time. This one guy, I went in to see him, and do you know what he said? He just glanced at first page of the outline and said, "Oh yeah, global warming, we've had hundreds of pitches like this the last couple of years. They're like confetti."'

'That's encouraging.'

'So I said, well, if there's so much interest in the subject, why didn't you make any of them?'

Caitlin smiled. 'I bet he liked that. What did he say?'

'I don't know. I'd already walked out.'

'Brilliant. You're going to go far in telly, Matthew. I can tell.'

They both grinned and the ice between them melted slightly. Smoke caught in Caitlin's lungs; she banged a fist on her chest. 'Nice weed.'

'Thanks. I grow it in my kitchen cupboard.'

'Yeah?'

'You just need a light and some nutrients,' Matthew explained. 'You can get them off the web.' But Caitlin didn't really care and neither, in truth, did he. 'Why d'you never get in touch?' he said instead.

'Don't ask me that.'

'But why?'

'You know what it's like.'

'But you could've done.'

'Then maybe I didn't want to.'

The joint was dead. Matthew pinched it out and tucked the roach into the pocket of his coat.

'It's good to see you,' he said.

Her expression didn't change. Her eyes. Her glass-green eyes. No one else had eyes like that.

'I miss you,' he probed.

'I can tell.'

'Caitlin . . .'

'Please don't, Matthew. I don't want to drag it all up again. It was painful enough the first time.'

'Then why are you here? Why are you staying with us? You must've known I'd come back. And Alex, too. Why did you even want me to come on this walk with you?'

'I didn't – you asked . . .'

'Oh come on!'

'I don't know, Matthew, I don't know what you want from me—'

She had turned away from him and he grabbed her shoulder and pulled her back around.

'I'll tell you what I want. I want to know. I want you to tell me who it was. Call me stupid, but I thought that's maybe why you'd come to see us. That maybe now your father was dead you could actually bring yourself to tell me.'

'Don't touch me! Do you think I need this? Right now? Do you?'

'*Who?*'

Caitlin stared at him, but she said nothing.

'It was Alex, wasn't it? That night he took you home. It was my fucking brother.' He grabbed her shoulders and shook her. 'Wasn't it?'

'Leave me alone!' She wrenched free of his grasp and strode off down the hillside.

'It was Alex!' he yelled at her retreating form, willing her to stop and turn. 'Wasn't it?'

But she just kept walking away.

When Caitlin got back to the house, sixty thousand pounds' worth of Range Rover was sitting in the driveway plump and smug as a carved stone lion, and lunch was about to be served.

'Hi! Just in time,' chimed Alex as they walked into the kitchen. 'Caitlin – you remember Mia, don't you? And this little guy is Rufus.'

Mia hopped to her feet and sashayed forward in her hipsters, describing sine waves with her pretty white pumps.

'Hi Caitlin.' She chanced a smile. 'It's been a while.'

'It has.'

'I'm so sorry for your loss.'

'Thanks.'

A silence followed, conveniently broken by Matthew coming through the back door and bringing the dogs in with him. As always Harry and Pandora transformed the scene, and suddenly there was much noise and activity.

'Come on, let's eat!' bellowed Miles, and grabbing a dish of roast potatoes from the side of the Aga and the bottle of Costières de Nîmes he'd opened an hour earlier to breathe, he led the way through to the dining room.

Despite Miles's effusive bonhomie, lunch was a quiet affair. Neither Caitlin nor Matthew said a word while the pork was carved and eaten, and Emily and Alex weren't too chatty either. Fortunately Mia was in a voluble mood, and prattled on happily about London life, and Rufus's new nursery, and how the architect they'd used for their renovation was now quite the rising star.

'He's building an amazing roof conversion over in Hoxton for Freddie Winston,' she told no one in particular.

'Isn't Hoxton a slum area?' Margaret frowned, the memory of a magazine article from the early 1980s faintly glimmering in her brain.

'Oh it used to be, but now it's very fashionable. I mean, loads of advertising agencies are opening there now, and lots of finance people live there because it's close to the City. And so there's plenty of nice shops and cafés.' She'd chosen 'nice' over 'cool' and 'cafés' over 'clubs' so that Margaret would better understand, not just because she and Alex hadn't actually been out clubbing since Rufus had been born. 'And there are some great properties. Freddie bought the top floor of this incredible old factory and has had the whole roof taken off and reinforced. He's having a pool and a dining pavilion built up there. It's absolutely amazing. The pool is going to be see-through, so if you're on the next floor down you can watch people swimming like in – what's that aquarium we went to, Alex?'

'Monterey.'

'In Monterey, that's it. And next to it, above it I mean, on the top, there's this pavilion which is going to be a pool house and hang-out most of the time, but if you flick a switch a dining table with chairs will rise up from the floor.'

'Wow,' Matthew said, finally hearing something he judged worthy of his comment. 'That's useful.'

'Now, now, Matthew, that's enough,' Miles said.

'But—'

'Matthew!' snapped Margaret, in a far sharper tone than her husband's. Knowing that resistance was futile, Matthew sat back in his seat and reached for his wine.

Sublime, unruffled, Miles began a fresh conversational strand. 'I don't want to discuss your father if it will upset you, Caitlin, but did you know that just before he died he bought the wood at the back of this house?'

'What, where we walked this morning?' Matthew said.

'If that's where you went,' Miles replied.

'No, I didn't know,' said Caitlin.

'I did a lot of work with him, you know, on the forestry project. I was quite closely involved.'

'What was it all about, Dad?' Alex said, feigning ignorance of the documents he'd seen that morning. 'Tony never struck me as the environmental type.'

'Maybe that's a question for Caitlin.'

Caitlin shook her head. 'I don't really know, to be honest.' She glanced at Matthew. 'He didn't really talk about it much. Dad had lots of projects.'

'I reckon it was a tax dodge,' Matthew said.

Margaret exploded. 'Matthew, that is enough!'

This time, though, Matthew wasn't in the mood for backing down. 'Mum, it's a perfectly valid suggestion. Loads of people buy land through offshore trusts as part of tax-avoidance schemes. It's happening all the time. We've already established that Tony was hardly an eco-activist. It wouldn't exactly be out of character if he'd done it for financial reasons.'

Miles stood and picked up the carvers. 'It's not a question, Matthew, of whether or not it's reasonable,' he said. 'It's a question of whether or not it's appropriate.'

'Quite,' said Margaret, her feathers smoothed somewhat by her husband's even tone.

'Who'd like some more meat? Caitlin? Can I tempt you? Emily, obviously not, but there's plenty more veg. Alex, I know you'll take some more. And Matthew, Caitlin's glass is empty – top her up, would you. And while you're at it you can go around the table.'

Social embarrassment successfully averted, the meal continued, discussion revolving around less inflammatory subjects, until the course was done. Nonetheless there was a sense of collective relief when Margaret stood and clapped her hands.

'Right, no levitating tables in this house,' she said. 'We're still very much at the manual stage. So come on everyone. All hands on deck.'

Mechanically efficient after many years of training, the family carried dishes, scraped plates, wiped surfaces, stored leftovers, filled the dishwasher and assembled the various components of dessert with barely a word exchanged. Then, just as Margaret was handing round dishes of rhubarb crumble and telling people to help themselves to cream, the low clattering of an unshielded petrol engine disturbed the prandial calm.

'Oh those wretched motorbikes,' she tutted. But the sound did not fade away and die, as it would have done had its source been some passing Kawasaki. Instead it came and went and came and went, changing direction as if moving in circles around the house.

As the volume increased for a third time, Matthew got up and walked into the front bay window to investigate.

'Matthew, we're still in the middle of eating.'

'I just want to see what . . .'

He broke off and ducked by instinct as something large and black flashed past the window.

'What the fuck . . .?'

'Matthew!' The admonishment came from Miles this time.

'Well it's not exactly every day a pair of legs falls from the sky into our driveway.'

Dessert was forgotten, and Margaret raised her hands in despair as her children all jumped up from the table and ran to the front door. Outside they found a man in a crash helmet standing on the property's large main lawn, the buttercup-yellow canopy of a paraglider fluttering above him, and what looked like a giant ventilation fan strapped to his back.

'Mind my roses!' Margaret yelled, as the canopy began to float down towards the borders, and in response the pilot began hauling on the suspension lines in an attempt to guide the delicate pillow of fabric to the safety of the grass. Now that he'd turned they could see his face. It was Jamie Blake.

'Hey!' he shouted cheerily. 'Thought I'd drop in!'

'Bloody hell,' said Alex quietly, voicing a thought shared by the group. 'This is a bit of a surprise.'

As they stood, slightly stunned, pondering the protocol for greeting someone you hadn't seen for twenty years when he'd literally dropped into your garden, a maroon pick-up truck rolled into the driveway with Sean Nolan at the wheel and a bearded man of around the same age in the passenger seat.

Sean got out and came jogging up, his face clogged with concern. 'I'm very sorry Mrs Wold. He wasn't supposed to land here. He hasn't caused any damage, has he?'

'Not for want of trying.'

Emily intervened. 'Oh come on Mum, lighten up. It's okay, Sean, really. Total losses amount to one cold rhubarb crumble and a few slightly bothered roses.'

Awed by the spectacle of something akin to a superhero flying in to say hi to his grandparents, Rufus had already decided that there was no point in standing on ceremony and had set off along the weathered stone path that led round the flower beds to investigate more closely. By the time the others caught up with him he was standing in front of the grounded paramotor trying to clip himself into the harness, Jamie's helmet balanced on his head.

'I want to go flying,' he said. He'd got hold of the throttle by now – a small metal trigger at the end of a cable – and was squeezing it repeatedly like a water gun.

Alex laughed. 'I think you're going to have to grow a few inches taller first, Rufe.'

'I could take him up,' Jamie said, giving Alex a wink. 'It would be fun. I could just strap you to my belly, Rufus, like a baby kangaroo.'

Rufus thought this sounded like an excellent idea.

'Can I go, Dad, can I? Mum? Can I go?'

Mia blanched. 'I'm not sure I'm quite so keen as you all are.'

Matthew glanced at the narrow gap between tree and house into which Jamie had descended. 'I don't think you've got the first idea how to fly that thing. You're bloody lucky you didn't disembowel yourself on one of the chimney pots.'

'Swear box Uncle Matthew, fifty pee,' chirped Rufus happily.

'He does know what he's doing,' Sean said. 'Unfortunately.'

Jamie grinned. 'Sean is referring to the fact,' he said, 'that Rick and I know he has promised Emily a flying lesson. And since I also know he'll never get round to asking her himself, I've come to ask her for him.'

Sean grimaced. 'Thanks Jamie.'

'My pleasure. So come on Emily. What about it? We've got a good few hours of daylight left.'

Everyone looked at Emily, but before she could speak, Margaret intervened.

'Emily, there's no way you're going up in one of those machines.'

That pretty much made up Emily's mind for her. 'Of course I am Mum. This is Sean and Rick's business. They make these things. They're perfectly safe.'

'Fantastic,' Jamie said. 'Caitlin, you'll come too, won't you?' he continued. 'Sean tells me you've been up before.'

Caitlin stared at him. In the general hubbub her presence had almost been forgotten, but there she was standing apart from the group, smoking yet another cigarette.

'Sure. Whatever. Let's go.'

'Hurray!' shouted Rufus, jumping up and down with excitement. But Alex shook his head.

'Sorry buddy, we're staying here. Your mother's right. Too dangerous.'

'But Dad . . .'

'No buts. Grandpa's promised to bring the box of Lego down for you to play with while your mum and I go out for a walk.'

Rick, Jamie and Caitlin took the truck and led the way; Emily followed with Sean and Matthew in the Wolds' old Renault 4. The car had been sitting in the garage under a tarpaulin for some years, but after she'd moved back from London her parents had had it serviced and taxed so that she'd be able to get around on her own.

'Bit weird, isn't it, for us all to be going flying the day after a funeral?' Matthew observed from the back seat.

Sean didn't turn around. 'Jamie thought it would take everyone's mind off things.'

Sensing where her brother was headed, Emily decided to ask the obvious question before he did. At least she could do it with tact.

'Sean, if you don't mind me asking, is Caitlin okay?'

'Yeah, I think so. Why?'

Emily glanced at him. The choppy swirl of his curls was highlighted by the low winter sun, which flashed into the car through gaps in the denuded hedgerows.

'I mean, what with her staying with us . . .'

'She's staying with you?'

'Yes. She came last night. You didn't know?'

'No.'

'That's odd. She said you'd all had a row about the will, and she'd walked out.'

'That's news to me. Jamie came back to my place and crashed out right after the ceremony. And as far as I know no one's even seen the will yet. I don't know how relevant it'll be, anyway. From what I've been told by Dad's lawyers, the probate could take years to conclude.'

'Really?' Emily said, beginning to wish she'd never asked. 'That's weird.'

'Par for the course, I think. Look, don't worry about it. We're here now. Time to do something more fun.'

They had reached the track that led to Sean's house. Emily turned in and trundled the Renault past the little gables of St

Leonard's Church, then at Sean's direction pulled into the field adjacent to the dark blue drier barn, where Jamie and Rick were already laying out the paramotors and their canopies on the grass. Caitlin stood leaning against the Toyota, Peruvian hat in her hands, blonde hair fidgeting in the breeze.

'You made it!' called Jamie, as they got out of the car. 'Well done. We thought you might have chickened out.'

Emily put a hand on her hip and feigned shock. 'Thanks very much! Before you know it matey I'll be giving you pointers, just you wait and see.'

'Not scared then?' he called back.

She grinned. 'Terrified!'

Sean fetched a helmet from the truck and took her over to the nearer of the two contraptions. Positioning her in front of it, he picked up the two cords that linked the harness to the wing, each of which terminated in a triangular plastic handle, and draped them over her shoulders.

'Okay. These are your main controls,' he said, threading his arms beneath hers and taking the handles in his hands so that he could demonstrate. 'They'll hang off the harness about where they are now, and you pull the one on the side you want to turn. So it's pull right to turn right, and pull left to turn left. Got it?'

Emily nodded and Sean handed her the throttle.

'This controls the prop. Don't think of it in terms of speed, think in terms of altitude. Pull the trigger to go up, release it to go down. And this red button here? If you really want to stop, hit that and the engine will cut out. Then you'll just start floating down to the ground. But try only to do it when you're pointing at a decent place to land.'

'Right. Pull: up. Release: down. Red: stop.'

'Great. Let's get you into the harness.'

Sean and Rick were hoisting the paramotor onto Emily's back when the whine of an engine a little further down the meadow signalled that Caitlin was preparing for take-off. They turned to watch as she pulled forward on her canopy. It twitched, raised an edge, then scooped itself aloft; craning her head to track its progress she walked forward until it was directly overhead, then gunned the motor and began to run. For a few paces she thudded heavily along and then her feet lifted free of the ground altogether and she was taking great long bounds in the empty air, bounds that took her clear of the tall hawthorn hedge that ran along the far side of the field and up into the sky.

'Wow,' said Emily, as Caitlin carved a turn around the barn.

'See how it's done? When the paraglider's right overhead, that's when you've really got to hit the gas and run like crazy. And don't stop running, not until you've cleared that hedge. Got it?'

'Got it.'

'Brilliant.' He blinked at her a couple of times, quickly leant in and planted a kiss on her cheek, then – blushing – retreated just as swiftly and made an 'O' with forefinger and thumb.

'Good luck!'

Emily smiled thinly and pulled the throttle, applying more force than she meant to. The propeller screamed into life and shoved her hard between the shoulders; she stumbled but recovered and now found herself moving forward with the canopy rising fast behind.

'Look up! Look up!' Sean's voice, now coming through the intercom, startled her with its immediacy. She lifted her head, felt the helmet cut into the back of her neck, and saw the bright nylon edge of the wing drift into her field of vision.

'Run!'

And run she did. Accelerating hard, she allowed the machine to push her forward and suddenly it was easy, the weight was gone, she'd been transformed, and her toes were lifting free of the turf. In her surprise she eased off the trigger and at once her trainers thumped back down to the ground.

'Keep going! Don't stop!'

She squeezed again and took another two or three giant steps, completing what amounted to a giant bounce. The hedge loomed in front of her. She put out a foot and it crashed through the tangle of hawthorn. And then she was over it and her next step struck into a void. Up she went as if borne upon a wave of pure exhilaration, and it wasn't until Sean told her to ease off the gas and level off her trajectory that the fear hit. Then, looking down, she had time to realise that she was high in the air – very high in the air – and that there was nothing at all between her and the field below.

Her legs dangled uselessly beneath her. Her right hand was gripping the harness so hard that her fingers had blanched and gone numb. A stave of telephone wires slid under her shoes. She didn't know where she was going, what to do next. The thought of moving her hands up to the control bars filled her with unspeakable dread. She was going to die.

'How do I turn again?' she yelled into the mike.

'Don't worry about that,' Sean's voice came back. 'If you carry on as you are you'll come round in a circle – it's the bias caused by the propeller. Just concentrate on getting your bum into the seat.'

The seat. She'd forgotten about the seat. The harness was fitted with one – less an actual seat than a sort of ledge that she could use to displace her weight from its present concentration on the straps slicing painfully into her armpits.

To get her backside onto it, however, meant releasing her grip, and that was hard to do: she was frozen with fear, dangling like a dead cat from her shoulders while the paramotor eased her in a circle just as Sean had promised. Over the neighbouring field, back over the telephone wires, over the barn, round by the river and back past the church, and all the time the notion that she should shift her position even a millimetre seemed utterly absurd.

'I'm scared, Sean.'

'I know you're scared. But don't worry. You can't fall. The worst that can happen is that you let go of the throttle and parachute to the ground.'

'Or crash into those telegraph wires.'

'That's not going to happen. Just concentrate on your breathing, okay? Do that for me. Breathe in, and breathe out. Breathe in . . . and breathe out.' Sean repeated this two or three times. 'Feel any better?'

Thirty metres up, Emily nodded. The focus on her breathing was helping, and now that her inactivity had resulted in nothing more dramatic than a couple of gentle laps of the meadow she was beginning to gain some confidence. She counted to three and slowly released her fingers, which complained as the blood flooded back into their joints.

There was no disaster. The paraglider didn't suddenly spiral out of control. Everything stayed fairly calm and stable, and she felt confident enough to work her hand up her chest and fumble for the shoulder strap. Got it. Okay. That's good. Now, move her right buttock just a little . . . She relaxed her shoulder, dropped her arm, and groped around until she'd managed to trap the edge of the seat between the heel of her hand and the butt of the trigger. When she had it tight she hauled with all her strength on the shoulder strap, pulling the seat forward and shoving back with her bum.

It worked. Suddenly the harness was taking all of her weight, and a pressure she'd been only half aware of was released from her groin and armpits as the shoulder straps slackened. Her circulation returned, along with a rush of euphoria.

'I did it!' she screamed, completely jubilant.

'Well done!' Sean's voice crackled over the intercom. 'That's a bit more like it. Feel good?'

'I think so.' Now that she was sitting down her situation felt entirely different. It was still scary, but in a way that was exciting rather than petrifying. She reached for the control wires and pulled a couple of breaths deep into her lungs. 'Wow. I'm flying. I'm really flying!'

'Do you want to try a turn?' Sean asked.

'Okay.' She looked about herself: the phone wires were some way away, and she was clear of the barn. Steadying her nerves, she gave a cautious tug on the right-hand control wire.

'Harder than that! You want to pull it down all the way to your waist.'

'Oh, right.' She gave the line a hefty yank; the canopy above her dipped and she swung out in an arc.

'Whoooah! This is awesome!'

She made a quarter-turn and then returned the controller to shoulder level. As the canopy straightened she swung back, pendulum-like, to the perpendicular.

The intercom buzzed. 'Looks like you're getting the hang of it.'

'Oh very funny.'

Down on the ground Matthew had wandered over to join Sean. 'She's getting on all right, isn't she?' he asked.

'Not too bad.'

'Caitlin's amazing though. Has she flown a lot?'

'Yeah, quite a few times. It's actually pretty easy to tootle about like this; otherwise we'd never let people up by themselves without lots more training. Things get more challenging as you go higher.'

Then, as they watched, something odd happened. Caitlin's canopy twitched violently, almost folding in half. It quickly recovered its shape and continued on its way, but with harness and propeller swinging free in an eccentric fashion. Eccentric, because Caitlin was no longer attached to them. While her craft hummed away on its own, she was falling rapidly to earth.

GULL

TONY NOLAN WAS STANDING in his socks on the patio at the back of his house in Shelfield, knocking dried mud off his wellingtons, his antler-handled walking stick leant against the large concrete planter beside him.

'Are you coming Sean?' he shouted back into the house, before perching on the lip of the planter and tugging the boots onto his feet. He was just getting to grips with the second one when his son emerged.

'Take your time, won't you?' Tony said.

'I couldn't find my gloves,' Sean explained.

'Gloves? What do you need gloves for? It's not that bloody cold.'

'It might be once we get up the hill.'

'Who said we're going up the hill?'

'Just a wild guess.'

Tony huffed his heel into place, levered himself upright, and set off in the direction of the paddock. At the edge of the patio he paused, leant his stick against his shoulder, and lit a Bolivar with a long-stemmed wooden match from a box he kept in the pocket of his Barbour for that purpose. This task accomplished, he snapped the match and flicked the two halves into a rose bed and then walked on, Sean bobbing at his side, a trail of sculpted tufts of smoke unfurling on the brittle air behind him.

In the paddock he made a small detour via the little stable block, pausing to inspect some work that had been done to patch up the shingles on the northern wall and murmuring something to Sean about poor-quality materials costing you twice as much in the end. Then he struck out for the gate that let onto the footpath behind the paddock fence and back down to the lane. Once through that it was only a short walk to the stile affording access to the arable field beyond, a field that stretched all the way to the foot of Round Hill, which was indeed their destination.

Tony, however, wasn't about to let himself be so easily second-guessed. His son's assurance had annoyed him, as had the generally cocksure manner Sean had displayed since his recent graduation, and to regain the initiative he cut across the field away from the hill and through the plough churn. This quickly caked their boots and made for heavy going as they took a turn around the eastern edge of the wood, coloured at this time of year only by the coppery carpet of leaves and the metallic highlights of moss and lichen that encrusted the trees' bare branches.

Eventually they reached Inkberrow Lane and followed it along what was now the north side of the wood, stamping the clay from their treads as they went and leaving manure-like trails on the pale grey tarmac in the process. As they neared the centre of the wood the narrow verge widened back into a clearing that in turn dwindled into a track leading south, and parked here were eight or nine distressed trucks and caravans. It was a travellers' camp, and one which showed few signs of life beyond the laundry hanging limply on the van-to-tree washing lines and the actions of an emaciated tomcat who was sitting on a stained plastic picnic table washing his face with his paw.

Tony's cigar was down to the nub now, and as they passed between the vehicles he dropped it underfoot and pressed it into the dirt. At that moment the door on one of the buses popped open and a heavy man wearing boots, jeans and a vest heaved out, pulling a plaid shirt up around his shoulders.

'Morning John,' Tony called. 'Didn't mean to wake you up.'

The man started, but grinned when he saw who it was.

'Morning Mr Nolan,' he said. 'What brings you this way?'

'Just out for a stroll. Have you met my son Sean?'

'I don't reckon I have.' John ambled over to them, and as he approached Sean could see that one of his eyes was strangely glazed and slightly smaller than the other. He shook the man's hand, which was as chapped and abraded as an old leather glove.

'Pleased to make your acquaintance, young man.'

He offered them tea but Tony declined, and he and Sean continued up the track through the woods.

'I didn't know you knew the travellers,' Sean remarked, when they were some way into the trees.

'There's plenty you don't know,' Tony said, and he eased his pace off a little now that he felt back in control.

The ground rose and the path wound to and fro until, quite abruptly, it stopped and they emerged onto a grassy ride, sliced through the wood to allow a line of telegraph poles to carry its wires clear of entangling branches. The shooting season was just commencing, and around them the birds ran thick along the ground, growing hungry now that the harvest was over and the days were growing colder and getting used to people coming this way on foot to bring them feed.

The ride took them over the crest of the contour and down the other side, and they followed the line of poles until the trees closed in again, the grass became hatched by muddy wheel ruts, and the track reappeared. Then they were out of the wood and crossing a patch of set-aside thick with fescue and meadow grass. During the summer this had towered ambitiously and harboured a dense peppering of wildflowers between its swaying peaks, but it had since been twisted into flattened swirls by the wild autumn weather. Ahead stood a smart aluminium gate, and beyond it Round Hill: they had come full circle.

They climbed the hill slowly. Even though this northern approach offered the gentlest gradients of any of the summit routes, Tony began to wheeze as they passed the ancient hawthorn that occupied a peculiar scooped-out hollow, like a tiny cwm, about halfway up the slope. Having already suffered one detour, Sean said nothing about the fact that he'd guessed where they were going; he also said nothing when his father lit up a Dunhill the moment they reached the small stone circle that sat on the hill's flat top like a rusted iron crown.

While Tony smoked Sean let his eyes run over the view to the southwest. The Warwickshire plain undulated away from them between the escarpment of Guy's Cliffe – curling like a crooked arm to their left – and the woods they'd just walked through, the space between these two margins crayoned in with a classic English patchwork of hedgerows and fields. This in turn was sliced into segments by lanes as sinuous as streams and pinned to its spot on the earth by the silage towers of Glancey's farm, standing like some ancient monument at the centre of it all.

'You're looking the wrong way,' Tony said. 'The other side, that's what I brought you up here to show you.'

Sean turned to see his father gesturing with his stick towards the northeast, in which direction another set of fields, flatter and much less picturesque, extended to the horizon. In the middle distance he could see their own house, at the far end of the little hamlet that dribbled away along Burford Lane.

'What about it?' Sean asked. The view was, after all, utterly unremarkable, merely another aspect of the one he saw every day from his bedroom window.

'I've bought it,' Tony said.

'You've bought it?'

'Well, not all of it. A lot of it though.'

'Who from?'

'The first chunk, which is way over there on far side of Wrokas bank by the river, that was from Pete Scrivens, when he decided to sell up and move out to Spain. Other bits and pieces I've added since. There's more, too. A band that stretches all the way across the Henley Road, past Bearley even.'

Sean whistled softly. Tony was talking about a great deal of land.

'What have you done that for? You planning on becoming a farmer?'

'Nope.' Tony put down his stick and reached inside his coat for his hipflask. 'I don't imagine those extortionate school fees I shelled out covered teaching you anything about the Forest of Arden.'

Sean sighed. The pointlessness of formal education, paid for or otherwise, was one of his father's favourite themes – although he noted that it was his school his father was choosing to target, not his university. He knew that Tony was proud of him for getting his degree, even though he would never actually admit it.

'Not exactly,' he said.

'No surprise there. Waste of bloody money.' Tony took a nip of his whisky and Drambuie mix and passed the flask to his son before taking up his stick again. 'Five hundred years ago it covered all of this,' he said, gripping the horn handle and sweeping the ash staff across the relevant quadrant of sky. 'Started this side of Stratford and went right past Birmingham, Coventry. All the way to bloody Tamworth.' An imaginary Tamworth was skewered with the stick's steel ferrule. 'Covered the whole damn county and more besides. All trees. Oak, elm, ash, larch. A lost world. Even the Romans were too scared to try and put a road through it. Coughton was the edge of it, that's as close as they dared come. You left the road there, you were on your own. Took your life in your hands if you wanted to get to the fort at Henley. Full of rogues and thieves it was. Outlaws, cutthroats. Like our friends back there in the caravans. Though Pig-Eye's a bit past it now.'

An image of the traveller's mild deformity flashed into Sean's mind.

'What happened to it?'

'What do you think? Cut down for firewood. Roof beams. Ships. The Elizabethans liked their ships, of course. And then they farmed the shit out of it. Enclosures. They wanted to clear the Catholics out. Robert Catesby and his gang. Gunpowder plot – presumably you've heard of that? That was all hatched round here.'

'And you're trying to recreate this forest?' Sean worked hard to keep any incredulity out of his voice. With his father, nothing was impossible.

Tony put his stick down and fetched out his cigarettes. 'Something like that.'

'Come off it, Dad. Even you're not rich enough for that.'

'I can have a damn good go.'

Sean laughed. 'Don't tell me you've had some kind of green conversion.'

Instead of answering Tony lit another Dunhill and smoked

distractedly for a minute or two. While he waited Sean took another pull on the hipflask and offered it back; when his father declined he placed it down on the flat top of the nearest of the standing stones.

'What do you know about NolCalc, Sean?' Tony said.

His tone had changed. So this is what they'd come up here to talk about.

'Not much, if I'm honest,' Sean replied.

'No, well you wouldn't, would you? I'll put it this way. What do you think, in the company, we spend most of our time actually doing?'

Sean pondered this, assuming a trap was being laid. He wasn't sure what it was, but he'd learned over the years that the best approach with such gambits was to act a bit dim and blunder right onto the tripwires rather than try to be too clever about trying to avoid them. He was more likely to find out what was really going on if he played to his father's vanity in this way, even if it meant swallowing his ego in the process.

'You make car phones?'

'Yes, well obviously. We do that. But mostly what we do is, we lose money.'

Sean raised his eyebrows. His strategy had got him straight to the heart of the matter all right. This was just not what he'd thought he would find there.

'But you sell bucketloads of phones, don't you? You're supposed to be the market leader, at least according to what I'm always reading in the papers.'

'Oh yes. We have a massive turnover. We just try very hard not to make a profit.'

'Why would you want to do that?'

'It's complicated.' Sticking to his strategy, Sean waited in silence while Tony stubbed out his cigarette on the standing stone and took a swig from the hipflask. 'It's basically because, like everyone else, we only pay tax on profits. If we lose money, we don't pay tax, and we can even claim rebates on the losses. So everything has to be structured to look like it's in the red, while actually remaining solidly black.

'It starts with NolCalc Limited being registered in Guernsey instead of here on the mainland, because the Channel Islands have much more lax laws around corporate ownership than we do. This allows it to be owned, not by me or my original investors, but by another company called Motherboards International, which is registered in the British Virgin Islands.

'But Motherboards International doesn't own itself, either. It's owned in turn by two companies called Summit Silicon and Third Bay, which are both based in Turks and Caicos.'

'Where the hell is that?' Sean had never heard of it, and from the name thought it must be somewhere in the Middle East.

'Caribbean. It's a British Overseas Territory. Technically it's ruled by the Queen but it has its own government that lets you set up companies with almost zero oversight.'

'Oh. Right. So who owns these Summit and Bay outfits then?'

'Well, that's where the dog bites its own arse. Ultimately the Nolans do, via a series of family trusts and holding companies some of which are in my name or which I'm a director of, some of which involve you, or Caitlin, or your mother, or your uncle Conor and your uncle Joe.'

Tony hadn't mentioned Jamie's name, Sean noted.

'So if that's what it comes down to, why bother with all the other stuff?'

'Why bother?' Tony allowed himself a laugh. 'Don't ever ask my accountants that. They'll give you an answer that'll last a week and when they're done you still won't understand what the fuck they're on about. But I'm going to tell you now, for free. I'm only going to say it once, and you're never going to find anyone else who'll be able to tell you without adding sixty-nine layers of bullshit on top of it and charging three hundred an hour for the privilege. So listen.

'The way it works is that the Turks and Caicos companies loan money, and I'm talking about lots of money, to the British Virgin Islands company, which has to pay interest on the loans. This interest can be lopped off its tax bill, as interest is a tax-deductible expense, and the loans are big enough that these deductions pretty much wipe out Motherboards International's entire tax liability.

'Motherboards International makes its profits by loaning money to NolCalc, along with inflated fees for "financial services", where the process is repeated: the interest gets deducted from its tax bill, and the fees suck up any profits that are left, effectively taking that money out of Guernsey.

'To oil the wheels there's another company, NolCalc Research, which is the only one registered here in the UK. Most of the people who think they work for NolCalc are actually employed by NolCalc Research. NolCalc subcontracts much of its work to NolCalc Research, which supposedly charges its services back to NolCalc "at cost". But those fees are also massively inflated.

'The result of all this is that NolCalc and NolCalc Research, which should both be hugely profitable, generally make an annual loss and so pay hardly any tax at all. Sometimes, as I mentioned before, they even earn rebates on some of their expenses from their respective Exchequers, meaning they *make* money from their governments – which in the case of NolCalc Research means from you, because you're paying for it, out of your income tax. Or you would be if you actually had a job.

'And so it goes on. There are lots of added complications, most of them blind alleys designed to confuse the various regional tax authorities and make it as hard as humanly possible to track where the real profits go and who owes what tax on them where. But what you end up with is a mass of wiring, like a booby-trapped bomb. Cut a wire to solve an issue in one country and you can suddenly find you've made yourself liable for all sorts of back taxes or fines in another. Of course there's an army of people on hand to make sure that this doesn't happen, all dependent on the continued operation of the machine for their eye-watering fees. Machine's probably not even the right word. It's more like some gigantic fucking fungus, eating itself at the same time as devouring anything in its path.

'I started it running, but I don't control it. The lawyers and accountants have that honour. In theory it's made me rich, but I risk losing a fortune in tax every time I put my hand into my pocket. To break free from it I really need to leave here and live abroad at least half the year, which is exactly what my so-called advisers would like me to do.'

'So why don't you?' The Caribbean seemed like a pretty good option from where Sean was standing, especially with a yacht or two thrown in.

'Because – I – like – it – here,' Tony said, jabbing the ground with his walking stick. 'Right *here*. I don't want to live in the fucking British Virgin Islands and spend my time playing tennis and drinking gin with other rich pricks like me. I want to be in Warwickshire. This is what I love.' He waved his stick at the sky again. 'This. Seasons. Mud. Apples. Swallows. Rain.'

'So that's why you're buying the land.'

'In a way. The land is . . . my revenge. I buy it via one of the Turks and Caicos companies and the lawyers let me do it because you don't pay tax on profits earned buying and selling land that's owned offshore. But it's a way to nail a piece of this monster I've created back down to the earth, and give me something I can fucking touch and fucking look at and fucking taste. And NolCalc doesn't know it yet, but I'm going to bind up that piece in a trust and plant it with trees and make sure it can never, ever be fucking sold, make sure it's here in perpetuity, my little monument to Arden Forest and old Robert Catesby. And you' – Tony planted the ferrule of the stick in the centre of Sean's chest – 'you are going to manage it for me. You with your expensive education.'

'I am?'

'You are. Now that you've finally graduated you need something constructive to do. I'm not having you lie around all day playing with yourself and pissing my money down the drain. So welcome to NolCalc, Mr Sean Nolan. First Vice-President of Forestry.'

Sean had had his own agenda for this walk. He'd wanted to talk to his father about something entirely different. As usual Tony's desires had taken precedence, but he still meant to give it a go. He might not get another chance. He was clearly in favour right now. It no doubt wouldn't last.

'That's great, Dad. I think that's an offer I can't refuse.'

'Well you could, but I wouldn't advise it. Drink on it?' Tony offered the hipflask.

'Absolutely.' Sean took a sip and passed it back, his hand trembling slightly with the weight of what he wanted to say. He didn't know how to say it, couldn't decide on a formulation that could be guaranteed to work, so rather than risk saying nothing in the end he just blurted out the words.

'But what about Jamie?'

'What about him?' his father said, apparently entirely unmoved.

'Shouldn't we do something to find him?'

Tony stood for a few moments staring east, then lifted his stick in a line. Sean thought for one terrible moment that his father was going to strike him, but instead he held the stick at the horizontal and looked down it like he was sighting some kind of pathway through the corridor of land he'd bought.

'Don't talk to me about Jamie,' he said. 'Jamie is the lucky one. Jamie is free. You're the one you need to worry about. You're stuck with NolCalc. You're stuck with me.'

Then he lowered the stick, drained the remaining contents of the hipflask into his mouth, and set off down the hill.

Bea and Luggie were end-of-the-beach kind of people. Bea was from Newcastle and Luggie was Welsh, and they'd met when they'd been teaching English at the same language school in Guatemala and decided that, whatever else happened, they didn't ever really want to go home.

When their teaching stint was over they'd travelled north into Chiapas and then meandered up through Campeche and the Yucatán peninsula, hopscotching between beaches, nature reserves and Mayan archaeological sites until they'd washed up in Cancún, where they had to spend a couple of weeks sorting out money and extending their visas. But as soon as they were able they fled its concrete sprawl and beachfront mega-hotels, whose trapezoid tiers of balconies and terraces formed such peculiar temporal echoes of the great stepped pyramids of Palenque, Uxmal and Chichen Itza, and headed south down the coast.

To rinse off the city they stopped in Tulum, a little resort favoured by backpackers, where they rented a simple cabana with hammocks for beds and the fine white sand for a floor. Here they spent a week sunbathing, touring the local ruins, and making snorkelling trips out to the little reef that snagged the waves about half a mile offshore. In the evenings they got stoned with the other travellers who congregated in the little clifftop restaurant, swapping stories of their trip for tales of the legendary all-night parties that took place whenever a bale of cocaine worked loose from the rafts floated ashore by drug runners and washed up on the beach. They knew the tales were true because at night while they stood in the surf carving trails of phosphorescence with their hands, or lay on their backs to let their minds wander along the dusty byways of the Milky Way, they could see the lights from the police launches that patrolled beyond the reef for precisely that reason.

After Tulum they continued down Route 15, taking local buses and stopping off wherever they felt like it, thinking to keep on like this through Belize and back into Guatemala before finally making up their minds what they were going to do with their lives. The further south they travelled the more insubstantial the road became, until it was little more than a tyre-compacted layer of grit and sand threading through a corridor of fan palms and desert willow as narrow and enclosed as that created by blackthorn and hazel on an ancient Warwickshire lane. By the time they crossed the land bridge that enclosed the Campechen lagoon and continued out past Zamach to the tip of Punta Allen it was almost impossibly fragile, but they'd heard there was a fantastic guest-house here, about as remote from civilisation as you could get in this region, and acting on the principle that they might as well head as far away from everything as they could before they were forced by circumstance to begin the slow hack back, they aimed for that.

Punta Allen, however, turned out to be more coherent than they'd anticipated, a settlement of thirty or forty dwellings that included several guesthouses and a hotel big enough to sport a tennis court. It was something they'd found repeatedly during their trip. Nearly every time they thought they'd headed far enough off the beaten track to have an experience that was new and theirs alone they found that the thing, whatever it was, had been in some way trampled and commoditised. Not necessarily in a bad way, just in a way that left their thirst for uniqueness, for striking out through virgin territory, tantalisingly unquenched. Sometimes, Luggie took to remarking, he wondered if he'd have found it easier to get off the map if he'd stayed in Wales.

They could hardly complain. The place was close enough to paradise as to be almost indistinguishable, and was certainly quieter and more remote than Tulum, where the ranks of huts had been dense enough to evoke an atmosphere of backpacker carnival. True to form they stayed at the smallest guesthouse at the farthest end of the settlement, just two thatched and whitewashed buildings divided into a kitchen and three guest rooms less than fifty metres from the sea.

And yet it wasn't far enough. This was supposed to be an adventure, not a holiday, and after a day spent recharging in hammocks slung between the coconut palms that grew almost to the water's edge, the logic of exploration kicked back in and they decided, after sourcing some provisions from the hotel with the tennis court, to hike out to the point.

At first they set off down the road, or what was left of it.

Route 15, tenuous enough when it had entered Punta Allen, emerged from it as no more than a path through the jungle barely wide enough to accommodate a jeep. But they'd been walking down it for little more than ten minutes when they came across a rusted metal gate hung with a hand-painted sign that said *Propiedad Privada*, and chained shut.

'End of the line, by the look of it,' Luggie said.

'Oh bollocks,' said Bea. 'What on earth is the point of having a "keep out" sign all the way out here? It's not like anyone's going to rat-run it on their way to the supermarket.'

'We could just ignore it. We're only going for a walk. If there even is anyone down here they're hardly going to care.'

Bea wrinkled her nose and peered through the undergrowth at the sea, which was close enough to be visible through the foliage. 'Let's just go along the beach. That way if anyone stops us we can just say we didn't see the sign.'

This seemed like a plan. Whoever owned the *propiedad privada* had not stretched to erecting any kind of fence to accompany their gate, so it was a simple matter to thread a path through the undergrowth to the shoreline and follow that south instead, even where it narrowed in places into less than a metre of driftwood-littered strand caught between the encroaching curtains of green and aquamarine.

By late morning the two of them had covered a good distance around the headland with little to mark the passing of the hours beyond the sun's slow climb into the sky, Yves Klein blue beyond a delicate comb of alto cirrus, and the appearance of a couple of wooden buildings. The first was a smart hunting lodge complete with a small jetty to which were moored two skiffs and an expensive-looking sports fishing launch, its tall flybridge bristling with outriggers and aerials; the second, some way further on, was a large but derelict triple-gabled shack, built on stilts, that looked like some kind of old-time way station.

Bea and Luggie had steered clear of the lodge, but this second building they explored, peering into dim rooms lit by the sunlight that streamed in through holes in the rotten roofs. They ate their picnic on what was left of the veranda while watching dove-grey gulls with long black beaks mine the waves for fish.

The day was baking hot, but by the time they resumed their walk the sun had passed its zenith and the narrow beach was now in shade, offering some respite from the glare. Not that they had far to go – after about half-an-hour more walking the beach widened to a final clearing in which a concrete lighthouse stood fenced around with chain-link. Beyond it, spreading right across what remained of the headland and blurring the boundaries between land and sea, lay an impenetrable mass of mangrove swamp.

'So this is why it's private,' said Bea, a little disappointed. 'It must all be owned by the government.'

Luggie pointed to the far side of the clearing. 'The track comes in over there,' he said. 'At least going back will be easy.'

'What a shame. I was hoping to see some kind of great panorama down the coast.'

'I wonder if we can get up it?' Luggie said, craning his neck at the lighthouse. A stone cylinder supported by four triangular flanges like vanes on a Futurist rocket, it stood a good seven storeys high. They couldn't see the entrance, but several small windows in the shaft marked the position of an internal staircase, and at the apex a circular balcony surrounded the lantern room. 'The view from the top must be awesome.'

'It's bound to be locked,' Bea said, with less enthusiasm. 'It's clearly in use.' She was peering at the small complex of blockhouses at the tower's base and had noticed that a set of solar panels, their newness in stark contrast to the greying paint of the buildings themselves, had been installed on the roof of one of them. Its door had been replaced and was fastened with a heavy-duty padlock. 'That must be where they keep the batteries for the light.'

'Why don't I just climb over the fence and take a look? It's not very high.'

'No, Lugs, I don't think you should.'

'Oh come on. When did you get so timid? There's no one here!'

'It just makes me nervous.'

Luggie ignored her, put his hands on the chain-link, and tested it with his weight.

'Luggie! Don't!'

And then another voice, quiet, but embossed with the unmistakable imprint of the English Midlands, spoke out. 'She's right mate, it's all locked up. You can't get up it.'

Bea yelped and turned; Luggie leapt down from the fence. Behind them stood a scrawny man, dirty and deeply tanned but clearly European, dressed in a pair of stained and patched hiking trousers and a hippy waistcoat, his hair and beard straggly and unkempt. The most remarkable thing about him, however, apart from his having apparently materialised out of nowhere, was that in his hands he appeared to be holding a live seagull.

'I didn't mean to make you jump,' he said. 'But you wouldn't happen to have any tape you could spare, would you?'

'Tape?' Bea said, disarmed by the sheer banality of the request. She slipped her backpack from her shoulder and started to unzip it. 'I might. What do you want it for?'

The man raised the seagull slightly. 'It's got a broken wing. I've made a splint but I haven't got anything that'll keep it in place.'

Bea dug out the little medical pouch she carried with her and retrieved a grimy roll of Micropore.

'Here,' she said, holding it out. 'Will this work?'

The stranger looked at them but didn't take his hands from the bird. 'Wow. Perfect. You don't want to help hold her while I do it, do you? We could go to my shack.' He nodded his head in the direction of the beach.

Bea looked at Luggie, who had come over and was standing beside her protectively. He shrugged.

'Okay then.' She zipped up her pack and slipped it back onto her shoulders. 'If it's close.'

'Yeah. It's just over there.'

The shack was indeed only a couple of minutes from where they stood, hidden so well in the palm-strewn jungle that the couple had walked right past it without even noticing. It had been a proper building once, probably from the same era as the one on whose stoop they'd eaten their picnic. Since then the walls had been patched with driftwood and the roof repaired with palm thatch held in place by a meshwork of salvaged fishing nets. Out front there was a well-used fire pit, set about with stones on which lay a griddle and a couple of blackened cooking pots; nearby a row of curling, metallic fish carcasses hung from a makeshift smoke line. There was also a large pile of discarded coconut husks, a couple of palm trunks for sitting on, and a clear plastic drum filled with what looked like clean water. But that was everything.

'Where do you get that?' Luggie asked, indicating the water.

'Oh, it's safe to drink. There's a tap at the lighthouse. It's piped down from the resort. Have some – there's some cups by the side of it.'

He went inside the shack, and while he was gone Luggie located a scarred plastic child's tumbler that looked like it had been found washed up on the beach and a glass adorned with the logo of the hotel in Punta Allen and filled them with water from the drum. 'Tastes okay,' he said, sipping from the cup. He passed the glass to Bea. 'Here, you get the posh one.'

Bea grinned. 'Ooh, fancy. I'm all class, I am.' She took a cautious sip. 'Do you think he's actually living here then?'

'I don't know. If he's got water he might be.'

Still holding the gull their host reappeared and manoeuvred an empty red and black plastic beer crate out of the doorway and onto the sand. He got it over to where Bea was sitting and then dropped to his knees.

'Okay, so if you take her from me,' he said, holding out the bird. 'She's stronger than she looks, so you need to hold her firmly and keep her wings pressed to her body – if she gets them free she'll try to get away. Once you've got her I'll hold the damaged wing and bind it up.'

'Okay,' said Bea, feeling nervous now. The gull's rigid neck and black, hemispherical eyes clearly signalled defiance. Bea had never held a wild animal before, but she'd grown up with dogs and cats and knew how powerfully they could struggle when they didn't want to be held. Her hands were sweating, she realised.

Taking a breath, she put down her glass and wiped her palms on her shorts before reaching out to take the creature, working her fingers beneath the stranger's as he slowly released his grip. The bird, though young, was still impressively large, and Bea's hands only scarcely reached around it. But it seemed docile enough, right up until the last moment of the transfer when, sensing a chance for escape, it tried to spasm away, raking Bea's wrists with its feet as it scrabbled for purchase. She nearly dropped it in surprise, but the stranger was close and clamped his hands back around it, restraining and calming the animal until she could re-establish her grip.

'Okay?' he said, when the gull was still again.

Bea nodded. 'Yep. I've got it now.'

'As long as you hold it firmly it should stay calm.'

'Right.'

She focused on the bird, now encased in her grip like a doll and staring at her as unblinkingly. It was warm, hot even, its belly soft and vulnerable, the carapace of its rachises ribbed like a cage, its motionless frame animated by the incessant vibrations of its heart, so short in phase as to feel almost electric.

'Ready?'

'I think so.'

'Let's do this then. I need you to release the wing. This one.' He tapped on the back of her right hand. 'Just ease your fingers back really slowly.'

Bea did so, and as soon as it was able the bird jabbed out its wing, attempted a couple of flaps, and then held it open, stiff with pain. The stranger wound lengths of tape between the splayed feathers until they bound the wooden splint he'd fashioned to the damaged humerus. Then, taking the gull back from Bea, he placed it in the beer crate he'd kicked out from the shack and put a ragged sheet of broken plywood on top, which he weighted down with a rock.

Bea crouched in the sand and peered at the bird through the holes in the plastic. It lay prone, panting, its damaged wing struck out, its beak half open. 'Where did you learn to do that?' she asked the stranger.

'I didn't. I just found it this morning on the beach. It was either try to help it or just leave it to die.'

'Do you think it's going to work?' she said.

'I don't know. I'll give it some water and fish a bit later. I want to let it chill out a while first. After that we'll have to see.'

Bea got up and went back over to her seat and glass of water. 'So are you, like, living here?' she asked, taking a drink.

'I suppose so,' said the stranger.

'How long for?'

'Not sure, exactly. A few months maybe.'

'On just fish and coconuts?' Luggie asked.

'Pretty much. I go up to the resort sometimes, to get other things. Rice and stuff. Biscuits. Beer.'

'Where are you from? I mean originally? You're English, right?'

'Yeah, of course.'

'How d'you end up out here?'

'Oh, you know. I thought it would be cool to live on a desert island. This is as close as I've been able to get. Hey, I haven't given you anything in return for the tape.'

Bea shook her head. 'Don't worry about it.'

But the stranger had already jumped up and disappeared back into his shack. When he emerged he was clutching a green plastic bag, which he brought over and set down on one of the logs.

'I don't know if you're into this,' he said, peeling the bag open until the contents were exposed, 'but if you are, help yourselves.'

Luggie and Bea came over to investigate. Splayed out for them to view was what looked like a handful of cat litter.

'Is that what I think it is?' Luggie said.

'Yep. Have as much as you want. I've got a whole bale of it stashed back in the jungle. I found it on the beach one night. The smugglers float it in.'

'We heard about that in Tulum,' Bea said. 'I didn't know they came this far south.'

'Oh yeah. They operate all down the coast. There's a kind of triangle that stretches from here out to the Cayman Islands and down to Colombia. Look – it's the real thing. Very pure. You only need a little hit.' The stranger reached into the bag and picked a small granule of the cocaine, ground it into dust in his palm then pinched it up and sniffed it like snuff. 'See? It's fine. I swap a few rocks now and then with one of the guys who works at the hotel in Punta Allen in return for the beer and the food.'

Eager to sample this unexpected bounty, Luggie leant in and did as their host had done. Bea, more circumspect, held back.

'Why are you telling us this?'

'Why shouldn't I?'

'But why us?'

'You seem like nice people. You helped with the gull.'

'But we could just steal your bale and run off.'

The stranger laughed. 'You don't know where it's buried. And even if you did, what would you do with it? It's more coke than you could put up your nose in a lifetime.'

'We could sell it.'

'Who to? If you sold to locals and word got back to the smugglers they'd probably track you down and kill you. And if the police caught you selling to tourists, well, the stories I've heard about Mexican jails, that might be worse than the smugglers. It's not so easy.'

'So what are you going to do with it?'

'Well some of it I'm going to share with you. If you want.'

'And the rest?'

'Bea,' said Luggie, 'go easy.'

'Sorry, but I want to know where we stand on this.'

'Okay,' the stranger said. 'Then the question is, can you sail?'

Bea looked blank. 'Er, no.'

'I can,' Luggie said.

'Can you?' Bea said, surprised.

'Yeah, a bit. I was in a club back home in Pembroke Dock when I was a teenager.'

'Good,' said the stranger. 'Because I can't. And I'm about to swap the bale for a boat. So it would be good if there was someone around to teach me which end is the front.' He looked from Bea to Luggie and back again, and then stuck out his hand. 'I'm Jamie, by the way.'

Jamie had taken the gull as a sign. The universe, it seemed, was fairly determined that he should try to fix whatever within him was broken, these two people who had appeared right on cue with their own unsatisfied yearnings and half a roll of Micropore were surely somehow meant to be part of the cure.

Because the timing was perfect. Only a few days before they'd showed up at the lighthouse Jamie had heard from Guillermo, his contact in the hotel, that he'd met someone who was prepared to trade the bale for a yacht.

The someone was Russian, one of a party of businessmen that had rented the larger of the two fly-fishing lodges in Punta Allen for a month – not the one that Luggie and Bea had passed but another one, a little further up the beach in the opposite direction. He and his friends had sailed up from Honduras in three boats, the smallest a four-berth gaff-rigged sloop called the *Chiriquí* that had seen better days. According to Guillermo he was more than happy to swap it for what amounted to a lifetime supply of high-quality cocaine with a street price many times that of the *Chiriquí*'s resale value.

With a sample in his pocket Jamie travelled out to inspect the yacht with his Mexican go-between. He knew nothing at all about boats, but this one was floating, had electronics and communications that appeared to work, had a sail locker with sails in it and a functioning engine, and had just made the trip from La Ceiba, so was presumably more or less seaworthy. He chopped out some lines on the table while the Russian served vodka and showed them the logbook and the registration documentation, all of which looked reasonably plausible. There was a bit of a wrangle when Jamie insisted on some cash on top of the yacht to cover his set-up and running costs and the Russian complained he didn't have that much money to hand. But eventually a sum was agreed and a deal was struck, with Guillermo agreeing to play middleman in return for a small share of the coke.

The Russian wanted the use of the *Chiriquí* for the remainder of his fishing trip, and it was during this period, before the deal was concluded, that Jamie had met Luggie and Bea. It had felt quite strange after being alone for such a long time to open himself to them so readily, but he needed help with the boat and he also needed reinforcements: it no longer felt particularly sensible to be living down by the lighthouse on his own.

Fortunately for him, hanging out on a deserted beach with a self-styled hermit and an unlimited supply of fine drugs was exactly the kind of offbeat travel adventure Bea and Luggie had been searching for. Within a couple of days they had moved out of the guesthouse, slung their hammocks in the trees next to Jamie's shack, and slipped into a kind of glorious castaway reverie, a desert island life with all the harsh edges smoothed away.

At the centre of their focus was the gull. She had started drinking water and eating scraps of dried fish, but kept moving her damaged wing, so they'd bound it to her body with a strip of bandage to give it a better chance to heal. They'd named her

Esperanza, a statement of their faith in her capacity for survival, and soon indeed she was hopping about their camp and taking titbits from their fingers, apparently unbothered by the loss of her ability to fly.

And then one morning Guillermo bounced down the track in the hotel jeep to tell Jamie that the Russian was ready and the deal was on. He sent Bea and Luggie back to Punta Allen with instructions to have a conspicuous lunch in the hotel, then went back into the jungle to retrieve the bale from its hiding place.

His hands were shaking as he dug it up. Until now the cocaine had been a weaver of dreams, a font of pure possibility from which all kinds of different futures could emerge, some of them pleasant, many of them not. But the act of digging it up and giving it to Guillermo was like opening Schrödinger's box to have a peek at its cat: the waveforms of fantasy were now all collapsing into a very concrete and defined channel of reality down which Jamie was being sluiced with little choice or control. At any moment he could fall through a trap or hit a solid wall, and there would be little or nothing he could do about it. For the first time since he'd left the Midlands he was really, truly, scared. Which was perhaps why he'd done this. Because it was also the moment he felt the return of an active desire to stay alive.

But on that day, it seemed, the universe was in a benevolent mood. Everyone behaved, the exchange was made, and within an hour Jamie had taken possession of the *Chiriquí*. With his survival instinct functioning again, however, he had no wish to hang around to wait for the Russians to change their minds or for tales of his encounter with them to spread. By nightfall he, Bea and Luggie had loaded up their stuff along with a couple of crates filled with supplies and, of course, Esperanza, who was delighted to once again be surrounded by water and hopped around the bows like the whole affair had been organised for her benefit. Then they headed south round the point, using the diesel engine and staying within sight of land until they had a chance to experiment with the sails.

The plan, in so far as they had one, was to hug the coast until they'd worked their way round to Chetumal, a resort tucked up inside a giant inlet and positioned smack on the border with Belize. Here they could sort out their paperwork, get some professional instruction, and spend a few weeks learning to handle the *Chiriquí* within the relative safety of the sound before risking any more trips out into the open sea.

In the event they stayed in Chetumal for nearly three months. Sailing a yacht across borders, which is what they wanted to do, proved more bureaucratic than they'd anticipated. Apart from updating the registration papers, getting the usual visas and drawing up a crew list, they needed clearance papers, but they couldn't get these without first buying insurance, which in turn could not be granted until one of them had a radio operator's licence. So while Luggie, as the best sailor, found someone to teach him to properly handle the boat and spent his days tacking to and fro across the sound beneath the watchful gaze of the Mega Escultura, the peculiar 70-metre-tall wafer of steel latticework that loomed over the bay, Jamie signed up for a communications course at a sailing school. To pay for all this he divided up the bag of cocaine he'd kept back in case of emergencies into wraps that he sold, very cautiously and somewhat against his better judgement, to the vacationing American sailors who passed through the marina, while Bea advertised her services as an English tutor on the notice-boards in the state university on the outskirts of town.

It was during this period, rather than in the couple of weeks they'd spent getting high on the beach by the lighthouse, that the friendship between the three of them was truly forged. They might have fallen into it more or less by accident, but preparing themselves and the *Chiriquí* for a proper trip down South America's Atlantic coastline was proving to need proper commitment and, for Bea and Luggie at least, difficult conversations with relatives back home about their intention to stay overseas.

More than once the couple discussed the sanity of chucking their lot in with this guy they hardly knew. In the end the pull of adventure always won out, but Bea's doubts didn't really leave her until the morning they woke to find the gull, having not exhibited any signs of ill-health beyond her inability to use her wing, lying stricken in the cockpit, gasping for breath.

'What's wrong with her?' Luggie asked, clambering up through the companionway to find Jamie cradling the bird in his arms.

'I don't know,' he said, his voice cracking. 'I don't know. I was painting the forward hatch yesterday and gave her some fish out of the fridge. Maybe I had paint on my hands?'

'I don't know if that would have done it,' said Bea. 'More likely she just got sick.'

Whatever the cause, Esperanza wouldn't eat or drink and grew weaker by the hour. By the evening, she was dead. Jamie was distraught. Luggie and Bea had never even seen him angry or upset before, but now he punched the side of the cabin until his knuckles bled before disappearing below. When Bea went to check on him he was curled up in his bunk, apparently sleeping. She went back on deck where Luggie poured them each a glass of rum and rolled a joint which they sat smoking in silence staring up at the sprays of stars, wondering what impact this was all going to have on their trip, while the dead bird lay beside them in a casket fashioned from an empty box of granola bars.

The gull had been their mascot; the thing that had brought them together and kept them together as they'd collectively nursed her back to health during their time by the lighthouse. They'd achieved that, and it had suggested to all of them that they could achieve more. Bea seriously doubted that if the animal had died in those first few days they would have had the faith to stick with Jamie through his crazy, risky boat deal and set off with him down the coast. But now she was gone, and her demise stabbed a needle into the balloon they'd inflated around themselves with their romantic, cocaine-fuelled fantasies of nomadism and escape. It was like when the drug wears off, and the house lights come on, and you see the club is just a sweat-stained room before you're propelled out into the street where it's morning, and it's raining, and you're hungry and your money's gone and there's no easy way to get home, and sensible people are hurrying past you with withering looks, desperate to get to the boring jobs that they do day after day, and that day after day help keep the world turning, and you're painfully aware that for all the energy you've just gone and expended, you've made no contribution at all.

Assailed by these doubts they were about to go to bed when Jamie appeared, eyes bloodshot, face puffy, but otherwise operational, and sat across from them in the little cockpit. Luggie handed him a glass of rum and began to build another joint. For a while Jamie sipped at the drink in silence, but then, when the joint was lit and had been passed around, he began to talk, telling them all the things he'd never told them, about where he'd come from and who he was, and most of all about why he'd left for South America in the first place. And this story changed everything.

They committed Esperanza to the waves out in the sound with full naval honours and a week later, Jamie's radio course completed, Luggie's competency established, and their documents all in order, they motored out of Chetumal's Terminal Maritime for the final time. Then they set the mainsail and the jib and headed past Belize into the Caribbean, glancing back periodically at the Mega Escultura as it slowly dwindled in size on the shore, until they looked up one last time to find that it had passed out of sight altogether.

For the next year they meandered past Honduras and Panama, Venezuela and Suriname, getting in and out of scrapes, moving where mood and weather took them, exploring themselves as much as the coast and learning all the time how to better handle the boat and the sea, until they arrived on Brazil's northern reach.

And there they discovered Rosaventos. On the continent's big bulge, not so far west of Fortaleza, cut off from the mainland by a dune sea and thus almost inaccessible unless you came in by water, it was the most perfect stretch of sand they'd ever seen. Vast, empty, fringed with a tassel of jungle and massaged for six months of the year by surfable breakers and a wind-sailable breeze, the place was a paradise.

They'd spent a week alone there the first time, sleeping on the beach, the *Chiriquí* moored at the sheltered end of the bay. Then, after a trip to Fortaleza to pick up supplies, they returned for a month, spending their days body-surfing and gathering food for their feasts in the evening: fruits and coconuts from the trees, fresh fish and flat bread from the little fishing village perched at the foot of a huge dune the locals called la Duna do Por do Sol, 'the

Sunset Dune'. It was so big that it had its own water table, which the fishermen tapped with a string of little pump wells they'd dug into its base.

But what next? They didn't know. They couldn't drift for ever. Though it hadn't really been discussed, they'd all been feeling the same thing – that in some intangible way their trip was over, that they'd started to outgrow life on board the little yacht.

'Something'll turn up,' Luggie had said, with classic stoner optimism. And in the past it always had. This time, however, the thought of trusting to chance made Jamie hot under the arms and cold round the shoulders. For the first time since he'd left Warwickshire he found himself wishing for a safe bet. He'd told Luggie and Bea the night the gull died why it was he preferred to be on his own, but being alone didn't mean he always had to keep moving, didn't mean he couldn't try and start to construct a new life for himself.

As it happened, however, Luggie was right. Something did turn up, in the shape of the besuited Brazilian who came striding towards them over the sand one afternoon as they lolled beneath the leafy boughs of a cashew tree. He said his name was Gomez and he represented some people who'd just bought a strip of land the boundary of which ran right through the tree in whose shade they were sitting. He was planning to grid it for water, sewage and electrics – the last could be brought in by pylon around the edge of the dunes – and selling off the lots for villas, hotels and restaurants. What did they think? Did they know people who came here? Did they know people who might be interested?

It was another gift from the gods. That evening, their imaginations well oiled with weed and rum, the three friends decided that they would pool together whatever cash they could, buy some plots off this guy, and build something real. It was what they'd been waiting for; it was what they would do. Because when they thought about it, it was perfect. The airport in Fortaleza was half-way decent, and though it took six hours by 4x4 to get from there to the fishing village, they realised that for the right clientele this would be a genuine plus. The journey would keep all but the most dedicated water-sports enthusiasts at bay, and speedboats and helicopters could whisk those seeking privacy and exclusivity to and from the understated luxury resort that they would build and run on the western curve of the bay.

So Jamie sold the *Chiriquí* in Fortaleza and pooled the proceeds with some savings Luggie had squirrelled away and a small legacy Bea had inherited from her father, who'd died when she was in her teens. And the three of them bought a plot, christened their new home the Club Vayu (after the Hindu god of the winds – Bea's idea), and embarked upon the not inconsiderable project of transforming it into a compelling place to come for a holiday.

Dinho Gomez Pereira – Jamie discovered his full name when he read it, many years later, in the court report of *Diário do Nordeste*. Before then, he and everyone else he met just knew him as Gomez. And Gomez was a handy guy to know. He was able to sort anything, pretty much. Builders, materials, vehicles, equipment, red tape – he seemed to be connected to everyone and understand the ins and outs of everything, his influence extending not just to the local tract of coast but as far south as São Paulo and Rio. There was talk of a family too, from what Jamie could surmise a wife and two boys parked in some Fortalezan suburb, though he'd never seen concrete proof of their existence.

Gomez was like that. Vague. He had proven as good as his

word to Jamie on many occasions, though the thing about Gomez's word was that it was never altogether precise. His accounts of events had the habit of being slightly self-contradictory, his facts slightly off, anecdotes left unresolved. And the more vague the details the greater the emotion with which he communicated them, as though the louder the skin of his passion the larger the void it was stretched across.

This was common with cocaine: Jamie had observed it many times. During his travels around South America he had come to see this kind of behaviour, voluble but dissembling, as a signpost indicating the direction in which to make further enquiries about the drug. Jamie was not of a mind to buy coke from Gomez, further complicating an already complex relationship, but that turned out not to make the slightest bit of difference, because in the end the cocaine came to him.

The first time it had been a small amount, a sugar-lump-sized rock that the Brazilian pressed into his palm the evening Jamie, Bea and Luggie met him for a game of pool in the hip Órbita bar in downtown Fortaleza to celebrate the completion of the first foundations they'd laid on their plot.

'Shhh,' Gomez hushed, gripping Jamie's wrist to prevent him from examining the object in the middle of the busy room. 'A little gift. To make sure you and your friends have a good time.' And a good time they had, bouncing around the dance floor long after Gomez had disappeared off to wherever Gomez went, releasing energy that would carry them forward into the next few months on a great wave of optimism, months in which they would be hard at work constructing the first of the Club Vayu's cabanas, its surf shop and its bar.

During this period they lived in tents, bathed in the sea and carted their drinking water from wells at the foot of la Duna until

Gomez got his pump station built and the pipes laid, at which point they were able to rig up some taps. It was immense fun to start with, but as the weeks wore on the challenges of the venture started to make themselves felt. In their naïvety they had completely underestimated the costs of building even the most basic of facilities, miscalculating both the manpower required and the quantity of materials. Jamie and Luggie had assumed they could do most of the work themselves, but this simply wasn't possible; and even when they managed to source the large quantities of concrete, rebar, piping, wiring, timber and various pieces of equipment and machinery they needed at a reasonable price, they couldn't get them across the dune sea without paying a hefty toll to Gomez's drivers to ferry them in on the aged flatbed trucks the Brazilian had procured for the purpose.

None of this had been discussed in detail when they'd purchased the plot. Being a bit more realistic than the boys, Bea had tried to raise these kinds of specifics, but Gomez had airily said that he'd provide transport links, and suppliers, and a utilities grid. What he didn't say was that there would be a fee for the trucks, a 'handling charge' for buying from his suppliers, and a levy for connections to the grid. It might have been okay if they could have shopped around, but all the suppliers in Fortaleza turned out to be Gomez's suppliers, as did all the workmen. Everything they touched seemed, in one way or another, to lead back to the Brazilian. There was no way around him, at least not one that didn't involve running up even greater costs and risk offending the man who had effectively become their patron. If he took against them then that would be it.

Running out of money and unable to see a better way forward, they decided that they had no choice but to talk to Gomez and try to negotiate better terms. The Brazilian listened, made a bit of a show of worry and disappointment at their lack of planning, and then – in a move Bea strongly suspected had been carefully premeditated – said that he was prepared to extend them credit at a reasonable rate of interest, with repayment deferred until they had started to generate income of their own.

None of them liked the idea, but it was either comply or walk away, sacrificing in the process all the time and money they'd already invested. So they accepted the offer and got back to work.

Two years passed. The Club Vayu had started taking in paying guests and the deserted beach where the three founders had once slept on the sand and feasted on papaya they'd plucked from the trees had become the focus of a buzzing little community. In between servicing the cabanas and running the restaurant with not inconsiderable flair, Bea had done wonders with the planting, bedding in Dominican bells, rain trees, Clivia and joewood, plants that were slowly turning the Club back into an extension of the jungle from which it had been hewn. Meanwhile Jamie and Luggie had grown into the role of water-sports instructors – the daily routine of schlepping boards in and out of the ocean and helping customers with their technique had given them the body tone and wetsuit-delineated tans of professionals, and had transformed their long hair and straggling beards from apologetic hippy, signifiers into the grizzled and authentic emblems of men who earned their living from the sea.

When Jamie wasn't taking classes or toiling away on the second batch of cabins he was throwing parties on the beach with the aid of a battery-powered sound-system he'd bought for next to nothing off a Swedish guy in Fortaleza marina who'd stripped it from his yacht. These events started out as small local socials, a focus for the frontier camaraderie that had established itself among Rosaventos's collection of tourist-trade entrepreneurs, but they soon grew in scale and reputation and started drawing people to the resort on their own account. Which was very much welcomed by all the businesses in the community – everyone was desperate now for a steady flow of customers.

But it wasn't enough, not yet. Even at Club Vayu, where they were running at reasonable capacity, they were barely breaking even. And now that tourists were coming Gomez was starting to make noises about the need for Jamie, Luggie and Bea to start paying down some of their quite substantial loan. Given that they were no better off financially, and had even more to lose than when he'd first extended credit, this ignited considerable consternation.

'Don't you see what he's doing?' Bea raged when the three of them sat down in their little office one evening after dinner to go through the accounts and formulate some kind of a plan. 'He's led us by the nose all the way. We're total patsies. We didn't just buy his plots, we've now built him a fucking hotel, on our tab! He could kick us out any time and take all of it in lieu of the debt, and we wouldn't have a leg to stand on.'

Luggie knew better than to go head-to-head with his girlfriend when she was in this kind of mood, so it was left to Jamie to remonstrate.

'Come on Bea, it's not like that. We went into this with our eyes open.'

'*I* went into it with my eyes open. You two went into it completely bloody stoned, if I remember. I warned you we couldn't trust him. But you didn't want to listen.'

'That's unfair. He hasn't even formally asked for a repayment yet. He's helped us out from the start, he's never let us down—'

'Jesus Jamie, get real! He hasn't helped us out at all! He's manipulated us. He saw us coming.'

'I think he deserves the benefit of the doubt.'

'Well you would say that, wouldn't you? You've only got yourself to worry about.'

Luggie looked at her for the first time since the exchange had begun. 'Bea . . .'

'Well it's true.'

Jamie looked wounded. 'You know why that is.'

Bea refused to be chastened. 'It doesn't change things Jamie. If he pulls a fast one you've lost your boat and a few years of your life. But me and Luggie . . .' She paused, her voice catching. 'You tell him Lugs.'

Luggie rubbed his face, his tanned skin lent a sepia cast by the light from the low-energy bulb that hung from the ceiling. 'Bea's pregnant, Jamie.' He took Bea's hand and cracked a smile broad enough to dam the course of the argument. 'I'm going to be a dad!'

But this news, momentous though it was, changed nothing, merely rubbing in the fact that they had to make the Club work. The question of how exactly to achieve that remained. Bea suggested offering diving as well as surfing, but there were already two dive shops in the resort and the costs of set-up and insurance would be huge, plunging them further into debt even if they were able to borrow the money. Luggie suggested paragliding, which he'd spent a season doing in Guatemala and loved, and that seemed like a better idea, although how much extra cash it would generate in the short term was debatable.

Whatever solution was suggested, it all in the end came down to the same thing: more guests, spending more money. And the best mechanism for achieving that in the short term seemed to be the extra cabanas and Jamie's parties, along with a plea to Gomez to extend the terms of their loan. So the next day Jamie called the Brazilian's mobile, left a message suggesting a meeting, then threw himself into the preparations for the latest event, which was to be his biggest and most elaborate yet.

A week of charging back and forth to Fortaleza, then, of meeting flights and getting people settled, averting crises, organising the music, erecting the awnings, sorting the bar. By the day of the party he was exhausted, and he had slipped away to his cabin to grab an hour's siesta when Gomez, with his usual uncanny sense of timing, knocked on the door.

'Hey my friend,' he grinned, his white teeth breaking through his puckered, plum-coloured face.

Rubbing his hands through his hair in an attempt to scrape back his tiredness, Jamie invited him in and fished two bottles of Sagres from his icebox. Gomez looked tired too, Jamie thought: tired and preoccupied, as if work was on mind. Which it probably was, Gomez being a man who was never seen out of his suit, even when he ventured onto the beach.

'You coming along tonight?' Jamie asked.

'I must apologise – I have a lot of business still to do today, then I will be looking forward to my bed! I think the same is true of you, my friend. I woke you from your siesta.' Although Gomez spoke with a heavy accent his English was excellent. Jamie had long ago given up attempting to speak Portuguese to him.

'I've done nothing but run round after thirty new arrivals since last Thursday. Who knew that people could do so little for themselves? I feel like a tour guide.'

Gomez laughed and took a slug of his beer. 'Your guests will love you for it.'

'I hope so. Did you get my message?'

'Yes, of course.'

'So then you know what I want to talk about. Shall we sit?'

There was one white plastic patio chair in the cabana, placed next to a bamboo chest that doubled as a table. Jamie perched on the edge of the bed and gestured to Gomez that he should take it.

'Look,' he said, when both of them were sitting. 'I don't want to mess you around, but the fact is we're not in a position to start paying down our loan.'

Gomez blinked, reached into his jacket pocket, took out a pack of cigarettes, and glanced at Jamie for permission to smoke.

'We're getting there,' Jamie said, passing the Brazilian a foil ashtray. 'We're just not there yet. I can show the Club's accounts if you like.'

'And how much longer do you think you need? To start to pay?'

'We're not sure. Another six months? A year maybe?'

Gomez drew heavily on his cigarette and shifted his weight forward, elbows resting on knees, until he was staring right down into the battered foil ashtray on the top of the chest.

'This makes things very difficult for me, Jamie. I have commitments of my own. Other people who need money from me. I am not a bank.'

'I know. I realise that. I'm – we're – very sorry. We didn't think it would take this long.'

Gomez removed the cone of ash from his cigarette by slowly rotating it against the rim of the ashtray.

'I have been generous, yes?'

Jamie nodded. 'That's not the issue. How about if we start paying off the interest? That's something we could definitely discuss.'

'It does not solve my problem. I have other projects, Jamie. Projects that need cash. They are waiting – and they cannot wait.'

Jamie took a swig of his beer and said nothing. He didn't know what to say. He felt light, much as he had the day he'd left Caitlin at the door of the pool house in Shelfield, or the day he'd dug up the bale from its hiding place in the jungle, or the time when the *Chiriquí* had been caught in a squall and pushed into a situation that was way beyond his and Luggie's ability to control. These were moments when he'd discovered that he was capable of relinquishing the process of conscious decision and moving into a space beyond panic, beyond fear, beyond even exhilaration, a space in which he was aware of one thing only: the need to keep pointing straight into the wave, whatever the wave was made of, and however big it might happen to be.

'Here.' Gomez reached into his other jacket pocket and produced a small parcel, wrapped in brown paper, which he placed on Jamie's end of the chest. 'You could help by doing something for me.'

Jamie looked from the man to the package, then walked over, picked it up, and unwrapped it. Inside, tightly encased in clingfilm, was more cocaine than he'd seen since he'd left Punta Allen.

'What is this?' he said, his pulse already racing.

'What is it?' There was a mocking tone in Gomez's voice that Jamie had never heard before.

'I meant, what do you want me to do with it?'

'You are having a party. There are many people coming, with a lot of money to spend. Help them to spend it.'

'And what do I have pay you?'

Gomez lit another cigarette. 'For this one? Nothing. This is my gift. Whatever you sell, I take it off your debt when you give me the cash. But the next one you buy, and you pay down the account with the profits. Is not that fair?'

'What if I don't want to go around dealing *branco* to my guests?'

'Then I think maybe it is time you leave Rosaventos, and go find someone else's money to take.'

For a while, it worked. The wealthy young fun-seekers who washed through Rosaventos were generally ready to sprinkle a little powder on their confections of sun, sea and sex. It was easier and infinitely less risky for them to buy from Jamie than go hunting randomly for a dealer in the bars of Fortaleza, and the cash the trade generated kept Gomez at bay. On top of that, many of the people who bought his drugs or attended Jamie's beach raves went on to sign up for one of his classes or stay at Club Vayu, even if they hadn't been his guests the first time around. And many more told their friends, who told their friends, and this word of mouth along with a steadily growing volume of pieces in the press helped keep the cabanas full and the business afloat.

Bea had her baby – a little boy she and Luggie named Finn – and the resort grew in reputation and scale. They finished the extra cabins and Luggie bought his paragliding kit and trained a couple of local kids as instructors. They extended the restaurant, had a website built to help handle bookings – still tricky because of their continued reliance on satellite comms – and picked up reviews in *Condé Nast Traveller* and some in-flight magazines.

Then, in the late Nineties, out of the blue, Sean got in touch. He'd been trawling the web for a couple of years for news of his estranged half-brother, finding every Jamie Blake in the world but the one he wanted. But one day one of the leads turned out to be real, and there on Sean's screen was a piece on Rosaventos from the Travel section of the online edition of the *New York Times*, along with a photograph of the man he was looking for.

He sent an exploratory email, Jamie responded, and soon after that Sean made the trip to Brazil. The day he arrived he had sat with his half-brother on the low wall that curtained the beach – both of them barefoot, Sean's toes pulpy and grub-like, Jamie's polished brown and smooth as pebbles by the constant interaction with sun, sand and sea – while Jamie reeled off the list of achievements: the club's windsurf shop, Day-Glo racks of boards and sails arrayed in the long lean-to beside it; an open, palm-thatched structure with an adjacent adobe block which together housed the restaurant and bar; beyond that, in a grove of cashew trees and carnauba, a group of cabanas: ten for guests, one for Bea and Luggie, and one right at the back, half-buried in the palm grove, in which Jamie lived. On the other side of the wall, of course, stretched the main attraction: the sumptuous vista of the Rosaventos bay, on whose beach knots of people were enjoying games of volleyball or frisbee while out on the water kite-surfers flipped on the breakers and sailboards sliced to and fro. And in the distance, boss of it all, the mammary swell of la Duna do Por do Sol pulsed with the heat of the day.

Sean's visit changed things. Once it had been established that both he and Jamie were equally intent on keeping their father completely out of the picture, they were able to pick up more or less where they'd left off over a decade before – with one crucial difference. During the course of Sean's stay they discovered that, perversely, the long period of separation had actually brought them closer than they had ever been as teenagers. Back then they'd been placed together by circumstance, and although they'd occupied the same house their lives had hardly touched. Now, however, they had a shared history, and Sean was in Rosaventos because they had chosen to share it some more.

So it was that Jamie found himself telling Sean how money Sheila had given him had got him as far as Punta Allen, where for a long time he'd basically just sat on the beach and contemplated suicide. When it transpired he didn't have the guts to keep swimming out to sea until he was too tired to get back, or rig himself a gibbet in a convenient palm tree, he'd tried to do it by just giving up: first, by running out of money and then, when he could no longer pay for a room or even a hammock on the beach, by walking as far he could down the coast until he reached the lighthouse. Poking around with the vague aim of getting inside it so he could throw himself off the top, he found the water tap. Then he found the hut in the trees, surrounded by a more or less unlimited supply of coconuts. Then, without really consciously deciding to do it, he'd gone back to the resort and begged or filched a machete, some fishing kit, and various other bits and pieces to help him get by, and soon he was spending the days in a kind of eternal present, catching fish and combing the shoreline for driftwood for his fire and any flotsam that might prove to be useful.

Then the bale of cocaine had shown up, and the Russian, and Bea and Luggie, and then, down here in Brazil, the mysterious Gomez, and then Sean, and now here they were, sitting talking on the wall at the Club, drinking a beer and watching the sunset, and feeling for the first time like brothers.

Some months after Sean's visit, Jamie met Gomez on the terrace of a restaurant overlooking the Praia de Iracema, Gomez dressed in his standard business attire of pressed short-sleeved white shirt, dark slacks and black leather slip-ons, Jamie in jeans, Havaianas and T-shirt.

'This was a very good idea, Jamie,' Gomez enthused, as the waiter poured them their wine. 'We should do this more often.'

'We should.'

They tucked into bowls of moqueca, the house speciality, a creamy stew laden with chunks of swordfish and prawn, and chatted about Vayu, about the tourist trade, how much Fortaleza was changing, how much Rosaventos had already changed.

Jamie waited till the food was finished and their espressos arrived before coming to the point.

'I need more cabanas, Gomez. A bigger surf shop. Better facilities. More staff. We need to grow. I want to buy more land.'

Gomez nodded, realising now what the lunch was about.

'And you have money for this?'

'I can get money,' Jamie said. It was something he had discussed with Sean. He'd have died before taking a penny of Tony's, and of course the inverse was also true – Tony would have killed him rather than give him one. But Sean had funds of his own now. During his stay they'd done some work together on the Club's financial projections, and he was interested in coming on board.

Gomez nodded, but his expression was one of sadness. 'The problem, Jamie, is not the money you still owe me. And the problem is not that I don't want to sell you more land. The problem is that there is no land left to sell. When we received the licence to develop Rosaventos, it was very clear: how much area, how many plots, what kind of buildings. And there are inspectors, everything. The idea is for an eco-resort. We are not allowed to build a whole town.'

Jamie nodded. 'I get all that. But there's that area at the far western end, just past us, beyond the palm grove. It's gridded for services, but it's never been built on. What about that?'

Gomez's eyes clouded slightly. 'That area is not up for sale.'

'Why not? Who owns it?'

'The developers.'

'Well can I meet them to discuss it? They're not doing anything with it. We've got more people coming through than we can accommodate. There's money to be made.'

'It's not for sale.'

'Everything's for sale, at the right price.'

'You couldn't afford the right price,' Gomez snapped.

'So there is a price?' Jamie persisted. 'Can't I even send them an email?'

'Email?' Gomez slowly shook his head. 'Jamie. I think you will understand this when I tell you. These are not the kind of people you email.' To emphasise the point he flared his nostrils and exhaled two columns of smoke, then glanced towards a table on the edge of the terrace, at which three men in their fifties sat enjoying an extravagant lunch. 'Do you see those guys over there? They're Porteños. Wealthy guys. Have you any idea what has been happening in Argentina?'

Jamie did – it had been in the news for months. The Argentine economy was in trouble. The pegging of the peso to the dollar by the Convertibility Law and the over-eager adoption of free-market reform had pushed the trade balance into deficit and unemployment up over 12 per cent. By 1998 the country had begun to boil dry. In 1999 GDP fell by 3 per cent. The deficit ballooned. Fernando de la Rúa replaced the ousted Carlos Menem as president, raising taxes and cutting spending radically in an attempt to pull the country out of the slump. As far as Jamie knew, the attempt wasn't working.

'My partners, the developers, they do a lot of business in Argentina,' Gomez continued. 'Like everyone else, like these guys here, they're very worried that the government will soon not be able to keep up the payments on its debts.' He gave Jamie a liquid look. 'A situation you will be familiar with.'

Jamie ignored this. 'What happens then?'

'What happens then is the government shuts down the banks and stops people getting to their money, in case it needs it for itself.'

'That's terrible.'

Gomez shrugged. 'That is South America. Terrible things happen all the time. We are used to it. And so we try to anticipate. The developers, they wish to take their money out of Argentina before this particular terrible thing happens to them.'

'That's very sensible of them.'

'Yes, it is very sensible. So I have been helping. Sometimes that is where I go. Argentina. To help bring out the money.'

Jamie considered this. 'In cash?'

'Yes, of course in cash. If we transferred it using banks it would be taxed when it left Brazil and taxed again when it was sent back to Argentina. Taxed twice! If we were even allowed to take it out of the country at all. And so the people whose money this is would only be getting it back after two governments had helped themselves. Tell me, is that fair?'

Jamie didn't have a chance to say whether it was fair or not, because at that point the waiter cruised up and Gomez asked for the bill.

'I thought I was supposed to be buying you lunch,' Jamie protested.

Gomez waved him away and slipped a sheaf of notes into the black leather folder that had been placed on their table.

'Another time, my friend, another time. Today, it is my honour. It's a beautiful afternoon. Shall we walk?'

They pushed back their chairs and the Brazilian led the way out of the restaurant, pausing to exchange greetings with the Porteños, clearly people he knew. Jamie hovered patiently – South American hellos were never brief – and when the Brazilian was done they descended the terrace steps, crossed the street, and strolled through the bands of shadow thrown by the palm trees across the sand-dusted pavement of the esplanade. For a period, they walked in silence. Then Gomez spoke.

'Jamie. The land that interests you.'

'Yes?'

'I have a proposition. I told you the problem that my friends have? All that cash from Argentina? I need someone to help me with it.'

'Help how?'

'I need a bank account. Somewhere the tax authorities can't reach out and—' Gomez made a plucking gesture in the air.

'You need an offshore account.'

'Exactly so.'

The skin on Jamie's shoulders twitched as the mechanics of Gomez's scheme suddenly became apparent to him.

'In my name, or in yours?'

Gomez shrugged another of his half-shrugs.

'Your name would be preferable.'

Jamie let out a small, involuntary laugh.

'So I set up this offshore account for you, pay in all this cash, then use the money to buy the land in Rosaventos off your friends at some crazy price? They get the money, I get the land, and I'm guessing you get a commission. Something like that?'

'As I always said, Jamie, you are a very smart man.'

'Do you need me to go to Argentina as well?'

'It is very likely.'

'Then there will be expenses involved. Lots of them.'

'Of course. You will need to take flights. Stay in hotels.'

'And I want a commission. Apart from the land. Same as you're getting.'

'I don't know if—'

'Okay, well then you write off the Club Vayu's debt.'

Gomez considered this.

'We can work something out.'

Jamie removed his sunglasses and blinked in the sunshine, wondering what he was getting himself into.

'All right,' he said. 'I'll think about it.'

When he got a telephone call from Brazil one Friday evening, Sean knew at once that something was up. Jamie never called. When he communicated at all it was over the Internet.

'Hey! Sean! It's me. What's up?'

Sean rubbed his face. It was late. He'd been locked into an epic session of *Tomb Raider* and hadn't noticed the time.

'I'm good. You know. Same old. You? Everything okay?'

'Yeah, fine. Look, I think I've found a way to get hold of that piece of land I told you about. But to do it I'll need to set up an offshore account in the BVI or the Caymans. Could you find out the best way to do that?'

'What do you want an offshore account for?' Sean asked, gearing himself for the moment, surely imminent, that Jamie was going to ask him for money.

‘A tax issue on the seller’s side. It’s too boring to explain.’

‘I know absolutely nothing at all about that kind of thing.’

‘I know you don’t. Nor do I. But if we can work this out then I may be able to get a deal, cover all the costs myself.’

‘What, of buying the land?’

‘Yeah.’

‘Oh well that’s good.’ Sean felt a distinct sense of relief. He had indeed discussed investing in the Club when he’d been out in Brazil, and it had seemed like a good idea when the sun was on his face and the surf was cooling his toes. But back in the colder, more pragmatic light of Warwickshire, it had started to seem like a rather less sensible notion. ‘I could ask the finance guys at Nol-Calc, I suppose.’

‘Are you crazy? That would go straight back to Tony.’

‘I wasn’t going to tell them it was for you – I’m not completely stupid. But yeah, questions might get asked. It’s not really ideal. The trouble is I don’t really know anyone in banking. It’s not exactly my scene.’

He racked his brains for a few seconds, drumming his fingers on the arm of the sofa and contemplating the figure of Lara Croft standing patiently on the edge of a precipice, ponytail swaying, awaiting his next command. The reality was that he had quite a narrow social and professional circle. Apart from his three years at university in Durham he’d never lived anywhere other than Warwickshire. He’d gone straight into the forestry management job that his father had created for him when he graduated, and after about three years of doing that Tony had shunted him into a lowly middle management role at NolCalc’s headquarters in Edgbaston. A squat postmodern hulk ornamented with pressed steel architraves and pediments that resembled oversized pieces from a child's building set, the building was filled with accountants, product designers and sales people. All the physical manufacturing took place overseas, mostly in China, and when Sean wasn't commuting to Edgbaston he regularly found himself listening to Mandarin language tapes at thirty thousand feet and waking up to pre-packaged 'Western-style' breakfasts in hotels that looked as they'd been constructed from the same AutoCad files as the NolCalc HQ. It was a routine that, while undoubtedly cosmopolitan in the broader sense, had not given him the wealth of contacts that a job in London might have done.

'How about Alex Wold?' Sean said, remembering suddenly that Matthew's older brother had gone into finance. 'Doesn't he work for an investment bank, or something? He'd probably know.'

'Can you ask him?'

'I don't think I have his details. I'd need to call his folks.'

'It's pretty urgent, Sean. The quicker the better.'

'All right, all right. Calm down, your ladyship. I'll do what I can. How's everything else?'

'Yeah, fine. Fine. Busy.'

'Lots of parties?'

'A few.'

'Got a girlfriend yet?'

'Nah. Too much else to do.'

Sean laughed. That was classic Jamie. 'Yeah, right.'

'I mean it! Hey. Look – I'm about to go to Argentina for a bit, on business.'

'Lucky you.'

'I won't be gone long. And I should be picking up email. So if you need me to call anyone about this bank account thing, then I can be available. Thanks man. Speak soon, yeah?'

Then he was gone and Sean found himself alone again with

Lara Croft. He stared at the computer-animated figure, swaying gently on the screen. Something about her – her hair, maybe, or her face seen in profile – reminded him of Alex's sister Emily. He hadn't seen Emily for ages. Maybe that's why he'd thought of Alex in the first place. Sean had his parents' number somewhere, Miles and Margaret's, in an old Filofax whose address function had long since been superseded by his palmtop. He'd need to call them. But where on earth had he put it?

Alex was happy enough to hear from Sean, but he didn't know anything about offshore accounts. Freddie Winston, however, could be relied upon to have a relatively detailed and strongly partisan opinion on the subject, and by happy coincidence Alex was having dinner with him the following night. He told Sean he would ask.

Dinner with Freddie was generally an extravagant affair. On this occasion they began in Soho with champagne cocktails at Kettner's, transferred by cab to Nobu on Park Lane for beef tenderloin tataki, then returned to Soho for whisky sours and cocaine in the toilets at subterranean jazz-age bar Titanic. After that it was imperative they go dancing round the corner at China White's, where they sailed past the enormous queue thanks to what Freddie pretended was his buddy-buddy relationship with the doorman but which Alex suspected had more to do with the absurd fee he paid for an annual 'VIP' membership.

Once inside they installed themselves at one of the low tables by the dance floor and ordered more champagne. While the drinks were being poured the conversation lagged, and casting around for something to say Alex remembered his promise. He'd meant to bring up the subject in the restaurant where it had been a little quieter, but he and Freddie had been too busy cock-measuring their various deals for an opportunity to present itself. Now would have to do.

'Know anything about offshore accounts?' Alex yelled above the music. With Freddie, blunt was best.

'There are such things. Who wants to know?'

'Old family friend. Well, young family friend, to be more accurate.'

'Where's he operate? The friend. Assuming it's a "he". Which jurisdiction?'

'Brazil, I think. Though also Argentina. South America, at any rate.'

'Ah,' said Freddie, reaching for the champagne bottle and topping up his glass. 'That kind of offshore account. Now all is clear.'

Alex grinned. 'He says it's for property deals.'

'I'm sure he does.'

'Seriously. He's got some land there already. Had it for a while – he runs a fancy little water sports resort. Windsurfing, water-skiing, all that malarkey. Apparently he's expanding. Tax is an issue, as is moving money around. So he needs a facility.'

'Water sports, huh?' Freddie leered, never one to miss a chance for innuendo. 'Well he's got you sold.'

'Apparently it's a bloody gorgeous spot, and he throws good parties, too.'

'I like the sound of that. Presumably he's also rolling in the finest chang.'

'I wouldn't know.'

'Oh come on. He must be. Why else move to Bumfuckão, Brazil, unless it's because it happens to be a llama spit from

Colombia? He must be up to his ears in dusky maidens, Cuervo Gold and fine white flake. And now he needs an offshore pot to stash his ill-gotten loot. Alex, my friend, there is only one thing for it.'

'What's that?'

'We have to go and see him.'

'We do?'

'We do. Call him up. Tell him we need to meet to, er, ratify the deal. Do due diligence blah blah blah. Tell him there'll be arrangement fees and expenses, then tell him we'll waive all that and do it gratis if he lays on the maidens, the nosebag and the Gold.'

Alex considered this, rather annoyed he hadn't thought of it himself. 'What about the windsurfing?'

'Fuck the windsurfing.'

Alex laughed. Sometimes Freddie could be genuinely funny, though if you threw enough shit at the wall some of it had to stick. 'So you can actually set up an account for him then?'

'Christ yes. We do it all the time through our Mexican division. They have a Cayman Islands operation. It's totally extreme. Known in the trade as the Marie Celeste.'

'Eh?'

'Thirty thousand accounts, zero employees.'

'No way? That's hilarious.'

'Absolutely. It was set up originally for the yacht-abiding fraternity, aka the Bermuda Triangle crew, so they could keep their dividends and capital gains floating in a virtual state rather than get them taxed back into reality every time they stopped off in port to stock up on ship's biscuits and gin. But these days all sorts of riff-raff get a look-in. They'd probably give your pal an account if he fell off the plane in Mexico City and asked for one. But don't tell him that. Not if we can score ourselves a free holiday.'

So Alex called Sean and Sean called Jamie, emailing him first to set up a time to talk.

'They want to come and visit,' he said, once he'd got his half-brother on the phone.

'What? Really? What about the account?'

'They'll sort the account. They'll bring the details with them. But I think they want you to show them a good time as a quid pro quo. They've heard about your parties.'

'They have? How?'

Sean cleared his throat. 'I might have mentioned something.'

'Ha, well, if that's what it took to get them interested, so be it. It's not a problem for me. Just let me know when they're coming. I'll sort them out. Fucking hell. Bankers. It's just like they say it is, isn't it?'

Sean had just put down the phone when his mother called, told him that Caitlin had come up from London for the weekend, and asked him if he wanted to join them the next day for lunch.

'I'm going to cook Lancashire hotpot after we get back from church, if you fancy coming over. I know it's your favourite.'

'Caitlin's not going to church with you is she?'

'I very much doubt it. I expect she and Mia will stay and hang out by the pool. If they can get themselves out of bed, that is.'

'Who's Mia?'

'A friend of Caitlin's. An actress I think. I haven't met her before.'

A friend of Caitlin's. An actress. Whenever Caitlin came to visit their parents, she seemed to bring a new friend. Even at Christmas. There was always some lost soul she'd found, someone who needed a temporary home. For a long while it had been her various boyfriends, never the same guy twice, each more random than the last. There had been that emo guy Leo, who hadn't been able to meet anyone's eye and had only eaten white food. There had been Paul, an advertising creative who dressed in Doc Martens, drainpipes and a dinner jacket and got into a very tense disagreement over dinner with Tony about golf, a subject he clearly knew nothing about. And then there had been Riichi, a Japanese tattoo artist whose extensive body art Caitlin had taken particular delight in describing in excessive and intimate detail.

Sean wasn't sure he could sit through another meal watching his father trying to keep a check on his tongue while Caitlin drank too much and continually drew the conversation back to whichever characteristics of her latest beau she judged the most likely to annoy him. It was hardly a surprise that none of the guys ever came back for a second visit. He'd once overheard the reaction of a boyfriend who hadn't enjoyed being goaded into the ring like that, a row that had turned into a full-blown screaming match up in Jamie's old room, which was where the visitors were usually cloistered by Sheila during their stay in a largely symbolic attempt to prevent fornication taking place under her roof. The row had not been pretty. A girlfriend could only be an improvement. Unless Caitlin was sleeping with her, of course, and was about to serve that revelation up for their father's delectation while their mother served dessert. Oh God not that, please not that.

But if Mia was Caitlin's gay lover neither of them mentioned it, and once he'd met her Sean found himself hoping fairly fervently that she was not: she wasn't only polite and apparently sane, but she professed to be both an actress and a model, a claim which was thoroughly credible. Girls like Mia didn't pass through

Warwickshire with particular frequency – at least not through Sean's part of it.

'Mia was in *The Bill* when I did my stint there,' Caitlin explained at lunch. 'But she's going to be at Stratford for a season. It's very exciting.'

'Oh,' said Sheila, who was a devoted theatregoer. 'What will you be playing?'

'Viola, in *Twelfth Night*,' Mia said proudly. 'Though we're also doing *The Cherry Orchard* in The Swan – I'm Varya.'

'How wonderful! We'll have to come and see it. Won't we Tony?'

Tony grunted a not particularly enthusiastic affirmative.

'It's amazing to be working with Michael Boyd. He's a genius.'

'Is he one of the actors?' Sean asked, vaguely jealous.

Caitlin cackled loudly. 'God Sean, you bloody philistine. He's the artistic director.'

Sean flushed. 'Sorry. I'm not really a theatre person. I don't think I've been to see a play since I was at school.'

Tony gave him a wink. 'We like our drama with balls, don't we son?'

'Tony! Please,' Sheila chided, misunderstanding.

'He's talking about sport, Mum,' said Sean. 'Does anyone want another drink?'

'There's another one of those on the side there,' Tony said, as Caitlin drained the last of the Valpolicella into her glass. 'You can open that if you like.'

Sheila's eyes flickered. 'Darling, do we really need another bottle?'

'It's not every day we have both the kids home. I say let them have what they want.'

Sheila let it ride. It was true. It wasn't often that they were together as a family. Rarer still for them all to be together without

Tony and Caitlin at loggerheads. She just hoped no one would spoil it by drinking too much, though by the size of the measure her daughter had just poured herself, it looked like she intended to try.

When lunch was over Caitlin, Mia and Sean took what was left of the wine through to the pool. It was a warm day and girls slid back the doors so they could smoke. The meal had left Sean feeling drowsy and he changed into his trunks and did a few gentle lengths in the half-hope of tempting Mia into the water. When this didn't happen he got out, put some music on the sound system, and came and sat on one of the white plastic loungers next to the girls, a towel draped round his shoulders.

Mia was talking about the theatre. Her shows went up in October and she was deep in rehearsal.

'Anyway,' she sighed at length, finishing a long anecdote about the irritatingly obsessive behaviour one of the more famous members of that season's company, 'to be honest I'll be glad of a break.'

'Are they giving you some time off?' Caitlin asked.

'Yeah. We've got a free week in September, thank God.'

'Nice.'

'After that it's heads down till April, so I thought I'd go somewhere nice and hot, and do ab-so-lutely nothing except lie in the sun. I've been in that rehearsal room the whole summer and I'm practically white. Look at me!'

Sean had been doing little else since Mia had arrived. Her mother was Senegalese, her father Scottish, and her buttery complexion looked just fine to him. But the notion that she might need to top up her tan gave him an idea.

'I'm going to this fantastic place in Brazil in September. For a beach party. You guys should come.'

'What party?'

'Remember Alex Wold, Matt's brother? I'm taking him over to see Jamie.'

Caitlin's head snapped around. 'You're in touch with Jamie?'

Sean had known this moment would come, and that when it did it would be difficult. At least this way, with a natural reason and an outsider present, there was a chance that a scene might be averted.

'Yeah. I tracked him down online. I actually went over to see him in Brazil back in February. Mum and Dad don't know, by the way.'

'I didn't know either. Why didn't you tell me?'

'I haven't seen you Cait. I wanted to tell you in person.'

Caitlin's hands were shaking as she lit a cigarette and tried to digest this piece of news. 'What's he want to see Alex for?' she said at length, struggling to keep a light tone.

'It's a business thing,' said Sean hurriedly, relieved that his sister seemed to be dealing with the revelations okay. 'Jamie needs some financial advice. Anyway, he organises these beach raves every month or so, and we're timing the trip to coincide with one of those.'

Mia felt that now might a good time to try to defuse some of the obvious tension in this little exchange. 'Sounds amazing,' she said. 'Who's Jamie?'

'Our half-brother,' Caitlin said.

'And what's this place of his like?'

'Oh it's unbelievable,' said Sean, pleased to have finally got Mia's attention. 'It's in the middle of a national park – there are no roads or anything. To get there you have to either go by boat or get a lift on one of these big-wheel trucks that drive you in over this incredible dune sea.'

'Wow. Caitlin – how come you've never told me about this?'

'I've never been,' Caitlin said quietly.

'I've only been once,' Sean said hurriedly. 'Jamie and Dad don't exactly get on, so, you know, it's been a bit difficult. It's best not to mention anything about it to our parents. Anyway, it's amazing there – they have surfing, parascending, diving, all that stuff. And the beach is beautiful. You guys should really come and see it. Jamie won't charge us to stay at the Club, and if you can pay for the connecting flights in Brazil, I reckon I can get three returns to Rio on my Airmiles. It'd be a pretty cheap holiday.'

'Are you even serious?' said Mia, her eyes wide. 'You would do that?'

'Sure. I get loads of points because of all the flying I do for work. To be honest I'd welcome the chance to spend them on something fun.'

Mia squealed and hugged Caitlin. 'But that is like, huge! Caitlin, your brother totally rocks. Oh my God, oh my God. This could be so fucking cool! We've got to go, come on Caitlin, we've got to!'

But Caitlin didn't look so keen. 'I don't know . . . I really wouldn't want Dad to find out.'

Sean put his hand on her shoulder. 'He won't know. Why would he know? I'll set it all up. There's no reason for either of us to tell him, and Mia's hardly going to say anything, are you Mia?'

Mia smiled her best smile – which was indeed a good one, reaching parts of Sean that smiles did not generally reach. 'My lips are sealed.'

The plan was for them all to meet at Heathrow, but Sean's Airmiles had only stretched to Economy seats and he'd reckoned without

Alex and Freddie booking themselves into First Class. Alex texted him to say they'd gone straight to the executive lounge when they'd arrived at the airport and would come and say hi after take-off.

The 777 was approaching the Canaries by the time the two bankers had finished their meal. With the darkening Atlantic sliding past below them like a sheet of hammered tungsten they rinsed down the last of the Sauternes they'd had with dessert, agreed it weathered the pressurised cabin better than the Beychevelle they'd drunk with the lamb, and decided they felt sufficiently fortified for a foray into the realm beyond the blue concertina curtains.

'Bet you're glad I insisted on First now, Wold,' Freddie hummed as they descended through Club World and World Traveller Plus into the claustrophobic confines of Economy.

'The lamb was good, but I'm not sure it was worth an extra grand apiece.'

'It's not about the lamb, you monkey – it's about the fact that down here you can't even breathe.' And he had a point: the amount of available light and air did seem to diminish the closer they got to the back of the plane. 'I mean, just check out the pong from those bogs. That's what the extra wad buys you. The chance to swap that for the scent of a decent Bordeaux. And a good night's sleep, of course. Given that we're going to be slumming it for the next few days, I say we should get in the creature comforts while we can.'

A hand and then a head appeared a few rows down. 'There they are,' Alex said. 'Let's go and say hello.'

Sean and the two girls were slotted into a bank of three seats by the window. Caitlin looked good, Alex thought. It was funny to think that when he'd last seen her she'd still been at school.

Now she must be nearly thirty, the fronds at the corners of her eyes and slightly papery quality of her complexion giving him the impression that she was capable and driven. Long production days combined with lots of late nights, probably. Classic media girl.

Mia, on the other hand, looked like she got plenty of sleep. She caught Alex's eye immediately, and he was encouraged by the fact that she showed a keen interest in things at the front of the plane.

'Oh man, I've never travelled First. Do you have, like, a bar and all that?'

'That's only in 747s,' Alex said. 'In the double-decker bit on top.'

'But we do have a gay Brazilian flight attendant called Erico, who brings us free drinks whenever we want,' Freddie informed her, loudly enough for anyone in the surrounding seats to hear.

'Yeah. Which is better than a bar.'

'Except when he asks if we need more nuts,' quipped Freddie weakly, but no more quietly.

'And you get those weird pod seats, right?' Mia asked. 'That you can lie down in?'

'Yep. We get those.'

'Oh wow. That must be so cool. I never get any rest in these ones. They're so damn uncomfortable.' She checked herself, and touched Sean on the arm. 'Not that I'm ungrateful or anything. Sean got us these flights on his Airmiles. How generous was that?'

Sean looked sheepish and Alex clocked that here he had a competitor for Mia's affections. He looked over at Freddie, who had been paying Caitlin the same kind of attention that he'd been giving her friend.

'Hey Fred. There were some empty seats when we came

through, were there not? What say we see if we can score these guys an upgrade?'

Freddie grinned. 'Got to be worth a try.'

'All right. Hang on.' Alex squeezed past his friend and disappeared back up the aisle. About five minutes later he returned, a pained expression on his face.

'No joy?'

'Well sort of. They'll do it, but they've only got two slots.'

'In Traveller Plus?'

'In Club World.'

The girl's faces lit up. 'Club World?' said Mia. 'That's like business class, right?'

'Yeah, pretty much. You get to lie down. And you get decent food and free drinks and all that shit.'

'Oh my God,' Caitlin said. 'That would be fantastic.'

'You don't get Erico, though. He's just for our benefit,' said Freddie, trying to squeeze a little more juice from his joke.

'And Sean would have to stay here,' said Alex ruefully. 'On his own.'

Both girls looked at Sean, who shrugged. 'Hey, I'm not going to stop you,' he said. 'If you guys go up front I can sack out across these three seats. I'll be fine.'

'Oh, you're so sweet. Thanks Seanie.' Mia threw her slender arms around his neck and gave him a hug. The brush of her breast on his arm and the pressure of her cheekbone against the soft flesh of his jaw set his heart racing, and for the next few minutes it felt like his small sacrifice had been worth it. But then she was gone, and Caitlin was gone, and three economy seats side by side still didn't make much of a bed for a man of his size, and he spent most of the night restlessly surfing the inflight entertainment channels and feeling that in some intangible way he'd been robbed.

By the time they landed at Galeão International Caitlin was in a terrible state. From her seat in Club World she'd led the others in a frontal assault on the cocktail list, and now she sat on an aluminium bench in the baggage hall with her head in her hands, sipping at a corrugated plastic bottle of mineral water while Sean retrieved her cases.

'That upgrade was wasted on you,' he sniped, not altogether pleased by her behaviour. 'I think we're going to have to get you a wheelchair if we want to make our connection.'

'Make that four wheelchairs,' said Alex, who was also feeling none too good.

'Better yet, get a courtesy cart,' said Freddie. 'Then you can just chauffeur the lot of us.'

The fact that the person with the worst seat had emerged from the flight in the best condition confirmed Sean's long-held suspicion that a surfeit of luxury was actively bad for you. Blinkered by sunglasses and incapable of conversation, his companions wandered along behind him as he led the way upstairs to the check-in desks, where they queued silently beneath the airport's dense white latticework of metal roof trusses before trailing back through security, along to the domestic gates, and onto the flight to Fortaleza. They all passed out before the plane left the ground and continued to sleep for the duration of the journey, leaving Sean alone with his book, a worn copy of Judy Leden's *Flying with Condors*, and the enticing permutations of the Brazilian coastline, intermittently visible between the frothy puffs of white cumulus that hung outside his window.

Their next baggage-hall experience was a more upbeat affair.

The four casualties had been rejuvenated by their naps and this time proved capable of collecting their own things and making their way to the terminal restaurant without undue assistance. Here they sat and guzzled Cokes and pizzas while Sean negotiated a price for a minibus to take them on the next leg of their journey: a five-hour drive up the CE-085 highway through a flat, rather unremarkable landscape of open scrub punctuated by tatty palm groves, linear villages, and herds of angular, heat-bothered cattle. The girls soon fell back to sleep while Alex and Sean read and Freddie engaged the driver in conversation using a combination of Portuguese, Spanish, English and internationally recognised hand movements, which seemed to work fine as long as the discussion didn't stray beyond the confines of football, women and politics.

Eventually, stiff-kneed and more or less on schedule, they pulled off the road and drew up beside a simple wooden-framed building clad with corrugated iron and shaded by a stand of susurrating eucalyptus trees, in front of which slouched a couple of geriatric flatbed trucks baked to the colour of dust and rigged with oversized tyres and crude passenger benches. The driver unloaded their bags and piled them up in the dirt and Alex paid him while the others wandered into the hut in search of help and cold drinks.

A few cans of Guaraná ('Well that tastes like shit' – Freddie) and a couple of cigarettes later they were off again, this time perched on the back of the marginally more lively-looking of the two lorries. As it nosed down a dirt track that led away from the highway the sense of anticipation they'd lost somewhere outside of Fortaleza began to return. And rightly so: just a few minutes later they crested a small rise and all of a sudden there lay before them an entirely new landscape of pillowy dunes rimmed by the blue crust of the sea.

'What do you think, Cait?' Sean asked his sister, as the truck fishtailed over the sand.

'Yeah. Amazing,' she said, sounding unconvinced.

'Are you okay?'

'Still a bit hungover.'

'Worried about seeing Jamie?'

'I don't want to talk about it.'

She shivered slightly, though the breeze coming off the ocean was warm and welcome after the stultified confines of the minibus. Sean slipped his arm round her shoulders and gave her a brotherly hug.

'Don't be. He's just the same. A bit more chill, if anything. It'll be fine. We're going to have a really fun time.'

The blistered red globe of the sun was perching on the horizon behind them by the time they had bounced around the base of la Duna do Por do Sol, wound their way through the sandy tracks that served the small beach town as streets, and drawn up outside the Club Vayu, their throats parched and their faces rimed with grit. A gaggle of teenage boys materialised from among the thatched cabins and screens of hibiscus to help with their bags, which they ferried between the two impressive palms that formed the Club's entrance and dumped in a heap on the wooden boardwalk that connected its various buildings. The group followed, bantering with the kids and fending off their requests to swap T-shirts until a lean, dreadlocked man dressed in a rash vest and Bermuda shorts came out and shooed the children away.

'Hey! Sean. You made it.'

'Luggie! Hi! Good to see you.'

They hugged.

'So – who are these guys?'

'Alex, Mia, Caitlin, Freddie. Everyone, this is Luggie.'

'All right! Welcome to Club Vayu! This' – Luggie indicated the slim weather-beaten woman with bright eyes who had just crossed from the bar area carrying a stack of clean laundry, a naked toddler in tow – 'is Bea. And that's Finn. Finn's the one who doesn't like clothes. You want anything done around here, best ask Bea. Not Finn. Or me!'

'That's about right,' smiled Bea, putting down her load on the reception desk and smoothing off her turquoise sarong.

'Amazing place you've got here,' said Mia, shaking her hand. 'I can't believe you guys built it from nothing.'

'Well it took a while,' said Bea, in a tone that suggested it was too early to say whether or not the project had been a success.

'A little slice of paradise, huh?' chuckled the rather more upbeat Luggie. 'Wait till you get a proper look around, it'll blow your mind.'

'How was your trip?' Bea asked.

'The last bit was the best,' said Freddie. 'I love the way you throw in that free spinal massage.'

The two hosts looked blank for a second, and then Luggie got it.

'Ha, sorry, it's a little bumpy isn't it? Well, it's all part of the experience. I'm just finishing up with a class, so why don't you guys get settled in? Bea will do the formalities, and I'll see you in the bar for a cold one in an hour or so.'

'Is Jamie around?' Sean asked, as Luggie turned to go.

'Oh, yeah. Not right now. He's in Fortaleza, sorting supplies for the party.' Luggie flashed another grin. 'He should be back tomorrow some time. He said to say hi.'

The Club Vayu bar and restaurant was built from carnauba wood and roofed with a thick gunmetal-grey cap of thatch plaited from the tree's long leaves. Open on three sides, it was a fine place to sit and enjoy a caipirinha while the sun set behind la Duna do Por do Sol and slowly turned the ocean to brass. Sean, Caitlin, Alex and Mia were doing just that when Luggie arrived and pulled up a chair.

'Where's your friend?' he asked, after they'd chatted for a few minutes and he'd noticed that Freddie was missing.

'He's got a bad stomach,' Alex explained.

'Something he ate?'

'He's blaming the pizza we had for lunch at the airport.'

'Wouldn't surprise me. The café there is notorious. I hope he recovers soon, because I've got a suggestion for you guys. We thought in the morning we'd give you a proper tour of the area. From up there.'

'From the roof?' said Mia, following the direction of Luggie's pointed finger.

'A little higher than that. Paragliders. It's one of the activities we offer. Anyone ever been paragliding before?'

All except Sean shook their heads.

'I've done a parachute jump,' Alex said.

'Well this is sort of the same. Except better.'

Mia looked worried. 'Won't we need some kind of training?'

'No – it's easy. We just strap you in and chuck you off. You'll pick it up as you go.'

'I think he's kidding, Mia,' Sean said, seeing the look of horror on her face.

'I am indeed kidding,' Luggie laughed. 'Of course we don't do that. We fly tandem.' He nodded his head in the direction of la Duna, now a giant absence looming in the twilight at the other end of the beach. 'We go from up there, catch the thermals, circle over the sand dunes and then swing out over the bay. It's totally epic. I took Sean up last him he came. How was it, Sean-o?'

'It was truly impressive. You've got to do it.'

'You can count me in,' said Caitlin. 'I'm up for it.'

Sean glanced at his sister, pleased to see she'd perked up.

'Ditto,' said Alex. 'This is what we're here for. What d'you reckon Mia? You game?'

Mia gripped her knees and grimaced. 'Arrrgh! I'm not so sure. It sounds a bit scary to me! Maybe I'll just watch.'

'Come on,' Sean encouraged. 'You'll regret it if you don't.'

'Hey, there's no pressure,' Luggie said. 'You can walk up with us tomorrow; we'll take a wing up for you so if you feel like going, you can. And if you don't like the look of it you can just walk back down again, no sweat at all.'

Although Freddie appeared at breakfast the next morning his stomach was still feeling ginger, so he passed on the excursion and instead installed himself in a hammock at the top of the beach while the others received a brief flight tutorial from Luggie. They then hefted the backpacks containing the gliders round to the front of the club and hitched a ride with one of the taxi trucks to the base of the dune.

Joined now by three other instructors, the group began to work its way up the great sweeping ridge that led all the way to the summit. The soft sand and the heavy equipment made for hard going and the hike took more than an hour; by the time they reached the crest the sun was well on its way to its zenith and they were suffering under its glare.

'Don't worry, you'll cool off fast enough once we get airborne,' Luggie said, breaking out some bottles of water and a couple of Ziploc bags filled with trail mix.

'It's quite a view,' Alex observed. And it was: they were high enough now to see the entire peninsula, revealed as a dun D-shape freckled with dunes, Rosaventos itself a livid green buffer speckled with the signature colours and forms – blue polythene sheeting, orange gas canisters, whitewashed walls, terracotta tiles – of Anthropocenic humanity.

Sean was gazing inland. 'Look – there's the truck. Right at the edge of the dune sea. There's the highway, see, and those trees – that must be where the taxi dropped us off.'

'I'm not sure I fancy walking back,' said Mia. 'The sand's already too hot to sit on.'

'Ha – all part of the plan,' Luggie said. 'Once you're up here, you realise that the best way down is to jump.'

He paired them all off with an instructor – 'Mia, you're sticking with me' – then quickly ran once more through the protocols for take-off and landing.

Sean and Demetrio went first. They were to launch off the windward side of la Duna, so Demetrio unfurled their canopy and laid it out at the top of the slope. Then he and Sean clipped themselves into their harnesses and hooked them together, with Luggie double-checking the straps.

'I feel like a pantomime horse!' Sean joked, as he and the instructor, now tethered together, sidestepped their way down the gradient until the control lines grew taut.

'Just be grateful you're at the front end!' Alex called back. And he had a point: to launch, Sean had the easy task of jogging straight forwards downhill. Demetrio on the other hand had to run backwards beside him while pulling the glider up into the air like a kite, then swivelling round and scooping his passenger up underneath him as the wing took flight.

Even though he'd done this before, Sean was amazed how instant and effortless the process could seem. Three or four steps and they were up and, within another moment or two, impossibly high, both from the speed with which the ground fell away and from the flood of adrenalin. That glucose rush was a feeling Sean loved, one that had always drawn him to sports of all kinds, and for the first time since Alex had poached Mia from under his nose on the aircraft he was able to let go and relax. This he could hold onto, this was reliable: the deep blue bands of the sea, the icing of clouds on the horizon, the clean cool air on his face, the sense of command over the territory below . . . it was all so much more comprehensible than the fathomless mystery of whether or not a girl might find him attractive.

Demetrio pulled them into a turn and they carved through the sky until the peak of la Duna came back into view.

'*Agora Filipe e Caitlin vão*,' he called, pointing, and as Sean watched the pair of them executed the strange little sequence of launch calisthenics and floated off the face of the slope just as he and his instructor had done. Before long all four tandems were up in the air, Luggie and Mia's included, and for the next hour or so the neon crescents hissed around the sky like storks bearing twins, hunting out thermals and tacking to and fro across the face of the breeze that flowed in from the Atlantic.

At length Luggie led them into land on the beach in front of the Club, where they helped pack up the harnesses while comparing notes on the experience. Mia, charged up with the zealousness of the recent convert, was particularly voluble.

'Glad you went for it in the end, then?' Sean asked.

'Oh yeah. I mean, I was completely crapping myself the whole time and when we took off I thought I was going to die! But Luggie was amazing and he talked me through the whole thing and after a while I just kind of forgot that what we were doing was totally insane and just started to think, God, this is just what it must be like, I mean really be like, to be like a bird, you know? Do you know what I mean?'

'Absolutely,' said Alex. 'The silence of it all, the fact that you're just kind of *there*.'

'Yeah, exactly,' Mia nodded.

Then Caitlin spoke up. 'Matthew would have liked it. Don't you think, Alex?'

'Yes,' Alex said, surprised. It was the first time anyone had mentioned Matthew during the trip. He'd been working on the assumption that the topic of his brother was strictly off limits. 'He really would have done. He'd like it here full stop, I'd think. It's his kind of scene.'

It was lunchtime so they headed back to the bar, commandeered a table, and ordered food and beer. They were halfway through their meal when Freddie wandered in.

'Well. If it ain't the Vulture Squadron. How'd it go?' he asked, and in reply received a chorus of happy responses. 'Aw, now you're making me feel bad that I missed it.'

'I'm sure Luggie will take you up another time,' Sean said.

'Don't pity him,' said Alex. 'I promise you Freddie will have been perfectly happy piloting his hammock at an altitude of several hundred millimetres above sea level.'

'Well, that's where I got the best view of this morning's girl-on-girl beach volleyball. Which was not to be missed, I can tell you. But as it happens, I wasn't in my hammock for very long. I've been busy. And I come bearing gifts.' He reached into the pocket of his shorts, pulled out a black plastic film canister, and placed it on the table.

Alex was the nearest: he picked the canister up, snapped off the plastic cap and peered inside.

'Easy does it,' Freddie instructed.

'Oh my goodness. Is this what I think it is?'

'It is. A present from young Mr Blake. Don't snort it all at once.'

'From Jamie?' asked Caitlin. 'He's here?'

'He was here.'

'Was?'

'He showed up after you'd gone. I spent most of the morning with him, sorting out, you know, the thing we came here to sort out. Anyway, then he had to leave. Said it was an emergency, had to fly down to Buenos Aires. Some business thing. He sends sincere apologies. And that, of course,' Freddie said, indicating the film canister. 'There's a big bag of grass too, if anyone wants any. He said to help ourselves to anything we needed, it was all on the house.'

'Is he not going to be here for the party?' asked Sean.

'I guess not. He did say that he'd be back before the end of our stay, if he could make it. His loss, right? He's got to work. We, on the other hand, have got to have a good time.'

There was a crash; Caitlin had knocked over her chair and was storming out of the restaurant and off down the beach.

'Whoa,' said Freddie. 'Was it something I said?'

'It's not your fault,' Sean told him. And he headed off in pursuit of his sister.

He caught up with her by the rocks on the peninsula's promontory, a steely outcrop of granite worn over millennia into a series of lenticular ovoids which resembled a pod of surfacing whales. Caitlin was sitting in the sand with her back to the base of the largest rock, keening. Sean sat down beside her, clearing a space among the briny strands of rotten bladderwrack and the clumps of fishing net knotted around pieces of wave-sculpted driftwood and shards of smoothed bone.

'Don't be upset,' he said, uselessly.

'Why would he do this, Sean? Why? When we've come all this way?'

'Like Freddie said, he's got to go away on business. It happens.'

'Oh bullshit! That's bullshit. It's been, like, thirteen years! We come to visit, and he's called away on business? Don't be so fucking naïve. You should be as insulted as I am.'

'He didn't disappear the last time I came.'

'Well then it's just me, isn't it? It's just me that he hates.' She picked up a splinter of driftwood and started grinding its point into her palm, turning it around and around as if she was trying to drill a hole through her hand. 'It's just like before, Sean. He's left me, just like before.'

'It's not like before. He invited us here. We can come back. It's easy for us. We have the money.'

'It *is* like before. You don't understand. He hates me Sean, he just fucking hates me. He doesn't want me.'

'That's not true.'

'Have you spoken to him about it? Have you asked him?'

'I—'

'No. You fucking haven't, have you? Because you know exactly what he'd say. You wanted me to come, Sean, you invited me. But he didn't invite me, did he? He didn't want me here. Go on. Deny it.'

Sean couldn't, so instead he said nothing and pulled his sister to him, stroking her hair while she cried it all out. The beach was busy now, with several hundred people arrayed across it sunbathing, diving in and out of the breakers, playing football. Out in the bay the windsurfers plied to and fro, drawing jagged slashes of colour across the whitecaps with their sails while three or four paragliders with tandem rigs soared overhead – Luggie, Demetrio and Filipe no doubt, repeating the morning's experience for a new set of guests. It seemed strange to feel sad on a day like this, when the sun was so high it left almost no shadow and the clouds he had seen from the top of la Duna that morning remained suspended above the horizon as if painted onto a screen. But sad he was, sitting there holding his sister's spasming body, asking himself what could be done to stop his long-cherished plan for family reconciliation from falling apart.

Then a movement caught his eye. A pair of red Bermuda shorts, running towards them between the groups of holidaymakers, unbuttoned denim shirt flapping in the breeze . . . It was Alex. And he was shouting.

'What's he saying?' Sean said to Caitlin, who didn't respond. 'I can't hear you!' he yelled down the beach.

Alex continued his run, feet puffing out little sprays of sand. The day was so bright Sean could hardly bear to look at him. As the other man drew near he released his sister and stood, hands shading his eyes, squinting into the glare.

'What is it?' he yelled again. But Alex didn't slow. He continued till he was right up alongside them then dropped to his knees.

'What's the matter?' Sean asked.

'You're not going to believe this,' Alex said, between gasps. 'In New York. Two planes have crashed into the Twin Towers.'

'You're kidding?' said Sean, his mouth suddenly dry. Even Caitlin looked up.

'I wish I was. Both of them have completely collapsed. We just saw it online. It's totally fucking unreal.'

EGG

MATTHEW HAD MET CAITLIN on several occasions as a teenager, but she hadn't made much of an impression on him – or him on her – until she changed schools from Stratford Grammar to Wardle's, a fee-paying establishment in Warwick, the same school that Matthew's sister Emily attended.

Emily, who was two years Caitlin's senior, had recently passed her driving test and was now doing the Wolds' school run. Every day she drove herself and Matthew, whose school was not far from Wardle's, the ten or so miles to Warwick and back in a somewhat comical red Renault 4 that had been Alex's before it had been hers, bought for him by Margaret and Miles without any consultation. He'd longed for a car and its promise of freedom from the confines of the countryside, but it was typical of his parents that they'd managed, with their unwavering ability to divine any currents of anti-cool in their immediate vicinity, to go out and buy the one vehicle that he wouldn't have wanted to be seen dead in. It was by a long chalk the crappiest set of wheels to draw up in the sixth-form car park every morning, and so Alex, in a pointless attempt to make it a degree or two more hip, had set about trying to trash it. But the boxy little vehicle proved as resilient as the indomitable French wagons from which it had evolved, and it survived him to pass into the hands of his sister, who treated it with rather more care and affection than her brother ever had.

One Saturday lunchtime that summer Margaret had fallen into conversation with Caitlin's mother, Sheila, over a gin and tonic in the King's Head. When she'd heard about Caitlin's move to Wardle's she'd asked in a characteristic fit of generosity – partly prompted by the flush from the vindication of her own choice for her daughter's education – if the Nolans would like to take advantage of one of the spare seats in Emily's car and share the journey to school. The matter was quickly settled: on weekdays Sheila would drive Caitlin from Shelfield to Snitterfield and drop her off at the Wolds' house for a quarter past eight. At a quarter to five, to coincide with the children's return, she would come to pick her up. Sheila would return the favour by doing the run if Emily was sick or had to stay late for extra-curricular activities.

Extra-curricular activities were pretty much the first thing that entered Matthew's mind when he saw Caitlin emerge from Sheila's car in his driveway the morning of their first shared journey. Angular and gangly, the grey panels of her ill-cut school uniform serving only to emphasise the litheness of her body, she hovered in the damp September dawn with one long arm rolling her school bag to and fro across her calf while the other pushed her long, tawny hair back from her lightly tanned forehead, as if she'd stepped straight out of one of Matthew's many wet dreams.

The effect she had upon him was so intense that beyond the most perfunctory grunts of greeting for the first week of the term he couldn't bring himself to speak to her at all although, Emily noted with amusement, he did at once forgo his usual place in the front for a seat in the back beside the newcomer. Then one October morning, when his sister was busy filling the car with petrol at a service station, Matthew asked the question.

'Hey, want to meet up at lunch?' Caitlin blinked, not comprehending. 'We could hang out in the park. It'd be fun.'

'I . . . I'm not sure we're allowed out.'

Matthew was ready for this. 'Who said anything about being allowed? Girls sneak out, you know. It's easy. No one really checks.'

Caitlin went red. She knew.

'Look, don't worry about it,' Matthew said, seeing that he wasn't getting anywhere. 'It was just an idea.'

'No, it's okay. I'll try. I want to. Where do you meet?'

Matthew's heart began to beat a little faster. 'Usually by the big fountain in St Nicholas's Park. Or in the café next to it. Café if it's raining.'

Caitlin turned to look at him and smiled. 'Or if you fancy a cup of tea.' Her embarrassment had gone, and happy, confident Caitlin had returned.

'That too.'

For the rest of the week Matthew spent the entirety of his lunch break in St Nicholas's Park, nervously scanning the paths and the café for a glimpse of the girl. But Caitlin did not appear that day, or the next, or the next. Not wanting to be seen as needy, he didn't bring the matter up with her when he saw her in the car, and Caitlin didn't raise it either, maintaining instead her usual aura of absent-minded intensity. For a while it was as if their earlier conversation had never happened at all. And then, the following Thursday, she appeared.

Matthew was sitting with his friends sharing a bowl of soggy chips and a cigarette, when Stuart broke off from the conversation and stared over his shoulder.

'I think there's someone here to see you,' he said.

Matthew immediately assumed it was one of the duty teachers, who occasionally launched a surprise raid on the park. He blanched and twisted around, expecting the worst.

'Hey,' Caitlin said.

'Oh,' he said.

'Don't sound too overjoyed.'

'No – it's – I just thought you were someone else.' He jumped up, ordered the boys to shuffle around, and reached for another chair. 'You with anyone?'

'Nope. Just me.' She sat down.

'This is Stuart. Pete. Ashwin,' Matthew said, awkwardly.

'Hi,' said everyone.

'Do you want a tea, or something?'

'Okay.' Then, as Matthew hadn't offered, Caitlin turned to Stuart. 'Have you got a fag?'

Stuart grinned excessively. 'Of course,' he said, whipping out his pack. 'Get the lady some tea then, Matthew.'

Matthew did, thanking his stars for Caitlin's arrival and cursing them for giving him Stuart Marshall as a friend. When he returned, the girl was sitting listening to an anecdote Stuart was telling about going with his father to buy a bull terrier from a car-wrecker's yard in West Bromwich. She laughed loudly at some detail as Matthew sat down, and he felt his throat constrict. Had he already lost her before they'd even got started? Because surely she preferred Stuart to him, Stuart with his moussed boy-band hair and his amusing life featuring comedy dogs and their comedy owners.

'Tea,' Matthew said. He tried to think of something to funny to add, but the eloquence he'd discovered on the back seat of the Renault 4 had deserted him.

'So,' said Stuart, happy to continue running point on the conversation. 'You two share car journeys, yeah?'

'Yup,' Caitlin said.

'That's very interesting,' Ashwin said, dunking a chip into a pool of ketchup.

'Very interesting' was the group's code for its exact opposite. Stuart giggled and kicked him under the table. He missed and caught Pete instead, who swore and kicked back. This meant war, and the table started bucking as the three of them hacked at each other's legs.

'Stop it you dickheads,' Matthew said, grabbing for his and Caitlin's cups in an attempt at damage limitation. He tried to sound annoyed, but in fact he was delighted. It was just the excuse he'd needed.

'Come on,' he said to a mystified Caitlin. 'Let's go outside.'

They left the café and walked down the crazy-paving pathway towards what everyone referred to as 'the lake' but which was in reality just a circular pond with a central fountain in which the local ducks liked to congregate.

'This was the scene of an awesome battle, you know,' said Matthew.

'When?'

'Last year. Fifth-form water fight. Seventeen of us got suspended. It was epic.'

'You got suspended from school?'

'Yeah, but it was ludicrous, and the teachers knew it. They thought it was a real fight, and by the time they worked out it was just a water fight they'd taken a stand and they couldn't back down. So they suspended us over half-term.'

'That sounds sort of pointless.'

'Exactly. They did it so they didn't have to really suspend us during actual school time, but also so they didn't have to back down and lose face. Except the school disco was on during that week, and we weren't allowed on the premises, so we couldn't go, which was a pain. So we got a sound system and set up a gig in Stuart's garden, which is just up off the Coventry road and has got this raised terrace like a stage. His parents were cool about it and we put the word out and everyone ditched the school event and came to ours instead. It was awesome.'

Matthew felt protective towards Caitlin, he realised. As the youngest of three he rarely got to feel protective about anyone or anything, unless you counted the guinea pigs that had lived in an old tea chest in the corner of the kitchen, a kind of rodent TV set that served primarily as entertainment for the family dogs. But it was a confusing feeling because he wanted her, too, wanted her naked against him, an impulse that seemed to contradict its more wholesome twin.

The paradox expressed itself right now in the desire Matthew had to brush the back of Caitlin's hand with his own and the fear that was preventing him from doing so. But Caitlin seemed to be waiting for him to do something, and the proximity of the tiny blonde hairs on her arm was causing patterns of what felt like static electricity to crackle between his elbow and his wrist.

A cloud slid across the sun and Caitlin shivered a little.

'Are you okay?'

'I'm kind of cold.'

'Why don't we walk down to the river? I'll show you the boats. And where the herons nest.'

'Okay.'

She followed him down to the water's edge, and although he still didn't touch her, while they wandered past the boathouse and along the river they walked really close, so close that Matthew fancied he could feel the warmth of her skin.

'Let's take a boat out,' she said as they looked across to the herons' island in the lee of the castle's high walls.

'That'd be cool. We could do it tomorrow, if you think you can get out again.'

'Not tomorrow. Now.'

'But it's nearly two. We've got to be back.'

'Listen to Mr Rebel Smoker. Don't be so dull. Who cares if we miss a couple of boring old lessons?'

Matthew hesitated. He could think of quite a few people who'd care very much if he skipped double French. He glanced at his watch, then back at the café. The lunch break was almost over, and Stuart had already started traipsing back across the park in the direction of the school. He looked Matthew's way, spotted him, and with a deep sweep of his arm gestured for him to come. But there in front of him was Caitlin, her face glowing with expectation, her eyes polished, a tiny skein of moisture dampening her upper lip.

'Okay, sod it. Let's do it,' he said, and taking her hand he walked with her back along the path towards the boathouse.

'I haven't got any money,' she said.

'Don't worry. It's only a few quid.'

It made him feel good, to be able to pay for her. He gave the money to the attendant who then led them along the boat-nuzzled jetty. A breeze plucked at the water as he helped them into one of the skiffs, gave them some oars, and cast them off.

Matthew took the oars and started to row. It was the first time he had been properly alone with Caitlin, and he was nervous: he caught a crab almost immediately, and then, because he was annoyed at himself for not projecting the image he wanted to project, he caught another.

'Do you want me to row?' Caitlin asked. 'I know how, you know.'

'I'm just finding my rhythm.'

'Have you actually done this before?'

'Yes! Tons of times. Isn't it obvious?'

Caitlin laughed, a sound that gave Matthew sweet release. 'Where are we going, anyway?'

'Let's go to the island. Then we can get out of the boat.' He had an image of helping her out onto the bank, her slipping in the mud and grabbing onto him for support, him bringing her face level with his. Then: kissing.

He'd watched too many films.

While he was fantasising Caitlin was craning her neck towards the castle ramparts, which reared up out of the water beyond the road bridge like the face of a giant dam. In their shadow was a tuft of land, thick with trees.

'Is that it?'

'Yeah.'

They drifted under the bridge and Matthew threw his head back to bounce an echo off its broad, shallow arch. Caitlin called out too, and their voices chased each other across the smooth surface of the concrete. Matthew closed his eyes for a few moments, the better to savour the effect.

When he opened them again he was looking not at the bridge, from beneath which the boat had now emerged, nor so much at the sky, although there was plenty of sky going on. What he was looking at was the ruddy complexion of a middle-aged woman, staring down at him over the edge of the bridge's stone parapet.

The complexion spoke. 'And what precisely do you think you're doing?' it said.

Matthew snapped upright and locked eyes with Caitlin, who was doing her best to suppress a giggle.

'Who is that?' he hissed.

'It's Ms Hinton, our deputy head,' Caitlin explained. 'I'm totally for it now. She's going to slaughter me.'

'Get over to the bank this minute!' said Ms Hinton, her voice sounding reedy after the rich echoes of their own.

Matthew picked up the oars and began to scull towards the riverbank, his mind darting like a rodent trying to flee a maze, while the teacher picked her way down the steep stone steps that zigzagged from the road to the water's edge.

'Your watch,' he said abruptly, as the teacher passed the half-way point on the stairway. Caitlin looked at him blankly. 'Quickly, turn it back half-an-hour or so. We'll tell her that it stopped, and that we didn't realise the time.'

'But what about your watch?' she said, as she fumbled with the winder.

'I'll ditch it,' Matthew said. 'We can't wind them both back.' And as the boat nosed into the bank he dropped the oars, slid the metal bracelet off his wrist, and let the handsome Sekonda, given to him by his parents only a few months previously, slip over the side and into the oily water.

Caitlin watched it go, open-mouthed.

'I can't believe you did that,' she said. 'This is never going to work.'

'Let's see.'

Ms Hinton huffed down the last flight of steps and strode across the path towards the boat.

'Names?'

They told her.

'And what precisely do you think you're doing out here at this time of the day?'

'But it's only half past one, Ms Hinton,' Caitlin said.

'Don't be ridiculous. You know perfectly well what time it is.'

'But my watch says half one, Ms Hinton.'

Ms Hinton looked at Matthew.

'And what about your watch?'

'I don't have a watch.'

Ms Hinton stared at him. Matthew stared back, trying not to blink, hoping she was going to ask him to turn out his pockets. If she didn't, he was going to look very foolish in a very short space of time.

'Turn out your pockets.'

He danced inside as he extracted the calculator, pens, diary, cassette tape and other bits of detritus that lurked about his person and offered them out to the teacher in his outstretched palms. See? No watch.

She didn't pat him down – there were some boundaries that teachers could no longer cross.

'The two of you shouldn't be out here on your own in any case,' she said.

'But we share school journeys Ms Hinton,' Matthew said. 'I had a message from my mum about a change in arrangements this afternoon, and she asked me to go and find Caitlin and tell her.'

'I fail to see how that necessitates a boat trip.'

Matthew contemplated saying something about only being able to talk to Caitlin when they were in motion, but checked himself. 'We just thought it would be a nice thing to do.'

'But you know perfectly well that these boats are out of bounds.'

'Not for sixth-form boys, they're not,' Matthew protested. 'We're allowed to go out in them, if we're sensible.'

'We were being very sensible,' Caitlin chimed. 'Matthew was taking me to see a herons' nest. It was very educational.'

Ms Hinton had made the mistake of soliciting answers from the two pupils, and now she was finding herself slowly but inexorably outflanked.

'That's as maybe. But it doesn't change the fact that you're both out of school during lesson time. Caitlin Nolan, you're to come with me. You' – she indicated Matthew – 'you're to go straight back to wherever you're supposed to be. And make sure that you do. I shall be calling St George's this afternoon to check up on you.'

'But what about the boat, Ms Hinton?'

'What about it?'

'I can't just leave it there. That wouldn't be socially responsible. I have to return it.'

Ms Hinton sighed. Having started this process thinking that absolute moral and judicial right were both firmly on her side, she was now going to have to tell this boy that the right thing to do was to get back into the boat.

'Well return it and then go straight back to school. Come on Caitlin.' And she turned and led the way back up the stone staircase before Matthew could tell her to do otherwise.

Caitlin owed him now, Matthew figured. On his side of the balance sheet: one boat rental, one watch, and a tricky situation coolly handled. He could sense the heft of these assets, and their weight gave him confidence. He felt more Caitlin's equal now, less of a supplicant kneeling at her feet. It was good, it was an advantage. He had to play it out.

That evening on the way home in the car he passed her a note that it had taken him what had been left of double French to write, even though it was in English and consisted of just a single sentence.

Meet me in Stratford next Saturday night?

Caitlin unfolded it and inclined her head to read it so that her hair fell forwards and hid her face.

'Okay,' she said.

Matthew now faced the crucial problem common to all teenagers living in the countryside: how to date without being able to drive. Before he even got around to asking anyone out, he had to make sure that someone in his family was available to be his taxi service for the evening in question. Real taxis were too expensive, as they charged a premium to venture out into the maze of lanes that began a few miles beyond Stratford's town limits. And buses were non-existent, with the nearest stop a good hour's walk away.

Even if he could get a promise from his parents ahead of time, or from Emily, or from Alex if his brother was around, it would invariably come with escape clauses and conditions attached. The driver could, and often would, withdraw the offer at any time, and Matthew would have no comeback. If he so much as looked disappointed they would point out that they were doing him a favour and whether they did it or not was up to them, which made his disappointment immeasurably worse, because they were, and it was.

And of course any girl that Matthew was trying to meet up with was likely to be in much the same situation. Factor these two sets of variables with the likelihood of getting an agreed date in the first place, and the possibility of having a successful encounter of any kind with a member of the opposite sex started to look vanishingly small. As for losing his virginity . . . Matthew tried not to even think about it, though in fact he thought of little else.

Having suffered so many let-downs in the past, for his date with Caitlin he'd broken with convention and asked her out before organising any kind of transport. Maybe it was a karmic thing, he'd told himself. By being too structured in the past he'd communicated his expectations of success to the universe, and the universe, being a shitty kind of a place, had stymied his plans and had a good joke at his expense. Perhaps if he pretended not to care the universe would waive its chance to trip him up, and the necessary arrangements would somehow fall into place with only gentle prodding.

Some hope. On Wednesday he'd asked Emily if she would drive him into town that night, but she had tickets to go and see *Good Morning Vietnam* in Leamington with a group of friends. If only he'd asked her earlier, she'd told him, devastatingly, she could have arranged to see the film a different night. He'd then asked his mother, but she was involved with one of her charity evenings and was going to be ferrying trays of vol-au-vents to some village hall the other side of Ullenhall, so no joy there. And with Alex away at university that left only his father. Did Matthew want his dad chauffeuring him out on a date? He did not. But it appeared he had no choice.

'What will you be wanting with Stratford?' Miles said, when he asked.

'Meeting up with friends.'

'Where would that be, then?'

'Not sure yet.'

'That'll make it hard to find them.'

Matthew sighed.

'Dad, will you just give me a lift?'

'How will you get back?'

'I was sort of hoping you'd pick me up as well.'

'Why not get a taxi?'

'Increase my allowance and I will.'

'Ah, so this is blackmail, is it? Give you more money, or be forced into servitude as your driver.'

'It's not blackmail, Dad. It's a lift.'

'What's in it for me?'

'The joy that comes from perpetrating a selfless act.' This was a favourite phrase of Miles's own, one he'd deployed against his children countless times.

Miles wasn't buying it any more than his kids ever had. 'What about a mowed lawn?'

'Oh great. I might have known.'

'You scratch my back . . .'

'All right, if that's what it takes. I'll do the mowing Sunday.'

'Saturday. Before you get your night out. I don't want you crying off with a hangover.'

'Oh fuuuu—' Matthew swallowed the expletive, knowing it was the kind of response that would kill the offer of the lift stone dead. 'I was going to watch the football.'

'Mow it in the morning. Then watch the football. On my television. And don't swear. Or no lift.'

Matthew had finished the patches of grass up in the walled garden and was manoeuvring the mower down the path towards the house's main lawn when he was distracted by the sight of Alex's burgundy Ford Fiesta, a reward from their parents for getting into Oxford, rolling into the driveway. If his brother had arranged to come home from university for the weekend, it was news to Matthew. How nice, and all that. How interesting, the consequent range of possibilities.

He engaged the clutch on the mower, slowed the two-stroke engine to an idle, slid off the seat and wandered down to greet his sibling.

'Hey,' he said, when he was well within earshot. He didn't want to seem too keen.

'Hey,' said Alex. He was unshaven and his hair, though not particularly long by the standards of the late 1980s, was longer than Matthew had ever seen it before.

'I didn't know you were coming home.'

'Last-minute thing. Had some weekend plans, they fell through, thought I'd take the chance to pop up and see Mum and Dad. And you too, of course, buddy boy.'

'How's whatshername? Vanessa?' Matthew asked, with the unconscious but unerring sense for a weak spot that only a brother possesses.

'Oh you know,' Alex said, going round to get his bag out of the boot of the car. 'Pumped and dumped.' He slammed the boot shut for emphasis.

'But she was so hot!' Matthew had met Vanessa only once, but she'd made a strong impression on him. A girl like that in his bed, he felt, and all his problems would be over.

'Lots of girls are hot. Doesn't mean they can't be a pain in the arse.'

Matthew could just not imagine this. Surely hotness excused everything else? 'I guess so,' he nodded, not wanting to seem naïve. 'Shame though.'

Alex shrugged. 'Plenty more where that came from.' This was over-egging it a bit – he wouldn't be able to get away with that in college. Matthew, though, snickered slightly. But then he also had an agenda of his own.

'Talking of which,' he ventured, 'have you got any plans for tonight? Because, well, I've kind of got this girl I need to give a lift into Stratford, and only Dad's free to do it, and he's being his usual pain-in-the-arse self about it all . . .'

'And you want me to give you a lift into town?'

'Pretty please.'

'I'm not even through the door and already I'm being press-ganged into service. I must be home.'

'Sorry,' Matthew said.

'Don't be so negative. I might've said I don't want to, but I haven't said I won't, have I? Look, don't worry about it, okay? You can tell Dad I'll run you into town. You and whatshername.'

His little brother had a girlfriend. This he had to see.

Although Alex had come home from Oxford that weekend because of Vanessa, the 'pumped and dumped' description of the end of their relationship that he'd given Matthew was not quite accurate. A pouting History of Art student with long slender legs and a generous trust fund, Vanessa had the effortless sense of entitlement that came from growing up in one of the plusher parts of Kensington. It was that, as much as what lay at the top of those legs, that Alex longed to possess, and ten months into their relationship Vanessa had started to feel it. She hadn't rationalised the notion – it would have offended her deeply if anyone had suggested that she might in any way be a snob; some of her best friends were, after all, working-class. But her instincts eventually told her that Alex was not of her pack and would, whatever else happened between them, always rank low within it. So she had conjured several excuses – his timekeeping, his annoying friends, her stage of life, her need for space – all of which amounted to telling him that it was time to move on.

The loss of face, even more than the loss of his lover, was more than Alex could bear. Rather than mope around college setting himself up as a target for pity or ridicule, he'd decided that the better strategy was to disappear for a couple of days and give himself time to lick his wounds and construct some armour. He hadn't counted on stumbling over the perfect antidote to his heartbreak, in the form of Caitlin. As soon as she'd climbed into the back seat and he'd glimpsed her profile in the rear-view mirror, his mouth had gone dry and his heart had quickened its pulse.

Matthew introduced him. 'This is my brother, Alex.'

'Hi Alex.'

He swivelled around to say hello. She flicked away the strands of hair that had fallen across her face and met his gaze. She was astonishing, even more so because she probably didn't know it yet.

'Nice of you to give us a lift,' she said.

'No problem.' Alex turned back and started rifling through the mess of mix tapes scattered in the front passenger footwell. 'Shall we have some tunes?'

He found the tape he wanted, clacked it into the player, and soon they were rolling along to the sounds of S'Express and Bomb Da Bass.

'Mind if I smoke?' Caitlin called above the music.

'Sure,' said Alex, who hated people smoking in his car and until that moment had always forbidden it.

Caitlin took out a pack of ten Marlboro Lights and offered one to Matthew, who declined. Then she leant forward between the front seats. 'Would you like one?' she said to Alex.

'Please.'

'I'll light it for you.' She indicated the cigarette lighter. 'Can I use this?'

'That's what it's for,' Alex said.

She pressed the light and remained crouched forward while it heated up.

'You've got a lot of tapes.'

Her scent, whatever it was, was almost effervescent, and it reacted with Alex's sinuses in a way that seemed to connect them directly to his groin. He angled his head, ostensibly to look at the tapes but in fact to bring Caitlin's chest within the ambit of his vision. She wore no bra, and her position allowed her breasts to hang down into the hammock created by her lime-green V-neck. Through the frame of the delicate gold chain of her necklace, Alex could clearly see how full and round they were, how snugly they'd fit into the palms of his hands.

'Yeah. They're kind of a thing, right now, at college.'

The lighter clacked out and Caitlin lit one of the cigarettes, leaned back, lit the other one off it, and passed it to Alex while he drove. Alex put the cigarette to his lips, hunting its tip for tantalising deposits of the girl's saliva.

He dropped the two of them off in Stratford as requested and then returned to Snitterfield just in time to join his parents for dinner. While his mother dished up lamb casserole his father asked him how things were going at university. Not wanting to talk about Vanessa, he mentioned instead that a lot of his friends were thinking of going into the City. The 'Big Bang' of financial deregulation that had taken place a couple of years before had opened things up. Firms were hiring, there was plenty of buzz.

'It's hardly a sensible way to earn a living.' Miles said. 'All these computers they're using have made the markets terrifically volatile.'

Computerisation was generally a recipe for disaster in Miles's view, a way to automate idiocy and let it flourish unbridled. He still had raw memories of deregulation's immediate aftermath: the Black Monday stock market crash in 1987 had wiped more than a third off the value of his pension and investments overnight. For Alex, however, Black Monday remained a largely abstract event, something that had been discussed much in the news and in his A-Level Economics class, but which had had no apparent impact on his material existence.

'There was a problem with computer trading,' he told his father confidently, 'around portfolio insurance, if I'm correct. But that was two years ago, and the technologies have matured massively since then. The trading systems are much smarter now and have all sorts of fail-safes built in. And without the City, how would the economy function? Credit is the blood of business, right? Seems like a pretty good way to make a living to me.'

Much of this, including its pompous tone, came from Freddie Winston, the college friend with whom Alex spent most of his time. But pomposity was something that didn't go down well in the Wold household. Especially frowned upon was a mixture of pomposity and petulance, and Alex's sign-off phrase had strayed into that territory.

'As we haven't seen you all term, Alex,' Margaret said, deciding that this conversation had gone far enough, 'I think we'll have a ban on politics at the dinner table. Can we please change the subject?' Which they did: to the current season of plays at the Royal Shakespeare Company – much safer territory.

After dinner Alex told his parents he had an essay to finish and went upstairs, lay on his bed, and thought about Vanessa. But his contemplations soon became infected by angst, and Alex didn't like angst. It was, he felt, not just unpleasant, but unnecessary. Shit happened. Learn lessons. Move on.

In order to do just that he got up and did a few sets of sit-ups in front of the full-length mirror on his wardrobe. It worked, sort of, but to complete the process he needed some chemical assistance. Cue the small pick-me-up he'd brought back with him from Oxford: half a gram of heavily cut cocaine wrapped inside a sock and buried deep at the bottom of his holdall. He dug it out and leaving his door open so that he could be absolutely sure of hearing anyone coming up the stairs, he laid out a small line on his desk.

The drug made him feel better – for a while. But then the glow it induced deteriorated into nerves and pent-up frustration, and with no TV to watch without going down and sitting in the living room with his parents he did some work on his essay in order to calm himself down. Strangely it proved the ideal activity, and he soon became absorbed in the task. Thanks to the stimulant the ideas flew at him; writing furiously he scribbled them down, forgetting the time in the process. It wasn't until he ran into trouble trying to tuck in a recalcitrant paragraph that he looked up from his pad and saw that there were only fifteen minutes before he was due to meet Matthew and Caitlin in Stratford, which was at least twenty minutes away in the car.

He finished his sentence, put on his jacket, grabbed the car keys, and – almost as an afterthought – stuffed the cocaine deep into one of his pockets. Just in case.

As he descended the stairs his father padded through the hallway dressed in his pyjamas, carrying two empty cocoa mugs back to the kitchen.

He glanced up. 'Ah, just the man.'

'Hey Dad. Just on my way out to collect the two lovebirds.'

'You couldn't do me an enormous favour?'

'I'm sort of running late.'

'It won't take a minute. I meant to pick up some post that was delivered to the Bearley cottage this week, but I haven't had a minute to get over there and it needs to be dealt with. You couldn't pop in on your way back from dropping Caitlin, could you, and fetch it? I believe it's on your way.'

Alex nodded. It was a peace offering. He had to accept.

'Sure. No problem.'

'Thank you Alex,' said Miles, using his son's name to acknowledge receipt of the olive branch. 'I'll get you the keys.'

Matthew had started feeling queasy during the journey into town. The smoke had set him off – three burning cigarettes, even with the windows half open, had created a toxic atmosphere inside the car. His brother's driving style didn't help. He'd forgotten about Alex's propensity to hurl any vehicle he was in charge of round every corner like he was competing at Le Mans. And he was sitting in the back, which made matters even worse. He'd wanted to be next to Caitlin, to recreate the situation of their daily school run, but now the need to concentrate on retaining the contents of his stomach deprived him of the energy for conversation.

He'd hoped things would improve once he got out of the car, but they didn't. Alex dropped them outside the McDonald's on Bridge Street and Matthew had two minutes in the fresh air to try and clear his head and settle his digestion before they were inside the restaurant and enveloped in another fug of smoke, this one laced with the miasma of greasy steam emitted by the food-processing machines behind the service counter.

Matthew hadn't really wanted to go to McDonald's. His perfect evening would have consisted of a quiet dinner somewhere where the food was guaranteed organic, then a drink or two in a pub that was lively but not too lively and in which they were unlikely to meet anyone that they knew, followed by a walk down the riverbank on the far side of the theatre, a shared spliff or two on a bench while watching the swans, all rounded off with some amorous petting and, perhaps, the loss of their mutual virginity on a bed of reeds under the stars.

But there was a social logic to teenage dates, he well knew, and that kind of slightly manipulative romanticism disrupted it. To impress girls, despite what all the love songs said, you needed not sentimentality and tenderness but access to fun, and preferably access to money if the fun in question required it. Matthew had already scored on one of these fronts by getting them a lift into town for the evening. He had another one snug in his pocket: money, enough of it to buy food and drinks for them both. Now he needed to be fun all evening, more so than anyone else they encountered. Which might have been fine: he'd proved himself capable of it during his and Caitlin's little boating adventure. But now he was feeling sick and he just wasn't sure he was up to it.

To compound the problem he soon discovered that he had stiff competition. The group they joined, drinking shakes and dipping fries in the smoking area, included several boys from Stratford whom Caitlin had known from her previous school. The picture he'd sketched of a lonely beauty trapped in glorious isolation in the wilds of the countryside, just waiting for her handsome prince to come and free her, suddenly seemed rather wide of the mark. By the way that she was greeted when she arrived, Matthew could see that she was far more in tune with Stratford's teen social scene than he was.

And so it proved. As they drifted from McDonald's to the Cask and Bottle at the bottom of Union Street, then across to the Vintner on the other side of the town centre – fashionable wine bars, rather than the pubs Matthew preferred – it appeared that everyone knew Caitlin and that Caitlin knew everyone. The shy schoolgirl of their shared school journeys was gone and in her place was a capable socialite, adept at surfing the attention of all those around her.

If she hadn't kept returning to him and folding him back into the flow of things, Matthew would have fallen behind after the first half-hour. But for some reason she did keep coming back, despite his lack of conversation and the pained expression on his face. In between his bouts of nausea and half-hearted attempts to converse with the other boys he spent a good deal of time trying to analyse why. It wasn't because she needed him to buy drinks – everyone offered her drinks, and the ones she didn't decline outright she barely touched. It could be because of her lift home, but that didn't require her to flirt with him, or touch him on the arm and shoulder, or introduce him to her friends in such glowing terms. Could it be, then, because she actually liked him? Could it be that she found him attractive for his own sake?

Before he could determine the answer to this most indeterminate of questions, the sickness that had been brewing in his belly welled up inside him and he was forced to repair to the toilets. When he emerged the group was getting ready to move on. Caitlin was nowhere to be seen; he eventually found her outside in the street talking animatedly with David Tate, who was a year Matthew's junior but was taller and more athletic.

'Oh my God, Matthew, you look terrible. Are you okay?' Caitlin exclaimed, when she eventually noticed him.

He played the sympathy card. 'I don't feel too good, actually.'

A look of distaste flashed across Tate's handsome face. 'Overdid it on the voddies?'

'I've hardly drunk anything. I think it must've been something I ate.'

'Oh you poor thing. We're going to the Slug. Are you okay to come?'

The Slug and Lettuce was back across town, opposite the Cask, where they'd been before the Vintner. Matthew could not see the point in traipsing all the way back over there when there were so many nearer bars to go to, but he wasn't in a position to argue, so he tagged along behind the group as it meandered through Stratford, stopping for chats with other teenagers it encountered on the way. By the time they reached the Slug he was ready to visit the toilet again. After that he felt too debilitated to do anything other than sit in a booth in a corner of the bar and wait for the evening to finish.

'What's wrong with him?' Alex asked, as Matthew collapsed on the back seat of the Fiesta.

'Sick,' Matthew mumbled.

'How much did you drink?'

'I think it was a dodgy McDonald's.'

Alex cackled. 'Oh yeah? I've heard that one before. You must have been a bundle of laughs. You're not going to throw up in my car, are you?'

Matthew shook his head, wound down the window, and leant his chin on the sill. 'Just get me home.'

Alex raised his eyebrows. 'You'd better sit in the front,' he said to Caitlin. 'You don't want him to hurl on you.'

He leant down to scoop the mess of tapes to the side of the footwell and was rewarded with a spectacular view of Caitlin's lovely legs as she climbed into her seat.

'So did you have a good evening, anyway?' he asked, pushing himself back upright.

'It was nice. We had a good tour around. Saw some friends. You know.'

Alex drove and they sat in silence until, a couple of miles outside the town limits, an unmistakable sound came from the back of the car.

'Hey – you haven't barfed have you?'

'Yeah.'

'Not in the car?'

'Out the window.'

'Bucket and brush in the morning for you, my friend.' Alex glanced over at Caitlin. 'Apologies for my brother.'

'Oh, it's not his fault. Poor Matthew.'

'I was planning to take you home first, but if it's okay I think we'd better take a detour and drop him off before he does any more pebbledash work.'

'That's fine,' said Caitlin, who wasn't tired.

Sensing an opportunity, Alex hung a sharp left past The Dun Cow pub and up the steeply winding entrance to King's Lane, a route that one mile and one turning later brought them to the gates of his and Matthew's home. He eased the car into the driveway and waited while his brother climbed out of the Fiesta and stumbled up to the front door.

'Goodnight Matty,' Caitlin called.

''Night. Sorry about everything,' Matthew mumbled back.

'That's okay. I had a good time. See you Monday.'

'Yeah. See you.'

His brother gone, Alex resisted the temptation to carve a doughnut into the gravel, executing instead a swift but sensible three-point turn before rolling off into the night, his prize at his side.

The most direct route from his to Caitlin's house was not back along King's Lane but through Snitterfield itself and then through Bearley, where the property his father wanted him to look in on was situated. It was an investment play Miles had bought a few years earlier, spent 'a few quid' doing up, and was now in theory letting out to cover the payments on the interest-only buy-to-let mortgage that he'd taken out to cover the cost of purchase. The rental agency that Miles's agency relied upon to find tenants was not, however, the world's most proactive operation, and the cottage currently stood empty. All of which, apart from the details of the mortgage, Alex knew.

'I'd have thought you and Matt would have been wanting to stay out later,' he said, as they drove through the woods that occupied much of the land between the two villages. 'I mean, if he hadn't been ill.'

Caitlin shrugged. 'Maybe. But where do you go?'

'I thought the Cask was open till one?'

'But it gets so rammed. And there's no dancing. If you want to dance, you've got to go out to the Wildmoor or the Tollhouse, then you need someone with a car.'

'I've got a car. And I like to go dancing.'

Caitlin looked at him.

'Seriously?'

'Sure. Why not? I've got nothing better to do. Shall we go to the Tollhouse? I haven't been there in years.'

She sat back and considered this for a minute.

'Hmm. Well, the Tollhouse is actually kind of lame. Maybe we should go to the Wildmoor. Though that's kind of lame as well.'

'It's Stratford. Everything's lame. While we think about it do you mind if I run a quick errand for my dad? It'll only take a minute.'

They were in Bearley now and he steered into a small terrace of nineteenth-century agricultural workers' houses, the last of which belonged to his father. Alex pulled the Fiesta into its diminutive driveway.

'Come on.' Taking the keys he got out of the car, walked up the two-metre path and unlocked the front door.

Caitlin followed. The place was furnished with careworn but good-quality items bought at auction, with one or two of the Wolds' cast-offs and a few flat-packed essentials mixed in. Not being occupied, it was empty of personal effects, and this gave it a strangely poised atmosphere, as if it were a film set on which a drama was about to be played out. Alex scooped up the pile of post from the hallway and took it through to the kitchen at the back, where he sat down at the small round table and began filleting out the junk mail and circulars.

'Won't be a moment. Make yourself at home. Hey – you know what?' He jumped up from his chair and went over to the fridge.

'Dad usually keeps some booze here somewhere, in case he needs to loosen up prospective tenants. Let's see . . . Aha! We're in luck.' He produced a bottle of white wine and lofted it triumphantly. 'Fancy a glass?'

'Okay.'

'Funny old place, isn't it?' Alex said, as he ferreted around for a corkscrew and glasses. 'Quite cosy, really. Look, there's a tape machine here. Shall we have some tunes?'

Caitlin sipped nervously at her wine while Alex went to the car and fetched a cassette. The moment he slotted it into the machine and pressed play, the cottage was transformed. Before, they'd been interlopers; now, the music made it theirs.

'Is it all right if I smoke?'

'Be my guest.'

She took her cigarettes from her bag and lit one while he fiddled with something on the sideboard. As she watched he bent forward and inhaled sharply before turning and offering her a rolled-up five-pound note.

'I thought we could use a boost, if we're going dancing,' he said, by way of explanation.

It took a moment for it to dawn on Caitlin what exactly he was suggesting. 'Oh, right,' she said, working it out. 'I've not done this before.'

'First time for everything. It's nice. Go on.'

He moved back to give her access to the line of white powder laid out on the sideboard; she balanced her cigarette on the edge of the worktop, tucked her hair behind her ears, and bent as he had done.

A hand in the small of her back, now, a hand on her hand.

'Hold one nostril closed. Inhale with the other.'

She sniffed, gently. Nothing happened. She tried again, harder this time. Half of the powder vanished. She hardly felt it go in. In a spot between and behind her eyes that she had not been conscious of before there was a tingle, a tickle, a slight burn.

'How was that?'

'Good,' she said. 'I think.' She took another sniff and finished the rest of the line, then stood up, trying to gauge if she felt any different. She didn't, particularly. She was a little light-headed, but that could have been the bending over. Her cigarette was smouldering away beside her; she picked it up, puffed on it, and then had a mouthful of wine.

'Okay?'

'Yes.'

She breathed, relaxed. Breathing was easy. She reached up and stretched.

'Um. Feels good.'

She giggled, then swayed, then stumbled.

Alex grabbed for her, took her by the arms.

'Whoa, you're rushing. It'll pass.'

Caitlin nodded.

'Can I have some water?'

'Sure. You okay to stand?'

'I think so.'

Slowly removing his hands, Alex filled a fresh glass from the tap. She took it in two hands, drank it in one draught, and gave it back to him. Then she rubbed her eyes. She looked a little better, he thought.

'Have you got any more?'

'Water?'

'No, that.' She pointed to the sideboard.

Alex raised his eyebrows. 'Do you think that's a good idea?'

'Yeah.'

'Okay . . . if you're really sure.'

She nodded, so he pulled out the tiny envelope of powder and cut another line, which she took. Alex looked on, wondering if she was going to teeter over again. But instead she turned to him, her eyes black and bright.

'Let's dance!'

She reached for the tape machine, turned the volume up, then started jiving round the kitchen. Alex joined her, slightly unnerved by her enthusiasm and wondering if he had perhaps made a mistake. The idea had been to seduce her, but now it was looking like she might in fact be more impressionable than he'd realised. He didn't want to do anything that they'd regret – and then of course there were Matthew's feelings to consider. What had felt like a bit of a lark half-an-hour before now looked like it might have some serious consequences.

Still, she was gorgeous. And she wasn't Vanessa. And she was turning her face up to his, her eyes closed, as if waiting for him to bend down and kiss her. Just a kiss . . . that wouldn't be so bad would it? What harm a kiss?

He leant into her, slipped his arm around her back, and guided her to him. She didn't resist and so, when their bodies were touching, he brought his lips down to touch hers, gently once, gently twice, then the third time firmly. Her mouth opened, their tongues connected, her hand went up to his shoulders, his hair . . . then she was grabbing, pulling him back, twisting away.

'What are you doing? What are you doing!' She was shouting, her fists clenched, the veins on her forehead livid with blood.

'I just thought . . .'

'No! No! No!' Vicious, cornered, she growled the words at

him then collapsed where she stood and curled up in a ball on the floor.

Alex spun over to the tape deck, switched off the music, and then crouched a little way from her, afraid to go too close.

'It was just a misunderstanding, okay?' he said, extending his hand. Nothing's going to happen. It's just the coke, it can be quite intense.'

She didn't respond, but he waited, and after a minute or so she gave an almost imperceptible nod. 'Okay, look, I can take you home, here . . .' He got up, fetched her cigarettes from the table and lit one for her. She slowly uncurled and pushed herself up onto her knees before taking it.

'I'm really sorry,' she said.

'Hey – a minute ago I was apologising. It's no one's fault. We just got carried away.'

'You won't say anything to Matthew, will you?'

'Me? God no, why would I do that?'

'I need him.'

Alex nodded, breathed out, and lit a cigarette for himself.

'He's a lucky guy,' he said.

The following Monday it was Caitlin's turn to pass a note. She crushed it into Matthew's hand as Emily's car drew up at the front gates of St George's School for Boys.

Call me at 9

He did call at 9. Caitlin was waiting.

'Hi.'

'Hi.'

'What's up?'

'Oh. You know. Stuff. I'm so embarrassed about what happened on Saturday.'

The words came out of their own accord. 'Don't worry about it Matty. It's fine, honestly. Look – do you want to get together next weekend?'

'Really? You want to go to Stratford again?'

'Let's not do that. Why don't you just come over here?'

'To yours?'

'You've got a bike, haven't you? Come on that.'

Matthew quickly did the calculations. It was about seven miles to the Nolans' place. It would take a while, but he could do it. They'd probably hang out by the pool. Just the two of them, with any luck.

'Is it okay with your folks?'

'I thought we could go for a walk.'

Right. So they were going for a walk. This was the countryside. Nobody under the age of forty went for a walk. But that's what they were going to do.

'Great. I'll bring a picnic.' Matthew cursed himself. What did he say that for? Why on earth was he bringing a picnic? They were going for a walk. Who needed a picnic? 'What time should I get there?'

'Lunchtime, I guess,' said Caitlin, who'd been thrown by the picnic idea. It reminded her of one of her mother's refrains: that it was typical for a man to think of his stomach in times of crisis. Of course Matthew didn't know the nature of the crisis, didn't know the trouble she was in. But she'd asked him to go for a walk. It was a weird request. He must have known that something was up. Boys were so dim.

Saturday came without further communication between them on the subject, despite several shared car journeys. Matthew woke at five and, like a child on Christmas morning, could not get back to sleep. For a while he lay beneath the covers contemplating the bedroom floor, head on the edge of his mattress, then got up and took advantage of the slumbering household to assemble some sandwiches and pack them, along with some pieces of fruit and a bottle of wine filched from the recesses of Miles's small cellar, into an old canvas backpack that he found in the brown cupboard room. He stashed everything in the garage next to his bike and carried on as normal until eleven-thirty ticked round. Then, tyres pumped, chores done and a History assignment out of the way, he lied to his parents about where he was going and set off.

It was a blustery autumn day. The brass barometer in the Wolds' hallway was pointing to 'changeable' and thick balls of cumulus tumbled through the sky, but it was warm nonetheless. Matthew cycled in and out of shifting patches of sunlight and shade, his mood switching gears accordingly. Shelfield was further away than he'd thought, and the trip was requiring much more effort than he'd anticipated. He'd never actually cycled anything like this far before, and it was already obvious that he didn't have the stamina for it. He'd barely got to Bearley before his calves were complaining and the straps from the backpack had started chafing his skin. And he still had another four miles to go.

Caitlin was watching for him from her bedroom, one eye on the lane, one eye on that week's edition of *Going Live!* on the portable TV Tony had given her for her birthday. When she saw Matthew toiling up the road like some wind-up metal toy she hurried downstairs and across the driveway to greet him.

'I thought maybe you weren't coming!'

'It took a bit longer than I expected,' he panted, almost falling off the bike in his haste to put down the backpack. 'I brought the picnic.'

Caitlin looked at her empty hands. 'I haven't . . . I could go and get some stuff from the fridge?'

'Don't worry. I've got plenty to eat. And wine. Let's just go.'

Matthew tucked the bike out of sight of the road then followed Caitlin down the lane to a T-junction marked by an old iron sign-post with a circle on the top. Behind it grew a dense clump of field maple, hawthorn and laurel, almost an extension of the Nolans' sizeable hedge, and into this the girl abruptly vanished.

Matthew did a double take, but when he investigated further he discovered that there was an entrance here, simultaneously obscured and created by two sets of interlocking branches. He slipped through and found himself in a natural archway formed by the trees, which framed a narrow footpath leading away between tall banks of treacherous-looking brambles. It was down this that Caitlin was now striding.

Matthew jogged after her, grateful to operate different sets of muscles from those the bike had strained. On they went, past the house, past the garden, and past the stable block – its shingles still untreated – that Tony had just had built for Sheila in the Nolans' small paddock so that she could realise her girlhood dream of keeping horses.

There the footpath ended, and by means of an oak stile bar-nacled with lichen and compromised by rot they passed into the field beyond, where the plough-churned clay lay like strips of gigantic metal swarf. Forced to pick her way between the docks and tussocks that formed the field's perimeter, Caitlin's pace slowed and Matthew finally managed to catch her up.

'If we go round here there's another stile and from there we can get on the back of Round Hill,' she said, indicating the dome-like mass that rose ahead of them. Matthew knew the hill well – it was the highest point for miles around. He had climbed it many times, usually in order to examine the ancient stone circle on the summit or to sledge down it in the snow.

They reached the stile in question and clambered over. The closely cropped grass on the other side made for easy going, and they strolled up the lower slope and around a sheep-notched contour until they were out of sight of the lane and the little row of cottages and houses that comprised the hamlet of Shelfield.

The sun was out more fully now, the day warming still further as the drifts of cumulus melted back from Warwickshire. The curve of the hill above him appeared to Matthew somehow cranial, as if it housed a giant dormant brain, the elm at the summit a neuron that had somehow escaped the confines of its skull and started to project itself towards the sky like some kind of biological antenna.

'This way!'

Caitlin headed down away from him towards a tyre-gouged track that led out of the field and into the wood beyond. There was a gate here, on the other side of which was a wild area of farming set-aside – their destination.

They waded through the swaths of fescue and meadow grass until they reached a wind-flattened patch, and here Matthew unpacked his picnic, surreptitiously cramming a couple of cherry tomatoes into his mouth to alleviate his hunger while he opened the bottle of wine. He glugged some into two plastic cups and passed one to Caitlin, along with a sandwich.

'This is so organised,' she said, tucking her legs beneath her and accepting the food with a smile. 'You're making me feel guilty.'

'Your turn next time,' Matthew said. He was hoping that at

some point Caitlin was going to offer other gifts, and far more precious ones.

They ate and drank in silence for a while, then Matthew lay down on the grass and squinted up at the Caitlin-shaped cut-out positioned between his eyes and the sun.

'I'm sleepy now,' he said.

Caitlin lay down on her elbow, her head towards his feet. She pulled at a clump of heath grass, running its stems between her fingers before beginning to fashion them into a plait. Matthew steeled himself. If he didn't kiss her now the moment would pass, and he might never get another chance. She wanted him to do it, surely? Why else would she have brought him here? It would be easy. He would sit up and put his hand on her hip. She would turn and her lips would part and he would lean in and embrace her and they'd melt together into the grass. And there, among the flax and the forget-me-not, the primrose and the burdock, they'd be together, properly, and his life would finally start.

It all seemed easy, suddenly. He sat up; he put his hand on her hip. She turned; her lips parted. He swivelled his legs and leant in as he'd planned . . . but then her hand came up to check him.

Matthew pulled back like he'd been stung.

'It's okay if you don't want me to kiss you,' he insisted. 'I didn't mean . . .'

'It's not that.' Caitlin pushed the heels of her hands hard against her eyes. 'It's not you, you're so sweet. It's me.' She paused, searching for the words. 'I've been so stupid, Matty.'

'What is it? What's the matter?'

Grabbing handfuls of grass she twisted them round as if to get a better grip upon the planet, then looked him directly in the eye. 'I'm pregnant.'

A trapdoor opened in the world and Matthew tumbled through it. He felt like he'd slipped into the fabric of a fairy tale, one in which a captured genie had tricked his way out of granting him his dearest wish.

'Pregnant?' The word squeaked out, compressed by the weight of its implications. 'But what are you doing to do?'

'I don't know! That's just it! I don't know what to do. I just needed to tell someone.'

Matthew's head spun. He wasn't sure what this meant, but at least she trusted him. That was something to hang on to.

'Okay, well, you can tell me,' he said quickly, trying to order his thoughts. 'Have you been to see a doctor?'

'No, of course not.'

'Well, wouldn't that be the first thing? I mean, if you need to, you know . . .'

Caitlin squeezed her eyes shut and shook her head. 'Don't say it! I don't know if I want that.'

'You want to have the baby?'

'Yes. No. I don't know. Oh God, I just don't know!'

'You can't have a baby, Caitlin!'

'Why not? Women do, you know. And my family's bloody Catholic.'

'But you're still at school! What about your A-Levels? And university? You wouldn't be able to do any of that.'

'Yes I would, or I could do it later. I mean, this is a person we're talking about.'

'It's not a person, not yet. Right now it's just some cells, multiplying fast, and making you really unhappy. It's not like you meant this to happen, right?'

Caitlin drew her knees up to her chest and wrapped her arms around them. 'No.'

Matthew felt ready to burst. Every urge in all the songs he'd listened to throughout his teenage years seemed to be prompting him all at once. Only one fixed point was discernible in the midst of the chaos: Caitlin needed his assistance. That is what she would value, and so that is what he would give her. It didn't matter who she'd slept with, whose child it was: it was pretty clear that she didn't trust the father as much as she trusted Matthew. And if she trusted Matthew more, then he could be more. He could be the better man. And he would be better; he would be. He would start by giving Caitlin that. And that way he would win her.

'It's going to be okay. We'll get through this. You can trust me. You won't regret it, I promise.'

He wouldn't ask her. He wouldn't tell her that he wouldn't ask her. But just as it didn't seem right to ask what she didn't want to tell, it didn't seem right not to tell what she didn't want to ask. So he mustered again all the energy he'd gathered when he'd first placed his hand upon her hip.

'You know I love you, don't you?' The words came out coarse and cracked. And yet they weren't quite the right ones, they might be misconstrued. 'I mean, you know I'm in love with you, right?'

Oh God, that was awful. He'd said what he meant, but it had sounded wrong. And yet it didn't seem to matter, because this time when he leant in to kiss her, she didn't push him away.

It seemed to Matthew another of the many personal insults issued to him by the universe that this kiss should have led him to the humdrum municipal space of the Arden Medical Centre, among whose pointedly upbeat receptionists and flame-retardant chairs he was now waiting while Caitlin spoke to a doctor.

On the wall black-and-white pictures of a herd of African elephants roaming through some picturesque patch of savannah alternated with posters advertising the dangers of herpes and chlamydia. On the low institutional tables back issues of women's magazines were muddled in with half-finished word-search puzzle books and public information leaflets. In the corner a water cooler stood beside a small drinks machine that vended desultory twenty-pence measures of watery coffee. A stained play mat lay strewn with a collection of broken, snot-smeared toys.

It was Caitlin's first visit to the Centre – they'd come here because consulting her family GP in Alcester was out of the question – but Matthew had been here many times over the years. Measles, minor burns, bronchitis, holiday jabs: since Stratford hospital had closed it had been the first port of call for non-emergency family ailments. To an external observer his visit with Caitlin would have been just another event in a commonplace series. But inside he was in turmoil, his mind jabbering with possible outcomes and permutations, with the prospect of what might happen if their parents found out. Even the celebrity weddings in *Hello!* and a 'twenty ways to get the best in the bedroom' feature in last month's *Marie Claire* couldn't distract from the churn of his thoughts.

Worst of all was the question of whether his presence was actually helping Caitlin at all. He told himself it was, but what were his motives, really? Was he truly here for her, or had he come to ensure the destruction of another man's unborn child because it lay in his way? Which was it? Both? Neither? He didn't know for sure but he suspected the latter, and the suspicion stretched Caitlin's ten minutes with the doctor into many hours' worth of torment.

And then she emerged and stood waiting for him by the exit looking pale and matter-of-fact.

'How'd it go?' he asked, as they walked out into the sunshine.

She shook her head. 'I need a cup of tea.'

They advanced down the street in silence until they reached a café where she sat at a vacant table while he went up to the counter to order. When he returned she was staring out of the window, an unlit cigarette and a balled-up tissue in her hand.

He sat down and watched her, sipping his drink while he fought back an impulse to tell her that she really should not be smoking.

'So what did the doctor say?' he asked eventually, striving for a neutral tone.

Caitlin lit her cigarette and took a lengthy drag. 'There's two ways to do it. There's medical, which is you take some pills which force a miscarriage, and it's messy and it hurts, and it takes a while. And there's surgical, where you go in, they put you to sleep, they do the procedure, and you wake up and go home.'

'Okay,' Matthew said, venturing a nod of encouragement.

'What do you mean, "Okay"?'

'I just mean, okay, so if those are the options, which one are you more comfortable with?'

'I'm not "comfortable" with either of them, am I?'

She rested the cigarette in the ashtray, unravelled the tissue, and blew her nose. She hadn't yet touched her tea.

'Sorry.'

'Well it was a fucking stupid thing to say.'

He stared at the bubbles floating on the surface of his drink, waiting for the squall to subside. Maybe she wasn't going to go through with it. Would that be so bad? At least they'd be together. And they could have other children too. It would be difficult, but they would find a way. There had to be a way. Other people did it, didn't they? Why shouldn't they make it work?

'Surgical,' said Caitlin. 'It has to be surgical. There's no way I'm doing medical. It takes too long. I might end up having to do it at home. With the surgical I can go in, a few hours later I can walk out, and apart from a few stomach cramps the whole thing's done with. We can even go in on a Saturday. They're going to refer me to Warwick Hospital.'

'That's great,' Matthew said, despite being nowhere near sure that it was. He'd just traversed the distance from abortionist to family man and wasn't at all certain he was ready to make the journey back again.

'I'm here for you,' he said, taking her hand. 'We'll get through it.'

Was she even listening? Her eyes seemed focused entirely inwards. Another thought occurred to him: that baby or no baby, she would not thank him for this, that on the contrary she would externalise her own guilt and project it onto him like a permanent mask of reproach, so that whenever she looked at him she could blame him for it. But if he didn't help her, who would? Who would have got her the appointment at the medical centre? Who would have got Emily to drive them into Stratford on the pretext that they wanted to go to the cinema? And who would find a way to get them to the hospital for this procedure that had to be kept an utter secret, never mentioned again, never let slip, never anything other than dead and buried, erased, and forgotten. Who, if not him?

In the event Caitlin was offered something better than a Saturday: Warwick Hospital could see her for an outpatient termination on the Thursday of the half-term holiday. By spectacular coincidence Matthew's parents had been planning a few days away that week, leaving him and Emily home alone. The timing could not have been better. To get Caitlin to the hospital all he had to do was borrow his mother's car. He didn't have a licence or insurance, but he'd been having lessons and he knew how to drive. The issue would be Emily, who would certainly stand in his way if she found out what he was up to. But a few steered conversations allayed that concern. On the date in question she was going to meet some friends at a point-to-point over near Ashorne, and would be out all day.

During the week that followed Matthew revised his plan repeatedly, trying to ensure he'd got every angle covered. In the end he was satisfied there was not that much to it: as long as the various other Wolds stuck to their own plans, as long as Caitlin met him in the lane as she'd said she would, as long as he drove the car without crashing it or getting stopped by the police, as long as the procedure went okay – as long as a million factors beyond his control unfolded more or less as they should – then by the following Friday this would all be behind them and the two of them would be free to move on.

Half-term came and Matthew's parents left on their trip as scheduled, once his mother was done with fretting over whether there was enough food in the house, and whether he had the number of the vet in case one of the dogs should swallow a stone?

'I don't know what you're getting so worked up about, Mum,' Matthew said. 'Em can drive to the shops if we need anything.'

'Yes, but what if she has an accident? She's only been driving a year and she's still very hesitant at junctions.'

'I am not hesitant at junctions!' shouted Emily, from the next room.

Margaret chose to ignore her. 'Now don't forget that there's extra bread and milk in the freezer and a lasagne too, though you'll need to take it out to defrost it at least four hours before you want to eat, so do try to think ahead.'

Matthew nodded mutely. His mother had already been through all this with him at least three times. It was ridiculous, and patronising, and tiresome, especially when his only true concern was the whereabouts of her car keys once she'd gone.

The moment his parents dragged themselves away he ran to check said keys were where they were supposed to be: in the Toby mug on the shelf in the kitchen. Then, feeling the need to do something vaguely rebellious to underscore his new independence, he took a beer from the pallet of cans on the floor of the freezer room and drank it with his feet up on the living-room sofa. This was intended to be relaxing, but it wasn't, as his thoughts kept inexorably turning back to the mission he would undertake next day. He tried watching some daytime TV, but that didn't distract him either. He needed to speak to Caitlin.

Fetching the cordless phone from its base station in the hallway he contemplated it for a minute or two – its shell of injection-moulded plastic, its telescopic metal aerial, the pattern of wear on its keypad, the nuggets of grime caught in the perforations of its mouthpiece – then dialled the Nolans' number.

Sheila picked up with a flustered hello.

'Is that Matthew? Hi Matthew. How are you, darling? Hang on, I'm not sure where she is. Caitlin! *Cait-lin!* You have a phone call. It's Matthew.'

There was a pause while Caitlin took the phone upstairs to her room.

'Hey.'

'How you doing?'

'Okay, I guess.'

She sounded calm. No. Subdued.

'You still okay for tomorrow?'

'Uh huh.'

She didn't say anything more, so Matthew pushed on.

'Mum and Dad have gone. I've got the car keys.'

'Great.'

'So I'll see you at ten then? In the lane? Where we said?'

'Yes.'

How painful this whole thing must be for her – he now regretted ringing her up. But at the same time he couldn't quite bring himself to terminate the call.

'Okay. Well, see you tomorrow, I guess.'

'Yep.'

'Bye then.'

'Bye.'

He pressed the handset to his ear in the hope of something more: a whispered 'Thank you,' would have been enough, even if an 'I love you' would be too much to expect.

'I love you,' Matthew whispered into the mouthpiece, saying it for her. 'I love you, I love you, I love you.' But his only answer was the steady electronic tone that signalled the end of the connection.

Matthew's sleep that night was disturbed by violent dreams. In the last of these, the one he remembered on waking, he was in a tower block in a war zone, a skeleton of a building gutted by shellfire and grenades. There were snipers on the upper storeys; they were on his side. He was there to relieve them, but his route through the shattered passageways was continually being diverted by falling masonry and collapsing floors, as well as by the families still living amid the chaos. Crouching in the rubble, huddled round fires made from broken furniture, they offered him saucepans filled with delicious-smelling food, begging him to stay and eat with them as he tried to pass.

When he finally did reach one of the snipers, he couldn't unpack his gun. It had somehow grown cumbersome and was proving difficult to assemble. As he tried to fit barrel and stock into one another they morphed and lengthened in his hands, while the threads of the components screwed together only loosely and kept undoing themselves at one joint while he was struggling to tighten up another. The rounds bursting into the room didn't help, their impact showering him with concrete and metal shrapnel and making it all but impossible to concentrate, while the sniper he was replacing was cursing him for messing up and putting them both at risk. And still the families kept coming by and offering him food. He lost his temper and shouted at them. Didn't they understand the danger they were in?

Before they could react a particularly violent volley of bullets tore into the ceiling above him and Matthew awoke to sunlight and a silent bedroom. He roused himself and stumbled downstairs in his dressing gown. Emily was already up and already on the phone, deeply involved in some conversation that was half gossip, half negotiation and to Matthew's eyes entirely an excuse to swan about parading her social life at that time in the morning, something she would never have done if their parents had been home.

The chat continued while Matthew dispensed raisin bran into a bowl and sloshed some milk on top; by the time he'd eaten it and made a cup of tea his sister was on her way out.

'Bye then!' she called. 'Don't forget to feed the dogs.' Again there was something theatrical about the way she said it, like she was starring in her very own soap, that got Matthew's goat in a manner distinct from her delegating him a task that she could easily have done herself. Then the back door slammed shut and she was gone and he was left alone with his irritation, the butterflies in his stomach beginning to flutter in anticipation of the day ahead.

One minute later the back door flew open and Emily blew back in.

'Bloody hell!' she swore, unusually for her. 'I've got a bloody flat tyre. I'm going to have to take Mum's car.'

Matthew, tea halfway to mouth, felt the room yawn out onto the infinite, a sensation he was getting to know too well. He sat, extended in time, unable to move, while his sister banged around the room, repeating the phrase 'Have you seen her keys?' over and over, as if she'd been programmed to inflict maximum damage on his psyche.

'You're insured, yeah?' he asked, in a hopeless attempt to divert the ineluctable procession of events.

'Yes, yes, of course,' Emily barked. 'Or if I'm not, I should be. Don't worry – I'll drive safely.'

It was pointless. It was better just to put himself out of his misery. 'In the Toby mug,' he croaked.

Emily found them, grabbed them, chucked her own keys on the sideboard, and left for a second time, her happy demeanour restored. Alone again, Matthew remained motionless while the noise of his mother's car's ignition puttered through the building. This was followed by the sounds of its tyres hissing across the gravel like a wave retreating down a pebble beach, a wave that had left one lone piece of flotsam washed high up on the shore: the keys to Emily's Renault 4.

Matthew stared at these for over a minute, abstracting their form and imagining the jumble of steel and rubber transformed to massive scale like some monumental industrial artefact, once immensely powerful and productive but now beyond salvage, welded into a solid form by weathering and decay.

And then something changed. The luminous flux of the morning light, a sigh and shift from the dogs in their box, the distribution of dopamine in Matthew's brain as caffeine from the tea he'd drunk found its way into his bloodstream – and the keys were once again key-sized and accelerating through the present and out into the future, no longer merely abstract, static objects but the origin of vectors describing powerful fields of potential activity.

Matthew reached forward, picked them up, and gripped them like a talisman. He'd never changed a wheel before. But how hard could it be?

Not that hard, it transpired. The only really tricky bit was deciphering the convoluted geometry of the collapsible jack. Once he'd got that figured out, raised the car a little and got the first nut turning, the rest of it was a breeze. He left home only twenty minutes later than he'd planned, and as his schedule allowed an hour of extra time for delays this was well within his zone of tolerance. There was an unexpected extra bonus, too: this forestalling of disaster with action had bred confidence. As he drove Matthew noticed that the nerves with which he'd begun the day had almost entirely evaporated, and he was able to contemplate the dirt ingrained in his hands and the nail he'd broken on the wrench with a fair degree of pride.

'I thought we were going in your mum's car,' Caitlin said, as she climbed in and fastened her seatbelt.

Matthew explained the situation with the tyre, careful not to boast about his resolution of the crisis, but not altogether eliding it. Perhaps he should have boasted, because Caitlin didn't seem to notice his act of heroism.

'This feels really weird,' was all she said. 'I nearly got in the back. I feel like we're on our way to school.'

The route they followed was indeed the one Emily took on their daily run, at least until they reached Wardle's where, instead of stopping and then turning down past the castle and over the river towards St George's, they carried straight on around the old town gate in the direction of the hospital.

They returned the same way some hours later, Caitlin lying in the back across the seats, groggy from the anaesthetic. Matthew drove a little faster than he should have done, in case of overlapping with his sister, but he needn't have worried. Emily showed up much later in the evening, long after he'd dropped Caitlin back at her parents' place.

When they'd parted there had been no kiss, not even an embrace. Matthew didn't think they'd exchanged more than a hundred words all day. Everything had been preordained: there'd been nothing much to say. The only sound that lingered from the whole grim process was the one he made when, on his way back through the lanes to Snitterfield, he'd had to pull over for a while to cry. But even as he did so he found himself wondering whether he was crying for himself, or for the dispatched foetus, or for Caitlin, or just because he felt that tears should be shed at some point on that day. And if he didn't know which of these was the reason, then was the crying any more genuine than Emily's social airs that morning, which had so irritated him? He simply could not say.

It was around a month later that the small brown envelope landed on the Wolds' front doormat. It was addressed to Emily but Miles picked it up and carried it into the breakfast room, holding it by one corner between thumb and middle finger and flapping it back and forth so that the cellophane window crackled.

'Ms Emily Wold,' he read, holding the envelope level with his eyes. 'From the DVLA. It looks like . . . could it possibly be . . . *some kind of traffic violation?*'

Emily grabbed the envelope and tore it open. It was indeed a speeding fine.

'What? I don't believe it. Forty-two in a thirty zone – fifty pounds and three points! Where did that happen?'

'I've always said you drive too fast,' Margaret chided. 'They hide with those radar guns, the police do. You don't see them.'

'Well I can assure you I don't remember being clocked by anyone.'

'Unless it was those new cameras they're bringing in,' Miles said. 'They're testing them in the West Midlands now. It's all completely automated – calculates your speed, photographs your number plate, tells a computer to send a letter out. Could have been one of those, in which case it's probably a mistake.'

Emily was reading through the letter again, checking she hadn't missed anything. 'It says here that it happened the day I went to Ashorne.'

'That was when we were on holiday, Miles,' Margaret observed. 'Clearly you weren't being as careful as you promised while we were away.'

'It's only forty in a thirty zone, Margaret,' Miles murmured, hoping that his wife wasn't going to remember that he'd received a fine for the same offence two years previously. 'It's easily done.'

'That's not the point. She should have been paying more

attention. What if a child had run out in front of her and she hadn't been able to stop? That's why we have speed limits, you know.'

But Emily wasn't listening. She was staring at the letter, brow furrowed, eyes flashing with an obsidian glint.

'It's not me that's not paying attention,' she fumed. 'It's the DVLA. I wasn't . . . Ow! What did you do that for?'

As he'd got up from the breakfast table Matthew had rammed the toe of his trainer into his sister's shin.

'Uh, sorry. Didn't mean to kick you,' he said, turning his head to glower at her and then rolling his eyes until they were looking pointedly upstairs.

Emily took the hint and held her tongue, but after breakfast she cornered her brother in his bedroom. Now she was the one waving the speeding ticket by its corner.

'What the hell is going on?' she demanded. 'How come my car was in Warwick that day?'

'I went to see a friend.'

'So that's why you fixed my tyre. You little sneak. You're crazy, you know. You haven't even passed your test. If you'd been stopped . . .'

'I wasn't.'

'But you were speeding, weren't you? It's a miracle they didn't pull you over there and then, they usually do.'

'Not having any insurance didn't seem to bother you much when you took Mum's car out.'

'I am insured. I checked.'

'Yeah, after. But you didn't know that at the time.'

'At least I've got a bloody driving licence! You're totally irresponsible.' She glowered at him, hands on her hips, but he just shrugged.

'You sound like Mum.'

'I know how she feels.'

'Look. I'll pay, all right? I'll pay the fine.'

'You haven't got any money.'

'I'll get some. I'll pay you back.'

'I'll hold you to that.'

'You can. I wouldn't have said it otherwise. But just chill out, okay? Or I'll tell her that you took her car, and then we'll both be in the shit.'

Matthew did pay back the money for the fine. He got a summer job working on a local farm and settled up with Emily out of his first wage packet. The trauma of the abortion had begun to fade by then, and things had settled down with Caitlin too. The farm was not far from Shelfield, which was mainly why Matthew had taken the job there in the first place. When he had a late shift running one of the corn dryers, which during the harvest needed to be manned around the clock, she would come and spend the evening with him. They'd listen to the radio, drink supermarket beers and smoke cigarettes while the noctules and pipistrelles jinked for midges in the twilight. Sometimes she'd let him kiss her, and maybe put a hand upon her breast.

By the time school resumed the following September there was no doubt that the two of them were a couple. Matthew passed his driving test and was able to ferry Caitlin to school himself in the Renault 4, which had passed to him now that Emily had started university, so most days they retraced the path of their trip to Warwick Hospital for reasons that had nothing to do with ghost children and medical procedures. Gradually these re-enactments, difficult at first, began to overwrite the memory of that awful day, and by the following spring it was as if the whole thing had never taken place.

But still Caitlin wouldn't sleep with him. She acquiesced to other things but drew the line at penetration and insisted that they kept their clothing on. Matthew tried hard not to press her, though he didn't always succeed. He understood how after what happened she'd be reticent about having sex. But his frustration was intense and he couldn't fully shed his resentment that Caitlin had given herself to someone else, but would not give herself to him. He stuck by his vow not to ask her who the other boy had been, but that didn't mean the question wasn't ever-present in his mind. He turned it over and over, and in the end, as much to retain his own sanity as anything, he decided on an answer: that she had in fact been raped, possibly by someone that she knew, and she wanted nothing more than to erase the entire incident from her memory. As well as explaining her behaviour, this had the added benefit of giving Matthew a mission. By setting his gentleness and patience in opposition to whatever violence had befallen her, he would help her rebuild her sexual confidence and learn to love again.

As their A-Levels loomed this indeed seemed to be happening. They discussed their plans for their life together at enormous length, starting with university and going on from there. They even decided to sync their UCAS applications, putting the same universities in the same order on their forms so that they should have the maximum chance of studying together instead of having to spend three long years apart. Caitlin told him she loved him, said she'd never been so happy, said she wanted them to be together for ever. Matthew felt like he'd been let into the most profound and glorious of all secrets. He wanted to sing his delight to every living being he came across; wanted to pin his heart to the moon. This happiness and the confidence it bred helped him to secure excellent exam results, which in turn meant good university offers, one of them from Cambridge. He hadn't wanted or expected an offer from that quarter. He had only really put the university on his shortlist because his teachers and his parents had said he should. Caitlin had followed suit, but they knew that the chance of both of them getting in to the prestigious university was close to zero.

Heart set on studying alongside his girlfriend, Matthew had been deliberately diffident and uncompromising at his interview, but it seemed that this very attitude had tipped the balance in his favour with the admissions tutors, swamped as they were by a tide of nodding, smiling hopefuls with little to say and less nerve with which to say it. Amidst this damp contingent Matthew's nonchalance and easy answers had, presumably, been read as intellectual bite.

Caitlin's results, however, were disastrous. She managed a D, an E and a Fail. Fails were almost unheard-of even from the worst students, and Caitlin had been tipped to get good results. She'd almost have been better off not turning up. There followed something of an inquisition. Her parents petitioned the exam board, the school. Her papers were recalled. But there was no mistake. She'd not even attempted answers for most of the questions she'd been asked.

When presented with the evidence Caitlin was impassive, saying only that she didn't know why she'd done what she did. She'd frozen when the papers had been put in front of her. She'd had plenty of knowledge spinning in her head, but couldn't write it down. When she'd tried it had all come out wrong. So she'd stopped trying.

Tony and Sheila asked Matthew to talk to her about it, but he couldn't draw any more sense out of her than they could. The oddest thing was that she didn't seem remotely troubled by what had happened – every time it was raised with her she dismissed it or laughed it off. Her lack of seriousness hinted at a profound gulf between them, an unseen tectonic fault, and it bothered Matthew more than outright rows or silences would have done.

Her parents felt the same way. Caitlin was sent to see an educational psychologist who diagnosed general anxiety disorder and suggested that she undergo cognitive therapy. The school agreed that she would be allowed to retake the year, as long as she continued with the psychologist. Caitlin said she would.

Matthew found these developments extremely difficult to bear. Caitlin refused to accept that they had anything to do with her termination, but he couldn't see how that could be so. He wasn't at all sure any longer that he'd done the right thing in helping her keep the whole affair secret now that it appeared that all the focus on the physical side of things had been misplaced and it was the psychological impact that was proving far more traumatic. But at the time he hadn't even considered that an issue.

What he couldn't do now, under any circumstances, was abandon Caitlin to her fate. Cambridge was the other end of a tortuous, three-hour cross-country drive, with no direct motorway and no direct train. If he went there he'd see her once or twice a term, if he was lucky. Given what had happened, there was no question about it. He simply could not take up the place.

He drove over to visit her one afternoon to tell her what he'd decided. She got in the Renault and he drove it a little way down the road and parked in a gateway so they could smoke.

When he felt the moment was right, Matthew gripped the steering wheel and took a deep breath. 'I called the Cambridge admissions office to see if they would defer my place for a year,' he said. 'They wouldn't, so then I called Warwick admissions, and asked them the same thing, and they said they would. So I've accepted Warwick and I'm going to take a year out.'

Caitlin felt giddy, even though she was buckled into the passenger seat. 'Have you told your parents about this yet?'

'I wanted to tell you first. It means we won't need to be apart. I can get a job around here, get some work experience or something, earn some money while you do your retakes. And then we can have a shot at going to Warwick together like we'd planned.'

'But I thought we'd agreed you'd be crazy not to go to Cambridge,' she gulped. She was finding it hard to breathe. She wanted to get out of the car, right now, and run back to her house.

Matthew started playing with his Zippo, flicking the metal lid open and closed. He couldn't look at her. There it was again, her desire for him to leave. It made him feel almost exalted to hear her confirm it because now, by staying in the Midlands, he was going to be able to find out whether or not she was being honest about her feelings for him. This was love he was talking about. *Love.* Wasn't it the most important thing in the world? Didn't it always boil down to just that? And shouldn't it, therefore, always come first? But did she love him, or did she just owe him? He needed to know which it was.

Matthew broke the news to his parents at dinner that night, and they were about as stunned as Caitlin had been. They objected of course, and his mother cried a little, but when he repeated his reasons calmly and rationally – he loved Caitlin, didn't want to leave her, he wanted some work experience and, conclusively, he preferred the course at Warwick, which he thought was more appropriate to his career – he found, somewhat to his surprise, that they actually listened to what he had to say. Usually his parents acted very much as individuals, their reactions to him different and characteristically unique. Now, though, he noticed that they seemed almost as one, their faces wearing identical expressions of apprehensiveness.

'Well you've clearly thought this through,' his father said when, eventually, he spoke. 'You're an adult now, Matthew. You have to take your own path. If this is really what you want, then good luck to you. I just hope you don't come to regret it.'

At these words Matthew felt happy and triumphant, but afterwards, after he'd hugged his parents and thanked them for their understanding, it was as if the apprehension he'd seen in their faces had been somehow transmitted to him, and he began to feel extremely anxious. He hadn't expected everything to fall into place so easily. On some level he'd expected someone to stop him: the admissions officers, Caitlin, Miles, Margaret, someone. But no one had. It was a shock to realise that people didn't have that power over him any longer. His father was right. He was an adult now. He could do as he liked – and suffer the consequences.

Another trapdoor was opening beneath him. He knew the signs this time. Action was required if he were to close it again. And so, before the week was out, he'd made contact with his local Friends of the Earth and Greenpeace groups and announced his intention to volunteer for whatever work they had going.

He spent much of the next twelve months fund-raising in town centres across the West Midlands, initially drawing social security to cover his expenses until his commitment and tenacity were spotted by a manager in the Greenpeace regional office, at which point he was promoted, put in charge of a team, and given a small salary.

As the world of charity work slowly began to reveal itself to him, however, his relationship with Caitlin became ever harder to negotiate. His plan to continue to drive her to school every morning proved wholly impractical now that he had to be on site first thing in the morning in Birmingham, or Coventry, or Leicester. And without that daily interaction and the social glue of school to bind them, the intimacy they'd shared began to fade. Caitlin's parents were insisting she focus on her studies, and Matthew was finding new friends among the activists he was working with. Mostly in their early twenties, they seemed more centred than any other group of people he'd ever met. Many of them were already veterans – or talked like veterans – of quite militant pieces of direct action that made his efforts standing on street corners handing out leaflets and rattling collection boxes seem paltry by comparison. They had an unshakable confidence that what they were doing was right, acknowledged no authority beyond the planet and what they judged was best for it, and communicated an intellectual excitement he'd not previously encountered.

On top of that, they opened his eyes to the tangled politics of knowledge. He'd always taken it for granted that scientists were scientists and that the reports and developments he read about in the papers or heard on the news were more or less accurate. But now he was learning that science was as riven and partial as any other area of human endeavour, and that little about it could be taken at face value, especially when it came to the environment.

The activists also smoked strong weed that many of them grew themselves in grow-lamp-equipped cupboards in the dilapidated rental properties they inhabited. Far more potent than the mild hash that had been traded at his school, the skunk chimed well with all this new relativity, transforming Matthew's surroundings into a pulsing sensorium that seemed both more vivid than anything he'd previously experienced and tantalisingly harder to grasp. It had a similar effect on his inner world, accelerating the flow of ideas into a torrent, at least while he was stoned. But each insight, however apparently lucid and self-evident it was at its inception, seemed to resist further examination, morphing like a cloud into another version of itself at the very moment it was probed.

Exposed to these influences Matthew soon became tuned to a constant state of reassessment, happy to replace what he now regarded as his parochial worldview with a more complex set of axioms. Certainties were now, he saw, part of the problem, unless they had contradiction built right into their heart. The world was changing and under threat. There was, in a way, a war going on, a climate war, a war in which he'd just enlisted as a mere grunt, the lowest of the low. He didn't expect to know anything much about it, not yet. He wouldn't be entitled to an opinion until he'd done a legitimate and recognisable tour of duty. In the meantime he needed to shut up and learn as much about it all as he possibly could.

Twice he shared some of the skunk he was now regularly smoking with Caitlin. On the first occasion it sent her mildly crazy. They were in Stratford with friends, hanging out in the Bancroft Gardens by the river, and she began running round and round in circles giggling, forefingers held extended by her ears, pretending to be what Matthew took to be a bull, an impression that was reinforced when she hit on the idea of butting him, prompting cries of 'Toro! Toro!' from the others along with much waving of imaginary capes. Matthew worked hard to see the funny side while Caitlin rode out the high, but the joke had been on him and he hadn't liked it. It killed his mood, which stayed dead for the remainder of the evening.

The next time he made sure the experience took place under more controlled conditions: just the two of them alone, one weekend, at his house when his parents were away. But this time it had the opposite effect. Instead of coming with him on a stoned walk through the woods like he had suggested, Caitlin stretched out like a cat on his bed and passed out, leaving Matthew bored, horny and frustrated, with nothing to do but lie next to her and read. Eventually she woke up with a headache and declared she didn't like skunk, and he figured it was just as well. It certainly hadn't made her seem any more inclined to sleep with him, though that afternoon she did promise that she would do once she'd finished her resits. And with this in mind he kept his eyes fixed on the prize of her getting good enough grades for a place at Warwick, at which point the two of them would be able to start things fresh.

The longer he held out for Caitlin, however, the harder Matthew found it not to feel that sex was something that she owed him. He had hoped to collect on the debt the night of her final exam, but when that day finally came she wanted to celebrate with friends rather than dive into bed – and that was fair enough, he could understand that, he could wait a little longer. It proved hard, however, to get her attention at all in the maelstrom of graduation. A week went by, and then another; she always seemed to have another party to go to, another friend to whom she had to say goodbye. He accompanied her to these socials even though they did little for him except emphasise how the gap between him and those in the year below, always difficult to bridge while he'd been at school, had been significantly widened by his experiences out in the world of work.

He had been them, just twelve months previously. In the mirrors of their dazed and excited faces he could see his old self, and it made him want to grab them and tell them that no, it wouldn't be like they imagined it, they weren't about to become bigger and more expansive and more inflated, that instead the opposite was going to happen: despite this great wave of change they were all convinced was about to break over them they weren't going to really change at all; they were just going to carry their selves forward into a new realm in which their inadequacies would be far more conspicuous than they had ever been during their education, and the lessons far more unfathomable.

Depressed and frustrated, Matthew finally had to all but insist that Caitlin let him take her out for a celebratory dinner. She liked Chinese food and there was a reasonable Szechuan restaurant on the first floor of the block on the corner where Sheep Street met Stratford High Street, right across from the Vintner. So he took her there.

At Caitlin's request they stopped for a preliminary drink in the wine bar. As soon as she'd said this, Matthew's heart had fallen. And just as he'd feared, a small group of Caitlin's friends was already sitting in one of the booths when they walked in. By the time he returned with a couple of drinks she was deep into her little scene.

Knowing full well that any sign of impatience on his part could capsize his plans for the evening, Matthew did his best to join in. The talking went on. There were more drinks. At half past eight he touched Caitlin on the arm.

'We should go.'

'You can't go!' said David Tate, who was one of the group. 'You've just got here.'

'We've got a reservation,' Matthew said.

'Oooh, a *reservation*. Fancy!'

'Matty's taking me out,' Caitlin said, rolling her eyes. Matthew couldn't tell if she was happy about the fact or taking the piss.

'We're celebrating.'

'Hey,' said Caitlin, eyes not rolling now but lighting up. 'Why don't you all come?'

Matthew started to panic. 'But we've only booked for two!'

'Oh they won't care,' Caitlin said. 'That place is always half-empty anyway.'

'Noodles, anyone?' said David, enjoying the look of horror on Matthew's face. 'Chicken chow mein? Personally I quite fancy a drop of bird's nest soup and a bowl of ducks' tongues.'

Caitlin evidently thought this was hilarious. It took Matthew another fifteen minutes to extract her from the bar and get her across the street to the restaurant, and then only once it had been established that everyone else, David included, had already eaten.

The place was half-empty, as Caitlin had said it would be. They took their seats at one of the tables overlooking Sheep Street and thus the half-timbered frame of Vintner. Not wanting to be dragged back there even mentally, Matthew cast his gaze around the room, trying to find reassurance in the arrangement of paper lanterns, black lacquer tables, carved wooden screens.

The waiter brought menus.

'What would you like?' Matthew asked, as he scanned through the dishes.

'I don't know if I'm that hungry, to be honest,' Caitlin said.

'Well, maybe something to drink. And prawn crackers. We should definitely get some prawn crackers.'

Caitlin shrugged. Matthew put down the menu and stared at her.

'What's the matter?'

'Nothing. Why?'

'Because, to be honest, you don't really seem like you want to be here.'

'Of course I do.' She picked up her menu, opened it. 'How about some ducks' tongues?' she giggled.

'Want me to go over the road and fetch David?'

'If you like.'

The waiter reappeared and asked if they were ready to order. Matthew sent him away.

'Come on Cait,' he said, trying to use the interruption to help him change tack. 'I just want to celebrate with you. It's a big deal for us, this is: you finishing your exams. In a few months we could be moving into a place at Warwick together. Think of that.'

Caitlin reached for her bag and began hunting for something inside it. Her cigarettes. She took one out and lit it.

'I don't think that's going to happen,' she blurted, between puffs.

Matthew sighed, exasperated. 'Well that's a pretty defeatist attitude. You've studied really hard. You're going to get good grades, I just know it.'

'Doesn't matter.'

'Doesn't matter? Why doesn't it matter?'

She sucked again on her Marlboro Light, exhaled, and looked at him. He didn't recognise the look. The Caitlin that he knew, she wasn't there.

'Because I didn't put Warwick on my UCAS form.'

Her words had come to him in disordered fragments, their phonemes utterly discrete, but once he'd deciphered what she'd said Matthew just got up from the table and walked away. Initially, thinking he might throw up, he was heading for the toilets, but he didn't know where they were and, unable to summon the self-possession required to look for them, he ended up heading down the stairs and back the way they'd come in until he found himself outside.

What Caitlin's action meant he did not know. It was the antithesis of meaning, meaning's antimatter: it rendered meaning void. The last year, the last two years of his life, everything he'd told himself and struggled for, all those hours and weeks and months he'd spent trudging the streets rattling a tin, all the jejune goals and romantic self-assurances he spun himself, all of this crumpled and collapsed into a psychological singularity so dense it seemed to suck in his entire soul.

Caitlin had followed him out and was now standing there in the small open plaza on the corner of Sheep Street talking to him. But it was like he was inside a television and she was standing in front of it yelling pointlessly at the screen. Why would she do that? Why would she even try to communicate? Did she not understand that what she saw of him was just a broadcast signal, that in reality he was standing many, many miles away, that there was glass, and antennae, and great tracts of open space between the two of them? He was beyond her now, and she beyond him. They were separate people, strangers. They would not touch again.

There were some issues, later, because he did not drive her home that night but instead abandoned her in town without the cash for a cab. Sheila and Tony called his parents to complain, but when Miles and Margaret brought it to his attention he simply told them the truth as he now saw it: that he did not know who she was. For a long time after that he refused to hear her name spoken in front of him. If anyone so much as mentioned her, he would just get up and leave the room.

He went to Warwick that September, or at least he packed his stuff and moved into his campus dorm. But that was about as far as it went. He didn't attend any lectures or show up at his seminars. He spent most of his time on the payphone in the hallway of his building or on the bus to London, making one of many trips to the Greenpeace head office where he was engaged in a relentless campaign to badger his way into a job, any job, even if it meant scrubbing the office floor. As it turned out, the time he'd spent running teams in the Midlands counted for quite a lot, and eventually he was offered an entry-level position.

He left Warwick without telling either the university or his family. Just packed up and left. For the next few years he was travelling continually wherever Greenpeace sent him, until a funding crisis meant cuts to his expenses and the already fairly minimal salary they were paying him. He heard about the EcoPath job from a friend, applied for it, got it, and off the back of it took out a 95 per cent interest-only mortgage on the flat in Oxford's Summertown.

The day after he took possession of the property a cat showed up in the backyard, half-starved, missing an eye, covered in fleas, and demanding food and attention as if by natural right. Perhaps he did have a right: perhaps he'd belonged to the previous owners and lived there already; Matthew never found out. But he recognised a kindred spirit when he saw one, and so he took the cat in, fed him, paid his vet bills, fixed him up. He named him Max, chosen for no other reason than it seemed to suit him. And Max must have liked something about the arrangement. At any rate, he stuck around.

STAG

TOBY STRAUSS WAS A DIRECTOR at Simple Eye, the production company that Caitlin worked for. He was also married and had two kids. Caitlin had met him when she'd been a line producer on *Beat Your Neighbour*, a property reality show in which two home-owners in the same street competed to see who could build an extension on their house the fastest and still add more value to their property than their rivals did to theirs.

Toby, with his floppy blond fringe, battered but expensive quilted jackets, designer jeans and suede walking boots had, in her mind, been an attractive but distant figure for most of the chaotic shooting schedule. Their relationship changed, however, when one of the couples they'd been filming turned out not to own their house at all.

This was a major crisis. The team was just a few weeks away from delivery and the couple – the Nashtons – were among the most televisual and entertaining of their subjects. They'd looked set to be the champions of the series, and now it transpired that not only were they not the owners of their property, but they had no planning permission for the extension they'd constructed. The local council was insisting that the extension be demolished at the expense of the actual owner, who'd been notified by the letting agency and who was threatening to sue both the Nashtons and Simple Eye for the damages incurred.

'It's a fucking disaster,' Toby moaned, head in hands, after he and Caitlin had been left alone in the Simple Eye boardroom by the deeply unimpressed Head of Commissioning. 'Our best strand. We're going to have to recut the whole series. We may even have to reshoot.'

Caitlin sat in silence, watching Toby's fine hair undulating between his fingers like seaweed between the spars of a wreck. He'd been gentleman enough not to throw her to the wolves in the meeting they'd just endured, but it was her fault that the paperwork hadn't been checked. Ever since the gaffe had been discovered she'd been writing apologies and resignation letters in her mind. So far they hadn't been needed, but now that moment had surely arrived.

Toby lifted his head.

'Let's go to the pub,' he said.

They went to the pub. Not the usual one, on the corner across from the Simple Eye offices, but another, a few streets away, the Nelson, which was quieter and more intimate. Better, Caitlin thought, for doing the deed. Though if Toby was going to try and assuage any guilt he might feel over her dismissal by buying her a drink, she wished he wouldn't bother.

Toby returned to the booth in which they'd settled with a beer for him and a white wine for her. He'd got a tube of Pringles too, which Caitlin couldn't help but feel was a little excessive. He was here to sack her. They didn't need nibbles.

He placed the drinks on the table, slid along the banquette, and took a gulp of his beer.

'What a prick he is,' he said, setting down his glass.

'I know it's all my fault,' Caitlin said. 'I know I've got to go. Please get on with it.'

Toby looked blank for a second. 'What? Don't be daft. You didn't take all of that seriously, did you?'

'But I should have done proper checks on the paperwork.'

Toby waved his hand. 'We're a production company, not a bloody bank. Listen Cait. You're the best line producer I ever had. You come early, you stay late, you work hard, you don't need reminding of the blindingly obvious and you're capable of handling more than one thing at a time, even when it's not your make-up or your boyfriend. You made a mistake, or, more accurately, you were fooled by some people who it turns out were basically mad. It happens. I'm not about to lose you over it, whatever Simon thinks.'

Caitlin didn't know what to say.

'Really?'

'Yes, really. Here. Have a Pringle.'

Their eyes met and they both grinned. The grim cloud hanging over them dissipated. Suddenly none of it seemed to matter very much.

'Christ,' Toby said. 'All this fuss over a shitty property show. I never wanted to do this, you know.'

'What, *Beat Your Neighbour*?'

'No. Well, yes, that too. I meant telly. I never wanted to work in telly. I mean, what boy spends his teenage years dreaming of making tedious reality shows about the housing market? I wanted to be a film director, like everyone else. Thought that directing telly would be a good route in. How wrong I was.'

'Well you're hardly past it.'

'Thanks. I'll take that as a compliment. But my chance has gone, I think. Especially given the state of the film industry in this country. The government has pulled all the tax breaks, you know. The whole thing, such as it is, is collapsing. It's like the nineteen-eighties all over again.'

'There's always TV drama. What's wrong with that?'

Toby faux-retched. 'God, where do I start?'

'Oh come on. There's lots of great series made all the time.'

'Name me one. Made in Britain – not America. And not a comedy or a costume drama.'

Caitlin hesitated. Suddenly comedies and costume dramas were all that came to mind.

'Told you. Incredible series are spilling out of the States faster than you can watch them, and here, what have we got? Big Brother and Jane Austen adaptations.'

'There's *The Office*.'

'Comedy. Doesn't count.' Toby tipped the last Pringles' shards into his mouth and crushed the tube between the heels of his hands. 'What about you? What brought you to the glorious land of TV UK?'

Caitlin looked away, as she generally did when asked about herself. Her story was well practised, but however many times she repeated it, it never sat snug. 'I – I don't know really. Sad, isn't it? I suppose I thought it would be interesting, and fun, and not all that hard. At school I really wanted to be an architect, but then I got scared off by the maths and the thought of seven years' training. I didn't know if I could face asking my parents to support me through that, only to discover at the end of it that I wasn't much good, or I didn't like it, or whatever. So here I am.'

'So you didn't have the self-belief to do what you really wanted to do.'

'Well, nor did you.'

'Touché. You're right. I didn't. And I still don't. We both live inside our own quiet tragedies, don't we? Another drink?'

'Oh . . .' Caitlin reached for her bag, but Toby was already on his feet.

'No, no. Come on. On me. You've had a shite enough day as it is. Same again?'

Caitlin nodded. 'Sure – thanks.'

'And here, while you're waiting.' He dug into his pocket and tossed something on to her side of the table: a small folded envelope of paper cut from a magazine. 'If you fancy it.'

Oh thank God, thought Caitlin. This would make things so much easier.

While Toby was at the bar she disappeared to the Ladies and helped herself to a couple of lines of the powder the packet contained; when she returned she passed it back to its owner, who then went off to the Gents.

They carried on in this vein for another couple of hours. Then Toby mentioned that he was living in a rented flat a few streets away, while he went through a trial separation from his wife.

Caitlin was drunk. 'You make it sound like surgery,' she said.

'It kind of is. Without an anaesthetic.' He motioned at his empty glass. 'Unless you count that.'

They giggled conspiratorially and their arms touched. Soon afterwards Toby placed his leg against Caitlin's underneath the table. She didn't move away. When they got outside, they both started walking in the same direction. Neither of them said anything about where they were going. Neither of them needed to.

Caitlin spent many evenings at Toby's place after that, though that first time was the only occasion they made love in the hallway. She would go there late, usually after a dinner eaten alone in her flat in Shoreditch, yoyo-ing up and down the Central Line in the process. The property production was soon behind them, the crisis with the couple that didn't own their house somehow resolved and faded to inconsequence, and they had moved on to new – and separate – projects. Toby was shooting outside London and travelling a lot; Caitlin had hoped he might request her as his production manager, but he didn't. She thought about mentioning it to him but decided against it: when it came down to it she knew he wouldn't want to mix business and pleasure, and she wouldn't either. It would be childish to make an issue of it.

But it did mean she didn't see a great deal of him, because he didn't seem to want to mix pleasure with pleasure much either. Their time together was always brief because his kids had to come first, which was fair enough. But after three months she still hadn't met them and they hadn't been told about her, as far as she knew. And he hadn't introduced her to a single one of his friends.

The excuse was the divorce. Toby didn't want his wife to find out he had a lover; it might play against him if things got messy and they ended up in court. Which was fine as far as it went, but after six months of making herself available, usually at short notice and often at what seemed like Toby's whim, Caitlin was starting to question their entire relationship.

She discussed the situation with Beth, the landlady at The Crusader, a pub that Caitlin frequented in Shoreditch, not far from her flat.

'He's using you,' Beth told her straight away. 'He needs to get real.'

'It's hard for him though,' Caitlin said. 'He's under so much pressure.'

Beth had no time for such limp empathies. 'I wouldn't put up with it. Has he told you when the divorce is due to come through?'

Caitlin shook her head.

'You want to be careful. He could be having you on. I don't want to slag him off or anything, but if you ask me I wouldn't be surprised if he was still sleeping with his wife.'

'They're barely on speaking terms.'

'Look babe, she's his wife. They've got two kids. Trust me, they're speaking. The only question is: are they still shagging? I mean, where does he spend his nights when you're not at his flat?'

'At his flat. Or in a hotel, when he's on location.'

'You're sure about that?'

'Of course. Why would he lie?'

Beth pulled on her cigarette and vented two long streams of smoke from her nostrils.

'Er, because he's a man, duck. That's what they do.'

Caitlin laughed. But the seed of doubt had been planted.

The next time Toby called her she told him she was busy and she couldn't see him that night. The plan, once she got off the phone, was to drive over and see if the lights were on in his flat. But now that the first step had been taken, she felt slightly ridiculous. Was she really going to get in her car and go and spy on her lover?

Well, yes, apparently so. Because here she was driving through town to Shepherd's Bush and parking across the road from Toby's block, within direct line of sight of his darkened windows.

The lights were off. This, unfortunately, proved nothing. He could have gone out for a meal or met a friend for a drink. He could be anywhere. What was she supposed to do now? Sit here on stakeout for the whole night? She did the first of several hits of coke from the supply she kept in her handbag and smoked the first of several cigarettes. She waited one hour, then two. This was ludicrous. She was freezing, ragged, high. She thought of Beth. Why was she taking advice from a landlady, someone whose job was to sell her alcohol, for Christ's sake?

Furious with herself, she started the car and was pulling out of the parking space when she saw Toby walking down the street towards her, arm in arm with a woman. Before she had time to change her mind she turned off the engine, got out of the car, and crossed the street to intercept them at the entrance to the block.

'Hello Toby,' she said, as he paused to reach into his pocket for his keys.

He jerked his head up, fringe swaying, face masked with surprise.

'Cait . . . hi . . . er . . . what you doing here?'

'Oh, you know. I was just passing.'

Toby removed his arm from the waist of his companion and swapped his keys from hand to hand.

'Er . . . this is Sophie. My wife. Soph – this is Cait. She works at Simple Eye.'

Sophie smiled and stuck out her hand. 'Hi. Do you live round here?'

Caitlin nodded. 'Yeah. Yeah – just over there. Funny coincidence.'

'I don't know how you do it. It's nice to visit, but I couldn't live in London.'

'Oh right. Where do you live?'

'Down near Haslemere. Much more relaxing! But Toby wasn't working and the kids are staying with some friends so I'm having a long-overdue night off.'

'Nice.' Caitlin looked back at Toby, who already had his key in the front door and was refusing to meet her gaze.

'Well, we'd best go up. See you at work, Cait.'

'Yeah. See you.'

'Bye!' said Sophie. 'Nice to meet you!'

Then they were inside and the heavy door had swung shut behind them and the lock had clicked back into place, and Caitlin was left on her own in a dark empty street in mid-January.

She got back in her car and sat staring forwards at the vehicle parked in front, at the reflections of the streetlights on the windows, at the plane trees lining the street, at nothing. How long she sat she didn't know, but at some point she became aware of a sound coming from her bag on the passenger seat. A buzzing. Her phone. She pulled it out and opened it.

'Hello?'

The call took a moment to connect.

'Caitlin – is that you?'

'Sean?'

'Have you spoken to Mum?'

'No. Why?'

'She's been trying to call you. We've got some really bad news.'

'What?'

'It's Dad. Cait – I don't know how to say . . . Um. He died this morning. Heart attack.'

Caitlin's hands began to tremble and she fumbled for her cigarettes.

'Cait?'

'Wait . . . I can't . . . I'm driving . . . I'm going to call Mum.'

She pressed the red button to end the call and dialled her parents' number. After one ring, Sheila picked up.

'Mum.'

'Caitlin – oh thank God. I've been trying to reach you for hours.'

'I was working late. We've been really busy.'

Sheila was crying. 'Did you speak to Sean?'

'Yes. How did it happen?'

'I went into his office to ask him if he'd be going to the golf club for lunch, and I found him collapsed on the floor. I called an ambulance. They said his heart had given out, and they took him away.'

'Is Sean there?'

'Not right now, but he's been over. He's coming back to spend the night. When do you think you can come home?'

'I'm not sure. We've got so much on. I'll come as soon as I can.'

Her mother's voice hardened. 'There's a lot to do. There's the funeral to organise, everyone to tell. We'll have the vigil here in the house. I could do with your help.'

'I'll be there for the vigil. When will it start?'

'Wednesday, but I really . . .'

'I'll be back for that, I'll make sure.'

'Caitlin, you should know. Your father, he'd been ill for a while. We hadn't told you and your brother—'

'Mum, I really need to go now – I'm about to get on the Tube. I'll call you tomorrow okay? Make sure you get some rest.'

'But Caitlin . . .'

'It doesn't make any difference now, does it? Tell me when you see me, okay?'

She flipped the phone shut, lit a cigarette and smoked for a couple of minutes, staring not out of the window this time but at her left hand, resting before her on the steering wheel.

Why had she not said something to Sophie?

She didn't know. And now it was too late.

She could not bear this thought, and to burn it from her head she took the cigarette from her mouth, pointed its tip at the soft pad that joined her left thumb and forefinger, and pressed it into the offending flesh.

Sheila had always teased Tony that he looked like Mario Lanza, but it was true; she'd thought it the first time she met him, and she thought it again when the coffin was brought into the house, placed on the dining table, and opened for her to inspect the work that had been done by the mortuary.

Tony hadn't had a bad tenor voice himself, though it wasn't a patch on the star's of course. But then Lanza had died at thirty-eight of a life too fully lived – one of the great tragedies of Sheila's teenage years – so her husband had done rather better on that count. When he knew he'd upset her over some trifle or other Tony used to croon her a passable version of 'My Wild Irish Rose', and when they were younger that had often worked some magic, making her laugh and putting their tiff into perspective. But the older – or drunker – he'd got the less effective that had become, until it stoked their arguments more than it calmed them.

But they hadn't argued that often, really, not in the later years. Tony might have continued being a tyrant at work, but Sheila had drawn a line after Jamie had left, and let him know in no uncertain terms that there was no way she'd continue to tolerate him acting like that at home, not unless he wanted a second divorce.

And he'd stopped. He'd changed. He'd listened and, if not mellowed, at least diverted whatever raging force it was that drove him. The tragedy was that he'd not been able to exercise similar limits on his smoking.

Cigarettes. If Tony could have slung them across his chest in bandoliers he would have done. He fired them up at the onset of hostilities – which for him began at about 6.30 in the morning – and kept going until last thing at night, jabbing them in sync with the *rat tat tat* of his phone conversations, flicking them in the street like red-tipped bullets or stabbing them into ashtrays to emphasise points. He was a smoker. It was who he was.

The oncologist had told them that Tony hadn't become aware of the lung cancer until it was quite far advanced because he also had diabetes. He hadn't known he had diabetes either, but apparently it was common in people of his age, people who'd spent a lifetime consuming foodstuffs filled with refined sugar and saturated fat. Late onset, they called it; there was a lot written about it in the magazines Sheila read and the lifestyle sections of the newspapers. But then Tony never looked at those: to his mind they were filled with trivia and aimed at people who didn't have to work for a living, though he'd learned not to say that out loud in front of his wife.

The cancer had caused a congestive heart failure for which Tony had been prescribed a drawer full of pills whose names Sheila could barely pronounce but which she'd had to organise and administer in order to keep her husband to his regimen: ACE inhibitors and beta-blockers and diuretics and digitalis and aspirin; at least she knew aspirin. The idea was to get the heart condition under control while they readied him for the removal of one of his lungs, which would be followed by courses of chemotherapy for his body and radiotherapy for his brain to stop the cancer from spreading, a development not unknown in cases like Tony's.

And then his heart gave out anyway, before they'd even started those courses, before they'd even steeled themselves to share the details of his condition with Caitlin and Sean, before they'd really absorbed the impact of any of this. It had only been a few weeks since he'd first felt the pains and gone in for the scans. A few short weeks. That's all it had needed to take Sheila from contemplating all her long-nurtured plans for Tony's retirement to contemplating this: a strangely kitsch mahogany casket perched on top of their oval mahogany dining table, the cost of these two things together equivalent to about five of the holidays they'd been planning to take.

She hadn't even liked that awful coffin. She'd regretted buying it as soon as she'd signed the order form at the funeral director's. But she didn't know what else to do. The oak had been nice, but she wasn't sure Tony would have liked it, and she knew for certain he'd have hated the pine. And she could hardly let him be buried in one of the cardboard ones, could she, though the wicker caskets had been nice. When her own turn came, she thought she'd choose wicker. She'd tell Sean and Caitlin: that would do nicely for her. Because in any event wasn't mahogany one of those rainforest trees they were supposed to have stopped chopping down?

The doorbell rang. Dabbing at her eyes with one of the tissues she had permanently to hand, Sheila left the morticians to their work and went to answer it. A trim middle-aged woman stood there, tidily dressed in dark blue leggings, a roll-neck sweater, black ballet flats.

'Mrs Nolan?'

'Yes?'

'The flowers you ordered. Would you like me to start bringing them in?'

'Oh! Yes, please.'

Sheila propped the front door open with the little stone statuette of a slow loris that she and Tony had bought on a roadside stall in Malaysia after she'd fallen in love with its pleading, doleful eyes. Cold sharp air invaded the hallway and sliced deep into the house's fug of warmth, making Sheila rub her hands as she stood in a corner and watched the florist and her assistant carry the long flat cartons of flowers, themselves rather like miniature coffins, in from their van. At the same time the morticians announced they were done and started to fold up their trolley and pack up their cases and shift everything out into the driveway.

Suddenly the house was busy with activity, and for a moment Sheila felt a prickle of the kind of excitement that she used to experience during the preparations for one of her and Tony's many parties. The silence that enveloped the place the last few days, that silver silence particular to winter in the English countryside, undiluted save for the cawing of a rook or two, had started to get to her. It had been too quiet, even, for her to be able to sleep.

She asked the florists if they'd like coffee, but they politely declined, so she went to the kitchen to pour one for herself and carried it back to the dining room. The room had already been transformed: just the two big displays of lilies, placed intelligently on the sideboard by the florist in the vases she had left for the purpose, were enough to lift the whole scene. And there was so much more to come – the cartons lay open now and from them spilled great clumps of yellow gerbera, cream carnations, buttery St John's wort, pale viburnums. And wads and wads of ivy, fern and moonseed, to buffer the colours with green.

The hallway and living room had to be set with flowers too, so the three of them had their work cut out. Sheila soon found herself absorbed in the task, snipping and tying alongside the two women, who turned out to be mother and daughter. For the next couple of hours she almost forgot herself for the first time since she'd gone into the study and found Tony stretched out on the kilim in front of his desk. A birthday present that rug had been, six or seven years back, but she'd already put it out for the binmen to take. She'd liked it, but she'd never been quite sure that he had. And she couldn't look at it now. Not after that.

'You have beautiful children,' the florist remarked while twining some strands of ivy around the pictures of Sean and Caitlin that were displayed on top of the Nolans' large teak media centre. 'Do they live local?'

'Sean does,' Sheila says. 'Just down at Lower Spernall, by St Leonard's chapel. Do you know it? He's got a lovely little cottage down there. He's been a great support, the last few days. Caitlin lives in London.'

'Is she going to be able to come home for the funeral?'

'Oh yes, of course. She'll be here tonight.'

'That's good. We'll be getting all the bouquets ready tomorrow so we can take them over to the church first thing Friday morning. We've not done a funeral in Wootton before. Is that where you're from?'

'No, not at all. Tony – my husband – he grew up in Walsall. And I'm from Sutton Coldfield.'

'Are you? Denise's boyfriend is from Sutton Coldfield, isn't he Denise?'

Denise looked up from the nest of cellophane, ribbon and trimmings in which she was kneeling and confirmed that yes, he was.

They chatted about Sutton Coldfield for a while, then the conversation moved along and then they were gone and Sheila found herself alone once more. At least now that the flowers were in place the house felt like it had escaped the awful stasis of the last few days. She primped and tidied a little, changed one or two of the things the florists had done that she hadn't much liked, and gradually worked her way back into the dining room. Still here, and so still, look at him, it didn't look like Tony, she'd never seen him still. Even when he was sleeping he'd always seemed to be shifting and flowing, undulating like some ocean creature, a walrus maybe, or a whale. That coffin, Mario Lanza all right, look at the size of it. Those hands, now they'd always be still. They hadn't been active, not like they once were, not for a long time.

But no need to worry about them, now. Not any more. After Jamie had left, it had been better. Before then, sometimes she didn't know how she'd kept it all from the children. Only really because he'd never gone for her face, apart from the night Jamie had gone, and then that was in front of them anyway, that time and that one time before. And perhaps just as well, because that's when he'd at last been able to see himself, and once he'd seen himself, he was able to stop. He wasn't a bad man. He just didn't know.

When.

To.

Stop.

Rat tat tat.

Sheila felt her heart leap in her chest, but it was just someone knocking at the window. She glanced up – it was Sean. Dear Sean. Gathering herself, she went round to the front door to greet him.

'Hi Mum.'

'Hello darling. You made me jump!'

'Oh – I didn't mean to. I just saw you in the dining room as I passed. It looks great with all the flowers and stuff.'

'Yes, it does. The ladies who did it were so lovely, and they've really done a nice job. They were from Sutton Coldfield.'

Sean came into the hallway. 'Looks splendid in here too. You have been busy.'

'Well it doesn't do to mope around.'

'I agree. Much better just to get on with things.' He paused, and smiled, not quite sure how to say the thing he needed to say next. 'So he's here then?'

'Yes, he's here.'

'They got him in okay?'

'Yes, but it was quite a job. They had this clever folding trolley they used to wheel him in on. I don't know how they'd have done it otherwise. Do you want to go in and see?'

'I think I'd better, don't you? Just quickly. I just want to say hello.'

That sounded funny to both of them, but what else did you say?

'You take as long as you want. I think I'll leave you to it if you don't mind. I've got some things to sort out in the kitchen.'

Sean. What would she do without him? It was just like him to come and talk about Tony like he was still a living, breathing person and make everything feel normal again. What would she have done without Sean to help her with the funeral arrangements, the vigil, with Tony's estate? She'd no doubt have managed well enough with the first two, but she wouldn't know where to start with the business, the assets, the probate. She wasn't equipped to deal with his lawyers, his brothers, his management team; she never had been. And how would she start that now, in the state she was in? She just thanked God for her son, who after all these years at NolCalc knew his way around that world, how to cope with all that. And would know how to cope with his sister, too, when she finally came.

'So have you heard from Caitlin?' Sean had reappeared in the kitchen and – apparently – had read her mind.

Sheila did her best to keep her voice level. 'Well, when I spoke to her on Friday she said she'd come up tonight.'

'And she hasn't called since then?'

'She has not. Has she called you?'

'Hmm. No. I hope she's okay.'

'I'm sure she's just fine. No doubt she's been busy with her many social engagements.'

'I'm not so sure, Mum. I think she'll be as upset as we are.'

'She has a funny way of showing it.'

Sheila started crying and pulled the tissue from her pocket to wipe her nose and eyes. A little awkwardly, Sean stepped up and gave her a hug.

'Oh Mum.'

'I'm sorry.'

'Don't be silly.'

'It's just that it's been so horrible, the last couple of months. I've felt so lonely. And we didn't want to tell you because we didn't want to worry you, but all that did was mean you didn't get the chance to say goodbye.'

Sean started to feel himself welling up now and lifted one hand from Sheila's back to rub at his face.

'It's okay. It's not your fault. It wouldn't have changed anything, really, even if we'd known – it all happened so suddenly. And you know how Dad hated the thought of anyone pitying him. He probably would have preferred it this way.'

Sheila sobbed and nodded and blew her nose and Sean dropped the embrace.

'I know. You're right. But I still feel wretched.'

'I think we're all going to feel pretty wretched for quite a while yet.'

'Yes.'

He looked around the kitchen for something else to do with his hands. 'Shall I put the kettle on?'

'Oh, yes. Please. I've got lunch if you'd like some. There's a fresh loaf and Connie went over to Evesham yesterday and brought back some lovely sliced ham.'

'I'm not really that hungry, to be honest. Just a cup of tea will be fine. Is Connie here? I didn't see her car.'

'I gave her the day off. She's going to have her work cut out for the rest of the week, so I thought it would only be fair. I had to practically force her. She wouldn't hear of it to begin with. She's such a dear.'

The kettle began to rumble and Sheila took the opportunity to sit at the kitchen table and collect her thoughts. This alone was unusual; Sean could not remember her ever sitting there and letting someone else make the tea. When he brought over a cup she was gazing out of the French windows and over the long patio at the fields beyond, on whose left-hand side you could just make out the summit and eastern slope of Round Hill rising anomalously out of the Warwickshire plain. The view of the hill was much better from Sean's old bedroom window, from which vantage point the house and the hedges didn't get in the way, and he had looked out at its silhouette every day of his teenage years. But there was something about that image that had been bugging him for the longest time, and now, all at once, it came to him. The shape. He'd have to check back through his photographs, but he could swear that the curve of the hill's dome was almost exactly the same as that of la Duna do Por do Sol as seen from the Club Vayu in Rosaventos. God, how peculiar was that?

'I called Jamie,' he said abruptly, before he could change his mind about broaching the subject of his half-brother.

Sheila reached for her tea with two hands.

'Did you? I was wondering if you would.'

'Tony was his father, too.'

'Yes.'

'Would you have preferred that I hadn't?'

'No. I don't know.'

'I've been to see him, you know. A couple of times.'

'Yes. I thought you might have done.' Sheila had set down her teacup again and was sitting brittle and motionless, as though the slightest vibration might crack her.

'Did Dad know?'

'I don't think so.'

'I didn't want him to know.'

'I think that was wise.'

'I didn't want to hurt him.' Sean swallowed, unsure how far he could go. 'I didn't want him to hurt Jamie.'

'No.'

'Or Caitlin.'

'No.'

'Or you.'

Around them the house hovered, listened, held its breath, and for a moment it was as if they were no longer on Earth but on a strange island spun from the tides of a far distant planet. And then Sheila reached her hand across this interstellar divide, clasped her son's fingers, and squeezed. As she did so, the doorbell rang.

'That will be the wine merchants,' she said. 'With the drinks.' She sighed, a momentous sigh that closed the wormhole that had, just for an instant, collapsed space and time. 'You couldn't be a dear, Sean, and go and let them in? They're going to need help.'

Sean smiled and pushed back his chair.

'Of course Mum,' he said. 'That's what I'm here for.'

Seven miles away in Snitterfield, Margaret Wold was staring at a tree through a window. The tree was one of the two large cedars that stood to the west and the south of her house, and the window was one of the many that formed the eastern wall of her aged conservatory. She was thinking about her garden and, by extension, the land all around: the woods, the rivers, the farms. She was thinking about the land and the sky, and the relationship between them. Thinking too about the rain, or rather the lack of it. Here they were, in January, the depths of winter, and there was a drought. It was absurd, but there it was. It was on the news. On *Gardeners' Question Time*. A hosepipe ban. That was the threat. In January!

She picked up a plastic watering can, tomato-red in colour but here and there gnawed grey by the dogs, and positioned it beneath a tap, lagged with rags, that poked out from the whitewashed conservatory wall. First the Argyranthemum, then the Dianthus, then the Datura. They didn't need much, this time of year, the poor things. Just to be kept damp while they were sleeping. The Ficus was already beginning to shoot, which was early. And the Clivia needed a drink.

A twist of her wrist – wrenching the usual twinge from her joints – and out shot a veined plait of icy water. It broke across the bottom of the drum and belched a methane-rich cloud of algae-stink up through the neck of the vessel.

It was a smell that never failed to trigger a memory of one of the many gardens Margaret and Miles had visited. On this occasion visions of Cornwall's Heligan, where the two of them had spent a glorious day just the year before last, rose up in her mind. Margaret felt the sap of emotion rise in her chest at the thought, and swallowed it back.

Miles. How strange that she should have met him because he handled the sale of the house in Walsall after she and Tony had finalised their divorce. She'd had no idea what she was doing and had gone with the first number she'd found in the Yellow Pages. What if she'd picked a different firm, or if a different person had picked up the phone the day that she'd called? Would Emily, Alex and Matthew never have been? Would all their troubles and trials, their achievements and upsets, the whole family tapestry they had woven together in this house they'd all shared, would that just wink out of existence? It had to be so. And how terrifying was that, how utterly, completely contingent? That everything she counted on to be most solid hung on the stitch of one random call. Well, that and the peculiar incompatibility of her and Tony Nolan's reproductive systems. They'd never known for sure what had caused it. More recently she'd read that a woman's immune system can attack and reject a man's sperm if it doesn't give out the right molecular signals, but back then no one knew anything about any of that. Back then things were so very different. Back then it was somehow her fault, her failure. And Tony's fault, in the eyes of his family, for marrying a non-Catholic like her.

It wasn't just his parents that had opposed the match – hers had too, although their prejudice had not been religion but class. The Nolans were descended from the wave of Irish labourers that had come to Walsall to work the limekilns and the gasworks in the mid-nineteenth century. They'd made good since then, had built up a small but profitable electromechanical business of their own, with solid contracts supplying the Lincoln Works, one of the town's biggest employers, and they lived three streets away from the Jacksons in a house of comparable size. But the taint of the western slums of St Peter's parish was hard to shift. Margaret's mother thought her dazzled by Tony's smile and Kerry wit; her father, a council architect and planner, wouldn't even grant her that, and had seen the whole relationship as some kind of token Sixties rebellion. And maybe they'd both been partly right, in their way. But Tony's sense of purpose, his raw intelligence, his profound aura of struggle, of determination – these things had touched her deeply. He had never seemed to her just another boy following his father into the family firm, and so it had proved. Half the county seemed to owe Tony Nolan something now, and countless more besides. Even her father, bless him, ended up teasing her that she might have been better off staying married to him.

But then he'd gone and betrayed her, hadn't he? And for that, all these years on, she really did still blame his mother. Margaret didn't like to speak ill of the dead, but she had not once managed to think a charitable thought about Ena Nolan. A short, oblong, armoured personnel carrier of a woman, Ena had waged a slow campaign of attrition against their marriage, needling Tony so incessantly and upsettingly about their childlessness that – in Margaret's view – she'd all but driven him into the arms of Janice Blake, just so he could prove to Ena that the fault was not his.

Margaret would never forget the expression of glee in her eyes when Ena broke the news. Yes, because it had been from her that she'd heard about Janice. That had been the culminating reason she'd left. Not the infidelity. She could have forgiven Tony that. Had done, in fact. But letting her find out from her mother-in-law? With a few decades' perspective she could see that he couldn't have known that Ena would do something so blatant, so base, and so – and here she checked herself at the politically incorrect content of the thought – so female in its raw emotional cruelty. And he'd said as much at the time. But that missed the point, and this was the attendant male naïvety that to Margaret's mind proved the gendered nature of the tactic: it was the fact that he even gave his mother the opportunity to do such a thing that so hurt and outraged her, more than the fact of its being done.

Ena hadn't been able to accept Janice either, of course, the illegitimate nature of the proof her son had offered had seen to that, and after Tony had torn himself to shreds discovering that he could make neither woman happy he had written to Margaret and asked if they could meet.

Margaret was engaged to Miles by then, and living in a room rented from a family in Alvechurch where she'd found a position as a primary school teacher, so she felt secure enough to agree to the request. But she couldn't very well have Tony come to visit her in her digs, so she suggested instead that they meet in Rackhams tearoom one Saturday.

On the date in question she'd travelled into central Birmingham on one of the city's fleet of black and cream Daimler double-deckers, buses that had always reminded her of humbugs, and got off at the stop right outside the department store. She loved Rackhams: its immaculate concrete corners and two-tone blue window panels were the most modern thing in Corporation Street and promised a future more clarified and convenient than the tough, constrained decades that had followed the war. So caught up was she by this notion that when she saw Tony waiting for her by the entrance she wondered if she'd made a mistake in choosing the store as a venue. Because he surely belonged to her past now, a part of all that messy stuff that stores like Rackhams suggested she could parcel up and leave firmly behind.

They went upstairs and found a table and the waitress took their order for a pot of Lipton's and a plate of shortbread. While they waited Tony pulled out his cigarettes and began to smoke, a habit Margaret had always abhorred.

'You haven't given that up then?' she observed.

Tony grinned apologetically. 'No. Do you want me to put it out?'

She glanced around. Half the people in the room had cigarettes in their hands, but the ventilation system seemed to be coping. 'It's fine.'

Their tea came. He pushed the biscuits towards her, toyed with his cup. He seemed unwilling to talk, which wasn't like Tony. In the end she had to prompt him.

'Come on then. What is it? You didn't bring me here just to blow smoke in my face.'

'No, I didn't.' Tony stubbed out his cigarette. 'The old man's had a stroke.'

'Oh Anthony. Oh that's terrible. Is it very bad?'

'Pretty bad. He's been paralysed down the whole of one side. He can't work.'

'Who's looking after him?'

'Ma, of course. She blames me though.'

No surprise there, Margaret thought. 'Why?'

'You can ask me that?'

'The divorce?'

'That. Janice too. She's refusing to have anything to do with me, still. Won't accept any help, won't even let me see the boy. I've heaped up a big pile of it, Maggie. A lot has been said.'

'You've had it out with Ena?'

Tony lit another cigarette. 'A lot has been said.'

That was the apology. If she had blinked she'd have missed it.

It was more like an admission of guilt, to be honest. But it was close enough. Immediately Margaret could sense the flux of anger that still pulsed within her begin to subside.

'I'm going to have to take over the business,' Tony continued.

'Do you want to?'

'I've got to. Patrick and Conor aren't ready for it.'

'All right. Well. If you want my opinion, I think you can do it.'

'I'll give it my best shot.'

'You'll be fine Anthony. I know you. And if you ever need any moral support around Ena – or Janice – you know where I am.'

Tony nodded. 'She wants to call him Jamie.'

'And what do you think?'

'It's a name, isn't it? Not my choice.'

Margaret saw his eyes, always so green and clear, blur briefly with fluid. She reached across the table, took his hand, gave it a squeeze.

'You can always call me if you need to. Miles won't mind.'

'Thank you Maggie. You're a good girl. Too good for me.'

She shook her head. Now it was her turn to fight back the tears. 'It just wasn't meant to be, that's all. Friends?'

'Yes. Please. Friends.'

They finished their tea, the waitress came by and they paid. As they were preparing to leave, Tony gave her another surprise.

'I've started going to church, you know.'

Margaret looked at him and laughed, partly with genuine amazement and partly with relief at the change in his mood. 'You haven't? After everything that's happened?'

'I was walking past one day and I found myself going inside. And just sitting at the back, you know. Thinking. Not doing confession or anything.'

'Did it help?'

'A little, maybe.'

'Good. Be careful though,' Margaret teased, attempting jest but failing to prevent it from being tainted by venom. 'They suck you in.'

On the humbug bus back to Alvechurch, a Rackhams bag filled with yarns from the haberdashery on her knee and a pretty mauve cardigan that had caught her eye round her shoulders, Margaret experienced a sense of hopefulness so distinct that even all these years later she could still vividly recall it. At that moment it had seemed that her life, which had earlier taken such a terrible and destructive diversion, was heading back in the right direction again, and that everything was going to work out for the best.

And so it had proved. She and Tony had indeed remained friends. She had gone on to marry Miles and have three lovely children; he to marry Sheila and father Caitlin and Sean. And of course Tony had not only taken over Nolan Engineering but had gradually transformed it into an electronics company of some significance, adapting what became NolCalc to the advent of the integrated circuit and the semiconductor and guiding it through the oil shocks of the early Seventies, Britain's entry into the Common Market and the Winter of Discontent. In the 1980s the company even produced a machine – the Torus – that nuzzled out a niche on a silicon savannah already alive with Lynxes, Commodores, Ataris, Sinclairs, Acorns and Amstrads, brands with which Margaret became familiar when she and Miles bought a couple of them as educational tools for their children, although to Margaret's disappointment they had seemed to use them largely for playing those awful video games.

By this time NolCalc had relocated to a business park in Edgbaston and Tony had moved his family to a house in Shelfield, which Miles had found for them just as the home-computer marketplace was swamped by the IBM PCs pouring in from America – a development that Margaret remembered as a cloud hanging over the sale at the time. But the experience of building the Torus had given NolCalc the ability to adapt, and Tony switched over to producing car phones just as they became a serious business accessory, a decision that made him a very rich man.

She and Miles hadn't done too badly either, Margaret reflected. Certainly they'd had a very comfortable existence on the back of the ever-inflating property market, although it wasn't a patch on Tony's success. But all those comfortable years, all those cars and houses and holidays and private educations, had it made any of them genuinely happy? Had her premonition on the bus outside Rackhams in 1968 actually, in the end, been correct? Because look at Tony, dead now, ravaged by lung cancer from all those horrible cigarettes he'd smoked, gone to his grave unreconciled with Jamie and barely on speaking terms with his daughter. And while she and Miles were stable enough, Alex and Matthew were forever at each other's throats and poor lovely Emily, the most sensible one of them all, was having such terrible problems finding a job, not to mention a husband. If anything, life for her children appeared to be getting harder and more complicated as time went on, and she worried for them now more than—

'Oh!'

The water had overflowed, she'd lost her grip on the can, and there was the Clivia in a clump on the floor: a molehill of soil crowned with terracotta shards and mashed, startled stalks, with the water pooling darkly around it and soaking into her deck shoes – Matthew's deck shoes, really, cast-offs from years before, though she'd got more use out of them than he ever had.

She shut off the tap and lifted the watering can in an underhand grip by one of its struts, feeling the muscles tighten down her back and pull on her hip as she did so. The hip sang out sharply with pain, a high note over the deep bass ache that never really went away. Nor would it ever, now, she supposed. Part of her wanted just to let go, to drop the can on the floor and leave the mess to its own devices. But that part had never been given much rein, and kick and scream though it might she didn't see any reason to give in to it now, bad joints or not. And there was the broken plant in the midst of it all, reaching up to her in supplication.

'Oh dear, oh you poor thing. What have I done?'

Talking to plants now, was she? A sure sign she was losing her marbles.

Then: Emily's voice, calling to her from somewhere inside the house.

'Mum? Is everything all right?'

A pause. Trembling hands.

'Fine, dear. It's all fine. Don't you worry.'

She went down on her knees, began to pick the sharp pieces of pottery from the damp rooty tangle.

It was all so damn silly and she didn't understand.

Emily's footsteps behind her. 'Oh Mum. Let me help.'

'No, no, it's all right. I'm just a clumsy thing.'

She'd cut herself on one of the potsherds, she now saw.

'You're bleeding, Mum. It's not all right. Come on.'

Emily knelt and started gathering the fragments and placing them into a bucket.

'Careful of the roots.'

'I am being careful. We'll find a nice new container for it. I'm sure it'll survive, if it hasn't been killed by the shock of the fall.'

Margaret stood and watched her daughter. She was a good girl, Emily. A strong back and good hips. And her hair. She'd often wondered from where she had got such beautiful hair. It wasn't from her or from Miles, that was for certain. Most likely was Miles's aunt Abigail, who had been something of a sensation at Emily's age. She'd died of TB at thirty-five, and all that was left of her now was the little sepia photograph that hung in the dining room, framed in an oval of inky black card, and the crocheted bedspread she'd once made that they kept in the oak chest on the landing, folded into a plastic bag to keep out the moths. One day, perhaps not very long from now, those too would be gone, and there would be no trace of Aunt Abigail left on the face of the Earth.

Already Emily had things tidied up nicely, had even managed to get the Clivia back in a pot. A plastic pot that was too cramped for it, yes, but it would serve for the moment. Margaret felt the clamp on her chest start to ease, and taking the plant from her daughter she returned it to its place on one of the wooden display stands, where she brushed off its leaves and pressed her thumbs reassuringly into the dark crumbles of soil round its stem.

Minerals flowed up her fingers; air tumbled into her lungs.

'You don't need to go to the funeral on Friday,' Margaret said, 'but I think you should go to the vigil. I think Sheila and Caitlin would like it if you dropped by. Caitlin works in television, you know. She's a producer.'

'Does she?' Emily's surprise was genuine. She never ceased to be confounded by the reach of the Warwickshire gossip network. Despite not knowing how to use the Internet and being incapable of operating a mobile phone, her mother managed to keep tabs on an extraordinary range of people and their various activities. 'I had no idea.'

'You could drop in tomorrow and say hello.'

'Yes, okay Mum. I get the hint. I'll go and do my civic duty.'

'You might enjoy it.'

'It's a vigil, Mum. Not a drinks party.'

'What I meant was, you might enjoy seeing Caitlin. You'll probably find you've got plenty in common.'

So it was that after lunch the next day Emily put on the dress and jacket that she kept dry-cleaned for interviews and drove over to Shelfield. She knew what her mother had been getting at by encouraging her to see Caitlin: because Caitlin worked in media, the thought process would have gone, chatting with Caitlin might help Emily find a new job. But Margaret had no comprehension of the cultural gap that separated the worlds of TV and print. It was a bit like suggesting that Wayne Rooney have a chat with the England rugby coach about the possibility of doing a stint as a prop forward. Just because football and rugby were both ball games, and Rooney looked a bit like a prop forward, it didn't mean his skills would transfer across.

The world had simply grown more specialised since her mother's generation had been in the jobs market, which had been buoyed for decades by the bottomless pit of baby-boomer demand and the consequent efflorescence of global trade. Things weren't like that now. Somehow careers had become codified into weird abstruse specialities that often seemed to defy any basic economic sense. Work was now a world of doubt that demanded that everyone buy into it with absolute unwavering conviction while simultaneously pretending that none of it mattered a jot, and Emily couldn't begin to claim that she understood the logic behind its most basic topologies. But one thing was for sure: it was no longer so easy to endlessly reinvent yourself with nothing in your back pocket but a liberal arts degree and an appetite for adventure. Not even if you worked in marketing.

On some level Emily was sure that property prices took some share of the blame. Finding a place to live was now a vertiginous activity fraught with risk, as ever-higher rents sucked up an ever-larger proportion of your income and the scale of the mortgage required to secure even a modest flat in a crappy area had grown dizzyingly large. Getting a foot on the housing ladder, they called it, and Emily supposed the theory was that this ladder would take you up. But whenever she heard the term she thought, not of sturdy wooden struts giving you access to higher things, but of ladders in her tights, unstoppable rips in the fine fabric of being that pulled you only downwards.

Part of Emily's own little rebellion against her parents had been to resist their mantra of bricks and mortar as the only sure core for a life and turn down their repeated offers throughout her early twenties of helping her to buy a small flat in London. And now – as her estate-agent father took every opportunity to remind her – the cost of even entry-level studios was so high, and her salary as a journalist – when she'd still had it – by comparison so paltry that she'd effectively missed her chance. She could have got a loan, that wasn't the problem: banks had been falling over themselves to lend to her while she'd been at *Hudson*. But the sheer amount of money she'd needed to borrow, not to mention the size of the monthly repayments she'd have to provide for, had been more than she'd been able to contemplate. Her only realistic option now was to let her parents buy her a property outright by selling something else in Miles's portfolio so that she could in effect live rent-free at her family's expense. They'd made it clear that this offer was available, but despite losing her job and moving back in with them while she looked for new employment, Emily had not yet been able to swallow her pride and take them up on it.

This was partly, she knew, because of what had happened with Laetitia. The whole episode had left her incapable of making anything that approached a life decision. She no longer knew what she wanted to do, or where she wanted to do it. All she did know was that she never wanted to deal with anyone like Laetitia ever again.

It had all started so well. Too well even – and perhaps that, in retrospect, had been the warning sign. Most people, in Emily's limited experience, began a new job with a certain amount of reticence and deference towards their new colleagues, at least until they'd learned the ropes and got a sufficient handle on things to be sure that their ideas and contributions were genuinely valid.

Not Laetitia. She'd had strong opinions on everything from the office decor to the magazine's design from the moment she'd got her knees under her new desk – and strong opinions about everyone around her, as well. She'd straight away placed Emily in the role of confidante and couldn't make a trip to the toilet without having some kind of encounter that she felt the immediate need to analyse in a stagey low voice across their desks or, if that was too undiplomatic even for her, via email or instant messenger.

'Oh my God, I just ran into so-and-so – you should have seen the way she looked at me! It's because of that comment you made in the meeting the other day about the beauty page. They just hate us, you know. They're so spoiled with all their free spa days and complimentary sample boxes, they don't know they're born . . .'

In the beginning this sort of thing was quite amusing. Her assistant's frequent cigarette breaks were an inexhaustible font of gossip of all kinds, and Laetitia's observations, while cutting, also seemed light-hearted and insightful. She had a satirist's eye for weakness and vanity, and after so long chafing under the features yoke in what practically amounted to solitary confinement Emily found Laetitia's Puckish willingness to say the things that she'd often privately thought about her workmates or the models and celebrities who danced their way across the pages of *Hudson* quite refreshing.

Part of Laetitia's confidence clearly stemmed from having worked directly with Heather Monk on another title, giving her a clearer view than Emily had of the corporate structure of which *Hudson* formed just one column. Indeed, it was merely one of a collection of titles that made up the women's 'vertical', as the various subcomponents of the small publishing empire were called, other verticals being cars, travel, design, technology and so on – a list that more or less corresponded to Emily's feature sections, but had entire buildings and the output of multiple editorial staffs devoted solely to them.

Two things about this made Emily uneasy. The first was that her job, indeed her entire creative output as a journalist and her romantic *raison d'être* for as long as she could remember, had turned out to amount to little more than a tiny market-tuned line item on some colossal financial spreadsheet. That all her hopes and dreams should have been so casually anticipated and captured in this way, Emily found depressing and somewhat demeaning. The second was the nonchalance with which Laetitia not only accepted this facet of reality without any hint of angst, but negotiated its geography as pragmatically as a parrot fish cruising around a reef in search of tasty bits of coral to nibble. Though she was only three years her assistant's senior, this made Emily feel almost geriatric by comparison. Here she was, a member of an older generation still riling against the inevitability of the capitalist status quo, her attitudes about as useful as a Zimmer frame in a marathon.

But if age was the issue Laetitia didn't seem to notice. She was evidently thrilled by all things Emily; a bit too thrilled, if anything. She was always a little bit too personal with her questions about Emily's background, thoughts, life; a little bit too ready to assume a bond between the two of them that didn't yet exist. And what started out as professional courtesy on Emily's part, making the newcomer feel welcome with a couple of trips to the nearest Prêt-à-Manger to grab some lunch and a couple of post-work drinks in the wine bar near the station, seemed to be interpreted by her assistant as a signal that they should always eat together, should always consult over social plans. It quickly added up to an over-familiarity that, while it had been touching to begin with, was soon putting Emily on edge.

Worse, though, was the turn Laetitia's gossip began to take after her first few months in the job: a slow but definite drift from the volleys of acerbic but randomly targeted *bons mots* to more focused patterns of fire that were clearly designed to delineate 'us' – 'us' being Laetitia and Emily – from 'them' – 'them' being everyone else, grouped according to various sub-labels that Laetitia had already dreamed up.

Emily didn't like this at all. She was, she told herself, happy enough not to pull rank on her one and only team member. Flat working hierarchies were cool – 'Hot or Not' had said so only two months before. But she was not a stirrer by nature, she got on well with most of her colleagues whatever their various shortcomings, and she had no desire to see tensions introduced into office relationships that she found it hard enough to manage as it was.

It didn't help that the quality of Laetitia's work was not exactly stellar. She'd come through her probation period well enough – the period in which, Emily now observed with hindsight, her charm offensive had been launched. But six months in and Emily was still pulling her up on operational basics regarding the software they used and the workflows they were supposed to adhere to, as well as chasing her continually to complete tasks – handling the contributors' invoices for example – that had been firmly defined as her remit.

It wasn't that Laetitia did nothing; it was rather that she saw her responsibilities as a kind of smorgasbord of options from which she could pick and choose at will, rather than a set menu that she was in fact supposed to be delivering to order. On top of that her timekeeping was terrible – she was late almost every day and pulled continual sickies. When she was in work and not on one of her many breaks, she was constantly checking various social media sites or making personal calls on her phone. And worst of all she'd managed to upset at least three of their best writers, creating rifts that required a great deal of soft-soaping on Emily's part to resolve.

In an attempt not to become a dictatorial boss, Emily dropped repeated hints designed to help Laetitia appreciate the fact that her behaviour was deeply problematic. Initially the assistant seemed to take these suggestions seriously, saying how horrified she was that she should have given such an impression and assuring Emily that things would get better. When they didn't, and Emily had to reiterate her guidance rather more assertively in their quarterly 360-degree review meeting, there was a scene.

'I can't believe you're saying that about me!' Laetitia spluttered when Emily directly criticised her for leaving the office at whim and spending working hours dealing with her personal issues. 'I thought we were friends.'

'We are friends, but I also have to be your boss and make sure we get our jobs done.'

'Well there's way too much to do, even for two people. I don't know how you ever coped on your own. They're exploiting us, you know.'

'That's not really the issue here.' *And we'd cope fine if you would just pull your fucking weight,* Emily thought. 'Look, maybe it would be better if I didn't come to that Tom Waits gig with you on Thursday.'

Laetitia looked at Emily with an expression that could not have been more stunned if she had taken the fire extinguisher from the corner of the room and dropped it on her foot.

'You can't, you can't do that!'

'I just think . . .'

'Are you completely crazy? He hasn't played here for seventeen years! I told Carter' – Carter was Laetitia's boyfriend, whom Emily had never met but about whom she had heard a great deal – 'I told Carter he couldn't go because I'd promised I'd take you. Have you even seen what those tickets are trading for on eBay? They're going for like £400!'

Emily had no idea why Laetitia slipped into a mid-Atlantic drawl when she was stressed or excited. Carter's influence, perhaps (he was Canadian). But she didn't like it and it made her even less inclined to spend another evening in her company. On the other hand, given the tension that was now in the air, maybe it didn't make much sense to ratchet things up any further. And she did rather want to go to Tom Waits . . .

'Okay. I'll come. I would like to. But you have to understand that I need you to take these issues seriously. I'm always here if you want to discuss anything, or if you've got problems and need to book some time off. But you must, must, must talk to me about things first instead of just disappearing whenever you feel like it. Otherwise it just makes it impossible for me to plan anything.'

Laetitia jumped up, came round the meeting table, and enveloped Emily in a hug.

'I do, I will, I understand. Things will be better, I promise. I'm going to take on board what you've said, I really am. I know how hard it must have been for you to say it, and how patient you've been with me. Things are going to change!' She disengaged and sniffed up a smile, then clapped her hands together like a little girl. 'Oh I'm so glad you're coming on Thursday! I really am! My friend Honor who got us the tickets says she can get us into the after-party. And some amazing people are going to be there. Thom Yorke and Jerry Hall, apparently . . . It's going to be awesome!'

The concert was indeed awesome, as well as awesomely loud, the singer's voice making Emily's brain vibrate as he ground his way through the set like some kind of giant industrial machine in urgent need of lubrication. Thom Yorke and Jerry Hall were indeed there – Emily saw them both – and so Honor clearly had the inside track, which wasn't surprising, since she turned out to be the tour's publicist.

'Thanks so much for the preview,' she beamed to Emily when Laetitia introduced them at the after-party, held in a little basement nightclub about five minutes' walk from the Hammersmith Apollo that had been booked for the occasion.

'Oh right,' Emily said, as the glow from the gig was extinguished by the sticky realisation that the tickets must have been a payoff for the preview piece Laetitia had written for the music section in *Hudson*'s latest issue. It wasn't a mortal sin, and most journalists in London wouldn't have given a second thought to accepting a freebie for an event they'd written up – this kind of perk was generally regarded as appropriate compensation for the low rates they were paid. But *Hudson*'s owners were American, and the Americans took a dimmer view of that kind of thing than the Brits did. Tickets for shows were supposed to be expensed and thus rendered visible to Accounts as a legitimised editorial cost, just as flights were. Books had to be returned to publishers, gadgets to PRs. Beauty products and booze were allowed to slip under the radar, as these couldn't really be tested without simultaneously being consumed. But tickets weren't in this category, although sometimes you could half convince yourself that they should be. Laetitia had clearly done just that, though Emily knew exactly what Bronwyn would say if she found out.

But Bronwyn didn't mention the tickets and nor did anyone else, and for the next few weeks things with Laetitia seemed to settle into a happier rhythm. She came into work more or less on time, did more or less what she was asked, and remained on more or less good terms with her colleagues. Emily took care not to overload her or push her too hard on minor infringements, figuring that in this particular circumstance less was most certainly more. But it was to prove a mere lull in the escalation of hostilities, and the last such one before outright war broke out.

The final act began one Monday morning, when Laetitia just didn't show up. Ten a.m. came and went without any sign of her. Ten-thirty, eleven, and still no Laetitia, not even a text to say she'd be late. By eleven-thirty Emily had called her three times and emailed her twice with no response on either channel. She was beginning to wonder if something genuinely catastrophic had befallen her assistant – she'd been stricken by a freak case of Ebola, or knocked down by a bus – when shortly after lunch in she wafted looking as battered and beaten down as a discarded fast-food carton blowing down a windswept street, and apparently as incapable of speech.

Unable to get any sense out of her in the panopticon of the open-plan, Emily steered her into an empty meeting room, in whose relative privacy she managed to extract Laetitia's latest tale of woe.

'Carter's left me,' she said eventually, once she'd stopped gasping long enough to catch a proper breath. 'We had a massive row last night, and about two o'clock this morning he just packed his bags and walked out.'

'Oh no,' said Emily, wondering how she was going to cope given that it was press week and Laetitia was now no doubt going to be no help at all. 'That's terrible,' she added. 'You poor thing.' And she stopped there, the despair that she felt rendering her incapable of expressing further sympathy. It was all she could do to feign sufficient interest to ask Laetitia what the argument had been about.

'Oh I don't know! Nothing! That's the stupid thing! Nothing at all! You know what these things are like.' Emily didn't, but knowing what Laetitia was like she could imagine the rest. 'You start out bickering because you've run out of milk and the next thing you know you're screaming at each other and throwing things. The fact is he's not been happy since I took you to that Tom Waits gig instead of him. He's been on and on about it, and it came up again last night. He thinks I betrayed him.'

'Over tickets for a concert?'

'You don't understand. Tom Waits is like Carter's total idol. He's obsessed.'

'So why didn't you take him? Why take me?'

'Oh but I'd had such a bad appraisal and I just wanted to make things better.'

Emily couldn't help it. She could actually feel the carotid artery bulging in her neck. If she didn't say something it was going to burst. Either that or the backpressure was going to give her a cerebral haemorrhage.

'Well that was your choice. If you recall I did point out at the time that all you needed to do was show up on time and do your fucking work.' She shouldn't have said fucking. She knew she shouldn't have said fucking. But it just squirted out like the plug of pus at the core of a particularly deep and angry zit, and when it did the release of pressure felt just so fucking good.

'But I have been, I have been! I've been trying so hard.'

'Yes,' Emily sighed, 'yes you have.'

'So why are you swearing at me? Why are you swearing? This isn't my fault!'

If the heads turning on the main floor were any indication, Laetitia's voice had reached a pitch capable of penetrating the meeting room's thick glass wall. In an attempt at damage limitation Emily jumped up and fiddled with the Perspex control rods that rotated the internal blinds. Two of them functioned correctly but the third had developed some kind of fault, a jammed pinion or cracked cog, and its slats remained stubbornly horizontal. She yanked at it in frustration and there was a soft crack as the rod snapped from its fixing and came off in her hand.

Gripping it like a whip, she turned back to face her assistant. 'But it's never your fault, is it Laetitia? When are you going to start to take some responsibility, huh? When?!'

Laetitia looked from Emily to the plastic rod and back again. Then, her face absolutely rigid, she retreated slowly backwards. When she reached the door she grabbed the handle, slipped from the room and fled down the other side of the glass partition in the direction of the lifts.

Emily was still standing holding the rod and trying to digest what had just happened when Miranda Walton stuck her head in through the open doorway.

'Is everything okay?' she asked, through a smile of precisely calculated benignity.

'Laetitia's in a bit of a state,' Emily flailed. 'Boyfriend issues.' She lowered the rod, glanced around for a bin to put it in, anything. 'And I broke this.'

'Well, if you need any help . . .'

'No, thanks. It'll be fine, I think. She probably just needs some time. I think I can cope.'

But Emily couldn't cope. Not with the way things progressed.

Laetitia didn't reappear that day, but she did turn up the next, arriving on time and getting on with her work. She was pale though, and almost completely silent. When she did speak she took care to keep the subject matter strictly limited to the task in hand and used a low, tremulous voice clearly and somewhat pathetically intended to evoke sympathy. Unfortunately for Laetitia, Emily rather liked this new assistant who kept her mouth shut and got on with her job, and she was able to avoid rising to the bait until the edition was put to bed at the end of the week.

'So, how are things?' Emily asked casually, as they were packing up for the day.

Laetitia shrugged as if the desperate need to emote was the last thing on her mind.

'Oh, you know,' she squeaked. 'Not great.'

'Did you patch things up with Carter?'

‘Nope. He came back and took the rest of his stuff while I was at work on Tuesday.’

‘Oh dear.’

‘It was his flat and he’s given notice to the landlord. I can’t afford to take it on, not on what they pay us here, so next month I’m homeless unless I can find somewhere else to live.’

Emily’s next ‘Oh’ was different. Things were clearly a bit more serious than she’d realised – perhaps Laetitia was genuinely in trouble.

‘I don’t know how I’m going to find a room in, like, three weeks. You know what it’s like trying to get a place.’ It was true. Getting a half-decent rental in London that was clean, convenient and secure and not hopelessly overpriced could take months of footwork. All the agencies had horrific waiting lists and anything good that was advertised in Loot or on Craigslist got snapped up within the space of a few minutes. ‘You live in a shared house, right?’ she continued. ‘I don’t know, maybe one of your roommates is moving out or something? If you hear of anything will you let me know?’

Emily gulped. ‘Yes, of course.’ In fact someone in her house had only recently announced their intention to leave, but the thought of living with Laetitia as well as working with her was more than she could stomach.

She might have dodged this particular bullet, but Emily would nonetheless find her life dominated by Laetitia’s flat-search for the next several months. She was not spared the details of each of the twists in the saga, nor the rollercoaster of emotions that accompanied them, nor the resumption of the random absences that inevitably ensued. And of course every time Emily dared to complain about the effect all this was having on her assistant’s ability to do her job there came the immediate rejoinder that none of it would be happening if it hadn't been for Emily's taking up that ticket to go to Tom Waits.

The situation was added extra piquancy by Emily's growing suspicion, weird though it admittedly was, that Carter didn't actually exist. For no reason other than the idle curiosity to discover what kind of person would have thought it was a good idea to ever have moved in with Laetitia, she Googled him one day and drew a complete blank, something which by that point in the history of the Internet was highly unusual. Her investigative appetite whetted, she hunted through some of the new social networking sites and found nothing on them either.

After that she began to make some subtle enquiries at work under the pretext of wanting to know more about this arsehole that had left her assistant homeless. But no one other than her had ever heard of him, or for that matter had even heard of Laetitia having a boyfriend. Not that this was grounds for anything – her colleagues' private lives were their own affair, and people didn't exactly bring their partners into the office to say hi. But it did seem odd that her voluble, neurotic and relationship-obsessed assistant, who spent so much of her time examining and discussing the minutiae of the lives of everyone around her, should not have mentioned the man with whom she had been living to anyone but Emily.

Whether or not Carter was real, the notion that he wasn't and had been invented by Laetitia – to make her seem more normal perhaps? More loved? – lodged itself in Emily's brain. If there had been no Carter, then there presumably had been no flat and no sudden crisis of homelessness. Had the whole split-up been an elaborate ruse to get Emily to feel partly responsible for Laetitia's domestic situation and generate an inexhaustible source of excuses for being late to work? It surely couldn't be possible. And yet it felt like it was. In order to further test her theory she wanted to probe Laetitia for more information about the mysterious Carter, but she couldn't think of a way to do it without appearing overtly suspicious, which perhaps confirmed that it was in fact pretty odd of her to be entertaining such a theory in the first place. People didn't go around inventing other people, did they? And people didn't go around imagining that other people invented other people.

It struck Emily, as she lay awake one morning with all this swirling around in her head, that the stress of working with Laetitia was getting to her. She was in the office longer hours now than she had been before her assistant was hired, as the job of managing Laetitia took up more time than Emily was saved by the younger woman's efforts, such as they were. And when she left in the evening the Tube journey home wasn't long enough to allow her to decompress from the stress of the day: that required at least two large glasses of the crappy wine she'd started buying in boxes from Tesco's and which she stored on a shelf in her room. She'd have preferred to drink in company but her social life had completely unravelled; she hadn't seen her friends for months and had fallen out of so many loops – most of which now featured babies – that the whole social structure she'd spent so much of her late twenties earnestly piecing together seemed damaged beyond repair.

On top of all that, or more likely because of it, she wasn't sleeping properly, nodding off whenever she took a moment to sit and read or watch TV, only then to wake several times during the night. Most mornings she snapped awake some time between five and six a.m. as exhausted as if she'd not slept at all and nursing a ball of acid foam deep in her belly. She then lay in bed stressing about the possible curve balls Laetitia was going to throw her that day, until the maddening circularity of her thoughts finally drove her out from under the duvet and forced her to find the willpower to assemble the cup of tea and piece of toast that served her for breakfast.

And then came the moment that she finally snapped. The trigger was something quite trivial: Laetitia's failure to put through the payments for yet another contributor. The journalist in question had rung up and given Emily a hard time down the phone. When she'd finished the call, despite knowing absolutely that she shouldn't, Emily swivelled round in her chair until she faced her assistant.

'Did you hear that? Did you? That is what happens when you fail to make sure people get paid. She says that's the fourth time you've forgotten her. But I'm the one that gets it in the neck.'

Laetitia continued typing whatever she was typing for a few long seconds.

'Who was it?'

'Martha Samuelson. Couldn't you tell?'

'Oh, her! She is such a pain. I can't believe you even put up with that kind of crap from her. If it was me I'd just tell her to go screw herself. I mean let's face it, she can't write for shit.'

Emily actually felt her jaw go slack at this. 'I cannot believe you said that,' she spluttered. 'The quality of her writing is not the issue here. She at least files on time. It's your repeated failure to actually keep up with the most basic paperwork that's caused this situation.'

'I can't help that. I do words, not numbers. I shouldn't have to handle that kind of stuff. That's Payroll's job.'

'Are you serious?' Emily had raised her voice, she realised.

'Yes I'm serious. You're always complaining about our workload, but it's that kind of bullshit that wastes our time. If you stood up for us like an editor should and got the people who were supposed to be doing that kind of thing to do it instead of bouncing it down the line onto me, then we wouldn't have a problem.'

Emily didn't know how to respond to this. Like so much of what Laetitia said the notion contained a quantum of truth, but it was being used as a spice to disguise the rotten nature of the major ingredients: her own work ethic and attitude.

'I cannot deal with this,' she said, far too loudly. 'I cannot deal with you right now. I need to, I just need to . . . I just need to take a break.'

Before she really knew what she was doing, Emily found herself doing a Laetitia: heading down in the lifts, out the building and across the street to the little park for want of anywhere else to go. She'd never really smoked, but now she bummed a Silk Cut off a man sitting on one of the benches and stood at the base of a large London plane tree, whose leaves she hoped would hide her from anyone looking down into the square from the office, and puffed away in the mistaken belief that a hit of nicotine would help calm her down. The cigarette, however, only succeeded in making her feel sick and light-headed and in need of something to remove the foul taste in her mouth. Leaving the square, she cut through to Buckingham Palace Road and strode past the souvenir shops and restaurants until she found a café capable of serving a reasonable cup of coffee. She briefly considered going into a pub and having a brandy but decided against it. It wasn't even lunchtime, and she was at some point going to have to go back into work. She allowed herself a mocha and a slab of rocky road instead and returned to the park to consume them before tackling the re-ascent to her desk.

Miranda intercepted her before she got past the door of the kitchenette.

'Ah, Emily. There you are. Can I have a word?'

'Um, sure.'

'Bronwyn's out today. We can use her room.'

Emily followed the deputy editor as she threaded her way across the production floor, reddening as she went – it all smacked of being sent to see the headmistress, and the fact that no one dared lift their eyes to look at her made it that much worse. Laetitia, she noted, was not at her computer, and she hoped to God that she wasn't already in Bronwyn's office waiting for Miranda to adjudicate their row. But the room was empty, and when they entered Miranda went and sat behind Bronwyn's desk in Bronwyn's chair and waved Emily onto the low two-seater sofa pushed against one of the walls opposite a giant framed print of the cover of the inaugural issue of *Hudson*.

The cushions were soft and Emily sank into them as she sat. She couldn't very well lean backwards and it wasn't possible to lean forwards either, so she was forced to sit bolt upright on the very lip of the seat, her body angled so that she could face the deputy editor, her legs folded so that her knees were above the height of her hips. It wasn't a position of strength.

'I'm sorry about earlier, Miranda,' Emily began. 'Maybe you were right to ask me if I could cope. Things have been very difficult with Laetitia. Actually I'm quite glad of a chance to discuss—'

Miranda cut her off. 'Emily, before you go any further I think you should know that Laetitia has made a formal complaint against you.'

Emily forced a smile. 'What, already? And then gone off home I expect. This is part of the issue—'

'Not today. After your last appraisal meeting. It's very serious. She says you've been subjecting her to an on-going campaign of bullying and victimisation. She says you threatened her with a plastic rod.'

Unable to process the whole of this statement, Emily made the mistake of reacting to the last thing Miranda had said.

'What? The thing you use to twist the blinds? That broke off in my hand when I was trying to give us some privacy. I mean, you came in and saw me holding it.'

'Yes,' said Miranda. 'I did. Right after Laetitia had run out of the room very clearly upset.'

'And she's saying I threatened her with it? But that's ridiculous.'

'She says that she felt physically intimidated.'

'Well it amounts to the same thing.'

'Does it?'

Emily swallowed, acutely conscious now of her disadvantageous posture. She wanted more than anything to stand up, but knew that would be a very bad idea.

'You must realise that these are very serious accusations, and that we have to take them very seriously.'

'But all I've done, ever since she started, is try to help her out!' Emily protested, her voice uncontrollably shrill.

'I'm afraid she doesn't see it that way.'

'I don't believe this. It's just beyond belief that she would do this. After all the slack I've cut her . . .'

'She also says that you've committed several breaches of our editorial code.'

'Like what?'

Miranda peered down at a piece of paper that was lying in front of her on Bronwyn's desk.

'Well, one of them was apparently to do with accepting some tickets for a Tom Waits gig.'

That was it. Emily could no longer restrain herself. She jumped up and strode across the room.

'That is a bare-faced fucking lie! She wrote that piece and got those tickets.'

'Apparently she claims you authorised it. That you knew the PR personally.'

'Only because she introduced me to her. Christ! What a total fucking bitch.'

'So you did know about it then? Look, you can say what you like in front of me, Emily, but I think you need to consider your position very carefully before you discuss it with Brendan and Heather.'

'You're not serious?'

'I'm afraid I am. Something like this . . . I'm not authorised to deal with it. I have no choice but to take it upstairs.'

'What about Bronwyn?'

'Bronwyn would say the same thing.'

'Oh please don't, Miranda. At least let me give you my side of the story.'

'It's too late for that, I'm afraid. They've already been informed. And it wouldn't make any difference anyway. Like I say, it's out of my hands. They'll be in touch with you about next steps within a day or two. In the meantime, you're going to have to take a paid leave of absence from work. It's the same for Laetitia. I'll pick up your duties in the interim. You can take me through everything today before you go home.'

Miranda stood up, came round the desk and put her hand on Emily's shoulder. 'Don't worry, okay? I'm sure this is all just a big misunderstanding. Heather and Brendan have a lot of experience of handling these kinds of issues. No one is out to get you. All they'll be interested in is trying to get everything resolved.'

For the first time since they'd met in the corridor Miranda smiled. It was a nice smile, not one of the deputy editor's calculated semi-grimaces but a heartfelt expression of kindness that transmitted real sympathy.

And that just made it worse.

Emily pushed the painful memory aside: she had arrived in Shelfield and needed to concentrate on finding a parking slot among the long line of cars drawn up on the verge in the lane. Once she'd done that she walked back along the line to the blocky, white, overbearing and – to her eyes – unappealing edifice of the Nolans' house to pay her respects.

There were a lot of people inside. In the living room, the hallway, the kitchen, in a small marquee erected over the patio. It was buzzier than she'd expected, more sociable. People stood chatting in knots of three and four, holding drinks and plates of food. The atmosphere was subdued, yes, but not overly serious or woeful. Maybe she'd been wrong about the drinks-party aspect. She wondered how many of the attendees were honestly grieving over the fact that Tony was dead. When a rich man dies, she supposed, plenty of folk stand to profit. Only those who walk away with nothing really get upset.

The cynicism of the thought made her check herself. She'd been a journalist too long. Reducing and generalising people's motives like that was the opposite of what this event was supposed to be about. She pondered going to say hello to Sheila, whom she'd spotted in the living room, but Tony's widow was deep in conversation with a jowly older man Emily vaguely recognised as one of

Caitlin's uncles. What she needed to do was to find Caitlin, but so far she hadn't seen her anywhere.

She was about to thread her way through to the patio when someone touched her on the arm. It was Sean.

'You haven't got a glass.'

Emily smiled apologetically. 'I'm driving.'

'I'm sure you can have a mouthful of something. It's nice wine, some cases that Dad had already bought. Me and Mum figured he wasn't going to drink it, so we might as well.' He led her over to the cloth-covered table that was serving as a bar and handed her one of the flutes of tawny liquid that had been set out in long ranks.

'So,' he said. 'How are you?'

'Shouldn't I be asking you that?'

'People have been asking me that all week long. Quite frankly, I'm sick to . . .' He paused and sucked his teeth. 'It wouldn't have been very tasteful to finish that sentence, would it?'

Emily grinned. It was strange. She'd completely forgotten about Sean. She tried to work out how many times they'd met. It couldn't have been more than a few. She recalled him as a quiet presence in the various country pubs they'd all hung out in as teenagers, hovering lightly behind the more charismatic figures of Caitlin and Jamie. He'd been shy and ungainly, not unlike Matthew in that way, ears and nose too big for his face, dark curls adrift and unmanageable, clothes that didn't quite fit. But unlike her brother, who still had an unkempt and puppyish air, Sean had grown into his features. Relaxed into them, if you like: he had the kind of good looks that didn't impress much at first but rewarded a second, more appraising glance. He was tidy without being rigid, smart without being uptight, and his once-chubby body now moved fluidly just below the surface of his suit. He was an inch shorter than Emily, too, which made him seem cute.

'You work for *Hudson*, don't you?' he asked, then added: 'Don't worry, Mum told me. I haven't been stalking you.'

'God, the Warwickshire mothers' network. Nothing escapes them does it?' Sean laughed at this, nodding in recognition. 'Well I'm afraid that for once the information is a bit out of date,' Emily continued, with a rueful expression. 'I lost my job.'

'Oh. That doesn't sound good,' Sean said, his smile straightening out, and Emily suddenly felt the full weight of the previous few months weighing upon her, something that Sean in turn seemed to pick up. 'What happened?' he asked.

'Long story.'

'Give me the short version.'

Emily had that rehearsed. 'I got into a bad situation with someone at work. An HR situation. It got really nasty and complicated and I didn't have a paper trail to prove my case so it ended up being my word against hers. I was offered voluntary redundancy as a way to make it go away and in the end it was just easier to take it.'

'Wow,' Sean said. 'That sounds like hell.'

'It was. That's why I left. It soured things so much that even if I'd fought and won I knew I wouldn't want to stay.'

'What are you doing now?'

'Nothing really, I'm ashamed to say. I looked for something in London for a bit but then I started running out of money. So I've moved back up here while I think things through, work out what I want to do next.'

'Can you find something on another magazine?'

'I don't know if I want to. The industry's not what it was. On *Hudson* we were so under-resourced all the time – that's partly what caused the problem in the first place. People don't see why they should pay for content any more, not when there's so much available for free on the web. We're losing readers hand over fist, and the advertising is all heading online.'

She expected him to apologise again on behalf of her circumstances – that's what most people did. But he didn't. Instead he said: 'That's hard. Do you have any digital skills?'

'Some. Not really. It's not like I can code. I was thinking of writing a novel,' she said, half-jokingly.

'You should do it! At least it'll put you back in control. I'll buy a copy! Hey – you know what? I sat up all night last night, did the vigil for Dad, and I've been chatting and handing out drinks all morning. I need a break and a change of clothes, and I'm about to shoot back to my place. Fancy coming along? There's something I'd like to you to see. It might inspire you.'

Emily was intrigued. It sounded more fun than standing around trying to make polite conversation. 'I should really say hi to Caitlin . . .'

'Oh, Cait's upstairs right now, getting some rest. She's doing the vigil tonight, so she's off-duty right now.'

'Okay. Well, then – why not, I suppose.'

As they left the house Emily found herself speculating about the kind of car Sean drove, and now she found out: his was the mud-spattered Toyota pick-up parked in the driveway, looking slightly incongruous among the Mercedes and Jaguars driven by the rest of the Nolan clan. While he backed it out she went down the road and eased her Renault off the verge.

Sean drew up alongside her and called to her through his open passenger window. 'It's really close. You know the bridge over the Arrow? Just before that.'

And then they were off through the countryside at local-knowledge speeds, haring down the luge-like cutting carved into Round Hill and playing cat and mouse along the ancient, sinuous curves of Spernal Lane, occasional flashes of low winter sun catching the crystals of frost in the parallel crests of the hedgerows and transforming the dull woody corridor into an effervescent maze of brilliant intensity, jagged with gleaming spectral light.

When the iron pipework of the little bridge came into view the Toyota duly slowed and indicated left, then turned down an unmetalled track. They passed the pretty gabled rectory on the corner which Emily had always rather coveted, and then the humble medieval stone peaks of St Leonard's chapel, long since deconsecrated, the yew by its porch taller than its little steeple, the tilting headstones in its tiny cemetery frozen like a symposium of druids scanning the sky for a sign. The two vehicles trundled along the track for a few hundred yards, the grit kicked up by their tyres noisily peppering their wheel arches, then pulled around a giant steel-framed grain dryer clad in dark-blue corrugated iron and into a square concrete yard bordered by a long cottage to the west and to the south, built from the same orange Darlaston brick, a low Victorian barn.

Emily drew up alongside the Toyota and got out.

'This your place then?' she asked Sean, who was lifting a bag out of the back of his truck.

'Yep. What do you think?'

'Great. What do you do in the barns?'

'Well the big one's not mine. That's owned by the local farmer. The dryer fans run twenty-four hours during the harvest, which can be a bit of a pain, but the rest of the time not much goes on there. This one, however' – he gestured towards the brick building – 'is mine. And that's what I want to show you. Come on.'

He led the way to the building's eastern end, which was fitted with two large grey barn doors. One of these was inset with a smaller, human-scale entrance, and through this they passed, entering a space dominated by a long central workbench that stretched the length of the building and was cluttered with aluminium propellers sporting viciously curved blades, luridly sprayed metal baskets, and all kinds of other components very few of which Emily recognised. The walls were lined with tools and webbing, there was a rubber floor the same colour as the doors, and track lighting pinned to the barn's rafters augmented the daylight streaming in through the rows of windows set into the roof. The whole workshop had the same homely air of efficiently managed untidiness as Sean himself, and this impression was further enhanced by the waft of freshly brewed coffee from a kitchenette at the far end of the space.

Sean dumped his bag and called out to a bearded man in a plaid shirt and denim dungarees who was standing rinsing mugs in the sink. 'Hey Rick! Smells like we've come at a good time.'

'Yeah man. Brew's up!'

'Crack out the biscuits, will you? We've got a guest.'

He led the way through the tangle of gear and offered Emily a stool at their little food counter.

'Rick, Emily; Emily, Rick. Emily's an old family friend. Rick is my business partner.'

'Hey. Pleased to meet you. How do you take your java?'

'Just a dash of milk please.'

Rick poured the coffees and passed them around.

'What do you make here?' Emily asked. 'Looks like air-conditioning or something.'

The two men chuckled in unison.

'No, not air-con. You're not the first to think that, though.'

Sean went over to the central bench where one of the circular steel baskets, as yet unpainted, lay on its side, its bruise-like welding scorches still visible. He stood it up. It was about a metre in diameter: a motor nestled inside the concavity, and from the convex side a harness dangled, quite an elaborate one, with shoulder straps and padding like those on an expensive mountaineering backpack. Emily had never seen anything quite like it.

'Behold,' said Sean, picking up one of the propellers and slotting it onto the stubby axle that protruded from the engine at the centre of the cage, 'a Dragon Paramotor. Special edition.'

'It looks like some kind of jetpack.'

Sean and Rick hooted again.

'Sort of. You do fly it. But you need a canopy too. You know, like a paraglider.' He pointed to a large poster on the wall showing a man soaring high above the Brecon Beacons in a fan-equipped harness, suspended from an orange nylon wing with a 'Dragon Paramotors' logotype emblazoned across it.

'And you do this for fun?'

'It is *so* much fun.'

'It looks terrifying!'

'It's different once you're up there – it's the best feeling in the world. Total freedom, really like being a bird. I'd love to show you some time.'

'Hmm. I think I'd need some convincing.'

'Convincing can be done, right Rick?'

'Oh yeah. We've taken all kinds of people up. As long as the conditions are good it's actually really safe.'

Emily listened while they recounted some of their more memorable flying experiences.

'I started it up because I needed a respite from NolCalc,' Sean explained. 'I mean, it was great, working for Dad and all. But at the end of the day I was working for Dad. Here I'm my own boss, even if it's only in my spare time.'

'Hey,' said Rick. 'I thought I was the boss?'

'Okay, well, I'm half my own boss. I fund it, he runs it, and we argue over all the decisions. But that's the joy of it. Dad was never much of a one for discussion. It was his way or the highway. Anyway,' Sean concluded, 'that's what I meant about, you know, writing a novel. Rick and me just did this because we wanted to do something of our own. It's just us and a couple of guys we've hired to help with the sales side and the metalwork. It's important to do that, to have something that's yours, even if it's just something small. Who knows? It might grow into something bigger. Maybe it will, maybe it won't, but you'll never know till you try.'

They were wise words and Emily felt a little embarrassed to hear them. She'd set out that day to show her support for the Nolans, and here instead was Sean giving her a much-needed boost.

'Thanks for the coffee,' she said, when they got back outside. 'And the advice. It's good advice.'

'No worries. Thanks for coming over. You helped take me out of myself. Take my mind off . . . you know.'

'Did I? Well then, I'm glad.'

They stood for a second and their eyes met.

'I'd drive back with you, but I've been up for nearly thirty-six hours and I'm fit to drop. Can you find your own way home if I go inside and crash out?'

'Yes, of course.' Emily opened the door of the Renault and climbed in. 'Good luck with the funeral. I mean . . . you know. I hope it isn't too tough.'

'Thanks. Hey – how about a drink? Sometime in the next few weeks?'

She turned the key, engaged the clutch, and put the car into reverse.

'Sure. I'd like that.'

'Maybe take you flying?' he called, teasing, as she pulled away.

'Yeah,' she laughed, shaking her head. 'Maybe!'

That night, long after the guests had gone home, Caitlin walked around the dining room examining the flowers. She fingered the ivy, the petals of one of the lilies: bright saffron pollen tumbled down onto her bandage. Lily pollen was supposed to be poisonous wasn't it? She wiped it off on her jeans, a yellow smear against the blue. Then she looked down at his face.

Once, at school, in Art, they'd made their own canvases, stapling the material onto little wooden stretchers before sizing and priming it. That's what his skin looked like – like it had been pulled taut over the bones of his skull and primed with a thin gesso ground. It was her father, but it was not her father. It was a perfect simulacrum, a masterpiece nested inside an expensive mahogany frame.

One thing was different. The jaw. The jaw was relaxed. It had dropped down into the neck, pulling the chin – in life always set firmly forward – backwards and down. This in turn dragged the lips into a slightly unfamiliar cast and gave his face a pensive expression: puzzled, but with no matching frown on the brow, as if he were trying to find his way out of a room in a dream.

No, not just one difference: now she noticed another. No cigarette. He had no cigarette. Well, that was easy to rectify. She went to her bag, retrieved her pack, took one out, then stood over her father's body wondering where to place it. The obvious location was his mouth, but that would be grotesque. She wasn't quite sure why she was doing this, but she wasn't intending to mock or defile him. Also, though, she did not want to touch him. So that left his hands, which had been laid, crossed, on his chest, leaving a conveniently sized gap between first and middle finger. Steadying herself on the table, she poked the cigarette into this slot and then stood back to view the effect.

'There you go Dad,' she said, breaking the quiet that had engulfed the house since her mother had gone up to bed. 'Not your brand, I know.'

The sound of her own voice surprised her, not because of how odd it was to hear it, but because of how natural. Until now the situation had felt entirely artificial, and she'd had no idea how to behave. What were you supposed to do? Sit silently in prayer? Throw yourself on the coffin and start ululating? Have a conversation? She'd tried the third option and had expected it to feel absurd, talking out loud to a corpse. But in fact it had normalised things. This was her father lying here, after all. Why shouldn't she talk to him? Perhaps for once he would listen.

She persevered.

'I'd light it for you, but I know Mum would freak. Though with half the garden in here I doubt she'd be able to smell it.'

Caitlin wanted a cigarette herself now. Maybe she could smoke out of the window? She picked up her pack and took one out, and with it the small fold of white paper that had been shoved in alongside. She placed this on the dining-room table next to the casket; it was the last of the wraps she'd bought from Peter in the early hours of Saturday morning, during the bender she'd been on since she'd spoken to Sean and her mother on Friday night.

She'd driven straight home after that, the pain in her hand shocking her into action. When she got in she'd switched on the TV, fixed up a dressing for the wound and consumed two large lines of cocaine along with the half a bottle of wine she had in the fridge. That helped with the pain but had the knock-on effect of rendering the isolation and claustrophobia of her little two-room flat in Redchurch Street completely unbearable. So she'd headed out to The Crusader, where she was sure to know some people and would at the very least get to see Beth.

The Crusader lay on the corner of Boundary and Austin Streets behind St Leonard's Church, which Caitlin had always thought ironic, as St Leonard's was also the chapel at the entrance to the track that led to Sean's cottage in Spernall. It was the church in the nursery rhyme, too, one she'd sung and skipped to in the playgrounds of her childhood:

Oranges and lemons,
Say the bells of St Clement's.
You owe me five farthings,
Say the bells of St Martin's.
When will you pay me?
Say the bells of Old Bailey.
When I grow rich,
Say the bells of Shoreditch.

These were the bells of Shoreditch. Mia had told her once that there was another Warwickshire connection, although Caitlin had never gone inside to verify it: Richard Burbage, the star of the King's Men, Shakespeare's theatre company, was buried here. Perhaps there was indeed some strange psycho-geographical congruence. Certainly this little area of Shoreditch behind the churchyard with its clumps of rangy pink roses huddled in tatty brick-bordered beds had always reminded her of Stratford-upon-Avon in general and of Sheep Street in particular. The Palladian lines of the church echoed those of Stratford's town hall, and the black-and-white Tudor frame of The Crusader itself strongly resembled that of the Vintner, the favoured haunt of her teenage years. Maybe that's why she always felt so comfortable in the place, despite its being only one notch above the area's nastiest strip pubs. Because The Crusader really was a total dive: its interior tiny and cave-like; its walls, ceiling and bar – even the glass panes of its windows – all crudely covered in the same matt black emulsion; its carpet like the scab on a graze; its atmosphere a dense beer-and-tobacco stink that you donned like a fetid overcoat as you walked in and carried with you for hours after you'd finally extricated yourself from its grip.

When will that be?
Say the bells of Stepney.
I do not know,
Says the great bell of Bow.

The Crusader also did lock-ins, legendary events that often lasted all night. That's what the blacked-out windows were for. Once the doors were shut, shortly after eleven, the place became a bunker, insulated from the world and protected from the prying eyes of licensing enforcement officers. Caitlin was a veteran of these events. They always ended messily, which was hardly surprising given the quantities of alcohol consumed, the open drug-taking, and the bolshie, libertine personalities of many of the regulars. All sorts of sordid things went on in the fabled backroom, which was even more like a bunker than the front bar. Once Caitlin had passed out in there. Not a good move: she'd come to on the little landing halfway up the stairs that led to the landlord's apartment to find herself being groped by a reveller even drunker than she was. She'd kicked him off then promptly thrown up, and was only rescued from her plight by Beth, who'd cleaned her up and parked her in the relative safety of their spare room for the night.

Here comes a candle to light you to bed,
And here comes a chopper to chop off your head!

The Crusader embraced her as she knew that it would, and when she told Beth about her father the drinks were on the house. Caitlin installed herself in a corner and proceeded to dispatch a long series of vodka tonics while cutting out line after line of cocaine to fuel conversation among the members of the small coterie that soon gathered around her in order to commiserate and talk through the stories of their own challenging fathers and families, thus sparing her the trouble of having to do the same thing herself.

She sought oblivion, but the more she drank and the more coke she sucked into her sinuses the more lucid she seemed to become. By three in the morning the drugs were all gone, all but the most stalwart of her companions had drifted away, and the emotional circuits being operated by those who remained had started to sputter. Someone suggested relocating to a party that was happening behind Broadway Market and this seemed like a good option, so they peeled themselves off from their seats and headed out into what was left of the night.

Up Hackney Road they wandered, past the wholesale handbag shops, the hipster graffiti, the jaunty coloured lettering that adorned the railings of the city farm. They hung a left behind the derelict children's hospital, cut through to the canal and crossed over the bridge, then turned right along the water's edge until they reached an unkempt 1960s factory block standing opposite two looming gasometers in the centre of a large and mostly empty car park.

Although the car park was ringed with security fencing the main gate had been left wide open, so in they went. The building was trimmed with faded red metal balconies and garlanded with cream paint that was peeling from its concrete substrate in great clusters that reminded Caitlin of hydrangea blooms. It looked a bit like it belonged, not in East London, but in the forbidden zone around Chernobyl, a Soviet-era high school perhaps, abandoned by its pupils – pencils dropped, textbooks left open on their desks – in their rush to flee the erupting radiation. This place was not deserted, though: they could hear the deep throb of bass speakers and see coloured lights flashing from a row of top-floor windows.

An industrial elevator gaped open at ground level: they got in, hauled shut the concertina door behind them, and stood around making smart comments while the lift clanked its way up the shaft. When they reached the top they stepped out onto an open walkway and made their way along to the entrance to the party.

While the others shuffled inside Caitlin hung back, the view having caught her by surprise. Her eyes were about level with the tips of the gasometers, and she could see past them through the clear January night towards the City, the river and beyond.

'You coming, Caitlin?'

'Yeah, in a minute. I'm just going to have a quick smoke.'

She fished around in her bag, found a joint she'd rolled back at the pub, lit it up and leant against the faded red rail. London stretched before her, its complex corrugations of shadow and light punctuated by the signature shapes of the capital's increasingly forested skyline, a gigantic hive generating a collective orange glow that infused the whole sky. But all this could not hold her gaze, which kept slipping down to the car park below and the patchwork of tarmac patches that made up its surface, which in the darkness looked almost like holes plunging deep into the earth.

'What's down there?' It was Peter, one of the people she'd come with. He had re-emerged from the party.

'Down where?'

He nodded down at the car park. 'You were leaning right over.'

'Was I? Oh, nothing. I was just thinking.'

'You don't want to be doing that. Thinking's bad for you.'

She laughed, but he was giving her an intense look. Was he making a pass? With Peter you could never quite tell.

'Here.' She gave him what was left of the joint. 'You can finish this if you want.'

'Thanks,' he said, taking it. 'Don't mind if I do. What did you do to your hand?'

Caitlin pulled her arm back and smoothed the dressing defensively. 'Nothing. Stupid cooking accident. Burned it on a pan.' She forced a smile. 'Bloody hurts though. What's the party like?'

'Oh, you know. There's an "art" band.' He made the quote marks with his fingers. 'Some stuff to drink. It's pretty radical. I think there's a real chance they might topple the government.'

Caitlin laughed softly. Peter was from Liverpool, and was one of the few people she knew who didn't take himself – or anything else – too seriously.

'It's freezing out here. I'm going in.'

'Yeah okay. See you in there. Try the anarchy punch. It's really good. You can have this too if you want.' He held out his hand; in its palm lay a wrap.

'Seriously?'

'Yeah. You look like you need it more than I do.'

Caitlin wasn't sure if there'd be a hidden cost to this, but she was way past caring.

'Thanks.'

'If you like it there's more where that came from. But you only get the one freebie.'

The coke brought her back up and pushed back the pain of the burn, and not long after she found Peter again and bought more – a lot more. The remainder of her weekend continued in much the same vein, switching from stimulant to stimulant, from pub to party, all the while dodging calls from Sean and her mother, until some time on Sunday she found herself exhausted enough to head back to her flat and pass out.

The clock was already nudging eleven on Monday when she woke. She felt appalling. She managed to fetch a glass of water from the kitchen and then, barely able to look at the screen of her mobile her head was throbbing so badly, she called Dawn Bradley, Simple Eye's office manager.

'Hi Dawn, it's Caitlin. My father's died and I'm sick. I won't be in this week.'

Dawn expressed sympathy, quickly followed by a request for a doctor's note. Caitlin half-expected her to ask for a copy of the death certificate as well.

'Just talk to Toby Strauss, okay?' she snapped. 'He knows all about it.' She threw the phone across the room and ran to the bathroom as her body began the process of purging itself of the copious amounts of alcohol she'd consumed over the previous two days.

Maybe it was self-inflicted, maybe it was some kind of bug she'd picked up, but a fever then took hold of her and she spent the next twenty-four hours largely confined to her bed, cramping and sweating and drifting in and out of bouts of hallucinatory sleep. It was lunchtime next day before she could eat anything, at which point she managed a piece of toast and a packet of soup. An hour after that she started to feel a lot better, at which point she craved more cocaine, which she duly awarded herself. But twenty minutes later she was in tears again, an abyss of self-disgust like one of those black-on-black tarmac patches opening up beneath her as the high wore off, and she had to take yet more coke to pull herself back, even though each hit felt like she was reaming her sinuses out with hot wire.

Thinking is bad for you, Peter had said, and he was right. She didn't need to think; she needed to clean. She stripped and showered, shoved her stinking pyjamas and bedclothes in the washing machine, pulled on fresh clothes, then went out into Brick Lane and bought smoothies, vodka and bagels. On her return she launched herself at her flat, which during the turmoil of the previous week she'd let slide into squalor. Powered by the cocktails and further lines of coke she cleaned late into the night, watched a film on TV, and then slept until lunchtime on Wednesday. The strategy had worked: she woke sufficiently calmed to eat the last of the bagels, put some things in a bag, buy a large cup of coffee on the way to her car, and begin the two-and-a-half-hour drive up to Warwickshire.

Sean was at the house when she arrived, thank goodness, which meant that she and her mother were less likely to argue over the fact that she'd effectively gone missing since they'd spoken on Friday. But it might not have mattered. Sheila was tired and distracted. Her face was drawn, she'd lost weight, and she seemed much older than Caitlin remembered, even though they'd seen each other at Christmas just a few weeks before. What was most shocking, however, was the way in which her mother treated her arrival almost as just one more thing to be ticked off the list of funeral arrangements, like the caterers or the florist. Sheila didn't even try to fuss over the dressing on her daughter's hand, and

Caitlin got the unsettling sense that it would have made little material difference whether she'd turned up any earlier or not.

Over a quiet dinner of lasagne that Connie had prepared and left in the freezer, Caitlin asked if there was anything she could do to help.

'I think it's all done, dear, really,' said Sheila, managing not to make it sound like an accusation. 'I'm just pleased that you're here. If you can help with the guests over the next couple of days, that's the main thing.'

'Who's coming?'

Sheila reeled off a list of names that began with Tony's brothers and surviving family and descended through various layers of business associates and friends until it shaded into the realms of people Caitlin knew she should know but couldn't even vaguely recall.

'What about the vigil? Doesn't someone need to sit with him at night?'

Sean and Sheila exchanged glances.

'I was going to do that,' Sean said. 'Keep Mum fresh for the day shift.'

'Well why don't I do it tomorrow?'

Sheila drew breath and nodded slowly.

'Well that would be nice, if you think you'd like to.'

'Yes. Yes I would.'

It was something, it was a contribution. Encouraged, Caitlin also volunteered to clear up the dinner things while her mother went and had a bath, and this offer too was accepted. She was putting the last of the dishes away when Sean wandered back into the kitchen.

'Hey.'

'Hey.'

'Mum's skipped her bath and has gone straight to bed. She said to say goodnight.'

'I'm not surprised. She looked shattered.'

'You should get an early night too, especially now you're going to be up late tomorrow.'

'You're as bad as she is. Fuss, fuss, fuss.'

'Oh come on.'

Sean's tone said everything. She'd been suspecting him of holding something back; now she knew he was.

'What?' Caitlin spat the word, daring her brother to come into the open. He took the bait.

'Jesus, Caitlin. What do you mean, "What"? Where the hell have you been?'

'I've been sick.'

'Off your face, more like. We needed you here.'

'Everything seems super-organised and under control to me. Just how you both like it.'

'What's that supposed to mean?'

'Why didn't she tell us that Dad had been ill, Sean? How dare she keep that from us?'

'So you didn't come because you were angry?'

'I told you, I didn't come because I was sick. Sick, get it? Fever, bed, throwing up? Sick!'

'That's very convenient.'

'Well maybe she made me sick. With her little secrets.'

'Oh grow up.'

'How can I grow up with a mother who insists on treating us both like children? Or did she deem you adult enough to confide in?'

Sean looked away. 'No. I didn't know either. Not until just the other day.'

'What was it then?'

'Lung cancer, basically.'

'Well there's a surprise. We could have guessed that. It's been on the cards for years. Why didn't they tell us? They could have told us at Christmas.'

'She said they didn't want to spoil Christmas.'

'What kind of stupid reason is that? This is what I mean about treating us like children. She didn't even bring it up this evening. I thought she might have done.'

'She thinks you're angry with her.'

'I am angry with her!'

'Well there you go.'

Spent, Caitlin slumped down at the table and pressed her palms into her face, waiting for tears that did not come. Sean went to the cupboard where the drinks were kept, reached down a bottle of whisky, sloshed a couple of measures into two tumblers, and came over to join her.

'Drink,' he said.

She did. The whisky was the most coherent thing she'd experienced that day.

'Thanks.'

'I've got something to tell you,' Sean said, at length.

'This better be good news. I don't think I can handle it otherwise.'

'Jamie's coming back for the funeral.'

Caitlin swayed slightly, her eyes lost their focus, and for a moment Sean thought that she might have been telling the truth and was genuinely ill.

'Oh yeah? Who says?' Her voice was hard and distant.

'He does. I spoke to him at the weekend. He's managed to get a flight into Heathrow first thing on Friday. He's going to catch the coach up. Should be here in time for the church.'

'Mr Reliable says that, does he? Where's he staying? Not here, surely?' Caitlin's bag was on the sideboard; she went over to it, retrieved her cigarettes, then went and opened the right-hand French window. With one foot in the kitchen, one on the patio, and the doorframe supporting her spine she lit up and blew smoke out into the pinched winter air.

'No. He's staying with me.'

'Does Mum even know about this?'

'She knows. She's fine about it. She thinks he should come.'

'Christ, more family secrets.'

'Well if you will insist on not answering your phone.'

'I told you, I was sick. I switched it off.'

Sean raised his eyebrows but otherwise decided to let this one slide. He sipped at his whisky while Caitlin smoked and stared out towards the dull mound of Round Hill, clearly visible in the moonlight, the dead elm on its summit a frayed cable that had been yanked out of the night. At length she shut the door, extinguished her cigarette under the kitchen tap and put the butt in the bin, then told her brother she was going to bed. By the time she came down the next morning the mourners had started to arrive and that was that, there was to be no further discussion – from then on everything was dictated by the logic of the event.

And now here she was, talking to her dead father's corpse. She didn't want a cigarette. What she wanted was coke. She opened the wrap, knocked a quantity onto the polished tabletop, pushed it into a rough line with one of the business cards the florist had left, and sniffed it up with the short length of drinking straw she kept in her bag for the purpose. Then she stowed away the straw, cleaned the table with the sleeve of her cardigan, and looked again at his face. Maybe the drug was affecting her vision, but he seemed less stretched now, more like he was simply asleep. On an impulse she reached into the casket, took the cigarette she'd placed between his fingers, and tucked it into the breast pocket of his suit, deep enough that it couldn't be seen.

'There you go, Dad. One for the road.'

And found that she was sobbing.

'Dad, Dad,' she whispered, wanting to scream the words but not wanting to wake up Sean or her mother. 'Dad, oh my Daddy, Daddy, oh my dear Dad.' She did touch him now, touched his cheeks, his hands, his brow, her fingers trembling, as splayed and desperate as the wind-worn branches of that dead elm on the summit of the hill. 'Oh Dad, Dad . . . I'm so sorry Daddy, I'm so, so sorry. I couldn't help it. I didn't want it, but I couldn't help it. Don't hate me for it Daddy, please don't hate me – I hate myself enough.'

Then it all tumbled out, years and years of it, like the words of an aria she'd been brought into the world to perform: how she couldn't help it, how she hadn't known how to stop it, how she despised herself for doing it, how she didn't know what else to do. How it was just because she'd loved him, Daddy, how she wanted to die to join him, Daddy. Because how could she choose? Please don't make her choose, Daddy, please don't make her choose – oh God forgive her – please don't make her choose, please Daddy please—

Because if this is what living was . . .

Then she didn't want to live.

Only Jamie moved as Caitlin fell. Sean had shouted but Jamie had moved, running twenty yards or so in her direction before coming to a halt. Watching her gave him instant vertigo – the path of her descent had become the axis around which the world now spun, the four men distributed as if pulled into an arc by gravitational forces created by the passage of her body through the air. Then she hit the hedge.

Dizzy and nauseous, feeling like he was being pulled both towards and away from her, it was all Jamie could do to stay upright. But a moment later he was running again, they were all running, speeding across the damp grass towards the gate in the corner of the field, deaf to any sound but the thump of blood in their ears.

Jamie reached the gate first and leapt over it. He caught his knee on the uppermost bar and landed awkwardly, his ankle folding under his weight, but if there was damage he didn't feel it and he was up again at once, arriving seconds later at the motionless form on the ground. The huge gash ripped open in the hedge – five full metres of elder, hawthorn and sloe – told him that Caitlin must have landed right on it before rolling out into the field.

He dropped to his knees beside her body and felt for a pulse at the base of her neck.

'Anything?' Sean panted, as he, Rick and Matthew ran up.

'I think so. But I can't really tell if it's her or me.'

'Christ, she's a mess,' said Sean, reaching into his pocket for his mobile. 'I'm going to call for an ambulance.'

'Caitlin!' Matthew urged. 'Cait! Cait!' But there was no response.

'Don't touch her,' Jamie snapped. 'Rick, is there anything in the truck we can use to keep her warm? Blankets or anything?'

'There's an old rug that my dogs use. But it's pretty filthy.'

'Get it. And then go park the truck at the end of the track and switch on the hazards. The ambulance will never find us otherwise.'

Just then there was the whine of an engine and a shadow slid across the field.

'Christ – Emily.' said Sean. 'She can't get down.' He handed his phone to Jamie and started running back towards the Toyota on whose bonnet, in the panic, he'd left his walkie-talkie.

Emily had seen the men rush over to the next field.

'What's the matter, what's going on?' she blurted as soon as Sean's voice crackled back into her headset.

'Something's happened,' Sean said blankly. 'We're going to get you down right now. Here's what I need you to do.'

Whatever the problem was, it didn't seem like a good moment to argue. Emily followed his instructions and was soon making a controlled descent into the centre of the meadow. When she had landed Sean ran over and took the weight of the cage while she unclipped herself from her harness.

'Why did you leave me up there?'

'We've got a problem. It's Cait.'

'What's the matter with her?'

'Over there. She fell.'

Emily's hands went to her mouth. 'Oh my God Sean.'

'Come on,' he said.

When they reached the others Emily fell to her knees alongside her brother, who had ignored Jamie's order and was sitting holding Caitlin's hand.

'She's not . . .'

'No, no, there's definitely a pulse.'

‘Oh Caitlin, Caitlin.’ Emily leant over the girl and with a tissue from her pocket tried very gently to wipe some of the blood from her face.

‘How long?’ Sean asked Jamie, taking back his phone.

‘At least another fifteen to twenty.’

‘Christ. That’s ages.’

‘Well they’ve got to come from Warwick. Nowhere local is equipped for something like this. The police will probably get here before that though.’

‘You called the police?’

‘Of course I fucking didn’t,’ Jamie snapped. ‘But they’re bound to show up. You’d better get your head around it fast. It was your equipment and you invited everyone. You could be liable.’

Emily turned to look at them. ‘It’s a bit early to be talking about legal action, isn’t it?’

Sean rubbed his face, which was drained of all colour. ‘Jamie’s right. The police won’t think so. We’d better prepare ourselves to give statements.’

‘You mean like match our stories?’ Matthew asked, incredulous.

‘No, that’s not what I mean,’ Sean said hotly.

‘I wouldn’t worry about it. We all saw her undo her harness, right?’ said Jamie.

Matthew stared at him, eyes hard as quartz. ‘You’re not suggesting she did this deliberately? That it was some kind of suicide attempt?’

‘I know what I saw.’

‘Well I didn’t see that. I saw her struggling with it, but it looked to me like she was trying to pull it back together.’

‘What, so I didn’t do it up properly, is that what you’re saying?’

‘Stop it!’ screamed Emily. ‘Just shut the fuck up, both of you!

Caitlin could die or . . . or . . . be paralysed, brain-damaged, anything. Has anyone called Sheila, or Alex and Mia?'

The three men shook their heads.

'No? Well let's get on with it, then.'

As Jamie had guessed, the police turned up and they were all obliged to give statements, though not before Sean had left with Caitlin in the ambulance. When they were allowed to go, Matthew and Emily drove to Warwick in Emily's car, and Rick and Jamie packed up the kit and followed on in the truck.

The two Wolds reached the hospital a few minutes ahead of the Toyota. They found Sean sitting alone in A&E, his sister long since moved to one of the theatres. Emily sat on the seat beside him and drew him into a long, tight embrace before asking what the doctors had said.

'They're not sure yet,' Sean replied, feeling both extremely detached and sick to his stomach. 'It'll be a while before they've got a complete set of scans. She's obviously got lots of broken bones. The question is whether or not she's damaged her brain or spinal cord. She was wearing her helmet, so that will have protected her head. But she might well have broken her neck. The weight of the helmet actually makes it more likely, they tell me.'

'Has she come round?'

'No. And she won't – they've put her in an induced coma. Apparently it's what they do if there's a severe risk of concussion. It reduces the pressure on the brain.'

Matthew balled his fists and began to smack them into his forehead.

'Jesus Christ,' he said. 'What the hell is going on here? What is happening to us? It's like some kind of curse.'

'Come on, Matt,' Sean said, getting up. 'It's not like that.'

'Don't tell me what it's like,' Matthew spat back, vaguely aware that other people in the waiting room were glancing his way. He wanted to lower his voice and behave more rationally, but he couldn't, and it seemed like an insult to Caitlin even to try. What had happened was a tragedy. It demanded an emotional response. It demanded that people be disturbed, feel compelled to look round.

'I need to see her,' he insisted. 'I need to see her right now.'

'You can't, Matthew,' Emily said. 'Have some sense. She's with the doctors.'

But he wasn't going to listen, and instead marched off across the waiting room and shoved his way through the double doors that led to the operating suites.

'What the fuck is his problem?' said Jamie, who'd just walked in with Rick.

'Isn't anyone going to go after him?' said Emily.

'He's your brother.'

'Jamie – Jesus,' said Sean, getting to his feet.

'Don't bother, really, either of you,' said Emily, pushing past the men. 'I'll go myself.'

Matthew hadn't gone far: she found him two corners away, sitting at the end of an empty row of grey plastic chairs.

'Come on Matty,' she said.

He shook his head. 'I just can't bear it, Em.'

'I know. It's horrible. We're all in shock. It's a terrible thing to have happened. And then having to deal with the police on top of everything else. It's just awful.'

'It's not that. I don't care about the police. I just care about her. I'm still in love with her Em. Don't you realise that?'

Emily sighed. 'I think I'd worked it out,' she said.

By the time Alex arrived, Emily and Matthew had returned to the waiting room and were sitting sipping paper cups of coffee with the others. Sean brought them up to date with what had happened.

'But when you say she fell,' Alex asked, zeroing in on the one piece of Sean's account that wasn't precise, 'what do you mean exactly? That the harness broke?'

Sean glanced over at Matthew, who was staring through the steam rising off his drink at the picture of a breaching humpback whale that hung on the waiting-room wall.

'There's a difference of opinion there, at the moment.'

Alex nodded. Emily had been reticent too, when she'd phoned to tell him what had happened.

'You say she did this deliberately,' Matthew said in a cavilling tone. 'Okay, so let's say you're right. Then why? Why do you think she would do this?'

'Matthew . . .' said Emily, trying to head him off from whatever stunt he was planning to pull.

'He knows,' he said, spitting the words at Alex, who recoiled. 'Don't you?'

'What the hell are you talking about?'

'Come on, why don't you tell them? It's about time.'

'Tell them what?'

'You – you slept with her that night you took her home, didn't you? Maybe even raped her, for all I know.'

'*What?*'

'What are you saying, Matthew?' said Emily, utterly thrown.

'I can assure you I have no idea,' Alex said.

'No, you don't, that's the trouble. You never had any idea. I made sure of that. Stupid Matthew here, always cleaning up someone else's shit. You got her pregnant Alex. Did you know that? Pregnant! And guess who had to help her while you swanned back off to university? I did! I had to organise her abortion, I had to help her through it. I helped her, I loved her, and she wouldn't even stay with me. She wouldn't even let me touch her! Two whole years I was there for her, and at the end of it she despised me, and it's all because of you!'

Matthew launched himself at his brother: flailing, punching, clawing at his face. Alex stumbled backwards into a chair, fell, and the two of them went down in the middle of the waiting room. Emily screamed, Rick and Sean dived in and started trying to separate the two of them, and the receptionist hit the panic button fixed underneath her desk.

Within seconds a security guard arrived and began trying to peel the roiling bodies apart. Rick and Sean immediately fell back, but Matthew lashed out at the new arrival and landed a couple of blows to his jaw.

'Right, you little bastard,' the guard muttered, then unleashed his gym-honed biceps and delivered a volley of short, accurate jabs to the kidneys of his assailant.

Matthew howled and creased in pain and the guard spun him round and frogmarched him out the main entrance and into the car park, closely pursued by Sean, Emily and Rick. Clutching his eye, Alex clambered to his feet and slumped into a chair.

Jamie came over and peered at his face. 'Are you okay?'

'I don't know. I think so. He's really hurt me.'

'Your nose is bleeding.'

'It's my eye I'm worried about – it felt like he dug his fingers right into the socket.'

'What was he doing?'

'I've no idea! He just completely lost it.'

'And what was all that about you and Caitlin? I mean, what he was saying . . . what was that?'

'It's just mad. I think he's talking about something that happened years ago. One night when I dropped Caitlin home after they'd been out on a date. But it's insane. I never slept with her. Nothing happened!'

'Are you sure?'

'Of course I'm fucking sure. What do you think, that I'm a rapist now? What is this?'

'But he says she was pregnant . . .'

'Well it's the first I've heard of it. If she was then I promise you it had nothing to do with me.'

At that moment Sean and Emily reappeared.

'Where's Matthew?' Alex asked.

'Outside, cooling off. Rick's trying to convince him to let him drive him home. What was all that about?'

'I have absolutely *no* idea,' Alex said firmly, still pressing the heel of his hand to his eye.

The receptionist called Sean's name and he approached the desk, flushed with embarrassment.

'You can go in and see Miss Nolan now. She's in Mallory Ward.'

'Can we all go?'

'Yes. But if I see or hear any of you behaving like that again, I'll have you permanently barred from the hospital. Understood?'

A male nurse buzzed them into the ward and asked them to clean their hands using the dispenser of alcohol gel fixed to the wall. One by one they worked the clammy substance around their palms and fingers and then, duly cleansed, they followed the nurse through the ward's communal area and past the eight-bed units into the small private room in which Caitlin lay cradled in bandages and the tubes and cables of various monitors and regulators, a ventilator strapped to her face.

They filed in through the door and arranged themselves around the bed, staring at the contours of her body as if they were those of an island upon which they'd all been marooned. Outside the window a chestnut fidgeted in the wind. One of the monitors beeped.

'Can she hear us?' asked Emily, at length.

'I don't know,' Sean said. 'I don't think so.'

The door opened and a woman in her mid-forties walked in and introduced herself as Doctor Odili. Her hair – chocolate brown, limed with grey – was drawn into a practical ponytail positioned high on the crown of her head, and her doughy complexion and puffy features told of long days without much exposure to daylight and short nights without much exposure to sleep. In her chapped hands she held a buff file thick with reports. She glanced from face to face.

'Next of kin?'

Sean looked at Jamie. 'Um, that's me I guess,' he said, so it was to him that the doctor addressed her assessment of Caitlin's condition.

It was the hedge that had saved her it seemed: if she hadn't hit it she would almost certainly have been killed outright by the impact with the ground. As it was, one of her ankles had been shattered, her left hip was fractured and her left femur had been snapped and driven up inside her leg. Her left arm was broken in three places and two vertebrae were cracked, as were three ribs. Her body was covered in lacerations from the thorns and twigs, and there was a large wound in her side where a branch had torn into the flesh and penetrated her breast. Something had also pierced her right eye, and it was likely she'd lose it, or at least lose its sight. The better news was that although she had severe bruising around several vertebrae she didn't seem to have damaged her neck or spinal cord. Most serious was her concussion: she'd need an MRI scan before they could ascertain its severity and the level of permanent damage to her brain. Because of the helmet there was a good chance this would be manageable, though they wouldn't know for a while; there were a lot of factors in play. The prognosis was therefore positive, but indeterminate. Caitlin hadn't fully hit the ground yet, the doctor said; in a certain sense she was still falling.

The doctor left and almost immediately the door flew open again. This time it was Sheila. She made straight for the bed, coat flaring behind her.

'What have you done to her?' she cried as she took in the sight of the figure on the bed.

'It wasn't anyone's fault, Mrs Nolan,' Emily began, although she stopped when Sean, now beside her, put his hand on her arm and shook his head.

'Oh my baby, my baby.' Sheila bent to embrace her daughter but was frustrated by the plethora of medical equipment, so she sought out Caitlin's hand instead. But that was bandaged too, and had a catheter protruding from it. 'Oh-oh-oh,' she moaned. 'I can't even hold you!'

Sheila took the hand regardless. Alex fetched a chair and manoeuvred it beneath her, and she sat for a while, bending Caitlin's fingers to and fro and pressing them to her lips in an instinctive, animal display.

'I hold you responsible for this, Sean. I've always said those machines were death traps. Right from the start, didn't I say? And now look. Look!' She gestured at Caitlin and let out another wail. 'Look what's happened to my baby!'

'I don't think it was Sean's fault, Sheila,' Jamie said. 'Caitlin didn't fall. She undid her harness and jumped.'

Sheila's eyes flickered as they hunted for purchase.

'Why would she do such a thing?'

Jamie looked not at his stepmother but at his half-sister, lying silently on the bed. How beautiful she was, how beautiful her skin, turned to alabaster by the flight of her will and the eerily even light from the diodes of the machines. He bent over her, guided a strand of hair back from her damp forehead and tucked it behind her ear.

'You know why,' he said.

Sheila stiffened. Her eyes stopped their saccades; her hands – still holding Caitlin's fingertips to her lips – paused in space. Even her tears seemed to halt their progress down her cheeks and hang poised in the moment like little beads of glycerine. Then the moment passed, she placed her daughter's wrist back down on the bed, stood up, and walked directly out of the room, the skin of her face glistening as if just turned from a mould.

As she pushed the door ajar it knocked into Margaret, who had been attempting to open it from the other side while carrying two large blue Tupperware boxes.

'Oh! Sheila,' she said. 'I—'

But Sheila just shook her head mutely and hurried off back through the ward.

'Oh poor Sheila!' Margaret said, as Emily came over to help her with the boxes and Sean rushed after his mother. 'She looks terribly upset.'

'She is.'

'I bought some sandwiches and fruit for you all,' Margaret said, indicating the boxes. 'Oh my goodness, look at Caitlin. No wonder Sheila's in such a state. Alex – you're here?'

'Yes.'

'But I could have sworn you passed me just now, as I pulled into the car park.'

'Nope, I'm definitely here.'

'It was your car, I'm sure of it. It's quite distinctive.'

A thought flashed through Alex's mind and he patted his pockets. 'My keys have gone! I must have dropped them when we had that fight.'

'What fight?' Margaret asked. 'Who's been fighting?'

'God, you don't think Matthew took them, do you?' Emily said, ignoring her mother.

Alex looked panicked. 'I bloody well hope not.'

'Do you want to go and check?'

'I think I'd better.'

So now it was Alex's turn to leave the room. He soon returned, flushed and out of breath. 'The car's definitely gone,' he said to the others, who despite themselves were eating the sandwiches that Margaret had pressed on them in his absence. 'Rick's truck's gone too, but I didn't see Matthew anywhere and I bet he didn't go with him. He must have taken it.'

'What do you want to do?' Emily asked.

'The Porsche came with a built-in satellite tracker. There's a bit of software on my laptop that will show its location. If you can go and get it from the house, you can fire it up and at least get some idea of where he is.'

'Why don't you just take my car?'

'I can't have that,' Margaret interrupted. 'He's not insured for it. We don't want any more of you driving around illegally, thank you very much. We've got enough on our plate as it is.'

'Okay, okay, Mum, I'll go. What's the program called?'

Alex told her and gave her some quick instructions on how to use it. 'Mum, why don't you go back with her?' he said, as Emily made to leave. 'Sheila's in the café near the entrance. Sean's there too, but I think he could use your help.' He glanced at Jamie, who was sitting with his head in his hands by Caitlin's bed. 'I can stay with these two.'

Sean was more than happy to be relieved by Margaret. He'd not been able to get any sense out of his mother at all. But when Emily suggested he go back up to the ward he shook his head.

'I'm coming with you,' he said. 'Or you'll be the only one without any moral support.'

'Oh I don't need it,' Emily replied, then quickly added that she was glad he was coming in case he took her too literally and changed his mind.

They left, and when they had gone Margaret bought two cups of tea at the counter and brought them back to the table where Sheila was sitting staring out through the café window into the brightly lit car park. She pulled up a chair, took a sip of her tea, then took out the little embroidery she kept in her handbag and began to work away at a half-completed flower motif.

'You got away lightly, Maggie,' Sheila said, when one petal had been finished and the next begun.

'You remember that night, that night I came to yours?'

Margaret shuddered. She knew which night Sheila meant.

'Yes. I remember.'

Sheila blew her nose on the serviette Margaret had brought with her tea. 'Well when I came back home, there he was, passed out on the sofa from whatever it was that he'd drunk. I went upstairs to check on the children and Sean was still fast asleep. But Caitlin . . . I couldn't find Caitlin.'

'She wasn't in her bed?'

'No, no she wasn't. I didn't know where . . . I searched the whole house for her, I was in a terrible panic, I thought she might even have set off down the lane to look for me and that something had happened to her, anything – God it was horrible.'

'But you found her in the end? You must have done.'

'She was in the back of her wardrobe, hiding behind all her dresses. She'd heard me calling for her but been too scared to come out.'

Margaret's mind was the one spinning awful scenarios now, conjuring possibilities she didn't want to contemplate. 'And she was, she was all right?'

'I told myself she was. But do you remember, my eye was so terribly swollen where he'd . . . She saw that and it brought it all back. She wouldn't even let me near her to comfort her. She made me get out.'

'Oh Sheila.'

'I told myself it would all sort itself out. But things were never the same with us, after that. Sean was fine, but Tony, and me, and Caitlin – after that it never really worked.'

'Did Tony ever hit you again?' Margaret asked. It was, she decided, important to say the words that for too long had been left unspoken.

'Oh yes. Not very often. And it stopped after Jamie left. That night was so terrible it shocked even him, and after that he really managed to change. But before then, yes, sometimes. You know how he could get. He'd get so het up about things, so fixated.'

'And you didn't think about leaving?'

'All the time. All the time.' Tears swamped the flow of words and Sheila took Margaret's hand while she sobbed. 'And just look what it's done to poor Caitlin. Look what it's done!'

'Shhh,' Margaret said. 'Shhh. You can't blame yourself like that. It wasn't your fault. You did what you could.' She was starting to cry herself now. They'd all known, of course. She and Miles and all of their friends. It had been whispered in the kitchen at dinner parties, in the lounge bars of the local pubs. But for all that, at least as far as she knew, no one had ever spoken to Sheila about it. In those days that was the attitude. It was their marriage, and thus their private concern. How stupid and naïve that seemed now. How wilfully blind. If this was indeed one of the reasons that Caitlin had done what she'd done, then it was all of their faults.

'Any of us could have said something,' she said, trying to articulate these thoughts as best as she could. 'We should have given you more support. Especially me, I really should have done. But I didn't want to interfere! I didn't want you to think, because I'd been married to Tony, that—'

'You couldn't have stopped it.'

'I could have at least let you know—'

Sheila cut her off and sat up. 'You couldn't have stopped what happened with Caitlin and Jamie.'

She wasn't crying now, and her voice had changed its timbre. Previously thick and rich with grief, it had now turned dry and cold.

'Why?' Margaret asked, worry once again rising up in her chest and displacing the guilt she'd been feeling. 'What happened with them?'

Sheila wiped her nose.

'It was wrong, Maggie. It was so wrong I . . . I couldn't . . . I never told anyone. But I think it's why Matthew – oh Maggie, I'm the one who should be apologising, not you. But you have to believe me, we just didn't know. We honestly just did not know anything about it.'

'What?' Margaret said, truly confused now, no longer sure whether to be worried, guilty or scared. 'What didn't you know? Please Sheila. Please tell me. What didn't you know?'

The daylight was already fading when Emily had arrived at the hospital; now that she and Sean were leaving it was properly dark. The two of them threaded their way between the ranks of cars glowing beneath the sodium lamps until they reached the Renault 4.

'Not exactly the world's best pursuit vehicle, is it?' Emily said apologetically, as they climbed into the sparse and functional interior.

'It'll do,' Sean said. 'I'm not sure speed is what we're looking for right now, in any case. We don't want to outrun him. We just want to find out where he is.'

‘Just as well. I’ll go through the lanes anyway instead of taking the bypass. In this thing it’s quicker.’

Though both of them were desperate to talk, neither was sure how to broach the subject of why Caitlin had done what she did. And what had Jamie meant when he’d told Sheila she knew? It was what Emily most wanted to ask and what Sean most wanted to tell, but neither could manage it. Instead, as they came down the hill into the centre of Snitterfield Emily dropped her hand to Sean’s thigh and gave it a squeeze. Their eyes met briefly and then, as she returned her hand to the wheel and turned into the road that led to her parents’ place, another vehicle, long and low, slunk past them in the other direction.

‘That’s bloody well him,’ she exclaimed. She jerked the car to a stop, slammed it into reverse, and steered them back around the turn before spinning the wheel back round, shunting the gear lever into first and setting off after the Porsche.

For half a minute or so the sports car stayed within sight, slowed by the speed bumps outside the village school. But once the road curved behind the Snitterfield Arms and became free of restrictions its tail-lights quickly dwindled into the night.

‘Is this as fast as it’ll go?’ Sean asked as the Renault’s engine whined under the bonnet.

‘Yes, unless you want me to tip it over the next time we go round a bend,’ Emily said. ‘If you fancy that then I can probably squeeze another five miles an hour out of it.’

‘Christ,’ said Sean. ‘Then we might as well give up. We’re never going to catch him. We’re better off going to get the laptop.’

Matthew was indeed long gone, not that he’d been trying to lose them. He hadn’t even spotted the Renault at the crossroads, let alone clocked that for a short spell it had been following him – he’d been far too focused on a mission of his own. He couldn’t tell how it was going to play out, but knew that the first stage involved the bag of weed he'd just retrieved from the backpack in his bedroom. Stage two was about finding somewhere quiet to stop and smoke it while he worked out what, now that he had control of his brother's prized possession, would be the most appropriate thing to do with it. Just lighting up a joint in the Porsche's luxurious leather-trimmed interior would be a retaliatory act in itself, of course, given Alex's terror of any such contamination. But there had to be something more, some other mechanism of revenge that would taste even sweeter.

He reached the junction with the Birmingham Road and pulled out carefully, aware that this stretch of highway was a notorious speed trap and regularly patrolled, then cruised down beneath the railway bridge until he reached The Golden Cross. At the pub he hung a left down Salter's Lane, the same route he'd cycled to see Caitlin for their picnic that fateful afternoon so many aeons ago. He didn't have to travel very much further to find what he was looking for: a tarmacked turn-off that led to Dockert's dump, where he used to come with Alex and their father to deposit their empty cans and bottles.

The access road was long enough to get the car out of sight of the lane, and he drove down it until he reached a set of chain-link gates that blocked his way. In front of these he stopped, turned off the engine, and sat for a couple of minutes soaking up the stillness before reaching for the pouch in which he kept his papers, marijuana and tobacco.

When he'd first got hold of Alex's keys Matthew's angry fantasy had been of spectacularly writing off the Porsche, steering it off a bridge or into a lake or a quarry and jumping out at the last minute, or perhaps even staying at the wheel in a suicide of passion that would somehow mirror Caitlin's fall. As he sucked smoke into his lungs he allowed himself to indulge these thoughts again, embellishing and annotating his earlier visions while knocking his ash into the footwell of the Porsche. But soon reality bit. It wasn't only to protect his upholstery and Rufus's lungs that Alex forbade smoking in his car. Very quickly the tiny cockpit had become completely fogged and Matthew was forced to open the door.

He got out, went over to the gates, and slipped the fingers of his right hand through the mesh. Reassured by the pinching sensation of the cold metal against his skin he peered through the links at the scene beyond, dim but discernible in the moonlight. And what he saw there took him completely by surprise. The dump of his childhood, with its landfill trenches, lines of yellow skips, dark green bottle banks, Portakabin offices and general air of squalor and decay, was all gone. In its place was a wide landscaped basin full of ranks and ranks of saplings. He blinked and ran his hand round the back of his neck as if to haul himself back into the present, then walked over to a sign clipped to the fence to the left of the gate which he'd hitherto ignored.

When he saw what was on it he started to laugh. The sign said the land was now owned by Tony Nolan and that these trees were his trees, part of his forest of the future.

'Jesus Christ,' Matthew hissed to himself. 'Jesus fucking H fucking Christ. There is just no escape, is there? There is just no fucking escape.' He bent down until his forehead pressed against the sign and stood like that, his neck taking his weight and his shoulders quite limp, while he took the last few pulls on the joint. When it was finished he very deliberately ground out the hot ball of embers in the middle of the metal plate, twisting it until the shower of bright orange sparks became a tumble of blackened tobacco.

Then, as he turned to flick the roach into the dirt, he found himself face to face with a fully-grown stag, staring at him down the line of the fence from a distance of some twenty metres.

A song popped into Matthew's head, one he'd heard somewhere years before about stags being the colour of bonfires, and even though the weak polarised light from the moon washed all the colours but greys, purples and blues from the scene he could see what the singer had meant. The animal seemed almost hewn from bark and fallen wood, seasoned by the weather, its antlers dried branches jutting from the great bole of its forehead, the bright mirror of Earth's satellite deflecting sparks deep into the knots that served it for eyes.

Presumably it had been chased out of the plantation, and now here it was patrolling the fence, preparing itself to push out and find a new territory. Not that there were many options round here, what with all the roads and railway lines and driveways chewing up what was left of the countryside. Matthew didn't know how the animals managed to survive in what hedgerows and small pockets of woodland still existed. It might have been rural, but it was hardly the Scottish Highlands or the wilds of Dartmoor. Maybe that was in the end why Nolan had started planting his forest – to bring back the deer and the boar. The irony being, of course, that nowadays you could only create free land by enclosing it and shutting those animals out, by making it into a policed slice of park.

Matthew punched the metal sign at the thought, rattling the chain-link and spooking the stag which turned and slipped away into the bushes as deftly as a trout into reeds. Then he let out a howl, venting his frustration at the peppering of stars that blinked, unmoved, overhead. Needing a more responsive outlet, he started kicking at the fender of the Porsche and was instantly gratified by the way its memory plastic buckled and re-formed with each blow, as if it were mutely acknowledging and accepting this punishment as fully deserved.

He knew then what he must do, and that of course was to take the car back to his brother. But he wasn't going to capitulate completely. He still needed some kind of token, some talisman of revenge, and crossing the Birmingham Road had given him an idea. He would run the speed cameras on the way home. Alex would get his toy back, but it would come with some points on his licence and a fat little fine. That was the very least he could do.

While Matthew had been getting high Emily and Sean had been firing up the tracking software on Alex's laptop in the Wolds' kitchen. Rufus was asleep but Miles and Mia had met them when they'd arrived, desperate for news about Caitlin. Matthew had said nothing when he'd turned up: just come in, gone upstairs to his room and gone straight out again.

'When I saw the Porsche I thought Alex must be driving it and was waiting for him in the driveway,' Miles had told them, very concerned. 'I should have thought he would have known better than to go driving someone else's car.'

'He's not in a good place, Dad,' Emily said. 'He was in a terrible mess at the hospital earlier. What happened today has really upset him.'

'Well, I know he and Caitlin used to be close, but it's still no excuse.'

'I think there's a bit more to it than that.'

'It doesn't matter, Emily! There are some things you just don't do, not unless there's a genuine emergency.'

The laptop had powered up now and Emily was too intent upon entering the password that Alex had given her to answer her father. As it was she got it wrong on the first two tries.

'Can everyone just be quiet for a minute? I need to concentrate!'

The third time it worked, and the Windows desktop assembled itself on the screen. Once that had happened, finding and starting the tracker was straightforward enough. It was already keyed to Alex's car, although it took a while for it to download a set of local maps from the server over the Wolds' slow Wi-Fi connection.

'Look, he's halfway to our place,' Sean said, peering at the ideogram of coloured lines and labels.

'Do you think he's stopped?'

'Looks like it, but I've no idea what the latency is on this thing. It could be sending a signal every ten seconds or every ten minutes. Did Alex say?'

'I don't think he knows. He said he set it up when he got the car and never looked at it again.'

'It isn't far. Shall we go and see?'

Emily nodded, and leaving instructions with Mia to watch the dot representing the Porsche and call her mobile if it started to move, she and Sean went back out to the Renault. They got in and as Emily started the engine he leaned over and kissed her on the cheek. It was completely unexpected but very much desired, and she felt herself flush.

'What was that for?' she said.

'Nothing in particular,' Sean said. 'Just for you being you.'

'Okay,' she said, then leant across and planted a kiss on his lips. 'And that's for you being you.'

They sat grinning at each other for a moment or two.

'You'd better drive,' Sean said, 'before we go off one another.'

'Well I wouldn't want that to happen,' Emily said. And she put the car into gear and pulled away.

They were passing through Bearley when her phone rang. She pulled it out of the pocket of her jacket and passed it over to Sean to answer. It was Mia.

'She says he's on the move,' he said, closing the handset. 'Heading up the Birmingham Road towards Henley, apparently.'

'That's annoying. I was really hoping we were going to catch him while he was parked.'

'Me too. Still, at least the tracker works. Now we know where he's going we don't have to be able to keep up with him.'

'I suppose not.'

They came to the junction with the main road and had just turned right in the direction of The Golden Cross as Matthew had earlier when Emily's phone rang again. Sean was still holding the handset and answered immediately.

'She says he's turned around and is heading back our way.'

'That's weird,' said Emily. 'Why would he do that? Unless of course the tracker's just not very accurate.'

'It could be that.'

'Let's see if we can spot him.'

The tracker was accurate and Mia was right. Matthew was now driving south. Having used the entrance to the cemetery in which Tony had been buried the previous day to execute a three-point turn, he was now heading towards them at over a hundred miles an hour in order to be sure to trip the safety-enforcement cameras positioned just up from the pub. There was no other traffic and he didn't intend to hold that speed for long, but as he came down the straight the stag he'd disturbed back by the plantation fence jumped the hedge that ran alongside the road and darted out onto the tarmac.

Not only was Matthew stoned, he had no experience of driving performance cars. Instead of braking he swerved to avoid the creature, managing to miss it but in doing so veering straight into the path of the oncoming Renault 4. Blinded by its lights he spun the wheel in the opposite direction, whipping the car back across the road so sharply that it caught the kerb with its front right wheel and rolled. Transformed into a boulder of unstoppable metal it tumbled sideways down the carriageway until it slammed hard into the side of the brick railway bridge that had been built by the Victorians to carry the trains from Warwick into Bearley.

ELEPHANT

WHEN CAITLIN AND SEAN were called into the living room for a conversation with their parents they assumed at once that they were in the deepest kind of trouble. Discipline in the Nolan household was generally issued either as curt, belligerent edict by their father or as lengthy explanation by their mother. The two styles conflicted, and the conflict often caused rows between the two adults that far outmatched the original complaint against the offending child. To have their parents manage to coordinate their strategy like this, in such a deliberate and premeditated fashion, meant that something serious was brewing.

They were asked to sit side by side on one of the sofas while Tony and Sheila sat across from them on the other. This too was out of character: Tony rarely sat down in anything other than his favourite armchair. Something was most definitely up.

'Your father and I have some important news,' Sheila began. It looked like she was going to be doing the talking, which was encouraging. 'As you know, your father was married once before.' This was hardly news; they both knew Auntie Margaret. 'And, well, we've never told you this,' their mother continued, with a glance over at her husband, who looked fit to burst, 'but your father had another child at that time.'

Silence.

'You have a brother. A half-brother to be accurate.'

So someone was after all in deep trouble, and it was their dad. Caitlin had never known him to sit quietly in admission of guilt like this. When he and her mother fought it was always Mum's fault, never his. The thought that it might be different this time embarrassed her. She felt embarrassed for him. And she couldn't bear that he might see that in her eyes.

Then Sean spoke. 'With Auntie Margaret?'

'No Sean, not with Auntie Margaret.' Sheila let that fact hang, presumably for Tony's benefit. There were plainly complications here that went way past the limits of what she regarded as suitable for the children. 'With another lady, a lady called Janice Blake.'

Sean spoke again, this time addressing his father. 'Were you married to her, too?' There was an insubordination in his tone that in other circumstances would have been quickly admonished, but Tony only cleared his throat and levered himself upright in his chair.

'No, Sean. Janice and I only had a short relationship. We did discuss marriage but, in the end, Janice felt she'd rather bring the boy up on her own. Which is what she did. I've helped out a bit with money and such, but we've not really seen each other since.'

'And then we had a letter with some very sad news,' Sheila said. 'Janice has been very ill for some time, and two weeks ago she passed away.'

'What was wrong with her?' Caitlin asked with genuine concern.

'She had a cancer, darling. It's very sad. Jamie is a little older than both of you, but still not old enough to be living on his own. He's staying with some friends right now, but we thought he should come here, to live with us. And we wanted to ask you two if that would be all right. Didn't we, Tony?'

Caitlin forced herself to look at her father. He had the air of a strong man, a boxer maybe, who'd just been repeatedly punched by someone even more powerful.

'That's right,' he said. 'Would that be okay with both of you?'

Caitlin couldn't ever remember hearing her father ask her or Sean's permission for anything. Of all the things she'd heard in the last few minutes, this was the one that unsettled her most.

Two days later Caitlin came home from school to find her father in the house and Jamie Blake sitting with Sean at the kitchen table. They were eating toast. Sean had been taken out of school for the day, but Caitlin had not. Sean was older and a boy, Sheila had explained, and he and Jamie needed some time to get to know one another. Caitlin would get her chance later. There would be plenty of time for all that. Caitlin had been asked instead to make Jamie a 'Welcome Jamie' card, which she had done the previous weekend. And now she had come to give it to him.

He got up from the table to be introduced.

'Jamie, this is Caitlin. Caitlin – this is Jamie. Jamie, Caitlin's made a card for you.'

Caitlin didn't feel the card was at all the right thing now. She'd made it for her brother, but Sean was her brother. This wasn't her brother. He was older than her brother. And bigger. He had long blond hair that hung down nearly to his collar. He could have been in one of the bands whose posters she had pinned to her bedroom wall. He'd think her card was stupid. It was stupid.

She held it out to him anyway. 'Hello,' she said.

Jamie took the card and smiled. He had a big smile, a nice smile, just like her father used to have.

'Did you make this for me?'

'Yes.'

'Can I open it?'

'Yes.'

He took it from its envelope and looked it over very carefully.

'It's beautiful,' he said. 'Thank you very much.'

'I'm sorry about your mum,' she said.

'Thanks,' he said, dropping his gaze to the floor. 'But now I've got you.' He raised his eyes and looked right into hers, and she felt like no one had ever truly looked at her before. 'All of you,' he said, glancing round at Tony, Sean and Sheila too. But Caitlin knew which of them he meant.

Caitlin's parents said that with the extra person in the house they needed more space, proper family space. So they were going to get an architect to design a big extension with a games room – and a pool! For the time being, however, Jamie was going to have the spare room at the end of the corridor. It was small, but Caitlin helped him paint it and make it nice. She helped him choose the colours and they did it together one Saturday. He taught her how to use a roller, the best way to hold a brush, how to lay masking tape to keep things neat, and how to use a razor blade to peel the tape away. He knew about things like that. He was hilarious and had her in stitches all the time. They flicked paint on each other and larked about, and he said he'd never wash the spots off his face but keep them there for ever.

Jamie was attending a sixth-form college near Bromsgrove, which was a long way to go every day, but he got driving lessons for his birthday and soon he was able to drive himself there in a car that Tony bought him. Caitlin made him promise that once he'd finished college he'd run Sean and her to school, and he did. She loved that, loved him driving her places. Sometimes she got him to drive her out at the weekends, or to the cinema – she always wanted to do everything with him. It became a bit of a Nolan joke, that Caitlin always wanted to do everything with Jamie. It had turned out that she was the one who made best friends with him, not Sean, who was in the sixth form himself now and had his own friends in school and was always out anyway at some activity or other.

'Goodness Caitlin,' Sheila would say, 'leave the poor boy be.'

'But Mum, he likes it,' Caitlin would protest, and Jamie would say: 'She's right Sheila, I do,' and then they'd go and do what they had planned to do in any case.

Sometimes Jamie even took Caitlin to Bromsgrove with him when he went to see his old friends over there. They were different to other people she knew at school or in the local villages. They were poorer, and tougher, and smoked, and mostly had jobs working in shops or garages, even though they were only sixteen or seventeen. Jamie smoked too, when he was with them. He didn't want her to smoke but she pestered him until he let her try.

'Don't for God's sake tell Tony,' he said. Jamie called him 'Tony', not 'Dad'. 'If he finds out I'm introducing you to my bad habits, he'll string me up.'

'He wouldn't mind. He loves you.' The evidence: the car, the laughter, the new extension, which was by now well on its way to being finished.

'Yeah, well. He doesn't love all this,' he said, gesturing at the run-down area of Birmingham they were driving through. 'Doesn't love this part of me. Thinks I might be a bad influence.'

'On who?' Caitlin asked.

Jamie swerved and blared the horn at a van that had pulled out of a junction just ahead of him. 'Are you blind?' he shouted.

'That was so dangerous!' Caitlin said. 'Even I could see that.'

'Too right it was. That's Bromsgrove for you.'

They drove on a short way. Then Caitlin said: 'Well, I'll be a good influence on you.'

Jamie smiled over at her. 'I'm sure you will, Cait.'

She didn't look back at him, kept staring ahead through the front window, but she stretched her hand across and briefly rubbed his arm. 'Mum says the builders will be finished in a couple of weeks. Then your new room will be ready. So I've got a surprise for you.' She reached into the back seat for her bag and pulled out a small folder stuffed with magazine clippings and colour charts. 'I've been collecting loads of design ideas. I thought we could decorate it together.'

Jamie hesitated. 'I'm not sure that's such a great idea.'

'What? Why not? We had loads of fun last time. And we did a really good job.'

'Yeah, we did.'

'Then why?' Again he didn't answer, though this time no van pulled out. 'Come on, it'll be fun!'

'I'm going to be too busy Cait. Tony's found me a job.'

The job was at the golf club Tony Nolan had built in partnership with several other local businessmen outside of the nearby village of Aston Cantlow, professedly in order that he could 'wear what I bloody well want to when I walk into the bar'. Jamie was given a slot in the pro shop selling clubs, accessories and other merchandise, but he didn't know or care enough about the subtle differentiation of irons, fairways and drivers to be able to muster much enthusiasm for the role. The reports that went back to his father via the shop manager were carefully couched – no one wanted to be seen criticising the boss's son. But Tony's managers knew how to damn with faint praise, and before long Jamie was re-located to the bar where his father could more easily monitor his progress.

Here Jamie seemed more in his element. He had an engaging manner and a sharp wit and could chat happily to almost anyone while pulling pints or uncorking wine. The customers liked him and he didn't seem too bothered when Tony tried to get him riled up, which he generally did whenever the opportunity presented itself. But that was Tony's way. 'Tough love,' he called it. He tested everyone, forever probing to see how deep he needed to jab to elicit a reaction. Jamie was determined not to fall for it. His instinct was not to get defensive but to jab right back. Which Tony liked. A smart response earned his respect. Act passive, and he'd steamroller you into the ground.

Back in Shelfield the extension was ready and Jamie moved out of the old spare room and into his new room over the pool. Despite his protestations Caitlin insisted on decorating it for him, though she toned down some of her wilder ideas and gave up on wallpaper after hanging it had defeated her. But in any case the excitement of the new bedroom paled beside the impact of the cuboid of water that lay beneath it. Jamie, Caitlin and Sean were in this amazing space whenever the opportunity arose. Caitlin, by now studying for her GCSEs, even tried to do her revision on one of the loungers until Sheila put a stop to it. Her mother also had an issue with the minimal nature of the bikinis she'd started wearing, and regularly told her to cover herself up. But they were just bikinis, everybody wore them. And as if to prove it, when Caitlin finished her exams they held a pool party at which, yes, all of her school friends sported similarly microscopic swimwear.

Sheila was not impressed. 'If that's how they all carry on,' she told Caitlin afterwards, 'it's just as well that you'll be starting at Wardle's in September.'

Jamie just said that he didn't see what all of the fuss was about. But there was more fuss to come. The day after the party two bottles of eighteen-year-old single malt were found to be missing from the drinks cabinet in the dining room, and Tony hit the roof. He suspected Jamie's friends from Bromsgrove, and said so. The row rapidly escalated into a full-scale screaming match that somehow became about Jamie's general level of ingratitude.

Jamie shut himself into his room for the evening and Tony made it abundantly clear that no one was to go up and talk to him. But later than night, when her parents were asleep, Caitlin crept down the main stairs, through the silent house and up the spiral staircase that led to her half-brother's room.

She found him in bed but awake, reading a football magazine.

'Hello. What are you up to?'

'I wanted to see if you were okay.'

'He'll kill you if he finds you here.'

'No he won't.'

'Then he'll kill me.'

She slipped into his bed and put her arms round him. 'So he'll have to kill us both. Switch the light off. I'll spoon you.'

'Cait, I don't . . .'

'Shh. Switch off the light.'

'Caitlin . . .'

'Shhh. I want to. It's my choice. Just let me.'

As tensions between Tony and Jamie continued to simmer, Caitlin's night-time visits continued. She and Jamie just held each other at first, but their encounters soon grew in intensity. A boundary had been crossed: the uncanny sense of mutual recognition they both had felt since meeting had now been acknowledged and left free to bloom. Borne along on a seething riptide of genes and hormones, neither of them felt in control of what was happening. Every touch, every meeting was vertiginous, joyful, suffocating. Being together was incredible, perfect, indescribable. And yet before the rest of the family they had to maintain the illusion that everything was just as before. Their fear of the force of their father's wrath if he should get so much as a sniff of what was going on enforced a strict cap on their activities. Jamie already suspected that the reason the extension had been built in the first place was to put some space between him and Caitlin. Caitlin thought he was being paranoid, but she couldn't argue with his caution – there was no question that what they were doing was wrong on pretty much every level. So although she wanted more and knew that Jamie did as well, she complied with his refusal to go any further than kisses and cuddles. In this way they found a kind of ideal love, illicit but uncorrupted, vivid but unconsummated: a shared reflection; a twinned existence – diffuse, unique, telepathic.

Inside this bubble they floated the whole summer long. Then came September and Caitlin entered the sixth form at her new school. It shouldn't have made a difference, given that Jamie was at the golf club most days and many evenings too, but it did. Staked down by the rigour of timetables and schedules, Caitlin soon found herself too tired to stay up and visit him during the night, and Jamie, once the reluctant partner, the one urging caution, the one who would always make sure that his half-sister was back in her own bed well before dawn, now began to feel the need to be with her growing ever more powerful.

Soon he could think of nothing else, and it began to affect his work. At the golf club he grew moody and short-tempered with customers. Word got back to Tony, who issued a series of reprimands that served only to make matters worse. And then Jamie crashed his car. One night on the way back from work he lost control and wrapped the little BMW his father had bought him around a tree. Except for a few bruises and some minor whiplash he was fine, but the car was not, and Tony was incensed.

In the row that followed too much was said. Tony accused Jamie of having designs on Caitlin; Jamie lashed back that Tony wanted her for himself. That was enough for Anthony Nolan – he grabbed his son by the throat and started slapping him hard in the face. When Sheila tried to intervene Tony hit her too, punching her full in the eye. Caitlin screamed and threw herself on her father's back; Sean had to pull her off. Sheila had to pick up the phone and start calling the police before she could get Tony to stop. Tony released the boy, but told him to get out and never to return. That suited Jamie just fine: free of his father's grasp he retreated to his room, threw some things into a duffel bag and set off up the road, not knowing or caring where he was headed.

That night he slept in a barn, making a bed atop a six-metre stack of freshly milled bales. He spent the next day there as well, cold and hungry but too exhausted by the effort of trying to think his way out of the paradox of his love for Caitlin and his hatred of Tony to go in search of something to eat.

The next night, however, he returned. The front door was locked and he had no keys, so he headed round the back of the house via an overgrown footpath that ran from the lane up the side of the property and round behind the stables in the paddock, where the fence was easy to climb.

There were security lights at the rear of the house but he knew a route that would let him avoid triggering their sensors. He reached the patio and tried all the doors that opened onto the pool and then the main back door itself. Everything was locked. He rubbed his nose and suddenly felt very tired and very, very hungry. He glanced along the line of windows that dotted the wall. One of them, a small vent light, had been left ajar.

His heart now beating faster, he felt inside the transom for the stay arm, which lifted smoothly off its pin allowing the window to swing open a little wider. With his knee placed on the sill he was able to lever himself up until his shoulder was jammed against the hinge and his arm just far enough inside to reach the fastener on the casement. That too opened easily, and a few seconds later he was squatting atop the tumble dryer in the utility room, embraced by the comforting smell of clean laundry.

There were some of his clothes here; he bundled them together then sneaked round through the lounge and up to his room, where he shoved them into a holdall along with a few more of his things. He was nearly done when he noticed a padded envelope on top of his chest of drawers, sealed but unaddressed. He picked it up and tore it open. Inside were three thick wads of banknotes. He had no idea how much money it was, but it was a lot. He sat on the bed a while thinking about this, then shoved the envelope deep into his bag and crept back downstairs.

Crossing back through the hallway and into the kitchen he opened the door on the double-fronted refrigerator and spilled a trapezium of light out onto the tiles. Inside he found an open packet of ham and half a sliced loaf, and set about folding several salty strips of meat and bread into his mouth at once, washing them down with great gulps of orange juice straight from the carton. He'd moved on to a pork pie and a hunk of cheese when there was a noise behind him. He froze, expecting his father's bellow to rip through the tension. But it wasn't Tony. It was Caitlin.

She ran to him and kissed him and they made love right there on the floor of the kitchen, lit by the light from the open door of the fridge. Afterwards Jamie tried telling her how he felt, but none of what he said seemed to carry any meaning, so he stopped trying to talk and went with her through to the pool, where they swam together and made love again then sat, nested in towels, kissing and hugging and crying, until dawn came and he tore himself away.

Caitlin watched him walk away over the patio and across the lawn, and after he'd turned for one final glance she threw herself in the water and lay face down trying to will herself to suck the chlorinated fluid into her lungs. Then Sean walked in for his morning swim and pulled her out and held her while she shook and puked and lay on the floor like a wounded bird, not saying a word about what had just happened and never mentioning it again.

The first missed period didn't alert Caitlin to her new condition. She'd missed periods before, usually when she didn't eat enough, which was fairly common, as she found food more a chore than a pleasure. But she'd never missed two in a row. And now she had.

It couldn't be, could it? Her belly clenched at the thought. It couldn't be. She slipped out from school in her lunch hour to pay a visit to the big chemist's on the town's main square, the one with enough cashiers and a high enough footfall for there to be a relatively minimal chance of being noticed.

Nonetheless Caitlin passed the shelf displaying the pregnancy testers two or three times without plucking up the courage to take one. The pharmacist, the girl at the beauty counter, the office workers at the sandwich cabinet – all of them were surely watching her. Even though she'd left her blazer in her locker she was still wearing her school shirt and skirt, and these marked her out as someone who should not be shopping for that kind of item. Someone would remember her; someone would give her away to a teacher.

The enormity of what she was facing hadn't, until now, really dawned on her. It was as if a cliff had reared up out of the ground in front of her: gigantic, crushing, impassable. She was nothing, a speck, an insignificance. Who could she turn to? Jamie had gone, she had no idea where. Sean? She couldn't drag him into this. Her school friends? She didn't really have any at Wardle's yet, and she didn't live close enough to any of her friends from Stratford Grammar to just drop round and see them, and anyway, there was not one among them she really trusted. Her parents, of course, were out of the question. The thought of what her father might do if he found out made her shake.

Her terror of not knowing was suddenly greater than her terror of being identified, and she reached up for one of the tester kits. Then, still not ready to take it to the checkout, she went to the chiller cabinets and grabbed a bottle of apple juice and a tuna-fish sandwich on the tenuous theory that the offending item would somehow be less visible to a cashier if it were bundled together with lunch.

The night that Alex dropped her back after she'd been with him in Bearley she must have made more noise than she imagined coming up the stairs, because as she reached the landing her mother called out.

'Is that you darling?'

'Yes Mum. Just off to bed.'

'Did you have a nice time?'

'Yes thanks, really nice.'

'Good. See you in the morning. Sleep tight sweetie.'

'Goodnight Mum.'

It made Caitlin want to cry, this little exchange, and once in the bathroom that's what she did: wept quietly for her mum, and for her dad, and for Jamie, and for how everything that had been so perfect had gone so terribly wrong. When the tears ran dry she washed her face and cleaned her teeth, then went to her bedroom, changed into her nightdress and got into bed in the dark, not wanting to look at her body. All night she lay awake like that, terrified, her mind racing from the cocaine, her limbs inert.

She had never been so frightened. She thought she'd known fear the night that her father had hit her mother and made her run off to the Wolds', and she thought she'd known it again the night Jamie left. But neither of those had come close to this, this terror so constant and complete that it hollowed her out and turned her into a shell of a person, a shell that the slightest blow would shatter.

The source of the terror, its seed, was the thing growing inside her, suspended in her empty interior like the cocoon of a silkworm slung from the forking twigs of a tree. As she lay in bed, rigid and awake, she imagined she could feel it turning and turning, walling itself in ever more securely with layer after layer of matter scraped from the inside of her belly.

It had to come out. Whatever it took.

She saw Matthew on the Monday as usual, and now it was her turn to pass him a note. Because what choice did she have? What other way could there be?

On a sunny day in May, four months after they'd stood on the Hungerford footbridge to get sight of the whale, Alex, Rufus and Mia emerged from Admiralty Arch at the end of the Mall and rounded the corner of Uganda House to see the Sultan's Elephant heading towards them down the length of Cockspur Street. With them were Miles and Margaret, who had been persuaded to come and stay for a few days. Despite not really wanting to, for Rufus's sake they'd made this trip to Trafalgar Square – he had pleaded with them to come, so they had. They did a lot of things they didn't really want to, now, for Rufus's sake.

The elephant's presence was immense – far more impressive than Alex had been expecting. He tried to count the number of people on board the thing: there were at least fifteen of them, mostly dressed in burgundy robes, either sitting in special alcoves at the head, mouth, trunk and tail, or gathered on the little balconies built into its flanks.

As the articulated trunk swayed to and fro and showered the crowd with water, Rufus went completely wild. He leapt up at his father and pulled on his arm, pointing excitedly at the giant form. *Dad! Dad! Look Dad, look! Look, Grandpa! Grandma! Look!* Maybe it was just that he was a few months older now, but Alex hadn't remembered his son reacting with this kind of enthusiasm when he'd seen the whale. Granted, there had been less to look at, but then the whale had been real, a living being, whereas the elephant, no matter how remarkable, was just an automaton, a human construction of metal and wood with no inner life beyond that of its drivers and creators, although ultimately, Alex conceded, they were living beings too. Still, it said something, didn't it, about the appeal of art over nature? It struck him that this was probably the kind of observation that his brother had made all the time, one of the things that drove him so crazy, and he stored that thought away.

Matthew had not survived the accident in Bearley. The Porsche's exceptional safety cage and airbags had shielded him at first, but the roll had caved the roof in, and when the car hit the bridge his head took the full force of the impact. Emily and Sean had been luckier. Emily had managed to wrench her car out of the path of the Porsche, which must have missed her by mere inches, and into the car park of The Golden Cross, which as chance would have it was largely empty. They went straight across it and straight through the wall of the pub, coming to an eventual halt with the nose of the Renault poking through into the lounge bar right next to the fireplace. If they'd hit the chimneybreast they would probably have died, but the wall they hit was an old one, built from a single thickness of weakly mortared bricks, and it absorbed much of their momentum. Emily sustained three cracked ribs where the steering column had been driven back into her chest; Sean had whiplash and a snapped collarbone courtesy of his seatbelt. Otherwise they both escaped unharmed.

For a period, then, there were four members of the two families in Warwick Hospital together. Sean spent a night under observation but was discharged the following day. Matthew was the next to leave, collected by a local undertaker and taken to a premises just a couple of hundred metres from the park in which he'd met Caitlin on the day of their boat trip. Emily stayed several days longer while she underwent an extensive series of scans and X-rays to check for organ damage and internal bleeding. And Caitlin emerged fully from her coma a few days after that, though it was several weeks before she was judged well enough to go home. Even when that did finally happen, there were outcomes to endure. She required extensive physio and would rely on a wheelchair for months. Her speech was slurred and also needed therapy. She had severe scarring on her face and torso, which might have psychological implications, and her hip was likely to give her trouble for the rest of her life. As Doctor Odili had predicted, she kept her right eye but lost most of its sight.

But she was alive, unlike Matthew, whose funeral bore little resemblance to Tony's. There was no sense of celebration of a life well lived, only that of a hole torn in the world. There was a short humanist ceremony, family only, at the crematorium, followed by a small reception for friends from school and colleagues from Eco-Path and Greenpeace held at the Wolds' home.

For the next couple of months the reverberations from Matthew's death, Jamie and Caitlin's affair and Caitlin's lost baby buzzed through the Warwickshire community. Then things went quiet for a while. Into the vacuum came rumours: that Jamie had taken Caitlin out to the Club Vayu while she was still in a wheelchair and that they planned to marry – it might have been illegal for them to cohabit in England, but it was apparently not against the law in Brazil.

The truth, however, was less romantic. Once there had been a door, a door that Caitlin would have gladly stepped through to be with Jamie, a door that had been swinging open on her trip to Rosaventos. But that door had closed. Caitlin did not now go to Brazil, although Jamie had begged her to start a new life with him. Instead she went to a small private clinic in Wiltshire where she was able to get the care she needed to recover from her injuries and free herself from her addictions to alcohol and drugs. She didn't find the regimen hard. Matthew's death had changed something in her, and given her the strength to make the choices she needed to make. When she was able to walk again she moved out of the flat in London and back into the family house in Shelfield, not so that her mother could look after her, but so that she could look after her mother, who was not coping well with the torrent of paperwork that had swamped her since the floodgates of Tony's probate had been opened.

There was to be a wedding, however, and it was one that would keep the gossips happy until it came along in due course: the wedding of Emily and Sean. Their bond had been sealed by the trauma of that day of dual accidents, much as Alex and Mia's had been by the collapse of the Twin Towers. The seed of attraction that had been planted between them at Tony's wake somehow managed to put roots down into the wasteland of grief in which it found itself, perhaps drawing sustenance from the feeling, shared by both parties, that the damage inflicted on the fabric of all of their lives could be at least partially sutured by a love that would at last see these two families, Nolan and Wold, properly joined after so many false starts.

Back in Trafalgar Square the elephant drew level with the Wolds, and they ducked and screamed as its great tusks tilted in their direction, its trunk lifted, and it drenched them all with spray. Now that it was closer Alex could see that it wasn't really walking at all: although its legs moved in an illusion of perambulation its weight was supported by a kind of giant trolley to its rear and a set of wheels positioned under its throat. It was ingenious but also somehow disappointing: he had wanted it to be a fuller realisation of an autonomous being, rather than just a kind of glorified carnival float. Intriguingly, when asked about it later Rufus didn't seem to have seen the wheels, even though they were obvious once you looked. He'd only seen an elephant.

How much had Alex himself had similar blind spots, that night he'd taken Caitlin to the cottage in Bearley, or in the face of the unfolding tale of her split with Matthew, or even when he'd witnessed her reaction to Jamie's absence in Rosaventos? He'd seen nothing of her inner turmoil then, but when he looked back – which, since her suicide attempt, he had often done – many of the signs had been there. And he'd seen nothing, either, of the demons with which his brother – his own brother! – had been grappling, despite having been, however inadvertently, the proximate cause of them, and despite having lived alongside them for years. What did that say about his own perceptiveness, about what he – or anyone – understood of the world and the way that things ultimately worked? Pretty much everyone at some point, it seemed, swam the wrong way up some uncharted river, and had to rely on luck, or strangers, or family, to help them to find their way back.

Well, the artifice was revealed now. Maybe all of them were just mechanical elephants, contingent mixtures of cobbled-together mechanisms that kept going as best they could until one day, because of whatever cascade of reasons and accidents, they could not. It was easy to make sense of things in hindsight; harder when you were riding the crest of time as it unfurled.

He didn't know any more. He'd left his sunglasses at home and sun was in his eyes and his head hurt and he needed to think about what they were going to do for dinner. If they ate at home he would need to allow time to pick up something from the supermarket, and if they ate out he must think of somewhere that would be suitable for everyone, not just for Rufus and his parents but also for Mia, who was in her second trimester and getting picky about food.

Alex felt another sudden wave of sadness for his brother. That's how it came now, in waves, although they were slowly getting smaller in amplitude as well as lower in frequency. Clearly he had still not recovered from the blow of Matthew's death, if indeed he ever really would. And if it was this hard for him, what could it possibly be like for his parents? Alex had visited them as often as he could since the accident, and was repeatedly struck by how fragile and slight they had grown – they who had once been so indomitable, so reliable and solid. Thank goodness for Mia's pregnancy and Emily's engagement, which had given them positive things to focus on. Because that was it, wasn't it? It was all about the flow of responsibility down through the generations, and Alex had had the very definite impression over the last couple of months that, sooner than it might otherwise have been, the baton had been passed. Like it or not he was holding it now, and while he did so it was his job to look after all of them – children, sister, parents, wife – regardless of whether or not they asked him to. And cat, of course. Because to distract Rufus from the loss of his uncle, Alex had agreed to let him take Max.

It was strange how life twisted round on itself. He'd moved to London years ago and had lived there as long as he had ever spent growing up in Warwickshire. And here he was standing in Trafalgar Square with his own family and his own very pressing concerns only a mile or two from the house that he owned. But he now knew that whatever happened to him in the future, however far he travelled, and however successful he should become, the Midlands was the one place he would ever truly call home.

Acknowledgements

In large part this book owes its existence to the unflagging support of all at the Port Eliot Festival, particularly to Catherine St Germans, Peregrine Eliot, Simon Prosser, and each and every one of the indefatigable Five Dials crew (you know who you are!). Every year since I first began *Midland* in 2006 you invited me back to read from what was then very much a work in progress, with no clear end in sight. Something that started life as an experiment in 'slow fiction' was thus able to grow into a long-running serialisation. When the scale of the task felt overwhelmingly nebulous and vast the annual festival deadlines encouraged me to keep pushing forward with the story in the small gaps I could find between the twin demands of my job and my young family, and very gradually I etched out various fragments and pulled them together into a coherent whole. Peregrine, sadly, passed away in 2016 – this small tribute to him is therefore *in memoriam*.

It was at the festival, too, that I first came across the publisher Unbound, which has given *Midland* such an excellent home. John Mitchinson and Mathew Clayton gave me a terrific welcome into their fold; and especial plaudits are due to Rachael Kerr, whom I first met when she did a heroic job on the publicity for *Habitus* way back in 1998, and who has now done similarly stellar service as the editor of *Midland*. Fiction's a long game, Rachael, and it's been an honour and a privilege to have you on my team from the get-go. Similarly Marion Mazauric and all at Au Diable Vauvert have stuck by me through the lean years, and let me have repeated use of their writers' residence on the occasions when I needed the space to focus on the book to the exclusion of all else. On my last visit there I managed to stop the whole place from burning down by borrowing a phone from a local farmer to call the *pompiers* when a fire broke out; I hope that goes some way to repaying the debt I owe you!

Publishing through Unbound is a group affair, and several people played a very significant role in the fundraising efforts: Francis Upritchard and Kate MacGarry (artwork); Gilo Cardozo and all at Parajet (video footage and flying trips); Harry Harris (music); Mark Bowsher (video); Andrew Kötting and Iain Sinclair (DVDs); Simon and Bea Bishop and Hackney School of Folk (events). My two hundred and twenty individual supporters also all deserve a mention for their generous contributions, which were of as much psychological value as they were financial. It's an amazing thing to see people step up to the mark to support an artistic project like this, and I can't tell you what it meant. You all, of course, get your names listed at the start and end of the book, but the real roll-call is the story itself, into which I channelled all the emotional energy that your encouragement gave me.

Thanks are also due to my agent, Jonny Geller, a man who doesn't blink at the prospect of a twelve-year wait for a manuscript, and whose support and early stage edits helped turn a decade of scribblings into a readable book, and to all at Curtis Brown; to Peter Carty and Amit Gupta for crucial reader services at crucial moments; to Ben Rapp for Porsche lore and offshore insights; and to Garth Edward, Ali Miremadi and all at the excellent Amplify Trading for their significant contributions to my understanding of financial markets of all stripes. Your information and advice was always one hundred per cent correct; the mistakes I've no doubt introduced are one hundred per cent my own.

As for inspiration, the good ship *Litenese* is loosely based upon the Earthwatch vessel the *Toftevaag*, which I was lucky enough to spend a few days on board while researching an article for *Time Out* some years before Matthew's excursion to Almería, and which as far as I know is still going about its important work. And the entirely fictional resort of Rosaventos is an amalgam of the beautiful Cabo Polonio in Uruguay, where I once spent a memorable holiday (thank you, Mariana), and the Brazilian beach town of Jijoca de Jericoacoara, my knowledge of which comes entirely from Google Earth.

Credit must also be extended to my lovely wife, Robyn Haselfoot, whom I met the month I began crafting a short story about a trader's encounter with the bottlenose whale on the banks of the Thames, and who has followed the developing saga with patience and forbearance ever since. Robyn has not only contributed many character insights and numerous nuggets of information, but was the person who first drew my attention to the rare and little-understood condition known as Genetic Sexual Attraction. GSA is thought to occur when biologically determined assortative mating drives are not dampened by the learned kin recognition constraint known as the Westermarck effect. The condition particularly affects siblings and half-siblings separated at, or soon after, birth, and goes a long way to explaining why Jamie and Caitlin behave as they do. Should the separated siblings meet again later in life the sense of mutual recognition can manifest itself as a powerful sexual connection, and once the individuals concerned have experienced this particular intimacy they can find it all but impossible to form subsequent successful romantic attachments.

For more information on GSA, Wikipedia is a good place to start; there is also a private online support group for those affected by the condition, which can be found at: http://thegsaforum.com/

Finally, I'd like to give a nod to the Warwickshire hamlets of Shelfield and Spernall, and the nearby village of Snitterfield. These are real places, if somewhat idealised and thoroughly repopulated for the purposes of this novel. In and around them I was fortunate enough to enjoy an almost stereotypically idyllic childhood, and in and around them, it seems, my mind still happily roams.

James Flint
London – Warwickshire – Vauvert
January 2006 to January 2018

A Note on the Author

Born in Stratford-upon-Avon, James Flint is the internationally acclaimed author of three novels: *Habitus*, *52 Ways to Magic America* and *The Book of Ash*. In 2002, his short story 'The Nuclear Train' was adapted for Channel 4, while his journalism has appeared in *Wired*, the *Guardian* and *Dazed & Confused* among many others. Formerly editor-in-chief of the *Telegraph*'s weekly world edition, he is currently CEO of the health communications start-up Hospify.

Unbound is the world's first crowdfunding publisher, established in 2011.

We believe that wonderful things can happen when you clear a path for people who share a passion. That's why we've built a platform that brings together readers and authors to crowdfund books they believe in – and give fresh ideas that don't fit the traditional mould the chance they deserve.

This book is in your hands because readers made it possible. Everyone who pledged their support is listed below. Join them by visiting unbound.com and supporting a book today.

Alejandra Aguado
Aladin Aladin
Benjamin Apfel
Fiona Arnold
Will Ashon
John Aucott
Liz Bailey
Fiona Banner
Richard Barbrook
Sarah Beckett
Alex Bellos
Sumant Bhatia
Derek Bishton
Nicholas Blincoe
Polly Botsford
Laura Brown
Matthew Brown
T Byfield
Ele Carpenter
Peter Carty
Jamie Cason
Carolyn Cemlyn-Jones

Monica Chadha
Dan Chambers
Alex Cheatle
Duncan Cheatle
Lana Citron
Jesse Cleverly
Dominic Collier
Lucy Cooke
Anthony Cumming
Piers Curran
Deborah Curtis
Lorrie Dannecker
Mariana Dappiano
Matthew De Abaitua
Josh de la Mare
William De Lucy
Diana DeCilio
Sebastian Doggart
Patrick Doherty
Martin DotMH
Ian Douglas
Jim Drury
Robert Eardley
Adam Edsall
Tim Edsall
Susan Elderkin
Richard Ellis
Karen Eng
Julian Evans
Peter Faulkner
Marcus Fergusson
Pete Fergusson
Charles Fernyhough
Steve Finbow
Nicholas Fogg
Kal Foley-Khalique
Jonny Geller
Vittorio Gherardi
Jules Glegg
Margarita Gluzberg
Marianne Goodson
John Grant
Daniel Grausam
Jim Gray
James Greenslade
Mark Griffith-Jones
Abha Gupta
Penny Haselfoot
Robyn Haselfoot
Chris Heath
Shirley Hellyar
Alex Hendra
Catharine Higginson
Tom Hodgkinson
Michael Hodgson
Leo Hollis
Grattan Hooey
Kirstan Horn
Sarah Hornsey
Heidi Horvath
Sophia Hughes
Daniel Jackson

Maxim Jakubowski
Antonio Jimenez
Jo Joelson and Bruce Gilchrist
Matt Jolly
Andrew Jones
Mehmood Khan
Dan Kieran
Paul Kieve
John Kjellberg
Krishna Kunzru
Rob La Frenais
Josh Lacey
Andrew Lane
Livy Lankester
Lottie Lawson
Alison Layland
Cath Le Couteur
Jessica Le Masurier
William Leigh Knight
Sam Leith
Toby Litt
Amanda Lloyd Jennings
Al Loehnis
Patty Long
Wilf Macdonald-Brown
Russell Mackintosh
Jim Mallinson
Chris Martin
Gareth McConnell
Glen Mehn
Anne Mensah
Christine Meula
David Mitchell
John Mitchinson
Ben Moor
James Mullighan
Monty Munford
N R
Carlo Navato
Charles Nduka
Jackie Neville
Courttia Newland
David Nolan
Lawrence Norfolk
Vasilis Ntiskos
Dan O'Hara
Imogen O'Surname
Josh On
Richard Page
Rowan Pelling
Daniel Pemberton
Samantha Perkin
Dan Peters
The Platform
Edward Platt
The Podcast
Justin Pollard
Gavin Pretor-Pinney
Dr David E Probert
Harriet Quick
Aliur Rahman
Terry Ramsey

Tim Rea
Martha Read
Zelda Rhiando
Sonja Robertson
Jeffrey Robson
Louise Rosen
Nick Ryan
Julie Salverson
Mark Sanderson
Ted Sandling
James Sandoval
Daniel Saul
Miranda Sawyer
Jess Search
Aaron Seymour
Sophie Slater
Mat Smith
Zadie Smith
Daniel Soar
Catherine St Germans
Katherine Stanton
Ellin Stein
Granville Stevens
John Stevens
Nick Stockdale
James Stocken
Sarah Such and Tony White
Chris Swales
Lucy Swanson
Jemma Tabraham-Johnson
Rabia Tasnim
Marcel Theroux
Paul Thomas
Lesley Thorne
Matt Thorne
Damien Timmer
Suzanne Treister
Nicola Triscott
David Tully
Jann Turner
Francis Upritchard
Hannah Upritchard
Nicola Usborne
Pauline van Mourik Broekman
Vikas and Christina
Stephanie Vizer
Saul Walker
Jonathan Wateridge
Hannah Whelan
Wiggins
Judith Youngquist